MARRY ME

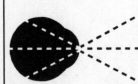

This Large Print Book carries the
Seal of Approval of N.A.V.H.

MARRY ME

JO GOODMAN

THORNDIKE PRESS
A part of Gale, Cengage Learning

GALE
CENGAGE Learning™

Detroit • New York • San Francisco • New Haven, Conn • Waterville, Maine • London

GALE
CENGAGE Learning

LIBRARY OF CONGRESS CATALOGING-IN-PUBLICATION DATA

Goodman, Jo, 1953–
  Marry me / by Jo Goodman.
    p. cm. — (Thorndike Press large print romance)
  ISBN-13: 978-1-4104-3476-0
  ISBN-10: 1-4104-3476-1
    1. Physicians—Fiction. 2. Young women—Fiction. 3.
Colorado—History—19th century—Fiction. 4. Large type books.
  I. Title.
  PS3557.O58374M37 2011
  813'.54—dc22   2010045471

Published in 2011 by arrangement with Zebra Books, an imprint of
Kensington Publishing Corp.

Printed in the United States of America
1 2 3 4 5 6 7 15 14 13 12 11

For Robin Harders —
a good person to have in your corner

PROLOGUE

Mrs. Theodore Easter
Above Easter's Bakery on Euclid
Reidsville, Colorado

Coleridge Monroe, M.D.
5231 52nd Street
New York City, New York

08 July 1884

Dear Dr. Monroe,

After careful examination of the particulars of your letter of interest and curriculum vitae the Reidsville Physician Search Committee is prepared to offer you a contract to serve as the Town Doctor. The contract is enclosed for you to review before accepting our offer. Our Lawyer for the Town assures us that it is a straightforward agreement, and we respect his opinion, as he knows the Town's Business.

As you may have many similar offers for your doctoring, the Search Committee

7

has asked me to convey their confidence in your abilities as stated in your letter. The Committee wishes you to know that you were selected from twenty-two candidates with like backgrounds and qualifications. Your letter, though, set you apart, and has eased our minds that you are personable and of excellent character. I will tell you that some members of the Committee found your missive charming.

With the unexpected departure of our dear Doc Diggins after twenty-four years of service to our Citizens, finding a replacement has been our priority, especially after Sam and Esther's baby had the rosy rash that none of us had ever seen. (All is well there now, you will want to know.)

Although you did not inquire about our Town, the Committee compels me to mention that Reidsville has some eight hundred forty-six souls, and they are all good folk. We are a Town of self-sufficiency and enterprise. The Calico Spur, an independent Railroad serves the Town. Reidsville has all the amenities and entertainments enjoyed by larger cities like Leadville and Denver. It's been more than a year since anyone was shot.

We eagerly await the favor of your reply and remain hopeful that your interest and circumstances have not changed.

Yours truly,
Ann Marie Easter
President, Reidsville Physician
Search Committee

Coleridge Monroe reread the letter before he separated it from the contract. Upon reviewing the terms, and finding them as straightforward as Mrs. Easter indicated, he set the papers on his desk and leaned back in his chair. Beneath the desk, he stretched his legs and absently massaged the corded muscles at the back of his neck.

He sighed. It offered some relief to the pressure building in his chest, but it was inadequate by itself. He needed to confront the problem.

"Whitley." He knew his sister was dawdling in the hallway outside his office, most likely with an ear pressed to the door in expectation of his reaction. Her eagerness these last few weeks to intercept the post began to make sense. She had been waiting for this letter and wanted to see it before he did.

He raised his voice just the level necessary to carry it beyond the heavy oak door. "Whitley. Come here."

To her credit, she did not push the door open immediately. She was cleverer than that. Her deliberate delay forced him to raise his voice yet again and pretend he didn't know precisely what she was doing. It was another moment before the door opened and a moment longer before she poked her head in.

"Did you call for me, Cole?"

In response, he crooked his index finger at her. She was looking particularly pretty this afternoon, slightly disheveled as always, but inordinately bright-eyed and puckish. Her complexion was a bit rosier than was its usual hue, a symptom, he knew, that could have many roots, but in this case was prompted by duplicity and some small sense of guilt. No longer in showy evidence was the spray of freckles across her pert nose and apple-shaped cheeks. He did not mention this to her for fear she would immediately seek out a mirror to confirm his observation. Worse, she might decide that the consequences of deception and remorse were worth the effort. The freckles were despised.

When she was standing in front of his desk, he pointed to the correspondence spread out across its scarred surface. "I am in receipt of an interesting offer, Whitley. I wonder what you might know about it."

"May I see it?"

The question concerned Cole. He arched an eyebrow and fixed Whitley with a look that made her shift her slight weight from one foot to the other. "Am I to suppose that you sent out more than one letter on my behalf?"

"You are not to suppose any such thing,"

she said stoutly. Shifting in place aside, she would not be cowed. "But you can imagine that I am not admitting to anything out of turn. Besides, any letter I might write would be on *our* behalf."

Cole's cheeks puffed briefly as he loosed another sigh. He hesitated, then pushed the documents toward his sister. "You forget with remarkable regularity that I'm the one charged with *your* care. I am the older brother."

Her perfectly bow-shaped upper lip curled with disdain. In every other way she ignored him while she read the letter penned by Mrs. Easter. "Oh, this is excellent, Cole. Really. And no one has been shot in over a year. That certainly speaks well of the town, don't you think? They are all good folk just as she writes. Did you read the contract? Is it satisfactory?"

"I read it. Whether it is satisfactory is unimportant. I've no intention of accepting."

"What? Why ever not? Did you read the part about the amenities?" Before he could reply, she braced her arms on the edge of the desk, leaned forward, and gave him a look that betrayed her irritation even as it implored him to reconsider. "You hate the hospital. No, don't deny it. I won't believe you. I see it in a hundred small ways when you come home, no matter how you try to disguise it. You'll never be allowed to do the research you want as long as you're there. They always have some other use for your talents. Dr. Erwin is no friend to you, Cole. He is jealous of your skill, not admiring of it, and he will never give you the opportunities you desire to do research and advance your work."

Stunned, Cole blinked. This was not a speech he could have ever anticipated his sixteen-year-old sister making. Her observations were accurate, and that troubled him. Was she listening at doors again, or had she managed to effectively make herself invisible so that his colleagues took no notice of her presence? Either was likely. With her flaming red hair always looking as though it needed the attention of a brush, the vaguely distracted expression in her green eyes, and her penchant for humming tunelessly as the mood was upon her, Whitley was often treated as though she was different in an odd sort of way, otherworldly, or slow-witted. At the Amelia Starcher Seminary for Fine Ladies, her fellow students thought they were very clever to give her the sobriquet Whitless.

"You've apparently given this a great deal of thought," he said.

She nodded, paused, then asked with quiet earnestness, "Wouldn't you rather be anywhere but here?"

He didn't answer, and he didn't bother to put the same question to her. He knew her well enough to understand when she was speaking from her own heart. Holding out his hand, Cole gestured for the letter in hers. She gave it to him and he reviewed it for a third time.

"Mrs. Easter writes that I am personable and of excellent character. Some members of the committee apparently found my letter of interest charming." He glanced up at his sister. Whitley's eyes immediately darted away. He wasn't fooled when the keen curiosity that had been her expression was replaced by something that was unfocused and distant. He let it pass without reprimand. He asked his question with a tone that warned her he expected an answer. "How is that possible?"

Whitley made a small, helpless shrug. Her mouth curled to one side as she worried the inside of her lip.

"No one has ever mistaken me for charming," he told her. "Me or my correspondence."

"I think you're charming."

"This is the first I'm hearing of it. Did you not call me obstreperous and overbearing at breakfast? I think you were doing more than trying out new words that begin with O." Her blush gave her away. "Confess, Whitley. I can't possibly consider this offer if you don't tell me what you wrote."

She grasped at the one word that gave her hope. "So you're saying you will consider it?"

"Consideration is different than acceptance.

You understand that, don't you?"

Searching his face, she nodded. The stony set of his features warned her that this small concession was the best she could hope for. He was *not* charming. He was obdurate — another O word that she should have used at breakfast. "I might have written something about the responsibility you recently acquired for raising your younger sister and the great trial she presents to you."

"Might have written?" he asked. "Or wrote?"

"Oh, very well, if you must have it precisely, I wrote it."

"With humorous anecdotes, I shouldn't wonder."

"Several. I'm sure you would find them amusing."

"Were they even true?"

She thought about that. "At their core."

"I see." It was perhaps better if he didn't know the exact embellishments.

"This business of sending a letter of interest and citing all your education and accomplishments seemed inordinately dry and altogether boastful. I thought you should have the appearance at least of being human."

Ignoring her impish smile, and shielding his hurt, he said quietly, "You know better than anyone that I am that."

Whitley's smile faltered, then vanished. There was gravity in her gaze. "You have to forgive yourself, Cole."

He didn't respond immediately. His eyes fell to the letter in his hand, then to the contract on the desk and studied both at length. Finally, reluctantly, he said, "It's not a matter of geography, Whitley."

Looking up to gauge her reaction, Coleridge Monroe found he was once more alone.

CHAPTER 1

Reidsville, Colorado
September 1884

"I reckon you're thinking this is a fool's errand."

Coleridge Monroe glanced up from closely watching his mare's progress on the narrow mountain trail. He was convinced that her steadiness was directly related to his sharp eye, that if his attention wandered for long, she would happily throw him off. "You don't strike me as a fool, Deputy," he said.

Will Beatty turned easily in his saddle to get a look behind him. "Now that's real kind of you to say so." One corner of his mouth kicked up when he saw how closely Monroe was watching the mare's step. The doctor had about as much schooling as a man could stand, but he didn't know his way around a horse. "No point to you starin' at her like that. I guess Dolly there knows this trail about as well as most trackers. Better than some."

17

"Really." Cole was skeptical.

"It's a fact. She's as sure-footed a mare as you're likely to find in Joe Redmond's livery, and she's been all over the territory more than once."

Cole dared to look off to his left where the side of the mountain seemed to have been sheared off by a single slashing stroke of the Almighty's hand. He thought of the mountains back east, the ones with the rounded tops and less dramatic inclines, and decided that for all the majesty of the Rockies, he infinitely preferred the gentler, aged Allegheny and Appalachian ranges. He didn't mention this to Will Beatty. The deputy was clearly comfortable with his surroundings. This climb was simply all in a day's work, and this day being Monday, it was his turn to provide escort up the mountain to the town's outliers and loners.

"You all right, Doc?" Will asked. His glance didn't miss much as it took in Coleridge Monroe. The doc was long and lean, but he rode like he had a poker for a spine — one that had been inserted right up his ass, if Sid Walker was to be believed. Sid, who suffered from crippling rheumatism, made this pronouncement after meeting with Monroe for the first time and not caring for what the doctor had to tell him. Worse, he informed everyone, "He's no Doc Diggins. Didn't even offer me a drink." Will was prepared to give

18

the doctor the benefit of the doubt, if not quite as much leeway as the women were. Every female in town seemed to like Coleridge Monroe just fine. Most of them had already found a symptom of one kind or another that required the new doc's attention.

Will didn't see that a thick head of hair the color of an old copper and a couple of green eyes were all that much to stamp the doc as handsome, but even his wife seemed to think different. Normally she was sensible about men, which served her well enough when she had been the town's sole madam, but now that she was his wife, she liked to tease him by waxing on about Coleridge Monroe's fine looks. Patrician, she called them. Outside of her hearing, he'd asked the sheriff what that meant. Noble, he'd been told. Women apparently said that when a man had a nose like a blade, a jawbone set so tight it could grind glass, and a certain remoteness that was not unattractive. Be that as it may, right now the noble doc looked as though he'd like to puke. Will thought that was probably why he took some pleasure in pointing it out. "If you don't mind me saying, you're looking a little peaked."

Cole refocused his attention on Dolly's progress. "Peaked. That's a good word for it considering our location."

It took Will a moment to catch the doctor's

19

meaning. When he did, he slapped his thigh. "Well, I'll be." He grinned, and two deep, crescent-shaped dimples appeared on either side of his mouth. "That ain't half bad. A little peaked." His smile faded when he saw Coleridge start to weave in the saddle. "Lean forward. Grab Dolly's mane. You gotta help her up the slope."

Cole was loath to release the reins, so he plunged his gloved fingers into the mare's ebony mane with the reins still wound between them. Dolly tossed her head at the suddenness of his move, but she held steady to the trail. Cole caught his breath, sucking in air between clenched teeth. Light-headedness faded.

"How you doin'?" Will asked. "Should we stop for a bit?"

"No. I'm good. Just some vertigo."

"How's that again?"

"Vertigo. Dizziness." He didn't explain it was a common enough symptom in response to heights. He doubted Will Beatty had ever experienced it. "I don't recognize this route we're taking. I had a map the sheriff drew for me the last time I attempted this."

"Oh, Wyatt wouldn't have sent you this way. Not on your own. There's another trail we could have followed, but that would have taken longer. I figured you were anxious to make the acquaintance of the Abbots and get back to town straightaway."

20

Cole would not let himself dwell on what route the deputy meant for them to take on their return. It would be a true measure of Will Beatty's compassion if he elected to follow the trail first suggested by the sheriff.

The deputy and his mount crested the ridge first, and Dolly dutifully followed. It took Cole a moment to realize they had ceased to climb. His grip on the mare's mane eased, and he sat up straight, shrugging the knots out of his shoulders and between his blades. Will slowed and allowed him to draw close.

"Not bad for a greenhorn," Will said. "You did all right, Doc."

Cole's tight smile was more in the way of grimace. "Thanks. I think."

"No, I mean it. You spooked me a little back there. Dolly, too. Thought you might slide right out of your saddle, but you held fast. I don't tell everyone this, but I had some of that vertigo once watching ol' Doc Diggins take a slug out of Wyatt's chest. Had to hold a bucket in my lap and my head over the bucket. I reckon that's the kind of thing that doesn't bother you at all."

Coleridge Monroe regarded the deputy a long moment, this time with appreciation for the man's forthrightness. "Was that the last time someone was shot in town?"

Will thought about it, then nodded. "Yeah, that'd be right. Guess that'd be a year and a bit now. We had a hangin' since then, but that

21

was after a regular trial. Judge Wentworth saw that everything was done proper. Anyway, Wyatt and me don't hold with lynchin', though Lord knows, it's tempting when you gotta wait a stretch for the judge to make his rounds."

Cole wasn't certain how he should respond. He elected to offer up a noise from the back of his throat that could be interpreted as the deputy saw fit. It turned out to be enough encouragement for Will Beatty to continue in the same vein.

"Now, outside of the town proper we had a couple of miscreants — that's the sheriff's word for them, and he does set store by a particular word now and again. You know what that means, don't you, Doc?"

"I do."

"Figured you did, you being an educated man and all. Columbia, is that right?"

"Yes. How did you know? You weren't on the search committee."

"No, but my wife was. Still is, matter of fact, if you don't work out like they hope. Contract's for a year, ain't it?"

"That's right."

"Well, don't you worry. I'll put in a good word for you now and again. I can see you got grit, comin' up here the way you are, 'specially after being shot at on your last trip."

Cole was fairly certain he didn't want to think about that. The bullet had shaved the bark off an aspen only a foot away. His mount, demonstrating more skittishness than the stalwart Dolly, unseated and abandoned him. He'd walked most of a mile before he caught up with the horse, wondering a good part of the way if he could expect a bullet in his back. "What about the miscreants?"

"Uh? Oh, those poor bastards. Forgot all about them." Will saw that the doctor was handling the pace he'd set well enough, so he increased it slightly as they rode the ridge-line. The goal he'd set for himself was to get where they were going and get home again with some daylight to spare. He didn't think Monroe or Dolly would do nearly as well after dark. "Let's see," he went on. "That was about four or five months ago. They say trouble comes in threes, but these two didn't need help. They rode out this way from Denver after getting drunked up and shootin' off their guns in a fancy house. Killed one of the girls, though no one's sure they meant to. Seems they were out of sorts with someone at their card table, and she happened to be sittin' in the fellow's lap. What I heard is that they finally got him and then they ran."

Cole glanced around. The landscape was as rugged and harsh as it was breath-stealing. Much higher up, snow-capped peaks glinted in the bright sunlight. Rocky crags made the climb to their summits appear unforgiving if not impossible. Around him, aspens shivered one after the other as the air stirred, their timing and execution as exquisite as a corps of ballerinas. Cocking his head to one side, Cole sought out the sound of a mountain stream. The swift rush of water made its own music, a steady percussive accompaniment to the occasional cries of birds and the murmur of the wind through the trees.

There was a terrible beauty to the vista that could make a man admire it and be cautious at the same time.

"Why did they come this way?" he asked, though he suspected he knew Will's answer. A man could get lost here.

"Lots of hidey-holes," the deputy told him.

That was another way of saying it, Cole supposed. In aid of suppressing a wry smile, he raised his gloved fist to his mouth and cleared his throat. "You found them, though, didn't you?"

"That's a fact. Sheriff's a member of the Rocky Mountain Detective Association. We went out as soon as we got the wire up from the Denver marshal, though I recollect now that there was a delay at the Denver end, and that gave them a good jump on us and every other lawman in these parts. Sheriff and I were out the better part of three days before we caught their trail. It wasn't hard after that, what with them circling back on themselves. When it was all said and done, Wyatt thought we could have saved ourselves a heap of trouble if we'd stayed in one place and just let them come to us. O'course, that wouldn't have really worked since they were dead when we found 'em."

"Dead," Cole repeated. "Shot?"

"Hell, yes. That's why I'm telling you this story, ain't it? You asked about shootings, remember?"

Reflecting on their conversation, Cole thought he probably had. There was a lesson in this, he decided, one of many he was likely to learn if he stayed in Reidsville: don't ask that no-account Beatty boy a question if you didn't have time for the answer.

"One in the face, the other in the crotch," Will said. "Wyatt thinks they had a falling out and turned on each other. Guns were right there beside them. The one shot in the face still had a cold grip on his. The one that took it in the privates dropped his Colt and was curled up like a baby, still clutchin' his balls when he died. Guess that comforted him some, knowin' he was leaving this world with his parts attached — even if he knew he was going to hell, which I think he must have suspicioned."

"I'm sure he did."

Will simply nodded. He pointed off to the right, indicating to Cole that he should start moving in that direction. "I guess it's not all that odd that it should come back to me so clear now."

25

"What do you mean?" asked Cole, ducking under the low spiny branch of a pine.

The deputy shrugged. "Don't know exactly, except that I can see their twisted selves like they were lyin' there on the ground in front of us. We found them in a scooped out section of hillside. Not properly a cave, on account of it not really going anywhere. Might have been a mine entrance once upon a time, though it didn't look as though it had ever been shored up with timbers. Probably abandoned right off when there was a strike somewhere else. That happened a lot in these parts in the early days."

Cole remained quiet, letting Will sort out his thoughts. A sideways glance revealed the deputy's contemplative profile.

"What I mean about it not bein' odd," Will said at length, "is that it wasn't but a piece from here that we found them. Seems like it might be natural to see it so clear like in my mind right now." He fell silent again, then said suddenly, "I could take you there if you want. That is, after we get you introduced proper to the Abbots. There's enough time for that, I reckon."

Coleridge Monroe had no idea what a proper response might be. He was saved from having to come up with one by the blast that reverberated through the mountain pass. He ducked instinctively.

Will Beatty was careful not to laugh, though

one corner of his mouth twitched. "Been expecting that," he said. "That'd be Runt warning us off."

Cole was prepared to say that perhaps they should heed the warning when Will drew his rifle from the scabbard and fired a shot in the air. His ears were still ringing as the deputy paused for a ten count and fired a second round.

"That'll let Runt know it's me," Will said, sheathing the rifle. "He won't know who you are, but he'll give you the benefit of the doubt 'cause I'm with you."

Cole looked to his right and left, peering back over his shoulder as much as he was able.

"Don't get all twisted there, Doc, and take a tumble. You won't see him until he's of a mind to let you. That's how it is with Runt. He's real cautious of folk. Always was more or less, but it's worse now that his brothers are gone."

"Runt? I thought the sheriff said it was Ryan Abbot that most likely took a shot at me the last time."

"Ryan. Yeah. He's the one. Call him Runt the same way folks like to call me that no-account Beatty boy. You get a name put to you around these parts and it pretty much sticks like pine sap."

"Things aren't so different where I come from."

Will thought he detected an undercurrent in the doctor's tone, not bitterness precisely, but something akin to resignation. "Reckon it's a universal condition, Doc, unless you got something in your little black bag for it."

"No." Cole shook his head. "No, I don't."

"Well, then, back to Runt. You can guess how he got his name."

"Smallest of the litter?"

"That's right, though there aren't but the three boys. Like I said, the older ones have moved on. Last I heard, Rusty — he'd be the oldest, about thirty-five or so, I'd guess —"

Cole interrupted. "Redhead?"

"What? Oh, his nickname, you mean. No, he was born Russell Abbot and has hair as black as a sinner's heart. He was called that on account of a crick in his knee that sounded like a hinge needin' some grease. Like I was saying, last I heard he found religion and two wives when a group of pilgrims came through here a while back. Settled himself in Utah."

"Mormons?"

"Seems like. If Runt's in a favorable mood, I might ask after Rusty."

The trail widened as they made a gradual descent. They left the relative protection of the trees for a gently sloping grassland. A scattering of black-faced sheep on the hillside suddenly huddled together and then moved as swiftly as a nimbus cloud toward a rough-hewn cabin and outbuildings set in the bed of the valley. Chickens ran in circles in the yard. A cow lowed mournfully.

Cole had come upon this scene before but not from this vantage point or at so close a distance. The shot that drove him away with his tail between his legs — if not his horse — had come when he was still on the periphery of the clearing, just barely revealed amidst a phalanx of aspens. He raised the brim of his hat a fraction and squinted against the sunlight glancing off the stream that ran through the valley.

"Where is he?" asked Cole. "I don't see anyone."

"Well, he sure as hell isn't waiting for us on that sad excuse of a porch. C'mon, we need to keep going."

"What about the other brother? You said he's not around either."

"That's right. Randy left about the same time Rusty did. Now, *he* had a way with the ladies. Always did, though I think they called him Randy 'cause his Christian name was Randall. Still, I remember people speculatin' on whether he just grew into his name, like the egg maybe came before the chicken."

Cole had been to Longabach's restaurant with his sister several times since their arrival. Estella Longabach's meaty stew was served with a side of speculation, giving her customers a double order of something to chew on. Cole could easily imagine the chicken and egg debate occupying the diners for an evening.

"Randy seemed the kind that would embrace his brother's new religion," Will said, "but he stayed a couple of months after that and took up with a half-breed Cherokee girl. Bought her from the trappers she was traveling with and moved on up to Leadville. Could be they have children now."

"So Runt cares for the place."

"His pa makes sure he does. He'll be the one in the house."

Cole tried to recall his conversation with the sheriff. "Judah?"

"That's right. But call him Mr. Abbot until he tells you otherwise. He's particular about that."

"Of course."

"You should know that Runt's ornery, and that he comes by it because he can't help himself. Judah's a hotheaded cuss and Rusty and Randy were just plain bad-tempered when I knew them. Both of them bullies, and with me being a few years younger, I felt the meanness in them more than once. That wasn't anything compared to how they carried on after Runt. My ma says that Runt had to come into this world with his fists up and flailing, just to make sure he survived. It didn't help that Delia Abbot died right off. I suppose there was a wet nurse for a while, but that was probably as much of a leg up as

Runt ever got."

"Could I have seen him around town?"

"No. He comes in maybe twice, three times a year for supplies. He hates leaving his rifle with the sheriff, but that's the law. Still, he's pretty good with his fists and doesn't back away from a fight. I've never seen him not get his licks in."

"So he's a brawler."

"No, not really. His brothers were brawlers. He did his share to keep up so they wouldn't turn on him, but mostly it takes some provocation to get him goin'. Someone, usually someone who doesn't know squat about him, gives him a reason to take a poke. He's never done any time in jail, and he's never been drunk. Wyatt just sends him off with his supplies and points out the doctor's office to the one that tangled with him." He gave Coleridge Monroe another glance and grinned this time. "Guess that'll be your problem now."

"Scrapes and bruises. The occasional black eye. It shouldn't be so bad."

"Dislocated collarbone or jaw is more like it. Cracked ribs. A broken arm."

Cole's dark copper eyebrows climbed his forehead. "He's the runt? Are you sure?"

Will chuckled. "He's that. Barely comes to my chin, and I know because he's given me a few pokes in the chest. His size, or the lack of it, is usually what starts the fighting.

31

Except for the ten-pound chip on his shoulder, he doesn't carry much weight on him. Used to be when the Abbots were still performing, Runt'd have to play all the girl parts. Lord, but he hated that. He cleaned up kind of pretty, especially for Juliet and that other one — the wife of the Moor."

"Desdemona," Cole said. "Othello's wife."

Will snapped his fingers. "That's right. Desdemona. Runt told me once that the only role he really liked was Portia."

"From *The Merchant of Venice*."

"That's the one."

Cole considered that. "Understandable."

"How's that?"

"A man playing a woman who disguises herself as a man. In Shakespeare's day, men always played the women's roles."

"Could be so, maybe it was, but around here, we like the parts that are all woman. You take my meaning?"

"I do."

Will thrust out a hand sideways to halt Cole's forward progress. "We'll hold up here. Wait for an invitation."

Cole flexed his fingers around the reins, relieving some of the stiffness that had crept into them. "Sheriff Cooper didn't mention that the Abbots were actors."

"It's been a while. I don't suppose folks think of it much. When Judah and Delia came to town they just had the two boys and called themselves the Abbot Family Players. They sang, danced, and performed recitations. I barely remember that. I was pretty young myself. After Mrs. Abbot died they didn't do a theatrical until Runt was probably six or seven. He did magic tricks then. Started playing parts when he was around eleven, I'd say. Quit everything . . . let me see, maybe six years back. He was probably seventeen or thereabouts. Couldn't take the teasing any longer, I guess. Better for everyone, most likely. He was bound to kill someone for tryin' to catch and kiss him. Don't know that anyone would have done it, but it never came to that since he couldn't be caught."

"So that was the sort of teasing you did. You *were* hard on him."

Will nodded. "Seemed harmless back then, just boys wanting to prove something we couldn't even understand about ourselves, but I feel proper shame thinking about it now."

"He's come to trust you, though, so that speaks well of you."

Will struck a thoughtful pose, rubbing the underside of his chin with his knuckles. "I wouldn't say that he trusts me exactly. Tolerates, is more like it. He likes the sheriff well enough, so Wyatt doesn't have to be as cautious. Of course, Wyatt always carries some of his wife's biscuits when he travels. Makes him kind of popular with the outliers." Will pointed to the cabin. "You might as well introduce yourself, Doc. Runt doesn't seem to be of a mind to show himself without you giving him your credentials."

Will tapped himself on the chest where his star was pinned to his vest. "I have mine right here." He gave Cole an encouraging nod. "Go on. Tell Judah about yourself. He's probably sitting on the other side of one of those dirty windows waiting to hear what you have to say. It's a sure thing that Runt is somewhere close by."

"Just talk?" he said, frowning. "About what?"

"Tell them who you are for starters. They know me, so it's you that's rousing their suspicions."

Feeling perhaps as foolish as he ever had, Cole raised his head slightly and called out. "Hel-lo! Mr. Abbot! Ahoy, there!"

One of Will's eyebrows kicked up. "Ahoy? We're not exactly at sea, Doc."

Cole very much felt as if he was. "It's a perfectly acceptable greeting at a distance, one I heard employed at a demonstration of the telephone." When Will simply stared at him blankly, Cole decided that explanation could wait. He tried again, shouting out so his voice would be heard clearly. "I am Coleridge Braxton Monroe."

Will could only surmise the doc was nervous because there was no other reason to give all three of his names. Braxton? Rose never mentioned the patrician features accompanied a pretentious name. Will managed to keep from rolling his eyes but suspected that somewhere Runt was fixing to fire another shot, probably across the bridge of Coleridge Braxton Monroe's noble nose.

"I'm the new physician for Reidsville," Cole went on. "I was recently hired by the town to fill the position vacated by Doctor Diggins. I understand that you and your son Ru—" He caught himself and heard Will's low whistle of relief. "Ryan may require medical attention from time to time. Sheriff Cooper encouraged me to get to know the outliers." He loosened the strap on his black leather bag and carefully held it up. "I brought my medicines and instruments. If you will permit an examination, I will better understand how I may be of service to you and your son."

There was no immediate reply, and Cole thought he would be forced to repeat all of it even more loudly. Will cautioned him to give it some time, and their patience was rewarded after a few minutes. The front door of the cabin opened and a man supporting himself with a cane limped out.

"Judah?" The question was reflexive. Even at his current distance, Cole could make out enough of the man's features to know he had to be the father.

"Judah," Will confirmed. "Don't be fooled

by the limp. He moves pretty well when no one's watching him."

"Why would he affect a limp?"

Will Beatty shrugged. "Acting's in his blood, I reckon."

It was as good an explanation as any, Cole decided, and he tucked it away until he had a better one.

"You invitin' us in, Judah?" Will called out. "No biscuits, but I have Mrs. Easter's rhubarb tarts. I know you like those."

Judah shuffled to the edge of the canted porch and leaned his left shoulder into one of the supports. Still holding the cane he cupped his hands around his mouth and yelled, "Does Coleridge Braxton Monroe come with the tarts?"

"Afraid so!"

Cole watched Judah's hands drop back to his sides. Apparently he'd done all the talking he was prepared to do across a distance. Judah turned away, but at the last moment, he flicked his cane in their direction and gestured to them to come forward.

"That's it?" asked Cole.

"That's it."

"What about Ryan?"

"He probably won't shoot us now, not unless his pa says to. C'mon. Let's go." He clicked his tongue and let his mount feel his boot heels. As they rode toward the cabin, Will opened up his saddlebag and took out a neatly wrapped parcel. He opened it up with one hand and passed Cole a tart. "You sure as hell won't get one of these out of Judah once I give them over. Better take it now. You'll thank me."

Cole did exactly that as they dismounted and tethered their horses. Mrs. Easter's delicious tart was settling nicely in his empty stomach. In anticipation of beginning his day on horseback, Cole had passed on breakfast. Whitley was disappointed, but he cared more about not being sick in front of that no-account Beatty boy.

He let Will lead the way across the porch and into the house. Judah had allowed the door to remain open just enough to confirm that his gesture with the cane had indeed been an invitation. Upon entering, Cole removed his hat, although he noticed that Will did not. He transferred his hat to the hand that also held his medical bag and stepped forward to greet Judah Abbot.

"It's a pleasure to finally meet you, Mr. Abbot," he said, holding out his hand.

Judah did not make to rise from his rocker or take Cole's hand. Suspicion was almost a tangible feature of his pale blue eyes. He looked Cole over carefully, taking his time, seemingly insensible of — or indifferent to — the rude nature of his regard.

Cole didn't retract his hand. He was used to being on the receiving end of Judah's type of scrutiny. At St. John of God's, it had been the steely-eyed stare of Dr. James Erwin that most of the young doctors feared. Erwin had a manner about him that was simultaneously demanding and disapproving. Pity the poor resident that surrendered to the pressure of answering a question quickly and got it wrong. Just as withering to a new doctor's confidence was the scornful look when the answer was right but too long in coming.

Judah Abbot, for all his cold and measured consideration, still had something to learn about intimidation from the head of surgery at St. John's teaching hospital.

Judah slowly extended his hand. His grasp was firm, Cole noted, and the palm was dry. Not unexpectedly, the older man showed some stiffness when he released his grip, and his thickening knuckles looked as though they might cause him pain from time to time. The index finger of his right hand was missing down to the first joint. It was an old injury, and the skin around the knobby digit was smooth and pink.

"I can't say that the pleasure's mutual, Doctor," said Judah. "Not at this juncture. Under the circumstances, it's appropriate to reserve judgment."

"As you wish."

Judah absently stroked his iron gray beard and set his chair to rocking slowly. His wintry gaze swiveled to that no-account Beatty boy.

"Didn't you say something about rhubarb tarts?"

"Right here." Will held up the parcel.

"Well, put them in the jar by the stove." He jerked his chin in that direction. "Then hide the jar behind the molasses in the larder."

"Keeping them from Ryan?" asked Will. "I don't know if Mrs. Easter would approve."

"She doesn't have to know."

Shrugging, Will did as he was asked.

Cole took advantage of Judah's inattention to continue his visual examination. His new patient's color was good, suggesting he did not spend all of his time indoors, although his lightly callused hands appeared to indicate he no longer did the hard labor. His long-sleeved chambray shirt and leather vest covered too much for Cole to make an evaluation. His eyes were clear, not rheumy, and while his facial hair concealed the true shape of jaw, Cole saw nothing that made him suspect Judah was hiding an extra chin. Cole had also seen enough past the man's tight-lipped smile to know that he still had most of his teeth.

Judah's physical presentation came as something of a surprise. During their journey, while Cole had been listening to Will talk about the man, he'd formed a picture in his mind. Except for the coldly suspicious nature of Judah's glance, he'd gotten nothing else right. Cole had been expecting a robust figure, a man with fists like cured hams and a chest as wide as a wine cask. He'd anticipated a man who had little sense of his own appearance and would be disheveled, if not slovenly. Cole realized he hadn't given enough thought to Judah's days as a performer.

There was a resonance to Judah's speech that Cole thought he must have used to great advantage in his Shakespearean roles. Even an actor whose audience probably first gathered in a tent would want to project his voice for better effect. Cole could imagine now that Judah had had little difficulty keeping attention on him.

Judah's clothes were faded from repeated washing and his boots showed evidence of a recent spit shine. On closer inspection, Cole saw the cane that Judah had used to wave them into the house was more properly a walking stick. It was a polished work of art; a column of chess pieces carved into ebony from the pawn tip to the crown knob, and would have been coveted by any New York gentleman for a turn in Central Park.

The interior of the cabin was clean and tidy, completely at odds with the disrepair and neglect that was the appearance from the outside. The thin film of grime on the windows added to the illusion, but on the inside those windows were framed by lace curtains, yellow with age, but nonetheless clean.

Cole did not know what to make of it, so

he continued simply to gather information for sorting out later.

Will returned from the pantry and pointed to one of the chairs at the table. "Mind if I sit?"

"As you like," said Judah. He glanced at Cole. "You, too, Doctor."

"Thank you, but if you don't mind, I'd like to begin the examination."

Will held up one hand as he dropped into his chair. "First things first, Doc." He regarded Judah levelly. "Where's Ryan?"

"Out."

"I know that, but where does he go? I couldn't make out the direction of his shot."

"Upstream a piece, I expect. He usually walks that way when his tolerance for my company is at its nadir. I send him out when my tolerance for him has reached the same low point."

"Which was it today?" asked Will.

"The latter."

Will nodded. "All right," he said, coming to his feet again. "I'll leave you two here and go find Ryan. Maybe I can convince him to come back long enough to meet the doc and have a go at conversation."

Cole thought Judah looked as though he wanted to object. There was just enough hesitation in his manner to suggest he was searching for a reason to keep Will in the house. He tried to set Judah's mind at ease.

"The examination is painless," he said. "And I'll be asking you to answer some questions about your medical history that you may not want the deputy to hear."

"I may not want you to hear the answers either," Judah said.

"That's certainly your prerogative."

Judah's eyes followed Will as he crossed the cabin. They lingered on the doorway after he ducked out.

Cole set his bag on the table, opened it, and removed a small clothbound notebook and pencil. He held them up so Judah could see and didn't miss the surprise in the man's eyes. Cole's tone was dry, the arch of his eyebrow ironic. "I don't think I'll be needing the bone saw just yet."

Will chose to stretch his legs with a brisk walk rather than look for Runt on horseback. He knew his quarry couldn't be too far upstream or he wouldn't have been able to see his and Cole's approach earlier. Every so often he turned, surveyed the point in the distance where he and Cole had been when they heard Runt's shot, and figured as long as it was in sight Runt was still within a shout.

If he'd come alone to the cabin, Runt would have joined him, no matter how out of sorts he was with his pa. Escorting the doc, though, made Runt even more suspicious than Judah. And that was quite a feat since Judah didn't trust his right hand with what his left hand was doing.

"Hey, Runt! Where the hell'd you get to?" Will waited a few beats, but except for his own soft echo, there was no reply. "Aww, c'mon, Runt. I had to bring the doc out. Sheriff's orders. Wants him to meet everyone, including you outliers. He's been to the Fabers, the Beauforts, and the Goodalls. He even went up to see Mrs. Minich on his own and managed to charm the old biddy. So far, you're the only one that shot at him."

Will sat down in the grass, stretched his legs out on the slope pointing toward the stream. He leaned back on his elbows and spoke conversationally to the trees at large. "The doc's okay, even if he does have three names and doesn't know much about anything 'cept doctoring." Will decided he wouldn't mention that Coleridge Braxton Monroe had at least a passing familiarity with Shakespeare. That wouldn't settle Runt's nerves. "He actually thought you meant to kill him, if you can believe it. I didn't have it in me to tell him that he'd be dead if that was your intention. I brought him up Colley's trail just to feel him out, take measure of his mettle. It wasn't right, I grant you, but he did okay. Stayed in his saddle and didn't puke. Didn't complain, come to think on it. Doc Diggins would have staked me out on the ridge and removed my entrails with a spoon for a trick like that."

"Lord, but you're grisly with your words."

Will hadn't heard Runt approach him from behind, but he had expected that would be the direction he'd choose. "Hey, Ryan." He glanced over his shoulder and nodded once in greeting. "I do paint a picture, don't I?"

"That's a fact. You always did."

"Have a seat." Will patted the ground beside him. "Now that you're here, there's no hurry. Your pa's being examined."

"More likely, it's the other way around."

Will chuckled. "Don't I know it." He looked back again. "You're not going to sit?"

"I don't think so."

Will's easy smile faded as he regarded Runt more closely. "Are you all right, Ryan? You're paler than the doc was on Colley's trail." Runt carried his prized Winchester rifle under his arm, but Will couldn't help but notice that his hold on it wasn't entirely steady. The barrel, while pointed downward, wobbled ever so slightly. So did Runt's legs.

This was where Will knew it got as tricky as trying to balance a shot of whiskey on his nose. If he pointed out what he saw, Runt was sure to take exception. He might even take himself off. Then there'd be hell to pay, especially if something was really wrong with him like Wyatt suspected. Keeping quiet, though, didn't seem like it had much to recommend it. Silence always suited Runt

44

just fine.

Will decided that accusing Judah was the way out of his dilemma. "Your pa take his stick to you again?"

Runt hesitated. "How'd you know?"

"Thought I saw blood on it."

"Could've been, I suppose. He walloped me pretty hard."

Will saw Runt shrug. That, and the way he spoke, seemed to make his words more of a statement of fact than a complaint. "What'd you do?"

"Can't say. Don't know."

"He didn't tell you?" He waited while Runt lifted his hat brim a notch and wiped his brow with his forearm. The sleeve of his flannel shirt came away damp and streaked with dirt. Will always thought that even if Runt was held down in a tub of suds, he'd still emerge the worse for wear. Dust motes hung in the very air around him, suspended like cigar smoke in the Miner Key saloon. The corners of his eyes were creased black, and there was a muddy smear on his right cheek. He wore gloves, but it seemed possible the grime had worked its way through the leather a long time ago.

Squinting up at him, Will said, "You know you can leave, Runt. Like your brothers did. Judah would learn to manage the spread, or he'd come back to town. Maybe mine for a spell. Take his share of what he can bring up

45

from the ground same as every other miner. I bet Abe Dishman would hire you to work on the spur. You could ride the rails between here and Denver for free."

"Sounds like you have my life figured out."

Will offered up a sheepish grin. "It's always easier to do with someone else's."

"You still married to Miss Rose?"

"I am."

"Then I think you're doing all right for yourself."

Will had to agree. "Thank you. I reckon I am." Runt had sidled closer so Will no longer had to look over his shoulder. Out of the corner of his eye he could still see the slight waver in Runt's stance. "How old are you, Runt?"

"Twenty-three."

"That's what I thought. You think much about gettin' hitched?"

"Now and again."

"There's some new girls at Miss Adele's. Could be there's someone for you."

"I'm not sure I want a whore. No offense meant."

"None taken. I made my peace with how Rose made her living before I started courting her. I can't see that you saying it outright is giving offense. Hell, the hardest thing she ever did was turn the fancy house over to Miss Adele. She cried off and on for five of the worst days of my life. I never saw a woman use as many handkerchiefs as she did, and I had to keep a couple or three spares in my pocket every time we went out. It wasn't the honeymoon I'd imagined."

Will heard Runt chuckle but noted it was a weak effort. "You sure you won't join me?"

"I'm sure."

Will wondered if Judah had waled Runt on the ass. Maybe that's why he didn't want to sit down. Will smoothly rose to his feet and brushed off his elbows. "Might as well go down then and meet the doc."

"I don't think so," said Runt. "Maybe next time. You go on, though. Don't let me hold you up."

Will wondered what he could offer as enticement. Runt's jaw was set stubbornly, and the look in his eyes didn't exactly hint at surrender. Even though Runt stood slightly higher on the bank, Will still felt as if he was towering over him. Not that Runt would give ground. Unless his knees were cut out from under him, he'd stay right where he was out of sheer cussedness.

"You know the sheriff's going to chew me out if you don't come with me."

"I sympathize but remain unmoved."

"The doc will probably complain the whole way back to town."

"And yet I am steadfast."

Will couldn't prevent his short shout of laughter at Runt's dry response. "Dammit,

Runt, you ought not to do that. I'm serious."

"But I am constant as the northern star."

That gave Will pause. "Those are somebody else's words, aren't they?"

Runt nodded. "Julius Caesar, Act III, Scene I, by way of William Shakespeare."

"I thought so. That man could sure strike a prose."

This time it was Runt who gave up a chuckle. "Go on. Make some excuse for me."

Will couldn't see that he was getting anywhere, so he finally gave in. "Everyone knows there's no excuse for you." Confident that he'd at least had the last word, he walked away. By his measure, he'd gone about twenty-two yards before a sound at his back brought him up short. He turned, saw Runt stagger, slip on his heels, then try to use his Winchester as a crutch. The rifle went right out from under him, and it was a shock to see him let go of it. He fell hard on his ass, clutching his privates like he'd been mule-kicked. Even more surprising than Runt losing his rifle was the holler that followed. Will didn't think he'd ever heard Runt cry out like that before, and he'd seen him take some pretty good wallops from his brothers. The Abbot boys hardly ever winced when they were in pain, let alone hollered like their hair was on fire.

Will Beatty's loping stride swiftly carried him back up the hill. He hunkered down beside Runt and tried to get a look at what was wrong. Runt was curled tight, his hands still between his legs. "What the hell's the matter, Runt? Let me see." He put his hand on Runt's shoulder and was immediately shaken off. He saw that Runt was biting down hard on his lower lip and still couldn't silence the moaning. "Jesus," Will whispered. "What did that bastard do to you?"

A deep shudder wracked Runt's small, wiry frame. "Leave me."

"Like hell." He reached behind him for Runt's Winchester, hauled it up, and stood. He stepped away from Runt and fired two shots in quick succession. The doc might not understand what he was hearing, but Judah would. Will was less certain if he'd come.

Will set the rifle down and knelt beside Runt. Without asking permission, he grabbed Runt's wrists and yanked them away. Will was still surprised by the resistance that Runt gave him. The accompanying groan was something awful to hear, and he couldn't stop Runt from jerking his knees all the way to his chest. It was a good attempt to hide the problem, but it came a hairsbreadth too late.

Will saw the blood soaking Runt's britches. The center of the dark, wet stain was Runt's privates, but the blossom had already spread to his thighs and lower belly. Will swore softly. "You sure you didn't shoot yourself? Lord, but you're bleedin' like a stuck pig. Let me at

49

least try to stop that." Even as he said it, he was shedding his vest. He tossed it aside and began unbuttoning his shirt. He came close to tearing it off his body as Runt fell quiet. Will thought it should have been a relief from the moaning, but it wasn't. The silence worried him more. He'd never heard of an Abbot boy passing out.

Will wadded his shirt into a ball and jammed it between Runt's rigidly held legs. His efforts elicited a jerky objection, but that small protest gave Will some hope. He looked off toward the cabin, wondering if help was on the way. He couldn't imagine that Runt would be able to walk the distance, and if he had to carry him, Runt would die of shame long before they reached the porch.

"I'm goin' back," Will said. "Won't take but a minute." He jumped to his feet. "Keep that shirt twixt your legs. And don't move." Will wouldn't have bothered with this last directive if he had been talking to anyone but Runt Abbot. He wouldn't put it past him to crawl off to some hidey-hole like any other wounded animal.

Will arrived at the cabin minutes later and flung the door open with enough force to shake the walls. Cole flinched, turning to face Will, but Judah's fingers never faltered as he buttoned his shirt, and when he looked up, he expressed no alarm. "Bring the bag," Will said, striding toward Judah's bedroom.

"Something's powerful wrong with Runt. I'll get some sheets. Take Dolly."

Cole thought he could have hesitated only the span of a heartbeat, but it was long enough for Will to bark another order.

"Go, dammit!"

Cole closed his bag and jerked it off the table. He didn't spare a glance for Judah, nor bother to ask Will what had happened. He felt the rush of Will's urgency roil through his own blood and was convinced he had to act. Following Will's direction, he mounted Dolly without taking time to strap on his bag. He held it close to his chest and managed the reins with one hand.

Will caught up to Cole at the edge of the stream. His arrival made Dolly pick up her pace. "Didn't you hear the shots?" The loose bundle of sheets under his arm flapped and snapped, forcing him to raise his voice. "I fired two, for God's sake."

"I heard them. Judah said you and Runt were trading target shots."

Will shook his head. "He knew better. The timing was all wrong." He could see that Cole didn't know exactly what that meant, but he gave him full marks for not asking. Up ahead, he could make out Runt's curled figure in the grass. "Damn, if he didn't try to crawl off just like I figured. He sure doesn't want to make your acquaintance, Doc."

Cole made no response to that. From the

impression Runt's body made in the short scrub grass, Cole guessed he'd crawled some ten feet from where Will left him. He was turned on his side, scrabbling at the ground with one bloody hand while the other was pushed between his legs. Before Cole reached him, he could make out the dark stain on Runt's trousers. The outer edge of blood was soaking his thighs.

Cole beat Will to the dismount and had already dropped to his knees beside Runt when Will joined him. He set his bag on the ground and jerked off Runt's hat and tossed it aside. Laying the back of one hand across Runt's forehead and then his cheek, he noted the cold and clammy condition of his skin, the effect of the blood loss and the beginning of shock. He circled Runt's outstretched wrist with his fingers and searched for a pulse. It was weak and thready. In spite of that, he felt Runt try to resist the grip. There was a measure of fight still left in the young man, and even if it ran counterpoint to Cole's own will, he considered it an encouraging sign.

Without looking up, he told Will, "Drop the sheets. I need you to take Runt's wrists. I have to see the injury."

Will winced at Runt's low keening cry and found himself hesitating.

"Do it now, Deputy, or you're no use to me or him."

"Sorry, Runt," Will whispered. He took

Runt's wrist from Cole's grasp then reached between Runt's doubled up legs and yanked.

Cole replaced Runt's hand with his own. It didn't require as many years of medical training as he had on his curriculum vitae to make his diagnosis.

"What is it, Doc?" He regarded Cole anxiously, certain now that the only thing worse than Runt's wounded animal cry was the doctor's stony silence. "What's wrong with him?"

Coleridge Monroe looked up from his patient and fixed Will with a glare that gave no quarter. "What's wrong with him is that he's having a miscarriage."

CHAPTER 2

Will knew he was staring like a fool at the doc, knew his jaw had gone slack and that his eyebrows were climbing toward his hairline, but there wasn't a damn thing he could do about it. He figured he was about as stupefied as a man could be and still draw breath.

Cole had no comment for Will's reaction. His attention had already returned to his patient. "Tear one of the sheets into strips," he said. "You can let go of her arms. Runt's not going to fight us."

"Then he must be dead." Will didn't realize he'd spoken aloud until Cole barked the order at him a second time. He dropped Runt's wrists like they were hot coals and grabbed one of the sheets. Using his knife, he quickly shredded it into bandages while Cole opened Runt's trousers and union suit.

"I don't see it, Doc," he said, stealing a glance at Runt's face. Not dead, just insensible. There was no belligerence or hint of challenge left in the set of Runt's mouth, no jut to the jaw or flare to his nose. The loose features weren't exactly peaceful either, and they resisted Will's effort to see the female in them. "You sure Judah didn't beat Runt's privates to bloody pulp?"

"I'm sure." Cole grabbed one of the bandages, folded it end over end into a pad and carefully placed it between Runt's thighs. "Help me lift and turn her. We'll use the slope to get her feet higher than her head. If I can slow the bleeding here, we might be able to move to the cabin."

Will slipped his forearms under Runt's shoulders and back. Cole supported her legs. On Cole's count, they lifted her just the few inches necessary to make the awkward half turn on their knees. Runt never twitched.

"Take a few of the bandages and wet them in the stream." Cole spared a glance at Will when the deputy didn't move quickly enough to suit him. If one got past the greenish tinge, Will's face was almost as pale as Runt's. "Are you going to faint, Deputy?"

Will rose unsteadily to his feet. "Touch of vertigo." He started off for the stream, remembered the sheets, and hurried back to get them. Coleridge Braxton Monroe rose in his estimation when he didn't comment on the lapse.

Cole removed Runt's boots, rolled down her trousers to her knees, then cut away part of her union suit with the knife Will left behind. When Will came back with the damp cloths he held out one hand for them. "Go wash out your shirt," he said, gesturing to the wadded and bloody chambray lying on the ground. "Then fashion some kind of sling we can use between the horses to take Runt back."

"I can make a litter. It'd be more gentle-like if we carried her back."

Cole considered the distance and the time and weighed it against the caution they would be able to exercise. "You're right. Make a litter."

Relieved that he wasn't needed at Runt's side, Will decided his shirt could wait. He grabbed his knife and went off in search of a couple of limbs long and strong enough to use as poles.

A grim smile flickered across Cole's mouth. In a whispered aside, he addressed his patient just as though she were able to hear him. "He'd never be able to look you in the eye again if he had to look at you now." The cotton bandage between Runt's legs was soaked with blood. Cole removed and replaced it, then began to mop the blood from Runt's belly and thighs. "I don't know if there would have been any satisfaction for you in seeing his face, but when he realized I was telling him that you're a woman, he looked as if he'd been poleaxed. I'm not convinced he believes me now."

The damp cloth in Cole's hand was already dark red with blood. He tossed it aside and picked up a clean one. "I'm not convinced that *you* believe me," he said quietly. The bloody smear on her skin was transparent enough now that Cole could see that some of what he'd assumed were streaks of dried blood were actually welts. The raised ridges ran diagonally on the flesh of her abdomen and upper thighs. Frowning, Cole set the cloth down and picked up Runt's right hand. He stripped off the bloodstained glove and examined her hand for defensive wounds. There were none, neither on the palm nor the back of the hand. He examined her wrist with his eyes this time, not merely with his fingertips. Evidence that she had been restrained was burned into her skin. He gently cleaned her wrist and found rope fibers embedded in her skin.

"Mother of God." Cole closed his eyes, but it was a brief indulgence. Setting Runt's hand aside, he continued to work to staunch the flow of blood. He eyed the shape of her abdomen, then laid his palm over her belly to gauge the distention. It was difficult to know the length of her pregnancy without speaking to her, but he didn't think he was wrong about the fact of it. The extent of the hemorrhaging concerned him. A woman in the first months of pregnancy could lose a child and only have ever had an inkling that she was carrying. The terrible proof that Runt's pregnancy had progressed beyond the first trimester was in the angry wales that marked her skin. Someone had tried to beat the baby out of her, which meant it wasn't solely her secret. Had she shared it, or had she been found out?

Looking at the raised stripes again, Cole couldn't help but wonder about internal damage. Concerned that a crude examination in this setting would do more harm, Cole elected to wait. Runt had to survive the transport first.

He called out to Will. "How's the litter coming?" There was a rustling in the trees off to Cole's left, but he didn't bother looking up. "Did you find anything you could use?"

Will came out of the woods dragging a trimmed and sturdy limb in each hand. "Sure did. I figure I got enough rope with me to lash a sheet to these poles. If I can tie it off, even better."

Cole nodded. He pointed to a spot some distance away where the horses were grazing. "Make it over there."

That no-account Beatty boy didn't have to be told twice. He gave himself a lot of clearance when he passed and spared only the narrowest of glances at Runt. "How's he doin'?"

There was no point in correcting Will's pronoun. "Just balancing on the brink of consciousness," Cole said. "The bleeding's slowed."

"Then he ain't been drained."

"No, Deputy," Cole said dryly. "He ain't been drained."

Will came close enough to grab a sheet and returned to where he'd dropped the poles. "Hell, you know what I meant, Doc. I didn't know a body had so much blood. I guess it's a good thing and all, but I never saw the like before. There've been gunfights in town with less blood."

"I assume the victims died quickly."

"Mostly, yeah."

"The heart's just a pump, Will. Once it stops, blood flow's only a matter of gravity."

"Oh." He thought about that. "Then Runt's got a strong heart."

"She does." Cole decided not to mention her wounds were probably more grievous than a bullet. He looked over his shoulder to see how Will was coming with the litter. "Why isn't Judah here?"

Will kept working. "You'll have to ask him."

"I will, but I want to hear what you think."

"Not that it makes any kind of difference to the truth, but I suspect he's not here because he's mightily peeved. He and Runt don't get along all that well. It's my recollection that they never did, leastways it was different than how Judah could tolerate Rusty and Randy. He didn't exactly warm to them, but he didn't cuff them every chance he got."

Will paused, struck by a thought that could never have occurred to him before today. "Do you suppose he knew Runt was a girl?"

It was the deputy's grave tone that kept Cole from ridiculing the question. He had to remind himself that Will was still struggling to accept a new truth. What Will had believed to be fact was, in fact, only perception. That no-account Beatty boy wasn't the first to mistake one for the other. The power of perception, now misperception, was evident in Will's discomfort and the downright idiocy of his last question.

"I think it's safe to assume that Judah knew the truth about his own child," Cole said.

Will flushed. "Yeah. 'Course he did."

"It might account for his dislike."

"Because Runt's a girl? What kind of sense is that? Girls are . . ." He searched for a word that would be the sum of all his scattered thoughts. "Nice," he said finally. "They're nice."

"I agree, but there are entire cultures that believe daughters are inferior to sons and have no value. The Chinese, for example."

Will wondered what explained Judah Abbot's thinking. The man was eccentric, but Will had never taken him for a fool, and he'd been married once upon a time. Had Judah held that same prejudice against his own wife? "I reckon there's no accounting for peculiar notions."

"Probably not."

Cole exchanged another bloody rag for a clean one. He saw Runt's lips part around a soft moan, but her eyes remained closed. He called to Will, "Are you about ready with that thing?"

"Just about."

Cole folded the last clean strip of sheet and placed it over the one between Runt's legs. He finished washing her, examining her flesh for more wheals. It struck him as odd that there were no welts on her hips. He would have expected her to twist violently to avoid the blows, thus raising welts on at least one side, depending on where the assailant stood. Realizing that her legs had probably been restrained as well, Cole rolled down one of the socks. Abrasions circled her skin at the ankle.

"Could Judah be the father of her baby?" asked Cole.

Will's stomach heaved. He waited for it to settle. "That's a hell of thing to ask me, Doc. I'm just gettin' used to the idea that he's a she. I can't think about how a baby got in him . . . her."

Cole didn't find the deputy's answer surprising. He rolled Runt's sock back up, loosely closed her trousers, and tugged on the stained tails of her shirt to give her some protection as Will drew near with the litter. "What about the sheriff? He was insistent that I come out here."

Will set the litter down as close to Runt as he could. "Are you asking me if Wyatt Cooper could have fathered Runt's baby? 'Cause if you are, that makes you about as thick as day-old porridge."

"I was thinking more along the lines of the sheriff suspecting that Runt was carrying a child."

"Then he had to have suspicioned Runt was a girl."

"That's right."

"He never said anything."

Clearly, that troubled Will. Cole said, "Maybe he thought you'd laugh at him."

"I probably would have." He considered what Wyatt could have possibly known. "Wyatt's got an eye for things, better than most folks, I've always thought. He started lugging his camera and equipment outdoors again, making photographs the way he used to before he became sheriff. His wife sorta insisted on it. She doesn't like him underfoot when she's working."

As a member of the search committee, and a woman of considerable influence in Reidsville, Mrs. Cooper was among those who greeted his train at the station platform. He knew she owned half of the town's mining operation outright, and all of the Calico Spur, but he learned these things later from others. She'd simply introduced herself to him as a

62

dressmaker.

"Has Mrs. Cooper ever come out this way with her husband?" he asked, gesturing to Will to support Runt's shoulders and back again.

Will moved into position as Cole did the same. They easily lifted Runt and laid her on the litter. "She's met all the outliers at one time or another."

Cole nodded but kept his own counsel. "Do you want to get your shirt before we leave?"

"Later. Once Runt's back in the cabin." He regarded Cole questioningly. "Unless you'll need me then."

"No. What I have to do is better done alone. Will the horses follow?"

Will put two fingers in his mouth and gave a shrill whistle. His mount tossed his head and turned in their direction. "Dolly will come by and by."

Cole decided to place his unopened bag near Runt's feet rather than trust either of the horses to carry it back. "Will you lead? I need to be able to watch her." Once Will agreed, they bent and raised the poles together, testing the strength of the litter before they straightened completely. It was more difficult for Will because of the awkwardness of gripping the poles slightly at his back, and Cole waited until he was certain Will had a good grasp and balance before he indicated they could set out.

Their progress was slow but steady, and they only halted once when Cole saw Runt's eyes flutter open. Her stare was blank at first, then so sharp with pain and accusation that Cole felt the edge of both. He thought she might have grimaced, but the dirt and blood smearing her lips could also have accounted for the misshapen curl of it.

Judah appeared in the doorway as soon as they reached the porch steps. He didn't move aside. His clear intention was to block their entrance. He thrust the tip of the walking stick at Will's chest, poking him hard. "You can't bring Runt in here."

"Move aside, Judah, or I swear I'll pick your teeth clean with that stick."

"You think I can't keep you out?" He gave the stick a flourish. "Do not underestimate my skill, Deputy. I honed my talents for the stage, but they're real enough. You have seen my Tybalt. He lays Mercutio out. And my Hamlet? The rapier is but an extension of my hand." Judah parried with his stick, jabbing Will in the abdomen. "You're not carrying a gun, I noticed. Just the rifle, and I think I can get to it first, what with you having to hold the litter the way you do." He looked past Will's shoulder at Cole. "You have something to say, Dr. Monroe?"

"Have you no compassion, Mr. Abbot? None? For your daughter?"

"So you know that now. Do you think it

makes a difference? Should I keep company with a whore just because she's my daughter?"

Will's knuckles whitened on the litter. "Put down that damn stick, old man."

Judah made a circling motion with the tip and lunged, driving the breath from Will's lungs with the sharpness of the blow. Will staggered, lost his footing in the loose gravel at the base of the steps, and bobbled the litter. Behind him, he felt Cole's grip change and thought they were losing Runt. It took him a moment to realize that Cole was lowering his end to the ground. The piercing whistle that followed made Will instinctively raise his shoulders to shield his ears. He noticed that the sound also halted Judah in his tracks and stayed his hand.

Will's horse trotted up and sidled close. Cole had Will's rifle out of the scabbard before Judah realized there was any danger. Sidestepping the horse, the litter, and the loose gravel, Cole raised the rifle and cocked it. His arm was steady, his aim true.

"You might find comfort in the fact that I know exactly where to fire a mortal round. There would be some pain but not much. I suspect you would be dead before you felt it." He paused, his eyes fixed on Judah's. "Now, move off the porch, Mr. Abbot, or I'll shoot you in the knee where you'll feel it the rest of your life."

Judah Abbot's mouth opened, closed, then opened again. He offered no response, however, and gradually lowered the walking stick. He used it to support himself as he moved sideways to the left lip of the porch.

"Go on," Cole said. "Jump." It was only a few feet, but Cole knew enough about the stiffness in Judah's hip to know the jolt would be painful and keep him from moving too quickly. As soon as Judah leapt, Cole laid the rifle beside Runt and picked up his end of the litter.

Will nudged the door open with his boot and went inside. "Judah's bedroom is over there," Will said, jerking his chin to the right. "Where I got the sheets. Runt and his brothers slept in the loft."

"Judah's room it is."

With some careful maneuvering, they were able to set the litter on Judah's iron rail bed. The springs creaked and mattress dipped alarmingly as Cole placed one knee on the edge to position Runt better. "We'll leave her on the litter for now. Fire up the stove and put some water on for me, then you can go get your shirt. Take the rifle and find a leash for that mad dog. Don't let him poke you with that stick again, and see if you can't get Runt's proper name out of him."

That no-account Beatty boy had an urge to salute smartly. He held himself in check, but only just. "Anything else?"

66

"Not now. Check with me when you get back."

Will nodded and started to go, pausing in the doorway to look back once. "That was some good thinking, Doc. You looked real comfortable handling that rifle."

Cole was brushing back a black shock of badly cropped hair from Runt's forehead. He looked up and caught the deputy's eye. "Perhaps I was." His gaze dropped away as he opened his bag, "Then again, perhaps I was acting."

"That's all right," Will said. "I like a puzzle." With that, he closed the door quietly and went about his business.

In preparation of this morning's visit to the Abbots, Cole had taken the time to pack his medical bag carefully. He wished now he'd known it would require a magician's skill to pull whatever he needed out of it. He owned three satchels: surgical, obstetrical, and one that Whitley called the kitchen sink. Believing that his goal today was to learn about his patients and provide evaluation and consultation, he brought the third bag for its general usefulness. It contained a mercury thermometer, a couple of scalpels and probes, one pair of scissors, sutures and a curved needle for suturing, tweezers, a razor, a binaural stethoscope, hand soap, a notebook and pencil, finger splints and a bandage roll, cotton pads, and five small cobalt blue bottles containing common medicines like pepsin and aconite tincture that had wide application. Almost as an afterthought, he'd added a saw and anesthetic vaporizer from his surgical bag. It never once occurred to him that he'd need any of his obstetrical instruments.

"It'll have to do," he told his patient. "I'll have to make it do."

Cole heard Will leave the house. Almost immediately there was a volley of expletives leveled at Will's head. Cole ignored Judah's colorful curses and accusations, confident the deputy could handle it, and began preparing his patient for a thorough examination by first removing the clothes that he could easily and cutting away the rest. The rest included the wide strips of linen wound around her chest like swaddling cloths. Cole's only response to making this discovery was to shake his head.

He carefully removed the bloody wadding from between her thighs and pushed a pillow under her hips to keep her pelvis on an incline. He covered her with a clean sheet.

The lack of good light in the room frustrated him. Drawing back the curtains revealed another window in need of a thorough scrubbing. Cole propped it open and examined the wadding. There appeared to be little new blood; most of it was in some stage of drying. This was borne out when he raised the sheet and glanced at the pillow under her buttocks. He was encouraged to see that bright crimson stains were minimal.

Cole tossed out water from the basin on the washstand and poured fresh from the pitcher. He found a stack of linen towels folded in the cupboard and removed one. Taking the soap from his bag, he made a good lather and washed his hands before he applied himself to the further care of his patient.

He retrieved his thermometer and slipped it under Runt's armpit, then he removed his pocket watch and observed her respiration for a full minute. After recording it, he checked her pulse. It was stronger than it had been when he'd first come upon her but not as steady as he would have liked. Cole took out his stethoscope and fixed the ivory earpieces in place. He lowered the sheet to uncover Runt's left breast and rested the ebonized wood bell over her heart. He listened carefully to the rhythmic contractions of the chambers, the rush of blood, and its smooth passage through the valves.

Runt stirred, moaned, and offered a modicum of resistance when he turned her on her side to listen to her lungs. After assuring himself that they were clear, Cole allowed her to lie on her back. He removed the thermometer from her armpit and read it. She had a slight fever. He set the thermometer on the washstand and recorded the temperature in his book as 100.4°

Cole put away his stethoscope and turned down Runt's sheet to the level of her waist. He tapped on her abdomen, carefully avoiding the welts, then pressed harder in the areas of the major organs, watching her face all the while for some reaction. None of her distress seemed to be associated with anything other than her pelvic region. He covered her up to her neck with the sheet and relocated himself closer to the foot of the bed.

Cole raised Runt's knees and pushed the hem of the sheet over them. He separated her thighs and pressed her heels into the feather tick until they found purchase. It was a stretch to reach the basin and towels, but he managed it and set them on the bed beside him. In order to learn the extent of her beating, he wiped away every vestige of blood. The labia majora were bruised and there were thin lacerations on the inner lips. Without a vaginal speculum, Cole could not make as complete an examination as he would have liked. He probed her vagina gently with two fingers, feeling for tearing and abrasions and believed he found both, suggesting the insertion of a foreign object.

Cole rinsed off his hands and rose from the bed with the basin in his arms. He emptied the basin out the window for the second time, then left Runt alone while he checked on the water Will was supposed to have left for him on the stove. It was boiling when he got there. At their current altitude boiling didn't necessarily mean it was hot enough for sterilization, but he decided it would serve his purpose.

He found some whiskey in the larder and tucked the bottle under his arm, and then carried it and the kettle back to the bedroom. He rinsed the basin with hot water, tossed it, and added more hot water. When it was tolerable to dip his hands in, he washed them again.

Situating himself at Runt's side, he replaced the pillow with two folded towels. Laying his warm palms over her lower abdomen, he massaged and manipulated the flesh in aid of expelling any placental tissue still trapped in her uterus. He worked for several minutes and kept a close eye on the bloody effusion that stained the towels.

When he was satisfied that the procedure had been as effective as it could be, he straightened and rolled his shoulders, loosening the hard knots between his blades. He reached for the towels, his glance swiveling sideways toward Runt as he did so. He knew a moment's hesitation when he saw she was watching him.

This was a lucid gaze. There was pain, certainly, but her slate gray eyes were not dull with it. There was cognition and comprehension. She held his stare unblinkingly but with none of the defiance he had glimpsed earlier. It required effort for her to speak. Cole would have only been surprised if she hadn't made it. Her voice was breathy, edged with a soft rasp that came from deep in her throat.

"Is it gone?" she asked.

Cole nodded.

She closed her eyes. "That's good, then."

"You're in a better place to judge than I am."

"God judges."

Cole did not disagree. He studied her face, the only part of her that he hadn't spared the time to clean. Looking past the smears of dirt to the structure of her face, Cole could see that she'd been given certain features that helped her hide her true nature. There was strong definition to her jaw and a natural thrust to her chin. Her mouth was a bold slash, the lips marked by beads of blood and scored from the biting pressure of her teeth. She had a nose that had actually been broken — perhaps more than once. If it had ever been delicate, it wasn't now, but the slight asymmetrical bent simply made her face more interesting, not necessarily more masculine. Her eyes were a tad widely spaced, and while she had thick lashes, they were also stubby. In the strictest sense, her most feminine feature was the absence of an Adam's apple, although Cole could imagine that cleaned up and given the proper application of stage cosmetics, she had favorably impressed her audiences as Portia, Juliet, and Desdemona. The heart-shaped face alone might account for it.

Cole slid off the bed. "I know you're not sleeping," he said, setting the basin aside. "I need you to be for what I have to do next. Do you understand?"

She didn't open her eyes, but she did answer him. "I can stand it, whatever it is."

"But I can't. If you've no pity for yourself, then show some for me." He didn't give her an opportunity to argue. "I have an anesthetic vaporizer with me. It's a kind of mask." Cole pulled it out of his bag. "Do you want to see it? No? All right. It has two parts, the metal holder that I'll place around your nose and mouth and the gauze that I'll stretch across the top and fix to it. I'll soak the gauze with some liquid ether. It will vaporize and you'll breathe it in. Slow, deep breaths. When you wake up, I'll be done."

He wondered if she would ask him what he meant to do and knew a measure of relief when she didn't. At no time during his stay at St. John's were any of the house doctors advised that they should explain themselves to a patient. Rather, they were cautioned to keep their exchanges with the sick to a minimum during rounds and discuss symptoms, diagnoses, and procedures with their colleagues. It was the generally held belief that the patients, even if they could understand what was being said, were not interested. They vested their faith in God and their doctors, and it was all the better, Dr. James Erwin told his interns, if they didn't know the difference.

Cole was never certain that the chief surgeon knew there was a difference, either. Erwin embraced the notion of his own infallibility. This thought rolled through his mind as he prepared the vaporizer. His hands were steady as he measured out the ether and poured it onto the gauze. He was not immune to uncertainty, even fear, especially when the procedure was one with which he had little experience, but he'd always possessed a talent for turning doubt into further inquiry and caution. He would act, but he would be exacting.

Cole placed the apparatus over Runt's mouth and nose and held it firmly when she instinctively tried to avoid it. He turned his face toward the open window to avoid breathing the ether fumes and spoke to her in a firm and steady cadence, encouraging her to take deep and even breaths. "Count backward from one hundred," he told her. By ninety-two, she was asleep.

Cole worked quickly after that. Using a finger splint and most of his own bandages, he fashioned a swab. He poured hot water and whiskey over it and then situated himself between Runt's raised legs. He carefully inserted the swab into her vagina and pushed until he felt the tip of her cervix. He cleansed her internal wounds by rotating the swab as he slowly withdrew it.

As soon as he was done, he discarded the swab and removed the vaporizer to the windowsill. He lowered Runt's legs and covered her, then pulled a chair up to the bedside, sat, and waited.

Cole heard the approach of Will's horse. There was another heated exchange between Judah and the deputy, then the cabin floor shook as Will thumped across the porch. A moment later, he was knocking at the bedroom door.

"Come in," Cole called.

"How is she?" Will hovered in the doorway. Water from the tails of his wet shirt dripped on the wooden floor.

"Did you even wring that out?"

"Twice." He waved more questions about his shirt aside. "What about her?"

"She's coming out of the ether now."

Will's lightly colored eyebrows lifted. "Glad I wasn't here then. If you needed that, it must've been bad."

Cole didn't argue. "What's her name?"

"Judah tells me we've been saying it proper all along, only we didn't have it right in our minds."

"How's that again?"

"It's spelled R-h-y-n-e. He said it was his wife's maiden name. Pronounced it like it was R-y-a-n, but with a little bit of a drawl. Rhyne. It's kinda pretty that way."

Curious, Cole thought. "When the family performed, did Judah print a playbill?"

"Not sure I remember." He removed his hat and plowed his pale hair with four fingers. "Reckon he did. Judah liked to be professional."

"It would be interesting to know how he introduced her."

"Runt Abbot."

Will and Cole turned simultaneously. Rhyne's eyes were still closed, but her lips were parted.

"Rusty, Randy, and Runt Abbot," she said quietly. "So there would be no mistake."

Cole dampened the corner of one of the towels and leaned forward to press it against Rhyne's parched lips. "Will you get her some cool water?" he asked Will. "And bring a couple of empty glasses. I don't know about you, but I could use a whiskey."

When Will disappeared, Cole addressed Rhyne. "Are you nauseated? Feel like you have to —"

"I know what it means. Keep a bucket close. We'll see."

"Pain?"

"What about it?"

"I can give you something for it."

She opened one eye, her regard skeptical. "Laudanum? I don't want it."

"I can't give you anything else. I have salicylate, but it will thin your blood. That's not a good idea right now."

Rhyne remained skeptical, but she didn't offer any resistance.

"As soon as I'm certain you're not going to be sick, I'll mix the laudanum for you."

Rhyne opened her other eye, turned her head carefully, and looked around. "Where's Judah?"

"Outside." He didn't mention that her father was tied up.

"He won't like me being in his room."

"I don't understand. Isn't this where he flailed you?" Cole had not intended to put the question to her so baldly, but he'd told his sister the truth when he said no one had ever mistaken him for being charming. Rhyne Abbot certainly would not misjudge him. What he did not expect, however, was for her to show no reaction. Will's arrival prevented him from asking further questions.

He held out his hand for the glass of water and edged his chair closer to the bed. Slipping one arm under Rhyne's head, he pressed the lip of the glass against her dry lips. "Easy. Easy now." He drew it back when she tried to make him tip it. "Ready?" When she nodded, he allowed her a few more sips before setting the glass on the washstand. "How about that whiskey, Will?"

Will plucked the bottle from beside Cole's chair and poured each of them a generous shot. "Wasn't sure you were a drinking man," Will said. "Sid Walker doesn't think you are."

"I'm not in the practice of offering alcohol to my patients, especially when their visit is prompted by that expectation." He picked up the thermometer from where he'd placed it on the washstand. "Here's what it's good for." He used the thermometer like a stirrer in his whiskey. "It cleans my instruments." Cole put the thermometer back in his velour-lined bag and tipped his glass at Will before he drained it.

"Will?"

"What is it, Runt?" He flushed. "Rhyne. I mean Rhyne."

"What's Judah doing?"

"Last time I saw him, he was pacing the ground and railin' at me. I've got him tethered to a tree by the privy, so you can understand the old bastard's not in good humor."

"You won't be able to let him go," she said weakly. "He'll kill you."

"I'm taking him in. He can cool off in jail. I figure that's the only way either one of us is safe. The doc isn't going to want to move you any time soon, and if you've got to stay in bed, Judah can't stay here."

That no-account Beatty knew what he was

about, Cole decided. "It's a good plan," he said.

"I thought I'd save you the trouble of explaining it to me." He finished his whiskey and rolled the glass between his palms as he went on. "I was thinking you'd want to stay here and look after her, but I know you'd have to make arrangements for your sister. I could ask Rose if we could take her in until you get back."

Cole weighed the needs of his patient against his responsibility to Whitley.

Will made another suggestion when Cole didn't respond, "Mrs. Cooper or Mrs. Showalter would do it, too, if you'd rather it was one of them."

Cole realized that by not answering immediately he'd offended Will. He knew all about Mrs. Beatty's former profession inside of two hours of his arrival. Rose made it a point to tell him. "It's a generous offer, Will, and I'll be relieved if Mrs. Beatty agrees. I hesitated because of Whitley. She thinks she's sufficiently mature to be left alone." She probably was, he allowed, but that didn't mean he'd allow it. "I think she'd be pleased to spend time with you and your wife."

"Good. That's settled." He stopped rolling the glass. "The sheriff makes his rounds on Thursdays. If you tell me what you'll need, I'll see that you get it. If you need it earlier, I suppose one of us can bring it tomorrow morning."

"Judah's about my size. His clothes will do. I'll want my obstetrical bag on Thursday. Whitley will show you which one it is."

Will nodded. "The larder's stocked. I peeked in the root cellar. You sure as hell won't starve." He glanced at Rhyne as it occurred to him that maybe he should apologize. "Pardon my language."

She sneered at him. "Damn you and your apology, Will Beatty. You can't leave me with him."

"I can't leave you with your pa."

"I want my rifle."

Will looked at Cole, saw the almost imperceptible nod, and agreed. "I brought it back with me when I got my shirt. There's nothing gained by leaving a fine rifle like your Winchester on the ground. I'll clean and polish it before I go, and I'll put it on the rack."

"I want it here."

"Bring it in, Will," said Cole. "She doesn't know she's supposed to be too exhausted to argue."

"Runt never did." Will realized his mistake, but he didn't correct himself this time. Rhyne wouldn't have thanked him for it, but she would have sapped her strength setting him straight.

Will took Cole's glass with him when he went. He poked his head out the door to check on Judah and got a double fist shaken

80

at him for his interest. Grinning, he ducked back inside, took the glasses to the kitchen, and got the rifle. Rhyne's Winchester repeater was a well cared for weapon and he was still admiring it as he carried it back into the bedroom. "I don't mind cleaning it," he said, approaching the bed.

"Take your time," Cole told him. "She fell asleep again."

Will found what he needed in the other room and set to work while Cole took some time to familiarize himself with the cabin. He climbed to the loft where Will told him Rhyne slept and found some relatively clean shirts, a pair of denim trousers, another flannel union suit, and five socks. "She doesn't own much," he said, showing Will what he'd found.

"No, I've never seen Runt in more than three of four different shirts."

"What about her stage clothes? Where do you think they might be?"

"Now, there's a question." He looked up from cleaning the rifle, a gleam in his eye. "You want me to ask Judah? It'd be a pleasure."

Cole shook his head. "Let me look around some more."

"Suit yourself."

The cabin only had three areas, and Judah's room was the only one that afforded some privacy. The small loft was open and looked down into the front room. The kitchen and

81

larder took up all of the space under the loft. Cole made his own inspection of the larder, saw that it was as well stocked as Will had said, and wondered if Rhyne was the one who made the preserves and pickled the beets. He chose a jar at random and read the label. The script was small and painstakingly neat: CHERRY CURRANT JELLY. The date indicated it was made last summer. Replacing the jar, he moved on, taking note of how precisely the shelves were organized and of how clean they were.

Judah's influence, he thought, but perhaps not his work. It was difficult to know, and he wasn't confident that Rhyne would see fit to answer his questions.

The door to the root cellar was set squarely in the middle of the larder. Cole lifted it and peered in. He found a lantern on one of the shelves, lighted it, and then eased through the opening and down the ladder. The smell of the rich, dark earth was pleasant, and Cole breathed deeply, inhaling the layered odors of onions, radishes, and potatoes.

Raising the lantern, Cole glanced around. He almost didn't see the trunk for the burlap bags piled around it. He didn't assume the intention was to hide the trunk, but rather that it had come to be hidden as a consequence of its lack of importance.

Cole cleared off the trunk and found that the key was in the lock. He turned it, flipped open a pair of latches, and lifted the lid. He called up to Will, "I found it!" Above him, he heard Will moving around. He looked to the opening and waited for the deputy's face to appear. "The costumes," he said when Will came into view. "There's a trunk of them here."

"I'll be darned." He leaned the Winchester against the wall. "You want some help?"

It took about twenty minutes for Cole to rummage through the trunk and pass what garments he thought might be useful up to Will. The work could have gone more quickly, but Will had some comment about every piece he examined, usually a vague, highly suspect reminiscence about the play or the role that had employed the particular costume.

"I don't feel so bad now about chasing after Runt. Seems to me that if I'd been able to catch and kiss him, I would've known he was a girl long before now." He held out a hand to assist Cole coming out of the cellar. " 'Course, I don't know if I'd have really kissed him. Truth is, I was always relieved when he got away."

"I can imagine," Cole said dryly. He brushed himself off and looked at the gowns and other garments Will had laid neatly over the backs of two chairs. "We have to talk about that, Will."

That no-account Beatty boy frowned. "Talk

83

about what? Tryin' to kiss Rhyne, you mean?"

"Not exactly." Cole closed the door on the root cellar and motioned Will to follow him into the kitchen. He kept his voice low so there was no chance that he would be overheard. "Have you thought about what you're going to charge Judah with?"

Will rubbed his chin. "Seems like there should be something. I know he beat Rhyne. She said he walloped her pretty good."

"That hardly describes what happened to her." The gravity of Cole's expression kept Will from interrupting. "What you say to people about bringing Judah in is your prerogative, but I'm hoping you'll be cautious about what you reveal — and to whom. It's going to be difficult for Rhyne when people learn Runt Abbot is a girl, but they don't need to know she was pregnant and lost the child. No one's health is improved by being the subject of that sort of speculation, and she's bound to learn of it."

"A lot of people know Judah has a temper, and they know Runt felt the hard edge of it most of the time."

"My point is that no one intervened. Ever."

"I can't say that anyone exactly witnessed it. More like they saw the evidence. There were the older boys, don't forget, and Runt, well, he wasn't complainin'."

"*She* wasn't complaining," Cole reminded him. "Then, or now. You must have noticed

84

that. When she asked about Judah, she was concerned for you. She still is."

Will couldn't argue with that. "So what are you suggesting?"

"Charge Judah with assaulting you. It's not a lie. He poked you with his stick, remember?"

Will rubbed his chest. "I'm not likely to forget." He didn't mention that he would have a bruise later. It paled in comparison to what Rhyne had suffered. "He took a couple of swings at me when I hauled him out to the privy."

"He also threatened you."

"That's true. I suppose what he did to Rhyne doesn't need to come into it."

Cole nodded. "Good." He saw Will hesitate, obviously uncomfortable. "What is it?"

"What about the other? The actual fact that there was a baby."

"What about it?"

"Well, we don't know who the father was. If it wasn't Judah, then it could be someone from town. It seems like I should be lookin' into that, most particularly if Rhyne tells me it was rape."

"She's not going to tell you."

Will thought Cole was probably right, but it was a disappointment that Runt wouldn't trust him. "She might."

Cole merely shrugged. He didn't offer that in his experience it was more likely that she'd confide in a stranger rather than a friend. "Are you all right with this?"

Will nodded. "I've got no problem with it. What about you?"

"No problem."

"Have you thought about what I should tell people when they realize you didn't come back with me? People are bound to need a doctor while you're gone. Seems like I should have something to explain it."

"You can say that we found Rhyne with a fever and I stayed behind to treat her."

"I suppose that'll do," Will said slowly.

"But you're doubtful."

"Folks expect to manage a fever on their own, not have the doc at their bedside for the duration. Maybe we should say she broke something . . . like an arm or a leg." Before Cole could speak, Will dismissed his own suggestion. "No one would believe you'd be the one to stay behind and help her with the place. I'm going to have to send someone out here to do that anyway. How about we say she was shot?"

"Shot? Who shot her?"

"Miscreants, that's who. People will believe anything about miscreants."

"I suspect they will," Cole said, his tone wry. "If you think that's best, Deputy, I can support that story."

"Good. I like it."

"Now, you mentioned something about getting me some help."

"You can't look after Rhyne and do her chores, too."

"I'm not incapable, Will."

"No, but you're city. Big city. I bet you never fended for yourself. Fed the chickens. Butchered your own meat. Milk probably came up right to your door and had the good manners to knock."

Cole could see that Will was enjoying himself. Folding his arms, he leaned against the stove and waited for the deputy to wind down. The mere suggestion of a smile lifted one corner of his mouth, and he found himself oddly entertained by the picture Will painted of his New York life. Much of what that no-account Beatty boy said was true, but it didn't follow that the picture was complete. To do that Will would have had to understand something about the demands of a house doctor, know the hours could be as long as a farmer's, the pay as poor as a ranch hand's, and the rewards as unlikely to be realized as those offered by the wanted posters.

"So what I'm saying," Will concluded after ticking off six additional points, "is that you're goin' to need an extra pair of hands. I figure the Longabachs can spare Johnny Winslow for a spell, and if they can't, then Ned Beaumont would probably hire himself out."

"Whatever you think is best," Cole said.

Will nodded. "One of them will be here in the morning." He picked up the Winchester. "I should take this in to Runt. She'll want to know that it's close by. I'll slide it under the bed."

"That's fine. Will you need help with Judah?"

"You might want to keep a watch for me out the window, but I'm not expecting there's much fight left in him. Lots of talk, mind you, but not much fight. I think we saw his final act when he drew that damn walking stick."

"I trust you to know." Cole pointed to the bedroom. "You go on. Say good-bye to her if she's awake. If she asks, reassure her that she's safe with me."

"She won't believe me." Will's quicksilver grin made his deep dimples appear. "I gotta tell you, Doc, Rhyne Abbot might just be the first female around here that doesn't think much of your fine patrician looks."

Rhyne felt as if she were being held underwater. Her lungs were near to bursting with the need to breathe. Panic made her want to flail and thrash; pressure from an unknown weight kept her in place. Sparks of pure white light appeared at the center of her vision, while at the periphery there was only unrelenting darkness. If she didn't draw air, she would die. If she did, she would die. There was no real choice, only the inevitability of death.

She decided to embrace it.

Cole jerked awake. His feet slipped off the iron bed rail and thumped to the floor. He sat up straight, alert. Something had changed.

Rhyne lay exactly as she had when he fell asleep in the chair beside her. The sheet covered her to her throat; her hands remained at her side. Her stubby lashes cast no shadows to add to the violet smudges beneath her eyes. She was pale, ethereally so, her shape defined by softly draping cotton.

And she wasn't breathing.

Jumping to his feet, Cole bent over her. He placed his cheek near her lips and laid his palm over her heart. "Rhyne!" He forced her jaw open and swept the inside of her mouth with his finger, searching for an obstruction. He could not feel anything, but his finger was wet and darkly stained when he withdrew it. Blood? The lantern light was inadequate to know with certainty, but no other cause came to mind. "Rhyne!" Turning her on her side, Cole gave her several hard blows between her shoulder blades with the heel of his hand.

She hunched her shoulders, gagged, and finally expelled the object caught in her throat.

Cole stared at the pillow. Not blood at all, he realized, but something deeply brown yet transparent, more like water in its consistency.

After a moment, it came to him. Tobacco spittle.

And lying just beyond the pillow where she had expelled it was the thing that had almost killed Runt Abbot: a black bolus of chaw.

Coleridge Braxton Monroe surrendered to both the consequences of adrenaline and the absurdity of his discovery. Slumping into his chair, he threw back his head and laughed until he was the one in danger of choking.

CHAPTER 3

It was a struggle to sit up. Rhyne supported herself on her elbows and stayed there while the first wave of pain ebbed. Grimacing, she inched backward until she felt the headboard pressing against her shoulders. With the iron rails behind her, she was able to rise to a full sitting position.

Her first coherent thought was that she was late beginning her chores. She'd seen the position of the sun from Judah's window often enough to know she should be bringing him breakfast now, not merely waking herself. She hadn't gathered eggs or fed the chickens. The horses needed her attention. There was no fresh water in the pitcher on the washstand and no kettle heating on the stove. Normally the aroma of brewing coffee would be filling the cabin, nudging Judah awake before she arrived at his door with his tray.

She'd tasted the coffee that the sheriff and Will brewed in their office, and it wasn't an invitation to linger. She couldn't imagine that the prisoners got a cup that was any better. That no-account Beatty boy didn't know what he'd taken on when he'd taken Judah in. Her father often set his mood by that first cup: bitter, black, and blistering hot.

Rhyne glanced at the empty chair at her bedside. She remembered waking once in the middle of the night and seeing the doctor sitting there, his head bent forward, his breathing slow and steady. At first she thought he was sleeping, then realized he had positioned the lantern and turned it down so that the circle of pale yellow light fell on his lap, or more precisely, on the book he had open in it. Even as she watched him, he turned the page. She considered telling him to put the book back before Judah discovered it was missing, but the recollection that it was Judah that was missing came to her before she spoke.

She fell asleep again before he turned another page, yet the memory of his hands lingered. She could see one of them folded around the book, the other lying flat over the page he wasn't reading. His hands were broad, the fingers long with nails that were trimmed short and scrubbed clean. The whole of his hands was clean, she recalled now: the tips, the palms, the creases of his knuckles. She imagined him rubbing them together over the basin, squeezing lather from between his fingers, reciting Lady Macbeth's best-known line, "Out, damned spot! Out, I say!" The vision of it made her lips twitch.

"Oh, you're awake." Cole stood in the open doorway, a tray in his hands. "May I?"

Surprised by his sudden appearance, Rhyne blinked. How had she not heard him? She couldn't believe he'd been that quiet, so she had to suppose her reverie had been that deep. She jerked her chin at the tray and regarded him narrowly. "I don't smell anything. What do you have there?"

"Broth and bread." He watched her curl her lip in disapproval. "It's what I believe you can tolerate."

"My stomach knows better."

Cole decided that conversation was an invitation and carried the tray in. He set it carefully on one corner of the washstand and then looked over his patient. The curl in her lip had disappeared, but her mouth was tight, suggesting she was in considerable pain. "I can give you some laudanum after you eat something."

"I don't want laudanum ladled down my throat. It muddies my mind."

Cole didn't ask about the circumstances that gave her familiarity with the opiate. Instead he said, "I'd like to examine you."

"I'll eat." Rhyne held out her hands for the tray.

"I wasn't trying to trick you into eating. I'll still want to examine you."

She said nothing and kept her arms extended.

Cole passed the tray and made sure she could balance it on her lap before he sat down. He propped his heels on the bed rail and folded his arms comfortably across his chest.

"You're going to watch me eat?" she asked.

"I thought I would, yes."

"If I had my rifle . . ."

"It's under the bed on your right. Would you like me to hold the tray while you get it?"

"You'd do that?"

"If it would make you feel better."

Rhyne wondered if she could believe him. His expression was grave, too grave perhaps to be strictly credited, and it occurred to her that he was secretly amused. It followed that she amused him, and while that didn't agree with her, it was better than being the object of pity.

She tore off a corner of bread and pushed it into her mouth, aware that his eyes followed her movement. Wrapping two hands around the cup, she sipped the beef broth. The crust of day old bread softened in her mouth and she swallowed.

"I don't remember your name," she said.

"Cole Monroe."

Rhyne tore off another piece of bread. This time she dipped it in the broth before she put it in her mouth. "What's the point of watching me? Doc Diggins never did."

"It's already well established in town that I'm no Doc Diggins, but it's possible that's not always unflattering. I observe all my patients."

"It's peculiar," she said flatly.

"You're right-handed. You have no fixed contractures of your arms and legs, allowing you full extension of both. No curvature of your spine, and also no evidence of *rachitis*." He responded to her raised eyebrow. "Rickets."

"You might have said so at the outset."

"Indeed, I might have."

He was practically daring her to shoot him, she decided. "That's all?" she asked.

"Well, there's no spasticity in your movements, no gross deformities of your hips or feet. Except for the fact that your nose has been broken, there are no apparent physical deviations of your face. Your respiration is normal, your fever appears to have passed, and you're able to make good eye contact."

"Maybe I'm just observing you."

He gave her a faint, knowing smile. "You've just proven that your gross hearing is within normal limits, as is your gross vision. Your color is improved this morning. There is no blue tinge to your lips or fingertips that would suggest a lack of oxygen to your tissues. As evidenced by the look you're giving me now,

I would say that you have coherent expression of thought and feeling."

"Are the hairs at the back of your neck standing up?"

"They are."

"Huh. I guess I do have coherent expression." She raised the cup of broth to her lips, watching him over the rim, and took another sip. When she set it down, she said, "So you're done examining me."

"Hardly."

She nodded slowly, having expected that answer. "I don't suppose I can talk you out of it."

"No. And it would be better all the way around if you didn't fight me, either."

Rhyne couldn't even pretend she had the strength for that. Feeling cowardly because she couldn't quite meet his eyes, she said, "I wouldn't mind some of that laudanum about now."

Cole didn't comment. He simply reached for his bag on the floor, opened it, and removed one of the cobalt blue bottles. Using the spoon he'd placed on Rhyne's tray, he measured out a half dose. "You can take it yourself," he said, "or I'll give it to you."

Rhyne looked down at her hands, saw the slight tremor, and knew she couldn't get the spoon to her mouth without spilling some of the medicine. It pained her that he must have also seen it, because the spoon was suddenly

96

poised at her narrowly parted lips. She opened her mouth and swallowed.

Without a word, Cole took the tray and removed it to the kitchen. He washed the cup and spoon, and then stepped onto the front porch to shake bread crumbs off the tray. Chickens pecked the ground around the crumbs. He'd already tossed feed to them, but they evidently liked the bread better. Shaking his head, he went back inside and laid the tray on the table.

Rhyne was still sitting up in bed when he returned. He counted it as a good sign that she wasn't pointing the Winchester at him but didn't fool himself into believing her disposition had improved in his absence. Fear was in the thread of tension he'd observed earlier. The slight tremor in her hands could have been explained by a host of conditions from delirium tremens to ague to exhaustion, but he didn't think he was wrong to suppose Rhyne Abbot's root cause was dread.

He imagined it was life experience that gave her the bravado to face him with her chin up and her jaw thrust forward. In her own way she was preparing for a punch, and in truth, she probably would have preferred one.

Her mind wasn't the least muddy.

Cole put himself between the chair and the bed. "I need you to lie down," he said. "Do you want help?" When she shook her head, he simply dropped into the chair and waited.

She moved carefully, in obvious discomfort, gritting her teeth so no sound escaped her throat. His sister made more noise getting up from the table.

"There's no hurry," he told her after she was flat on her back. Last night he had been able to remove the litter poles and dress Rhyne in a clean shirt, but she was still lying on the bloodstained sheet that had carried her in. A fresh pillowcase had taken care of the tobacco juice. "How long have you chewed tobacco?"

The question startled Rhyne. She stopped staring at the ceiling and tilted her head in Cole's direction. "About half my life. How did you know?"

"You choked on a chaw last night. You could have died. You don't remember?" He wasn't surprised when she shook her head. "Do you chew in earnest or for show?"

She smiled slightly at the question. "All the world's a stage."

He liked her answer. "You fooled a lot of people."

Rhyne said nothing for a moment then offered quietly, in the manner of a confession, "Sometimes I fooled myself."

Cole saw that she regretted the admission as soon as it crossed her lips. He didn't doubt that it was the soporific effect of the laudanum that made her less guarded. "How do you feel about people in town learning the truth?"

Rhyne bit into her lower lip and turned her head away.

"You should prepare yourself," Cole said. "You're going to be a curiosity."

"There's nothing new about that."

Cole thought he heard a faint catch in her voice. He was better prepared to face her anger than either her shame or her distress. "No one will know about the baby unless you want to tell."

Rhyne remained quiet.

"No one will know about the baby's father."

"You don't know about him, either."

"No," he said. "I don't." Cole waited to see if she would tell him now. "You can't live out here with Judah."

"He's my father. I take care of him."

The way she said it was not precisely a protest, Cole thought, but more of a statement of fact. "He'll kill you some day. I think he meant to."

She shook her head vehemently but still didn't look at him. "No, you don't understand. He didn't. Wouldn't. It was the baby he hated."

Cole didn't offer his opinion to the contrary. He'd seen Judah's eyes when he called his daughter a whore, glimpsed the loathing that made him raise his girl as if she were his son. Perhaps it was Judah that Rhyne had fooled most successfully, not that he didn't know she was female, just that she had been able to make him forget — right up until the moment he realized she was carrying a child. That had removed the scales from his eyes and unleashed his fury.

"We'll leave it until later," he said, getting to his feet. "I'd like to begin my examination."

Cole accepted Rhyne's permission as the absence of an objection. He took the thermometer out of the bag. "May I open your shirt? I want to take your temperature." At her faint nod, he unfastened the first two buttons, slipped the material over her shoulder, and placed the thermometer under her arm. "It will take some time." He withdrew his stethoscope. "Your heart now."

"I thought you observed it was fine."

"This just makes me thorough."

"I liked observation better."

"Liar." Cole placed the bell over her heart and listened. "Now your lungs." He helped her on her side. "Can you cough for me?" She did, but it was painful and caused her to draw up her knees. "That's enough. Just breathe in and out, deeply and slowly. Good. Like that." He eased her onto her back. "I want to see the welts." He saw her tense and waited it out before he folded down the sheet. "Do you want to lift your shirt or shall I?"

It gave Rhyne some small comfort that he asked. "I'll do it." Closing her eyes, she scrabbled at the fabric with her fingers until the flat of her abdomen was exposed.

"I'm going to swab them with a tincture of mercury and salicylate that I asked Chet Caldwell at the pharmacy to prepare for me when I came to Reidsville. It will be wet and a little cold." He prepared a cotton pad with the tincture and swept it lightly over each of her wales. She shivered slightly but otherwise didn't move. "I have to remove the wadding between your legs." He did this quickly, examining it for blood. There was very little evidence that she'd bled after the last change, but he replaced it with a clean cotton cloth anyway. "I think we can put you in a pair of drawers now."

Rhyne nodded. She kept her eyes closed and threw up barriers one after another to keep humiliation from tearing out her soul.

"I have a pair here," Cole said. "I found them in a trunk in the root cellar. I aired them out on the back stoop."

"Just my regular drawers," she said.

"You only have a union suit," he said, lifting one of her legs. "I don't want to cut another one off of you if there are complications."

She didn't ask about complications. She didn't speak at all, accepting this was another argument she had no strength for. Although she had never had a doll, she knew what they were and how young girls cared for them.

Now she allowed herself to be cared for in exactly that manner, lying back without dignity or complaint, dressed in lace-trimmed undergarments that made her feel extraordinarily vulnerable.

Rhyne imagined she should have felt some relief when he finally pushed them over her hips and drew the strings taut at her waist, but she only felt exposed, more naked now than when she'd had nothing on.

"Are you all right? Have I pulled them too tight?"

She batted his hand away then laid her forearm over her eyes. The thermometer slipped under the sleeve of her shirt, and she had to lie still while he probed under the chambray.

Cole read the thermometer. "Almost returned to normal."

If only that were true, Rhyne thought. She tugged on her shirt, fixing it over her shoulder and smoothing the fabric across her belly. She allowed Cole to pull the sheet over her, mostly because she couldn't stop him from helping her. She wanted to wail.

"When are you going to let me get up and get on with my business?"

"Let's talk about it tomorrow."

"I can't stay in bed all day."

"If you get up now you won't be able to stay out of it for the next three days." It was an exaggeration but not much of one. "You need to rest. You're strong, healthy, there's no reason you can't move around tomorrow. Nothing strenuous, though."

She lifted her forearm and glared at him.

"Will's sending out someone to help with the place."

"Who?"

"Johnny Winslow was his first choice. Ned Beaumont was the runner-up."

Rhyne groaned. "Not Ned. He'll get half the work done in twice the time. I can't afford him."

"Then hope that Johnny shows up."

Rhyne supposed that was all she could do. "You're not going to sit in here all day, are you?"

Cole shook his head. "Not if you tell me what's to be done."

"I meant that you could go in the other room, maybe get some sleep. You look haggard."

Remembering Will's comment about Rhyne finding no favor in his fine patrician looks, Cole's mouth twisted in a wry smile as he bent to retrieve his notebook and pencil. He recorded Rhyne's temperature and then turned the page. "Give me your chore list," he said. "First to last."

Rhyne found that obeying the doctor's edicts was downright disagreeable, but she didn't really doubt that he understood her limits better than she did. She only had to recall how she'd slept the morning away after giving him the list. Cole Monroe had been forced to shake her awake when he brought her lunch: more bread and broth, and to prove that he wasn't trying to starve her, a soft-cooked egg.

Lying in bed, she could hear him chopping wood. Try as she might, there was no angle from the bed that allowed her to see more than limber pine and blue sky through the window. Rhyne took her sense of his activity by listening to it. He didn't know how to swing an ax or efficiently set and stack the wood. She found herself holding her breath at times, quite literally waiting for the ax to fall. Sometimes the wood would split; sometimes Dr. Monroe would swear. He couldn't find his rhythm, so he did a great deal of swearing.

Rhyne didn't mind the swearing. It made him ordinary in a comfortable sort of way, reminded her that he was flesh and blood and bone. He hadn't seemed so regular the first time she'd had him in her rifle sight. On that occasion, coming through the trees on horseback, he'd put her in mind of a warrior king. She'd only seen drawings of men like Alexander, Charlemagne, and Marc Antony in her father's books, but Cole Monroe was one of their ilk: proud, straight, and tall, with features struck from marble with tools only

104

the gods could have used.

She'd pulled her shot on purpose, sending it just wide of his perfectly cast ear. Rhyne recalled that he hadn't been able to stay in the seat of his startled mount, but perhaps not even warrior kings could manage a beast like Becken. The stallion was known to be the most powerful — and the most skittish — animal in Joe Redmond's livery, and Rhyne believed Joe had sense enough not to send Becken out with a greenhorn. If nothing else, respect for the horse should have stopped him.

Rhyne knew now that by giving Joe the benefit of the doubt, she'd allowed herself to set Cole Monroe firmly in the pages of Judah's history books. There was comfort in that, too, or at least there was safety. If he wasn't real, then neither was the danger.

It had been foolish, she supposed, to believe the doctor wouldn't come calling again. If she'd known that Sheriff Cooper was behind it, she would have been prepared. Most likely, she would have made herself scarce so that even that no-account Beatty boy couldn't have found her. Instead, she'd walked directly into the trap the sheriff set for her and put herself at the mercy of the warrior.

Rhyne remembered lying in the scrub grass, helpless to defend herself when Cole Monroe knelt at her side. Sunlight at his back cast his face in shadow but didn't obscure the strong definition of his features. They were still visible, even through the haze of her pain. His jaw, square and vaguely aggressive, was set so tightly that a muscle worked in his lean cheek, and each time he drew a breath there was a slight flaring of his nostrils, just enough to make her think of dragons and dragon slayers and wonder which he was. She recalled that moment when his hat fell back and sunshine glinted off his dark copper hair. She'd had the fanciful impression of a halo of fire, an impression that wasn't dispelled by the flash and fury she saw in his eyes.

She listened to the ax fall again and smiled faintly at the muttered curse that followed. Since it seemed unlikely that he'd exhaust his repertoire of cuss words, Rhyne figured Cole Monroe would have to learn to hit his target squarely before he cut himself off at the knees.

Cole set down the ax and paused to shake out the kink in his right shoulder. He massaged his upper arm, rolling the shoulder one way then reversing the motion. He felt the strain on muscles he'd forgotten how to use. It wasn't unpleasant, but then he knew the deep ache wouldn't begin for hours. He had no objection to physical labor and no bias toward those that engaged in it for their livelihood. Most people didn't appreciate the hard work that hospital doctoring entailed: lifting and transporting patients; standing for hours in surgery; walking the wards in an endless loop; climbing stairs two at time and upward of thirty times a day. There were orderlies to assist, but it was Cole's experience that they had a gift for being elsewhere when they were needed most. Some doctors would rather spend their time following an orderly's trail rather than move patients or attend to their most basic needs, but Cole was rarely one of them.

Still, chopping wood was strenuous in an altogether different manner than he was accustomed to. It didn't help that he wasn't very good at it. Raising the brim of his hat, he swiped at his brow with his forearm and looked off in the direction he expected help to appear. He scanned the crest of the ridge and saw nothing that made him think he could pass off this chore onto someone else.

He was on the point of picking up the ax when he heard Rhyne cry out, and he was already turning when the hard thump and clatter reached his ears. Cole took off on a run, covering the ground to the cabin in short order.

He had a picture in his mind of what he could expect when he reached Rhyne's room, but there was no satisfaction in being right. She was lying on her side on the floor, her feet tangled in the sheet that she'd dragged from the bed. The washstand was overturned beside her, and he judged by its position that it had missed her by the narrowest of margins. That explained the thump. He attributed the clatter to the basin and pitcher that were lying just out of her reach. Water had spilled from both, forming a pool that was slowly moving toward Rhyne's head. One sleeve of her shirt was already damp.

"I told you not to get out of bed." He didn't try to mask his annoyance. "Don't be surprised if I shoot you first. I can get to your rifle a lot quicker than you can."

Rhyne pulled her arms under her and tried to push herself up.

"Don't move. For God's sake, just lie there and catch your breath." He bent and picked up the washstand. Towels had spilled from the cupboard under it. He shoved those back inside and closed the door, then he replaced the basin and pitcher. Dropping to his haunches beside Rhyne, Cole helped her turn on her back and lifted her to a sitting position by supporting her shoulders.

"What was so important that you had to get up?"

She stared at him mutinously. "Are you mule-stupid?"

"I must be."

Rhyne shook her head, disgust, not embarrassment, defining the line of her mouth. "I'm about to burst," she said tightly.

That took some steam from Cole's boiler.

He knew he should have thought of that and left the pot within her easy reach, or better yet, made certain she emptied her bladder before he left the house. "Where's the pot?"

"Under the bed."

"All right. Let me untangle you and get you up to your knees." Cole pulled the sheet out from under her legs and tossed it on the bed. He allowed Rhyne to struggle a bit changing position before he offered help. She needed to have a better sense of her own limitations if she was going to heal properly. While she caught her breath, he lowered his head to the floor to look under the bed.

He guessed that she'd probably pushed the pot deeper when she first tried to grasp it. Making a sweep with his arm, Cole pulled it forward. He also captured two lengths of rope. He knew immediately he was holding what had been used to bind Rhyne's wrists or ankles to the bed frame. A second sweep would likely produce another pair. Instead of reaching for them, he passed the pot to Rhyne and pocketed the rope out of her sight.

"I'll leave you," he said. "Call me when you're finished."

Standing on the front porch, Cole examined the rope in the sunlight. Dried blood flecked both lengths but not enough for Cole to conclude that they had been used regularly as restraints. He raised his arm in preparation of pitching both ropes as far as he could, but in the end stayed his own hand. Returning them to his pocket, he leaned back against the rough-hewn cabin wall and waited for Rhyne to summon him.

"It burned," she told him when he arrived in the room. "Making water's never burned before."

Cole nodded, helping her to her feet. "Your urethra's inflamed, and there are scratches and fine tears on your labia."

"Oh."

"Do you have any idea what I just said?"

"No, but plain speaking isn't your strong suit. I'm learning that about you."

He let Rhyne's nails sink into his arm as she lowered herself to the mattress. "I take it Doc Diggins spoke differently."

"I never traded too many words with him," Rhyne said. "But I don't recall that he ever said something I couldn't comprehend. He set my nose once and I know he just called it my nose."

"Always a good choice," Cole said dryly.

"Well," she demanded, "what else is it?"

He eased Rhyne back and laid the sheet over her again. "Well, in my case, it's a proboscis."

She regarded him suspiciously. "Why in your case?"

"Because it's prominent." He gave Rhyne his profile and let her judge for herself.

"It's noble."

Cole chuckled softly. "Did that no-account Beatty boy tell you to say that?"

Rhyne shook her head. "No, why would he?"

"That's a good question." Cole straightened, placing his palms at the small of his back. "So how did he come by that name? I don't have an answer for that either."

"Did you ask Will why folks call him that?"

"No. I thought I'd like to work it out on my own."

"Then I won't tell you."

"You know?"

"Of course I know. I've known him all my life."

Cole folded his arms across his chest as he studied her. She had a kitten-in-the-cream smile turning up the corners of her mouth. In that moment it was difficult to reconcile the fact that she had managed to pass muster as a boy, then as a man. "Is there any chance he was responsible for breaking your nose?"

Rhyne had to clutch her middle to contain the pain as she laughed. "Will Beatty? Lord, no. If there was a fight, he mostly stood in the ring of spectators. His mother taught piano for a lot of years, you know, and Will can play. Ma Beatty would have been plenty disappointed if he broke his hands."

"Is that so?" Cole didn't try to check his amusement.

Rhyne nodded. "He's good, too. I heard

111

him play a couple of times at the Miner Key. He knows songs with words and lots of them that don't have any."

Cole's smile deepened a fraction. "I couldn't have guessed."

She shrugged. "I think it depends on where you're standing to know a thing like that."

"And I'm still outside looking in."

"And I'm inside out." She laughed a little self-consciously. "You know what I mean."

"I do, but that's an indication that you need to rest." A second indicator was that she didn't argue with him. He picked up the ceramic pot to dispose of the contents and left the room, shutting the door quietly behind him.

Johnny Winslow arrived at dusk. He shared a talent with the deputy for making a short story long and a long story dramatic, so Cole was out of patience by the time the youthful Mr. Winslow came to a halt. The gist of the tale was that his horse lost a shoe and Johnny had to turn back to have the blacksmith repair it. He was offered another mount by Joe Redmond, but refused to take Becken because of the stallion's reputation for recalcitrance and leaving his riders dusting off their britches.

"There's not much you can do now," Cole said, looking Johnny over. The young man had a restlessness about him that did not make him a quiet companion even when he wasn't talking. "Take your roll up to the loft. We can share the space."

"I don't mind bunkin' outdoors. Prefer it, in fact."

"That's up to you."

Johnny nodded. He had to push back a lock of hair that immediately spilled over his forehead. "There's no rain expected. I checked with Sid. His rheumatism is the same today as it was yesterday."

Cole had learned that Sid Walker's joints substituted for a standard barometer in Reidsville. By all accounts, his predictions were reliable. "Well, then, I suppose you can have your pick of places to sleep."

Johnny set his roll on the floor. "I reckon you're probably hungry. I can make dinner." He started walking toward the stove. "What's your pleasure? Will told me that Runt had everything I'd need."

"You can cook?" Cole hadn't expected that. He'd only ever observed Johnny in the completion of routine chores at Longabach's restaurant.

"Sure. I've been watching Estella and Henry for years. Lately, Estella's been letting me have a turn. You haven't been at the restaurant much, I noticed."

"Whitley likes to cook for me." Cole refrained from confiding that his sister wasn't particularly adept at it. "She should be doing other things. I'm thinking of hiring a house-keeper that would also cook for us."

"Doc Diggins did," Johnny said. "So what do you want for dinner? Should I ask Runt?"

"No, Runt's resting. I saw ham in the curing shed. Start there and surprise me with the rest."

Johnny paused as he was checking the stove's ash pan. "Now you know the Longabachs' serve plain fare, not that fancy food you get at the Commodore."

"Plain is fine, Johnny. And I haven't been to the Commodore except to attend to a guest's appendicitis. I can promise you that after a day of doing Runt's chores, I'll eat anything you put in front of me."

"Then we'll be fine, Doc. I'm good at this."

Cole didn't allow Johnny to take the meal he prepared to Runt. He carried it in instead, settling the tray on her lap after she sat up. "How do you feel about seeing Mr. Winslow?"

Unsure, Rhyne slowly picked up her fork. "Does he know about me?"

"I can't say. He asked how you were getting on and seemed satisfied with my answers. He didn't show more curiosity than that."

"Maybe Will didn't tell him."

"Maybe not. Maybe he left it up to you." Her uncertainty was palpable, and Cole let her wrestle with it. "You don't have to decide this minute. I can hold him off tonight, but know this, Rhyne, I'm not getting you a rub of tobacco to pouch in your cheek or letting you apply dirt and sweat like you were making an entrance from stage right."

She didn't reply. She didn't think she could make him understand how naked she felt.

"Eat what you can," he said, rising. He was all too aware that he'd spoiled her appetite. "I'll come back to get the tray."

Johnny Winslow entertained Cole with a series of circular tales about the denizens of Reidsville. Some were funny, like the time Gracie Showalter locked her husband out of the house buck-naked in retaliation for tramping mud all over her clean floors. Some were poignant, like the passing of Wyatt Cooper's first wife while he was out in the back of beyond making photographs. Still others were cautionary, as when Foster Maddox, heir to the California-and-Colorado railroad line, tried to take over the Calico Spur and the town rallied to take it back.

In spite of his flagging energy, Cole remained interested. While his contract with the town was straightforward, the actual arrangement was unique, and so he gathered the threads of Johnny's stories as material for the tapestry that explained Reidsville.

The town gave him a home for which he did not have to pay rent. Moreover, at the end of a year, the house would be his outright if he and the committee agreed upon his continued stay. If he left after that, he could sell the house back to the town and was guaranteed a fair price for it. He arrived with his own instruments and a few medical journals, but a reference library, surgery, and examining office were all provided for him. Mrs. Easter had taken great pride, as well she should have, in pointing out the new microscope on his desk.

"Doc Diggins had one like it," she'd told him. "For show, mostly, because I never saw him look in it, but one couldn't help but feel more confident about him for having it."

Reflecting on Mrs. Easter's words now, Cole was reminded how true they were. Too often doctoring was more showmanship than science. It was Cole's aim to change that, at least in Reidsville.

"You look about ready to call it a day," Johnny told Cole. "You want me to get Runt's tray?"

"No, I'll do it."

"Okay." Johnny stood and began clearing the table. He was almost done by the time Cole got to his feet.

Rhyne looked up when Cole slipped into the room. She held out the tray. "He's going to think I didn't like it."

"I'll tell him you just weren't hungry. That's true, isn't it?"

"It's true," she said. "But I want to tell him myself."

Cole arched an eyebrow. "Really?"

She nodded. "I'd rather do it without an audience. Johnny and me. Alone. He never paid much notice to me when I was in town. He was polite and all, just not one of the ones who liked to rile me and stir things up."

Now it was Cole who hesitated. "If you're sure."

"I am. Go on. Send him in."

Cole set the tray down. "Not until I bandage your shoulder." When she looked at him oddly, he explained. "It was Will's idea to tell folks you were shot. He came up with that to explain why I stayed back and he returned to town."

"Shot?!" Her dark eyebrows darted toward her cap of badly cropped hair. "Who shot me?"

Rhyne's clear indignation was not unexpected. Cole held up his hands, palms out, absolving himself of responsibility. "Miscreants, Will said."

"He's ridiculous."

"Maybe, but he warmed to the story so quickly there was no turning him from it. I'm just going to put a sling on your right arm and shoulder. Keep it still and don't let Johnny get too curious about your wound. What you want to tell him about the miscreant that shot you is your business. My advice?

Say the least you can. He'll have no difficulty making the story his own. You won't recognize it when you hear it again."

Cole adjusted the sling, running a finger under the knot at Rhyne's neck to make certain it wasn't too tight. He felt her seized by a sudden tremor and realized he shouldn't have touched her without seeking permission. "I should have warned you," he said, his tone curt.

"Which do you hate more?" Rhyne asked, watching him closely. "Making a mistake or apologizing for it?"

Cole pretended he hadn't heard. He stood, retrieved the tray, and bid her good night, leaving the door open. "Runt wants to say hello," he told Johnny, passing off the tray. "Don't stay too long."

"You goin' to bed?"

"Soon. I thought I'd step outside for a while."

Johnny was unsuccessful at masking his surprise, but he didn't say anything. "Suit yourself."

Nodding, Cole did just that. The evening air that greeted him was clear and cool: another successful forecast for Sid Walker. Breathing deeply, he set his shoulder against one of the supports and waited. He didn't know the precise nature of what he was waiting for, only that he would understand what to do when it came to him.

118

As it turned out, it was laughter, and once he heard it and knew Rhyne would be fine, Coleridge Monroe turned in.

"Johnny says you got him good," Cole told Rhyne. "And he didn't appear to be bothered by it. If his reaction is any indication of what you can expect from others, the town is going to be much more astonished that you were shot than by the fact that you're a woman."

"Will should have never said that about me."

Cole shrugged as he put his stethoscope away. "I told you, he suggested a broken limb at first, but it grew like Topsy from there."

Rhyne's slate gray eyes narrowed a fraction as she plotted revenge. "I'll settle up with that no-account Beatty boy. Just see if I don't."

"I have no doubt," said Cole. He helped her sit up in bed and rearranged the sling for her comfort. It did not escape his notice that her stiff movements were accompanied by a grimace. "Where do you hurt?"

"Are you going to be a burr under my saddle about it?"

"I am."

She sighed. "My belly."

"Inside or outside?"

"Outside."

"The welts, then. Do you have any ointment? Liniment?"

Rhyne looked pointedly at his medical bag, one dark eyebrow raised.

"I have tinctures for infection," he explained, "but your welts are beginning to heal, and the discomfort is because your skin is being pulled taut. Most people have some salve or liniment in their homes, so I don't carry it with me."

"There's a bottle of Mr. Caldwell's special liniment in Judah's chest of drawers." She watched Cole cross the room to the narrow chest. "First one."

Cole rooted through Judah's handkerchiefs and socks and finally found it. "Do you know what's in it?"

Rhyne shook her head. "Cat piss probably. That's what it smells like."

Having been forewarned, Cole removed the cork carefully and gently fanned one hand over the bottle. The scent that wafted toward him made his head jerk back and his features contract. He jammed the cork back into place.

"Told you," Rhyne said. "Judah uses it on his hip when it's grieving him. He swears by it."

"Really?" He was skeptical, but he carried the bottle over to Rhyne anyway. "There's camphor in it, and more than a little alcohol, but I have no idea what Mr. Caldwell uses to create that peculiar odor. Not many compounds can overpower camphor."

Shaking her head, Rhyne took the bottle from his hand. "It's better if you just keep it away from your proboscis. I'll put it on myself, thank you."

Cole didn't argue. "I should go help Johnny. He got an early start on me."

"He told me you were still sleeping when he brought me breakfast."

"I suppose I was," he said stiffly.

"There's no need to take offense, Doctor. None was meant."

He knew she was right. "Whitley says I'm thin-skinned about all the things I *can't* do."

"Sounds about right. Who's Whitley?"

"My sister. She lives with me."

"Do you take care of her or she of you?"

Cole didn't have to think about that. "It's both."

"That doesn't sound too bad."

"It's not," he allowed. "Most of the time."

"Is she bossy?"

"She's sixteen. She's devious."

"I was thinking she was older than you."

He shook his head. "No. There are thirteen years between us." Cole moved away from the bed to end the conversation. He suspected that boredom was provoking her questions, and that meant she was ready to engage in mild activity. "Is there something I can get you to read? That's an extensive collection in the other room."

121

"They're all Judah's."

"He collected them, you mean."

"I mean they're all his. No one's allowed to touch them without Judah's permission, and he's stingy with it."

"He's in jail. I don't think he'll know."

"He'll know. He always finds out." Rhyne rolled the bottle of liniment between her palms as she considered the consequences of defying her father. "*Nicholas Nickleby*," she said finally. Getting a switch across the back of her legs for Dickens was not the worst thing. "I've always liked that one."

Cole nodded and left to get it. By the time he returned, Rhyne had applied the malodorous liniment and was setting the bottle on the washstand. He wrinkled his nose. "I'm going to leave you with Mr. Nickleby and lend Johnny a hand. I was thinking I'd like to get you up and moving around." He saw by her hopeful expression that she would willingly abandon the book in favor of leaving the bed. "Later," he said firmly. "At lunch. I can help you to the table and maybe out to the porch after that."

"We should do it now," Rhyne said. But Cole had already turned away and she was talking to his back. He must have known she'd never throw the Dickens at him because he didn't even try to hurry.

Cole found Johnny sitting on the corral fence.

He had a saddle balanced on the rail beside him and saddle soap in one hand and a rag in the other. He was watching Dolly scratch her neck on a fence post. When Cole came up beside him, he pointed to the mare. "Did Joe Redmond suggest that you take Dolly or was that your idea?"

"Joe's. Will told me that Dolly is familiar with the trails."

"That's because she's about the same age as dirt. If you don't mind me sayin' so, she couldn't pull an old whore off a piss pot."

There was an expression he hadn't heard before. "Colorful."

"You take my meaning, though."

"I certainly do." He looked over the other horses. "Which one did you ride out here?"

"The spotted gray. That's Sassafras. Sassy to those familiar with her temperament. She likes to toss her head and pretend she's ignoring you."

"A coquette, then."

Johnny pulled a face. "Ain't that one of those fried potato and lamb balls they serve at the Commodore?"

"That's a croquette. A coquette is a flirt."

"Huh." He rolled that around in his mind for a moment, then gave Cole a suspicious, sideways look. "I thought you never ate at the hotel."

"They have croquettes in New York, Johnny. Banana. Oyster and macaroni. Salmon.

123

Sweetbread. Chicken and mushroom."

Johnny's mouth watered in appreciation. He glanced up at the sun. "Still got some time before lunch, I reckon. Too bad about that. I've got a powerful taste for some fritters."

Cole chuckled. He put one foot on the lower rail and hoisted himself up beside Johnny. "Do the other horses have names?"

"Probably do. I only know Twist — the cinnamon gelding by the trough. That's Runt's horse, leastways it's the one he, I mean she, rides into town when she's not coming for a season's worth of supplies. She has to bring the wagon for that. The two mares pull that."

"I was under the impression she only ever went to Reidsville when she needed supplies."

Johnny shrugged. "Mostly that's it, but I've known Runt to come in for powders from Caldwell's or to pick up leather goods at Wickham's." He held up the saddle soap. "Or something like this at the emporium." He folded his palm around the soap again and rested his forearm on his knee. "I suppose I took notice because Mrs. Longabach makes me sweep the walk in front of the restaurant three or four times a day. Right there in the center of town, I don't miss much."

"No, I don't suppose you do."

"In and out like the wind," Johnny said. "That's the way Runt moved. I always thought it was because she didn't want trouble, though Lord knows she never ran from it."

"And what do you think now?"

"I reckon Runt just didn't want to be found out." Johnny shook his head slowly. "Peculiar, ain't it? Her pretendin' all the years to be Judah's son, I mean. Can't help but wonder how old she was when she found out different. I didn't ask her; didn't think it would be polite on account of she's a girl now, but I did wonder it. I have three sisters and a brother and we got around to comparing parts eventually." He felt his face go hot. "We didn't do nuthin'," he explained quickly. "Just looked. Got a lickin' for it, too."

Cole was hard-pressed not to grin. "Children are curious, and they usually get punished for it. Fortunately, it doesn't make a lasting impression."

"Maybe your mother wasn't using the right switch." Johnny had an urge to rub his posterior even now. "I can tell you, willow leaves an impression."

"I meant that we don't stop being curious," Cole said. He stared across the corral at Twist.

"I guess that's true. I got me a girl now. Mary Showalter, but folks call her Molly. I get powerful curious about her."

Cole did smile now and kept his own counsel. There wasn't much point in explaining that curiosity was the precursor to scientific inquiry or that it had a far broader application than discovering what was under a woman's skirts.

Still, Cole found himself wondering how old Rhyne was when she learned it for herself. And even more important, what happened next.

CHAPTER 4

Rhyne was the first to see Wyatt Cooper riding along the ridge. She was also the first to remark that he wasn't traveling alone. "That's his wife he's got with him."

Cole and Johnny exchanged glances as Rhyne pitched the potato she was peeling into the bucket at her feet. She tossed the paring knife in after it. Cool spring water splashed all around.

"I'll need another spud," she told them, wiping her hands on her trousers. "Two would be better. Lord, but I hate peeling potatoes."

Johnny said he'd get them, but Cole didn't believe for a moment that his offer was prompted by either graciousness or gallantry. He just wanted to escape the sharp edge of Rhyne's temper. The porch shook slightly as he hurried across it.

As soon as Johnny disappeared into the house, Cole stopped snapping string beans and looked up at Rhyne. She was sitting on the edge of the porch, he on the step below. "Is it really the potatoes making you set your teeth? You volunteered, remember?"

"I wanted to be outside in the fresh air with a knife in my hand."

Cole plucked one of the potatoes from the bucket and held it in his palm. She'd crafted it like an owlet. "If you wanted to whittle baby barn owls, you might have just said so."

Rhyne set her mouth stubbornly and retrieved her knife. She picked up the last unpeeled potato, or at least the last one she had at her side, and began to remove the skin.

Cole dropped the spotted owlet back in the water and returned to the string beans. He waited her out, not because he was particularly patient, but because nudging her never yielded answers.

He glanced toward the ridge. Wyatt and Mrs. Cooper hadn't started their descent. Neither of them appeared to be in a hurry to do so.

"I don't want to leave," Rhyne said. "He's going to make me go. I know it. He's tried to convince me before. So has she."

So that was it. It wasn't about Rachel Cooper at all, or not only about her. Rhyne must already sense the pressure the two of them would bring to bear. At the risk of having the paring knife thrust in his shoulder, Cole reminded her what he thought. "You won't be safe here. I shouldn't have to put

128

any other argument in front of you. On your own, you can keep trespassers out, but once Judah returns it will be different. He owns everything. You'll be the trespasser."

"He won't throw me out. He needs me. No one else will work for him."

"That doesn't mean you should."

Rhyne fell silent. She stared at the potato in her left hand, then at the knife in her right. "What else would I do? This is what I know."

"You're familiar with this place," Cole said. "But you know a great deal more than that. You could —"

Johnny stepped out of the house juggling three small potatoes. "Here you go, Runt." He tossed one toward her, and she snagged it out of the air with the point of her paring knife. Johnny was delighted. He dropped to the space beside her. "Now there's a skill that don't get near enough attention."

Rhyne looked at Cole. "Yes, indeed," she said quietly. "There's such a great deal that I know." She handed the knife and the potatoes to Johnny. "You finish up. I'm going in."

Rachel Cooper dismounted in front of the cabin. She passed the reins to her husband and he continued on to the corral. Johnny tipped his hat at her and then went to help Wyatt.

"Mrs. Cooper," Cole said, getting to his feet.

"Rachel, please." She held out her hand. "I was relieved to learn you stayed behind, Doctor. Doc Diggins saved my husband's life, so I'll always be grateful to him, but I know he wouldn't have stayed with Runt unless Will had run off with all the horses. Doc was never much for walking if he could ride, and never much for riding if he could drive his buggy."

It was the first time Cole had heard the slightest criticism leveled at the doctor's head. "I rode out on Becken the first time and learned I preferred walking." Cole found himself appreciating Rachel Cooper's soft laughter. She was a tall, lithe woman, poised but not rigid in her carriage. She had graceful gestures, not expansive ones, but her smile was generous enough to spark her dark brown eyes.

"I heard that Joe gave you Becken."

"Is there anyone that doesn't know?"

"I don't think so. It's that kind of town."

"Was it a test of some sort, or did I do something to offend Mr. Redmond?"

"No." She shook her head. "Nothing like that. He told me that he meant to accommodate your skill. Your introductory letter, remember? You described yourself as a bruising rider."

"Whitley." It wasn't the first time his sister's name had served as a curse.

"How's that again?"

"Nothing," he said, turning to give her his

130

elbow. "Shall we go inside?" He escorted her up the uneven steps and across the canted porch. She seemed to glide.

Cole had never seen the sheriff's wife in anything but sharply tailored dresses that were vaguely masculine in their cut. It was a style that balanced her softer, feminine features, and lent the impression that she'd be at her ease marching off to battle. Today, however, she was wearing clothes that Runt might have envied — if Runt had ever wanted anyone to know she was a woman.

There was no mistaking that's what Rachel Cooper was. She wore loose, comfortable trousers that still managed to suggest there were a pair of elegant ballerina's legs beneath them. Her shirt was pale blue chambray but in no manner was it a man's discard. The soft cotton had been fashioned to fit her narrow frame, and the cuffs ended at her wrists, not well beyond them. She wore a dark brown leather vest and boots that showed scuff marks and a cursory spit polish. Like a man, she removed her hat when she walked in the door and placed it on a hook beside Runt's battered one. A heavy plait of coffee-colored hair fell down the middle of her back. She took off her leather riding gloves and dropped them on the table.

"Is Runt up there?" she asked, pointing to the loft.

Cole tore his eyes away from her fallen

braid and shook his head. "Judah's room." God help him, at least he didn't stutter. He felt the warmth of her gracious and gentle smile and had no doubt then that she was used to reactions like the one he'd just had and that they meant absolutely nothing to her. Cole imagined her husband had had to learn to be tolerant.

"Do you think Runt will mind if I go in?"

Cole laid his hand on Rachel's forearm, halting her forward progress. "It was you, wasn't it?"

"Me? You'll have to be more specific, I'm afraid."

He studied her face, trying to look past the features that carefully guarded her thoughts. "You were the one that wanted me to come out here. Your husband insisted, but I think that was at your prompting."

"Really?"

He nodded. "You weren't raised here."

"No. Sacramento."

"So Runt was a stranger to you, not someone you grew up seeing in town, or on the stage, or getting underfoot."

"That's right." She waited expectantly, a faint smile playing about her generous mouth. "You have a point, I take it."

"You saw it right away, didn't you? Whether it was because you were a stranger to the community or whether it was because your business is the female form, you knew Rhyne was a girl from the first."

"I'm impressed, Dr. Monroe."

"And what about the rest?" he asked.

"The rest?"

Cole couldn't say it. Confidentiality stayed his tongue.

"I suppose you mean, did I know she was pregnant?" She removed her arm from under his and this time laid her fingers on his sleeve. She didn't make him respond to her question. "The last time I saw her was shortly before you arrived. I knew then. Don't ask me how I knew; I'm not certain I could explain it. I just did." Her voice fell to an even softer whisper. "She lost the baby, didn't she? No one shot her like Will said."

"Ask her."

Rachel breathed deeply, girding herself. She nodded once. "I will. Excuse me." She paused a few steps away and turned back. "I never kept my suspicions from Wyatt. You should know that."

"I didn't expect that you would, Mrs. Cooper, but thank you for telling me just the same."

Rhyne considered pretending to be asleep when Rachel Cooper came in, but she couldn't dismiss the notion that it was a cowardly act. There was a time that she'd have rather faced down the Wickham boys or maybe three or four of Sid Walker's grandsons

133

than carry her end of a conversation with someone like Mrs. Cooper. The hard truth was that she didn't think she wanted to meet up with the Wickhams or the Walkers again.

It had always been her preference to be left alone. Rhyne winced as the front door banged shut. She heard Johnny chattering and the sheriff asking what was for dinner. Closing her eyes, she let her head fall back against the iron rails. If any more people showed up she was going to charge for the sideshow.

"It's getting crowded, isn't it?" Rachel said, closing the door behind her. She leaned against it as Rhyne's head snapped up. "I imagine you'd like all of us to leave."

"I can't pretend otherwise."

"You could," Rachel said, not unkindly. "You're an excellent actor." She pushed away from the door and approached the bed. "Still, I'd rather you didn't pretend at all. I would like it if we could proceed with honesty."

Rhyne was certain she didn't like the sound of that. "You can't make me go back with you. The sheriff, neither."

"Well, that's honest." Rachel's gentle smile didn't waver. She pointed to the chair at the bedside. "May I?"

Rhyne shrugged. "Suit yourself."

"I will, thank you." She could not have been more polite if Rhyne had offered her tea and tarts. She lowered herself and settled back, resting her arms on the curved arms of the chair. "Is this where Dr. Monroe sits when he's with you?"

"When he's not pushing his thermometer at me or listening to my heart sounds." Rhyne knew her recalcitrant tone made her sound like a child. Her mood was not improved for the self-awareness.

Rachel pointed to the sling. "What's that for?"

"Will told you I was shot, didn't he?"

"Yes," she said. "He told me." Rachel did not allow Rhyne to escape her gaze; she followed her, ducking her head to keep the contact when she had to. "Honesty, remember?"

Rhyne took umbrage. "I haven't lied."

"No, but you haven't really answered my question."

Swearing softly, Rhyne yanked the sling from her arm and tore at the bandages that Cole had finally wrapped around her shoulder. "I told Cole no one was going to believe I let myself get shot."

"*I'm* not going to believe it, Rhyne, and neither is Wyatt, but you'll have to put that all back on for Johnny. He doesn't know what happened, and he doesn't need to know."

Rhyne snorted. "I've heard that before."

Rachel took a deep breath and forged ahead. "Did you lose the baby?"

Stricken, Rhyne's hands curled into white-knuckled fists. Sheer effort of will kept them

135

at her side when what she wanted to do was hit something . . . or someone. "How did you know?"

"No one told me," Rachel said. "If that's what you're thinking, put it out of your mind. The truth is that it wasn't long after Wyatt introduced us that I realized you weren't a boy. Minutes, Rhyne. Not hours or days later. I couldn't understand why Wyatt had never seen it. Or anyone else, for that matter. It's not important now. My husband came around to my way of thinking, although it was a struggle for him. You were very good."

"Not so good that you didn't see through me."

"Yes, well, Dr. Monroe has a theory about how I was able to do it, and I'm inclined to think he's right."

"Then tell me how."

Rachel understood that Rhyne needed the answer as much for her own protection as out of straightforward curiosity. "It's because of who I am and what I do. I was a stranger in town, you know that, and I'm a dressmaker. The first made me open to forming my own opinion about the people I was meeting, and the second made me something of an expert on the female form."

Rhyne remained suspicious, but she relaxed her bloodless fists.

Watching some of the tension seep from Rhyne's shoulders, Rachel felt as though she was finally making herself heard. It was not so different than going head-to-head with Wyatt when he dug in his heels. "As for the baby, I noticed the change in you when I was here a couple of months ago."

"You couldn't have. I didn't know it myself."

That didn't surprise Rachel, but she refrained from saying so. "It's not unusual to misread the signs. Indigestion. Nausea, but not only in the morning. I've been told there might even be some bleeding in the first and second months." Rachel wished she could report these things from personal experience, but after more than a year of marriage, it remained a disappointment that she had not yet been able to conceive. "There are naturally changes in a woman's profile, but that comes later. The glow, though, can begin at any time."

"The glow?"

Rachel shrugged helplessly. "Perhaps Dr. Monroe will explain it to me, but not understanding it doesn't mean that I discount its existence. A woman's physical appearance is altered by subtle changes in her skin, her nails, and her hair."

Self-conscious, Rhyne plowed one hand through her raggedly cropped hair. Unable to help herself, she glanced at the back of her hand then gave a cursory look at her nails. "I guess I noticed all that." So had Judah, she

137

realized. Here was the explanation for why he'd begun watching her so closely that she could hardly stand to be around him.

"Well, I noticed it," said Rachel. "I convinced Wyatt that he had to send Dr. Monroe out here. I hope you'll believe me, Rhyne, but the first inkling I had that you'd probably lost the baby was when that no-account Beatty boy came back to town with Judah and that ridiculous story about you being shot. Since he wasn't saying that it was Judah who shot you, I got it in my head that something else had happened."

"So you were right."

"There's no satisfaction in it for me." Rachel leaned forward. She set her forearms on her knees and threaded her fingers together. "You should know that Dr. Monroe wouldn't answer my questions. He kept your confidences, Rhyne, and told me to ask you. Doc Diggins wouldn't have been so respectful."

"I wouldn't have let Doc Diggins get this close."

Rachel smiled appreciatively. "I don't doubt it. It rather begs the question, though, of how Dr. Monroe was able to manage it. I know you ran him off the first time."

"I would have run him off again, but he showed up with Will. I had it in my mind to leave until they were gone, but Will came looking for me." She lowered her head a moment, closed her eyes. "I was scared," she said, the confession offered most reluctantly. From beneath her black, stubby lashes, she glanced sideways at Rachel. "Don't let me ever hear you told anyone that."

Rachel pressed two fingers to her lips, promising silence.

Reassured, Rhyne's gaze returned to her hands. "I thought I was going to die," she said on a thread of sound. "That's what scared me. It was nothing but pure soul-shattering fear that I was dying that made me walk out to meet Will, and nothing but hard-nosed pride that kept me from telling him anything was wrong. As it happened, I didn't have to say a word." She fingered the edge of the sheet. "One moment I was standing, then I wasn't. There was so much blood. I couldn't stop Will from going for help, and I couldn't get away."

"I'm so sorry, Runt. I know how much you wanted to protect your secret."

"You *don't* know," Rhyne said. "And you can't guess. You don't have the imagination for that. No one does."

The scorn edging Rhyne's husky voice pushed Rachel back in her chair. "Perhaps you're right," she said at last.

"I didn't want the baby."

Rachel felt Rhyne studying her for a reaction, determinedly hoping to put her off with defiance and misdirection. "No," she said after a long moment. "But I did."

Rhyne's head jerked up. Her lips parted, then closed.

"It's all right," Rachel said. "I hardly know what to say myself. It was probably selfish of me to tell you. I didn't plan it."

"I provoked you."

"You did, but that doesn't excuse me." Rachel pulled her long braid forward and fingered it absently. "It came to me slowly after I realized you were pregnant, but I thought we might come to some agreement that would benefit both of us. I worked it out in my mind that you would allow Wyatt and me to raise your child. No one would have had to know where our baby came from. No one except you and Judah and Dr. Monroe would have known the truth about you. You could have kept your secret, and I could have kept your child."

Rhyne glimpsed a thin film of tears in Rachel's dark eyes before they were quickly blinked away. Rhyne wanted to say that it was right and proper that someone was crying for her baby, but the words stayed lodged in her throat. She hadn't been able to shed a single tear on the baby's behalf and didn't know if she ever would.

"Judah would have wanted money," Rhyne said because she didn't want to think anymore about what might have been.

"Wyatt thought he might. We agreed we would pay. Not because he had any right to it, but because we believed it would make things easier for you."

Rhyne frowned. A small vertical crease appeared between her eyebrows. "It's not so bad here. Things could be harder. Plenty of folks have it hard."

It was the opening Rachel had been hoping for. "No one else has Judah Abbot for a father. I've only had a short acquaintance with the man, but I know he's so full of himself, and so full of meanness, that he can't see past his own nose to what he has in you. Maybe he was different with your brothers or before your mother died — there are some who say that he was — but what he is now is all I've known. I don't mind who knows that he scares me, or that I've been afraid for you long before I knew you were pregnant."

"Is that why you think I should live in town? Because you're scared?"

Rachel laughed. "If only that carried some weight with you. No, Runt, I think you should live in town because you've only ever known this one thing. You should make your decision about where you live after you've given yourself a real choice. The way I see it, you've been denied your nature. If you don't at least learn something about being a woman, then you'll be the one denying it."

"I guess I know a thing or two about being a woman," Rhyne said tightly. "What I learned, I didn't much like."

One of her fears confirmed, Rachel nodded slowly. The question of paternity hovered on her lips, but she didn't give it voice.

"It wasn't Judah," Rhyne said. "The doc asked me. Guess that makes him brave or stupid."

"So I'm a coward."

"Or smart," Rhyne reminded her.

"Do you want to tell me who raped you?"

"I haven't wanted to tell you anything, but you have a way about you." To be certain Rachel didn't mistake it for a compliment, Rhyne added dryly, "Puts me in mind of a bloodsucker."

Rachel grinned, unoffended. "Wyatt will appreciate that."

Rhyne pulled out the pillow that was supporting her back and smoothed it on her lap. "I'm kind of tired, Mrs. Cooper."

Getting to her feet, Rachel took the pillow from Rhyne and plumped it for her. "It would have been more convincing if you'd looked me in the eye." She handed back the pillow and left.

"Well?" Wyatt asked when Rachel came up behind him and set her hands on his shoulders. He twisted his head to look up at her. Seeing her face, he had answers to questions he hadn't asked. He reached back and laid a hand over hers, then addressed Johnny who was sitting across the table from him. "Would you mind giving us a few minutes?"

Johnny jumped to his feet. "Sure. Stir the pot, will you, though? Don't let the taters burn. Comin', Doc?"

Cole was already rising but stopped when Wyatt shook his head.

"I need him here," said Wyatt. "If you'd gone to medical school, I'd need you, too."

"Medical school," Johnny repeated, grinning. "Sheriff, you know Mr. Cassidy passed me out of the eighth grade as a mercy to himself."

Chuckling, Wyatt jerked his thumb toward the door. "Get out of here, and close the door behind you."

The silence in the room lasted until Cole saw Johnny pass across the yard on his way to the privy. He turned to Rachel. "Are you all right? You look a little pale."

Rachel waved that aside. She released her husband's shoulders and pulled a chair beside him. "It was a disappointment, that's all. For Rhyne, too, I think. Not that she said it in plain words, but it seemed as if she wanted to."

Wyatt took Rachel's hand and squeezed it gently. "I'm sorry, Rachel." He spoke to the question in Cole's eyes. "We were prepared to raise Runt's baby if she would have agreed."

"I had no idea."

Raking back his tawny hair in an absent

gesture, Wyatt explained, "It's not unheard of in Reidsville. There's plenty of precedent for it. Will Beatty, for instance. John and Janet Beatty raised him from birth."

Cole had already met quite a few members of the widespread Beatty clan. By and large they were redheads, relatively short in stature, and tended to have deep-set green eyes. His own sister was more likely to be a shoot off the Beatty family tree than the deputy was. It was surely love and affection that bound Will to the family, not blood, and Mendel's law of genetics had to apply. With his pale blue eyes, hair the color of corn silk, towering height, and a pair of deep, crescent-shaped dimples that Cole hadn't seen in anyone else, the answer was suddenly clear: on no account was he a Beatty boy.

Cole hadn't realized he'd spoken aloud until he heard Rachel's appreciative chuckle.

"I lived in Reidsville a lot longer before I figured it out," she said.

"You never did," Wyatt reminded her. "I had to tell you."

Cole didn't allow them to be sidetracked by the fact that he had finally solved the puzzle. "Do you think Rhyne would have agreed to give up her child?"

Sobering, Rachel nodded. "Wyatt and I had more questions about Judah. In the best of circumstances, he can be difficult. We were prepared to offer him money."

"Did you tell Rhyne?"

"Yes. She also thought he'd want money." Rachel leaned her shoulder against Wyatt. "I'll never believe she would have asked for anything like that for herself. She wanted to be left in peace. We could have promised her that."

Wyatt glanced at Rachel. "Was it rape? Did she tell you?"

Rachel sat up straight. "We talked about this, Wyatt. You said you wouldn't be the sheriff here."

Watching him, Cole tried to imagine a situation where he would promise not to be the doctor. It would be like shedding his skin. Wyatt's struggle seemed to be the same. It was visible in the tightening of his jaw and the ripple of tension through his shoulders.

"But if there was a crime, Rachel, I should . . ." He stopped because she was shaking her head.

Rachel touched her husband on the underside of his chin and tilted his head in her direction. "I swear to you, Wyatt, Rhyne never said she was raped. She never mentioned there was force. And she told me in no uncertain terms that Judah was not the father. Let it be." She let her hand fall away while Wyatt wrestled with his conscience. He was regarding her closely, examining her features as he considered her words, looking for the lie, and because there was none, she

145

resolutely held his gaze.

"All right," he said at last. What he left unsaid was his hope that he didn't regret it. Wyatt lifted his hands, palms up, and shrugged lightly as he turned to Cole Monroe. "That's that. Tell us about Rhyne's health. Can she travel?"

"Tomorrow, I think. Saturday, certainly. But whether she will is another matter. How long can you hold Judah?"

"Judge Wentworth will be here on Monday. I'd like to let Judah go before then. I don't want to put the matter before the judge, and I'd like for Judah to think we're doing him a favor."

"You are, aren't you? He attacked your deputy."

"It's a little embarrassing for Will to pretend Judah got the better of him. Judah is thirty years his senior. It doesn't matter how hot-tempered or unreasonable Judah can be, it's still Will's job to take care of him. Normally we wouldn't take Judah in for waving his stick around, whether it poked one of us or not." Wyatt set his arms on the table and folded his hands. "Will's been tight-lipped about what went on out here, and I figure that's because you asked it of him. He generally has a lot more to say. I've been thinking you could fill in some of the details, Dr. Monroe."

"I only asked him not to talk to anyone about Rhyne's miscarriage. It wasn't clear to me then if you and Mrs. Cooper knew that Rhyne was female, let alone that she was pregnant. I was thinking of my patient. I wouldn't have insisted that Will keep it from you had I known."

"That's all well and good, but now you *do* know."

"Information has to come from Will, or better yet, Rhyne."

"How did she lose the baby, Doctor?"

"You must know that it happens, Sheriff. Even to healthy women."

"Runt's had injuries that didn't put her in bed for three days."

"This was different. She was hemorrhaging. There was significant blood loss."

"That doesn't happen all the time."

"No, but it's not unheard of."

Rachel slapped the table sharply with the palm of her hand. "Stop it. Both of you."

"Wyatt, you're reneging on your promise right in front of me, and Dr. Monroe, you're twisting my last nerve." She stood up. "I'm going to stir the potatoes before they burn."

Wyatt and Cole watched her go. They exchanged glances, and neither of them was so foolish as to say or do anything that would bring her back to the table in a hurry. They sat in silence, pretending interest in the shelves of books on the far wall.

Rachel took her sweet time at the stove, finding other things to occupy her besides the potatoes. It was almost comical, the way they sat there like chastened schoolboys. She loved her husband, and Cole Monroe was rising steadily in her estimation, but lord help her, they were struck from the same piece of steel. She was still determining how much longer to leave them there when the decision was taken from her.

Rhyne felt everyone's attention shift to her as she stepped into the room. She walked steadily toward the table and was proud of the fact that none of them, not even Dr. Monroe, could guess at what it cost her to make that short journey.

"I'm not deaf, you know. You really should have told Johnny to take me with him, or left yourselves." Her glance swiveled to Rachel at the stove. "I've been thinking about what you said, Mrs. Cooper, about me making a decision once I've had a real choice. I've decided I'd like to try that. Living as a woman for a time, I mean. I know I can't do it here — Judah would never allow it — so that means I have to go to town. If you think you can help me find some kind of work, then I'll be ready to travel tomorrow, just like the doc said I could."

"I *think* you'll be ready tomorrow," Cole said quickly.

Rachel dropped her spoon at the stove and advanced on Rhyne, prepared to hug her. She stopped abruptly when she glimpsed Cole shaking his head, warning her off, and threw her arms rather awkwardly around Wyatt as he was getting to his feet. Wyatt was glad for the attention, but he had to withdraw the hand he was extending toward Rhyne and use it to steady himself.

Cole stood and pushed his chair toward Rhyne. "Sit here."

She didn't hint at how grateful she was to have a seat under her. She hadn't expected that standing at the door for as long as she had would so completely sap her strength. It didn't bode well for making the journey on horseback, but the thought of riding in the back of the wagon was equally unbearable.

Wyatt gently disengaged himself from Rachel's arms and excused himself to go out on the porch and call for Johnny. He waited there, rocking back on his heels as he marveled at his wife's powers of persuasion. When Johnny came loping across the yard, he walked back inside. The table was already set for dinner. He'd timed it perfectly.

There was some awkwardness among the diners at first. Johnny Winslow managed to cut through all of that by entertaining them with one improbable adventure after another, many of them having to do with his courtship of Molly Showalter. Cole's eyes often strayed to Rhyne — until she ground the heel of her boot on his vulnerable instep. After that, he watched the unspoken exchanges

149

between Rachel and Wyatt: the smiles that hovered briefly when they silently shared their amusement, the sideways glances that spoke to their complete awareness of the other, and the subtle way they traded touches when one of them passed the salt or held out a plate for a second helping.

He knew a stirring of envy, and the power of it caught him unawares. When he looked away, he saw that Rhyne was watching him. Her expression was inscrutable, but he doubted his had been the same. He wondered if she knew how to interpret what she'd glimpsed in his face. How could she possibly guess that he didn't covet Wyatt Cooper's wife when he was only beginning to understand that what he coveted was Wyatt Cooper's life?

Cole held a small bowl under Rhyne's chin. Her lips were frothy with the soda paste he'd mixed for her to clean her teeth. She looked vaguely rabid. He took the brush from her when he decided she'd done enough. "Spit."

Rhyne did. She reached for the water glass on the washstand, rinsed, and spit again. She clicked her teeth together to show him her shiny pearlies. "You're like a mother hen. Worse, actually." She shooed him away from the bed. "Where's everyone sleeping tonight?" After dinner, she'd excused herself and gone immediately to lie down. If there was conversation about her at the table, this time she had been too tired to care. She woke up when Cole entered her room carrying another black satchel. "There's room in this bed for Mrs. Cooper as long as she doesn't take it in her head that I'm the sheriff and try to hug me. Did you notice that it seemed like she was going to when I was standing at the table? I was braced for it, but lord, I don't mind telling you that would have hurt. It was a pure relief when she targeted her husband instead."

Cole regarded Rhyne curiously. They only had a short acquaintance, but he couldn't recall that she'd ever strung so many sentences together. He didn't attribute that to her feeling better because she didn't strike him as a talker. That left another explanation. "Are you nervous?"

Rhyne's head came up, but her eyes darted away. "Nervous? No."

Following her glance, Cole saw that his second medical bag was in her line of sight. "I asked Will to send that bag out with Wyatt." He bent and picked it up. On the outside it was almost identical to his more practical traveling bag. "It carries most of my obstetrical instruments."

"Ob-stet-ri-cal." The word rolled awkwardly off her tongue, and she misplaced the accented syllable. She said it again, getting it exactly right, but with no comprehension of its significance. "I don't know that word. What's it mean exactly?"

"It's from the Latin. *Obstetricius.* And also, *obstetrix.* Having to do with midwifery. For our purpose, everything associated with childbirth." The lantern light gave Rhyne a ghostly glow as she blanched. He set the bag on the floor again. "I'm not going to do anything with it this evening," he told her. "I want better light. Tomorrow morning will be fine. I'll know how well you'll be able to travel after examining you."

Rhyne turned on her side and put a hand out for the bag. "Let me see what's in there."

Cole used his heel to nudge the satchel out of her reach. It came to rest beside his other bag. "Tomorrow," he said firmly. "You asked where everyone was sleeping." He wasn't sure she was listening to him any longer, but he answered her earlier question anyway. "The sheriff and Mrs. Cooper are going to be in the loft. Johnny's making a roll for me on the porch. He says he's been sleeping just fine out there."

"Johnny can sleep standing up while he's holding a broom. I've seen him nodding off in front of Longabach's."

"For someone who doesn't go to town frequently, you seem to know a great deal about what goes on there."

She shrugged. "I pay attention. It's useful." She turned on her back again and stared up at him. "For instance, I noticed you looking at Mrs. Cooper like you wanted to pass on the potatoes and eat her up instead."

Ignoring her, Cole gathered up the spit bowl, washcloths, and his satchel. "In the morning, Rhyne."

She let him go without saying good night. Pleasantries would have aroused his suspicions, and he might have turned back. Rhyne was quite sure she didn't want anything to delay his exit or prompt him to realize that in his haste to avoid explaining his interest in Mrs. Cooper, Cole Monroe had picked up the wrong medical bag.

The heady aroma of strong coffee brewing on the stove carried Cole to wakefulness. He sat up slowly and wiped sleep from his eyes. Johnny Winslow still lay a few feet away, snoring softly. Cole looked out into the empty yard, then to the corral. Wyatt was tending the horses. That meant that Mrs. Cooper was probably responsible for the coffee.

Cole threw off the wool blanket and got to his feet. Yawning, he shook out his stiff limbs. The morning air was damp, and thin fingers of fog covered the mountaintops in the distance. Ignoring the steps, he hopped down from the porch and crossed the yard to the pump. He rinsed his mouth and washed his face. The cold water finished the job of waking him up.

He returned Wyatt's greeting, then started back to the house, raking his hair with his fingers to give it some sense of order. Upon entering, he breathed deeply, infinitely more invigorated by the coffee than he had been by the fresh air.

Watching him, Rachel Cooper smiled appreciatively. "That's how Wyatt faces the day." She was sitting at the table, her hands wrapped firmly around a cup that was raised to her lips. "I prefer tea, but I couldn't find any. I don't think the Abbots drink it."

"You're probably right. Rhyne never asked for it." Cole crossed to the kitchen to get a cup for himself. "Is she up?"

Rachel shook her head. "I didn't hear her moving, so I checked on her a few minutes ago. She's still sleeping soundly." She rested her cup on the table and turned slightly so she could see Cole at the stove. "Do you really think she'll be able to go anywhere today? She seemed so tired last evening. Her eyelids were drooping at the table."

Cole had noticed that, too. "I'll be able to tell you after I examine her." He hesitated briefly, then went ahead when Rachel's glance seemed to encourage him. "I've been thinking about what you said last night . . . about wanting to raise Rhyne's baby. I wondered if you spoke to Doctor Diggins about conception or submitted to an examination." He saw her color. "I suspect I was too

154

forthright," he said brusquely. "I apologize."

Rachel waved a hand dismissively. The heat in her cheeks subsided. "It was unexpected, is all. I thought we would be discussing Runt."

"After last evening, I think it is better not to speak behind her back or fool ourselves to believe we are out of her hearing. Perhaps we should discuss this at another time."

"No," she said quickly, surprising even herself. "No, I wouldn't care if Rhyne over-heard." She took a steadying sip of coffee. "I went to Doc if I had a cough I couldn't seem to chase away or a steady ache in my fingers that kept me from sewing, but I didn't have confidence in him to help me with what he called female problems. From time to time he'd deliver a baby, but mostly he left that to Mrs. Cromwell or Mrs. Best."

"Midwives?"

She nodded. "They're very good, and you won't regret relying on them, but they don't have the breadth of knowledge you do — or at least that I believe you do. You submitted an extraordinary *vita,* Dr. Monroe. The committee was especially impressed with your tenure at St. John of God Hospital. It was our belief — rightly or wrongly — that it broadened your experiences, making you knowledgeable of the range of illnesses and conditions that you'd find here."

"I believe that it does, Mrs. Cooper, but I

hope the committee hasn't forgotten that I entered into the agreement with the understanding that I would be able to continue my research."

"Yes. Yes, of course. There is no question of that."

Cole leaned his hip against the warm stove and drank from his cup. "Come to see me after we return," he said. "It's unlikely that there's anything wrong at all. It could be that you simply want it too much."

"How can that be?"

"Honestly, I don't know. It just seems to happen that way sometimes. Have you ever tangled your sewing threads because you're trying to hurry?"

"Yes."

He shrugged. "It's like that, I suspect."

Rachel considered his imperfect metaphor. She wondered what parts were tangling.

"There is also the possibility," Cole said, "that the problem with conception lies with your husband."

"No," she said. "I know it doesn't. Wyatt's first wife was pregnant when she died. Please don't repeat that. No one knows."

Cole was vaguely insulted that she thought it was necessary to caution him. "I think I've demonstrated that I honor confidences."

"I'm sorry. Of course you have." She looked away, embarrassed. "Old habits."

"I need to wake Rhyne," he said. "I may

ask you to assist me, Mrs. Cooper. Would you be willing to do that?"

Rachel had no experience with what he was asking her to do. She had never been present at a birth and what she understood about her own body was limited to her relations with her husband. She realized she was astonishingly ignorant.

"If you think it will help Rhyne," she said.

"It might. We'll see." He poured a second cup of coffee for himself and a small one for his patient. He set both cups on the tray he'd been using and balanced it carefully in one hand while picking up his medical bag in the other. That left him without a hand to open the door to Rhyne's room. "Would you?" he asked, indicating the door with a thrust of his chin.

"Of course." Rachel rose and preceded him to the door. She let it swing open and stepped aside to allow him to enter. It wasn't her intention to linger, but what she glimpsed from her vantage point at his side rooted her to the floor.

A Winchester in Runt Abbot's hands was a deadly thing.

"The only step you better be taking, Dr. Monroe, is the one that puts you on the other side of that threshold."

Cole didn't move. "I thought we were past you trying to run me off, Rhyne. Put the rifle down."

"Not a chance. I saw what you have in that bag." She nodded toward the satchel on the floor. "I've been waitin' for you."

Cole hefted the bag in his hand. The weight of it spoke to his error. "Let's discuss this," he said calmly. "I brought you coffee."

"So help me God, I'll shoot you where you stand if you come in here. Put the tray on the floor, take your cup, and go."

Cole held on to the tray and let his medical bag thump to the floor. "I'm not going anywhere." He passed the tray to Rachel and told her to back out of the way.

"I think you're safer if I'm standing here."

"I wouldn't count on it," he said wryly. "Go on. I'll be fine." He returned his attention to Rhyne. Her grip on the rifle hadn't wavered yet. She was kneeling on the bed, her thighs slightly splayed for balance. It was difficult to know which was more rumpled: her shirt or her hair. A deep pillow crease marked her cheek, and the flush of sleep still suffused her complexion. The danger posed by the weapon was a marked contrast to the pair of lace-trimmed drawers she was wearing.

He was in a standoff with a feral kitten.

"I'm not going to examine you against your will, Rhyne."

"I won't let you put that mask on me again."

"I only put you to sleep to spare you more pain. That wouldn't be the case today.

There'd be discomfort, but not pain."

Rhyne jerked the rifle at him. "How would you know? I bet no one's ever poked you with something like what you've got in that bag."

"You're right. I only know what my patients have told me."

She still wasn't satisfied. "They probably lied. Did you think of that? I bet they didn't want to disappoint you, you being so plainly easy to look at and all."

Cole sighed. "May I please come in, Rhyne? Johnny and Wyatt will be here soon. There's no reason to include them in this conversation."

"Maybe they'll want to know what you do to women. It might even be against the law. That's what I'm thinking."

"Oh, for God's sake," he said impatiently. It was easy to call her bluff when he concluded the better choice was for her to just shoot him. A single long stride took Cole far enough into the room that he was able to slam the door shut behind him. He walked over to the bed, jerked the Winchester from her hand, and expertly removed the cartridges. He pocketed them and returned the rifle. "Don't ever point that at me again. You won't like what happens to it the next time."

Rhyne cradled the Winchester protectively.

"What the hell's wrong with you?"

She liked it when he forgot himself and spoke like a regular person, not a professor-doctor-scientist. *Et tu, Brute.* She knew Latin, too. "I reckon I got a little squirrelly."

"Squirrelly."

"It means demented."

"I *know* what it means." He sat down in the chair and plowed one hand through his hair. "What caused it?"

That raised her eyebrows. "Have you looked at those things in your bag?"

"Yes." He pointed to the bag at his feet. "May I?"

Rhyne laid the rifle beside her and sat back against the iron head rail. She regarded the bag uncertainly but finally gave her approval.

Cole set the bag in his lap and opened it, displaying the instruments for her to see. "These are delivery forceps," he said, pointing to the curved metal tongs. "To help ease a baby out. All of my obstetrical instruments are blue gun steel so they can be sterilized. That means I can heat them to a temperature that destroys bacteria and reduces the chance of infection. Bed fever, for instance."

"I've delivered animals before," she said. "I used my hands when I had to."

"Yes, well, this is the preferred procedure for women giving birth."

Rhyne wondered about the poor baby's soft head getting squeezed like a ripe melon, but she kept the picture that made to herself. "What's that?" She pointed to another instrument. "That part looks like a duck's bill."

"It's a trivalve speculum."

"Does it go where I think it does?"

"In your vagina, yes."

"Vagina. You've said that before. Is that what the front hall's called?"

"Front hall?"

"My brothers told me that's what it was. Front hall. Back door. Rainspout. All the parts."

"I see," he said carefully. Cole recalled Johnny telling him about comparing parts with his sisters and brother. It was difficult not to smile. He wondered if the nomenclature the Winslows had employed was as illustrative as what the Abbot boys used. "Yes, the front hall is the vagina. The literal Latin translation is sheath."

"Sheath." Perhaps there was some value in learning more Latin. Judah had never seen the point of it. He thought Greek and English were the voices of the poets. Homer and Shakespeare were his favorites. "What exactly does it do? Not the vagina, I mean. The speculum."

Cole wondered if he could have such a frank discussion with anyone other than Rhyne. Her curiosity was not restrained by embarrassment. He was bound not to do harm, and in this circumstance harm would be done if he made her feel shame. He removed the speculum and demonstrated how it opened. "Once this is inserted into the

161

vagina, I can open it and look into the canal. I would be able to see your cervix — that's the tip, the neck, of your womb. I'd better understand what injury had been done."

Rhyne frowned. "I don't know what you mean."

Now it was Cole's brow that creased. "You remember the beating, don't you?"

She nodded, but there was hesitation and uncertainty in the small movement. "The marks haven't gone away," she said. "Of course, I remember."

"All of it?" He watched Rhyne's confusion fade to fear, and he knew then that she had passed out under the force of Judah's blows. He spoke quietly, but he also spoke the truth. "When the beating didn't produce an immediate abortion, Rhyne, Judah used his walking stick inside you to force one."

CHAPTER 5

Cole threw back the covers on his bed and put on his slippers. He shrugged into his robe, belted it, then left his bedroom in search of warm milk and brown sugar and maybe some of Mrs. Easter's rolled oats bread if Whitley hadn't sneaked the last of it.

He made his way through the dark house without incident. He'd discovered that Whitley was easily disturbed by these increasingly frequent excursions, and the quickest way to alert her was to light a lamp. As long as nothing was left out of place when they retired for the night, he could manage the route without stubbing his toe.

When he reached the kitchen he finally lighted a lamp and fired up the stove. He swung a chair around and straddled it while he waited for the milk to heat. He wondered if what he really wanted was to go to sleep. He could always go to the surgery and lose himself in his work. There were nights when that was a better choice.

Footsteps behind him in the hallway had Cole glancing over his shoulder. "What woke you, Whitley?"

She shrugged. "I don't think I was really sleeping. I keep listening for you."

"I wish you'd stop doing that."

"I wish you'd stop doing this."

He sighed. They were at an impasse. "Would you like some milk? I can add more to the pot."

"No."

"Did you eat the last of the oat bread?"

"There's still some in the box. Would you like me to get it for you?"

He let her do it because she wanted to be useful. He watched her slice off the heel — his favorite part — and smear a bit of butter on it. She placed it on a small plate painted with delicate red poppies and passed it to him.

"Did you look in on Rhyne?" he asked.

She nodded. "I always do."

"How is our patient doing?"

"She sleeps much better than either of us. She never stirs when I go in."

Cole knew that didn't necessarily mean Rhyne was sleeping, but he refrained from sharing that with Whitley.

"What happened to her, Cole?"

"Whitley."

"If I knew, then maybe I'd know how to talk to her."

164

It was a familiar argument over these last three weeks. "You talk to her just fine."

"But she hardly says anything."

"She will when she's ready. She's not a chatterbox like you."

Whitley dropped into the chair at the head of the small table. She pulled her hastily braided hair forward and began to rework the plait. This occupied her for a bit longer than a minute and helped her sustain her silence until she was compelled to point out that his milk was scalding.

Cole jerked upright, almost tipping the chair as he stood. He grabbed a towel to wrap around the pot handle and removed it from the stove. The milk beaded and sizzled as he poured it into a cup already containing a teaspoonful of brown sugar.

"I like her," Whitley said. "Even if she doesn't talk much. You're right about me. When I have to, I can carry both ends of a conversation."

"Mr. Cassidy says you do a lot of that in school."

"Mr. Cassidy is ancient, Cole, and he only wants to talk about ancient things."

"Greece, perhaps? The Roman Empire? Those kinds of ancient things?"

"Precisely." She pushed out her lower lip, but Cole wasn't watching and the effect was lost. She sucked it back in and absently rubbed the spray of freckles on the bridge of her nose. "I already know about those civilizations. We studied all about them at Miss Starcher's, and since they're ancient, they really don't change, do they?"

Cole gave her full marks for being able to coax a smile out of him. "We had an agreement, Whitley. If you did not settle well in school here, then you'd have to go back to Miss Starcher's Seminary while I stayed behind to honor my contract. I thought you might be bored in Mr. Cassidy's classroom, but from what I have seen, he appears to have challenging studies for all of his students. Are you falling behind?" He gave her a sideways look when she didn't answer. "What? You're suddenly having trouble with your end of our discussion?"

She blew out a large breath, making her lips vibrate, and tossed her fiery braid back over her shoulder. "Let's end our discussion."

"Let's," he agreed. "Go to bed, Whitley. We'll talk about school in the morning."

"Well, that is certainly something to look forward to." She kissed him on the cheek and then made a dramatic exit, practicing her flounce for her own amusement.

Cole listened to her climb the stairs. Her footfalls echoed softly as she went down the hallway to her room. He gave her ample time to crawl into bed again before he left the table. Droplets of hot milk splashed the back of his hand as he carried the cup and crust to the library. It was more likely that he'd fall asleep there while reviewing his notes than if he returned to bed. Standing at the closed pocket doors, he realized he'd left the oil lamp behind. It was that oversight that allowed him to glimpse the narrow band of light in the seam of the doors.

There'd been no lamp burning when he passed the room earlier, and he was certain Whitley hadn't doubled back. There was probably only one good explanation for the light, and he toed open the door to see if he was right.

Rhyne was curled in the chair that he'd planned to occupy. She was wrapped in a dark green woolen shawl and had one of his heavy medical books open in her lap. The pool of light at her side allowed him to see her intense concentration. There was a small vertical crease between her eyebrows, and her shoulders were hunched forward. He couldn't see what she was studying, but he knew it wasn't an illustration because her index finger moved steadily down the page.

The final testament to her complete absorption was that she had not acknowledged him; indeed, she did not seem to know that he had joined her.

Cole took advantage of her lack of awareness to observe her a moment longer. A few days after coming to town, Rhyne had quietly submitted herself to Rose Beatty's scissors.

Her ragged crop of hair had mostly been trimmed to a smooth cap. Here, in the middle of the night, Rose's work was not in evidence. Much of Rhyne's short black hair stood at attention, although not with the precision of soldiers on the parade ground. This was a scruffy troop of new recruits who had never marched together. When she absently rubbed the side of her head, it only made things worse.

She looked like a rumpled pixie.

Her lowered eyes allowed Cole to see what was perhaps the most surprising transformation in her heart-shaped face: the dark, thick sweep of her eyelashes. According to Mrs. Beatty, Rhyne admitted that her stubby lashes were the result of some painful plucking and an occasional trim with a pair of shears that could have put her eyes out. Upon learning of it, Cole could only think that Rhyne Abbot had reached a very low point if she was owning up to such a thing.

Standing there, Cole wondered how he could make his presence known without frightening her. It occurred to him that he would not have given Runt Abbot the same consideration. He cleared his throat. Rhyne stiffened, but she didn't flinch.

"Would you like your chair?" she asked, looking up.

"No. Stay there." He held up his cup and

plate. "Hot milk and bread. Would you like some?"

She shook her head. "That would put me to sleep."

"Exactly."

Her smile was faint, and faintly self-mocking. "I don't want to sleep."

He nodded, understanding. "May I join you?"

Shrugging, she said, "Suit yourself."

Cole would not allow her to put him off with that affected, careless air. "May I join you," he said again, more deliberate in his tone this time.

She hesitated, searching for the honest answer. "Yes," she said finally. "I would like that."

Cole moved to the writing desk and sat in the cabriole chair behind it. He set his cup and plate on the blotter. Stretching out his long legs under the desk, he found the upholstered footstool and propped his heels on it. "What book do you have?"

Rhyne closed it enough so that she could read the spine. "*Foster's Anatomical Reference and Surgery Guide.*"

"You said you didn't want to sleep."

"It's not Dickens," she admitted. "But it is interesting. It hasn't put me to sleep yet."

Cole picked up the cup of milk and eyed Rhyne over the rim. The placement of her index finger between the pages suggested that she'd read better than a third of the book. It was an impressive accomplishment given the short time she'd been in his house. "How do you get past Whitley?"

"I wait until she's with you, then I leave. Why does she look in on me before she goes downstairs?"

"It eases her mind."

"I don't understand."

"It's important to her to know that you're there and that you're safe. It's why she follows me. She needs to know I haven't left."

"Why would she think you'd leave?"

"Because I have."

Rhyne watched him tip his cup and carefully test the heat of the milk against his lips. He must have found it to his liking because he took a large mouthful. Her eyes strayed to his strong throat and the way the muscles in his neck moved when he swallowed. "Sternocleidomastoid," she whispered to herself.

Cole lowered the cup and looked at her oddly. "What did you say?"

"Sternocleidomastoid. The muscles in your neck. Am I saying it right?"

He nodded slowly, pointing to the book. "You remember that from there?"

"Uh-huh." She added quickly, "But I don't remember everything."

Cole didn't think he'd be surprised if she did. "What *was* your education, Rhyne?"

"Judah schooled me. Same as Rusty and Randy."

"He had his own ideas, then, of what was important for you to know."

"That's right."

"You studied all the classics."

"He read them to me and my brothers."

"How did you learn to read?"

"Rusty and Randy taught me."

Cole tried to imagine the boys risking Judah's wrath to sneak books into the loft to share them with their sister. It didn't fit easily with what others had told him about the older Abbot boys, but apparently there were times when they weren't beating the hell out of her.

He took a bite from the heel of bread and washed it down with another swallow of milk. "Will it bother you if I review my notes? That's why I came in here."

"You usually work in your surgery."

It was true. That's how she'd avoided being found out. "I finished the last set of experiments. I need to look over my documentation."

"Of course." She immediately ducked her head and opened the book.

Cole could only interpret her readiness to resume her own reading as evidence of her considerable relief. Since she had just exchanged more words with him than she had since her arrival, Cole did not indulge in feel-

171

ing slighted. Instead, he was marginally optimistic.

He opened the middle drawer of the secretary and drew out the notebook he was using for this round of his research on bacterial staining. Squaring off the book, he opened it to where he had recorded information on the last group of experiments. His meticulous drawings of what he had observed under the microscope were helpful in reviewing his conclusions. They provided substantiation of the bacilli cultures he was trying to identify.

He made a few notations, but more often simply tapped the tip of his pen against his lips. The milk and bread were not touched again.

In spite of her intention to ignore Coleridge Monroe, Rhyne found herself stealing the occasional glance. He never surprised her by looking up from his work. She found herself fascinated by the way he gave over all of his attention to the thing in front of him. He didn't seem to notice the dark copper hair that had fallen forward over his brow. In any other circumstance, he would have pushed it back with an impatient gesture. Now, it just lay there, another shadow crossing his quiet features.

She knew he still struggled with the rightness of his decision to tell her what Judah had done. He must have seen something in her face that made him question his judgment. She remembered only that she'd stared at him. From her perspective it seemed that she'd had no reaction at all. She couldn't move for the numbness. It was exactly like the last moments before she fell asleep under the spell of the vaporizing ether. She was anesthetized.

He'd put away his instruments and walked out with both bags, one under each arm. Rachel had come to her then, but Rhyne knew Cole hadn't explained what had taken place in the room. Rachel didn't ask a single question. She just sat in the chair Cole vacated and stayed there until Rhyne slept. In Rhyne's mind, at least, she stayed much longer.

They had traveled that same day. The decision was made while she was sleeping, and that suited her fine. She didn't raise an objection to riding in the bed of the wagon and didn't complain that she could walk to the wagon when Johnny and the sheriff said they would carry her. Rachel packed some clothes and personal things, and Rhyne let her do it without giving her any direction.

She heard snippets of their conversation, but most of it was merely a harmless buzzing in her ears. She had no real interest in what they had to say.

When they arrived in Reidsville, they went directly to Cole's home. She recalled a flutter of something then, an inkling of doubt, perhaps, just enough to know that she would not always be numb. She hammered the feeling down.

She floated through her days, vaguely detached but carefully polite. At night, she roamed. Too restless to sleep, she explored the house, moving quietly in the hallways so that even Whitley didn't hear her. She spent time in almost every room, from the overstuffed comforts of the front parlor to the spartan surgery. She wandered through the kitchen and poked around in the larder. Sometimes she removed the slippers Whitley gave her so she could feel the tasseled rug in the dining room under her feet.

Her favorite room was the library. The shelves were crowded with books, not only medical tomes, but biographies and novels, histories and illustrated travelogues. The space smelled of leather and paper and lamp oil. The window facing the street was framed by heavy velvet drapes the color of wild grapes. If she had to spend time indoors, this room would make it better than tolerable.

No one had said how long she might stay here, and she hadn't asked. Whitley seemed oddly fascinated by her. Rhyne didn't know whether to be flattered or annoyed. Cole, when she saw him, was courteous but reserved. Mostly, she was glad of it.

He never broached the subject of another examination.

She didn't leave the house for ten days.

During that time Will and Rose Beatty came to visit and Rose cut her hair. Mrs. Cooper came and went a great deal. Sometimes she brought Molly Showalter along. They measured the length and breadth of her, then showed her a portfolio of sketches that Mrs. Cooper had done especially for her. Dresses. Jackets. Gowns. Hats. They asked her to choose. It was overwhelming.

She recalled how Cole had come upon them in the parlor: Rachel, Molly, and Whitley sitting still as stone while she examined the drawings one by one. She could feel their eyes on her and knew the pressure of their expectant silence. Cole had grasped the situation immediately and relieved her of the portfolio. In less than two minutes he made all the decisions. Whitley pronounced him overbearing. Molly cowered a little in his presence. Rachel looked up at him, smiled as if she understood something she had not before, and accepted his judgment.

Rhyne had not known what he'd selected for her until Mrs. Cooper returned for the fittings. She came alone, while Whitley was at school, and it was just the two of them. Talking did not seem so much like a chore.

The first time she ventured out it was because Whitley wanted to go to the emporium for licorice and Cole wouldn't let her go alone. Sitting in the parlor, Rhyne had been able to hear Whitley wheedle and coax.

Cole never raised his voice, but he never changed his mind, and he finally removed her from the surgery and closed the doors. She'd come to the parlor after that, feet dragging, chewing on the tip of her braid. Rhyne already had her coat ready.

She had no enthusiasm for walking through town or the energy to deflect the stares, yet she managed it because listening to Cole's sister whine jangled nerves that were better left for dead.

Rhyne belatedly realized that her occasional glance in Cole's direction had become a straight-on stare. It had been a long time since she'd turned a page. The last time she had watched him so closely, he'd been in her rifle sights.

"You were right to tell me," she said suddenly.

Cole looked up. He rubbed his eyebrows with his thumb and forefinger. "Pardon?"

She found it strangely reassuring that he could be dog-tired *and* mannerly. He must have had a good upbringing, or at least not the one she'd had. "I said, you were right to tell me. I'm talking about Judah, in case you didn't know."

"I was working that part out." He pushed the notebook away and leaned back in his chair. "Why are you telling me now?"

"Shouldn't I?"

"No. No, this is fine. I'm just taken . . . I

don't know . . . it seems . . ."

Rhyne tried to remember if she'd ever known him not to finish a sentence. "I was thinking about the last time I pointed my Winchester at you. It just occurred to me that you deserved to know you made the right decision."

"What makes you think I didn't know that?"

She shrugged. One corner of the shawl fell off her shoulder. She pulled it and the sleeve of her nightgown back into place. "The way you watch me, for one thing. The way you don't sleep, for another."

"Apparently I don't watch you closely enough," he said. "I didn't know you were moving around at night."

"I know how to track and hunt. I can move so you can't hear me unless I want you to."

"I guess I've learned that." He folded his arms across his chest and studied her. "So if I did the right thing, why can't *you* sleep?"

"Because I still think about it when I close my eyes. Isn't that curious? I don't remember it. Didn't know it happened. And I dream about it anyway."

"Forgive me, but I don't see how you can say I acted properly."

"You just turned over the cards I was dealt," she said. "It's still my hand to play. That doesn't make it easy; it just makes it mine." Rhyne saw that he wasn't entirely convinced. "Judah might have taken it in his

177

head to taunt me with it. That would have been worse. I don't kill the messenger, but Judah wouldn't be the messenger exactly, would he? Here's a word for you, Dr. Monroe, with Latin roots: patricide. I reckon you know what that means."

Hair stood up on the back of Cole's neck. "I reckon I do," he said softly. He'd always thought that keeping Rhyne away from Judah was protecting her. She was making it clear that it worked the other way as well. "There's no reason for you and Judah to cross paths."

"That's fine by me. I'll move to the other side of the street if I see him first."

Cole knew it didn't follow that Judah Abbot would do the same. Will Beatty escorted the man out of town the morning after Rhyne arrived. Judah had the spread to himself now; for the first time in his life he was well and truly on his own. There existed the strong possibility that he would eventually come looking for Runt.

Rhyne closed the book in her lap and laid it on the side table. She pulled the shawl closer and tucked the hem of her nightgown around her feet.

Cole got up and added wood to the small stove. He stirred the embers and then brushed off his hands and returned to the chair. "Late summer nights here are chilly, I'm learning."

"I like them. All the stars are out. The sky's

open and wide. I bunked outside most of the time. It seems strange to sleep every night with a roof over my head."

Listening, he smiled faintly. "Perhaps too much has been made of having a roof. The sky has a great deal to recommend it."

"You slept on the porch," she pointed out. "It has a roof."

"Not much of one."

"True."

They fell silent. It didn't take long for it to stretch toward awkward. Rhyne glanced at the book she'd put aside. Cole fiddled with his cup. As often happens, when they spoke, it was at the same time.

"Go on," Cole said. "Ladies first."

Hearing that expression, one that she had uttered to females all her life, tickled Rhyne. She stared at Cole for a long moment absorbing the idea that what he'd said really applied to her. She felt her lips part as the urge to laugh began to swell inside her. It erupted from her throat as something husky and hearty, eventually bringing tears to her eyes before it became a choking fit that required Cole's assistance to contain it.

He pushed her forward in the chair and tapped her lightly on the back with the flat of his hand. "You don't have a chaw in your cheek, do you?"

Rhyne shook her head hard, squeezing out a few additional tears. She swiped at them and gasped, trying to catch her breath. "Stop. Don't. Say. Anything."

Chuckling, Cole pressed a handkerchief into her hand. "Better?"

Through her tears, Rhyne could see that the linen was monogrammed. The embroidery floss was emerald green. Someone had chosen that color because it matched his eyes. The stitches were fine, the script elegant with flourishes and curlicues: *CMB*. She started to push it back at him, but he insisted she keep it.

Rhyne touched it to her eyes, then the corners of her mouth. She refused to put it to her nose. She folded it in her fist and sniffed hard.

Cole didn't comment, nor did he laugh. In truth, he was touched that she found something so ordinary worth extraordinary care. He stood abruptly so that his hip was no longer resting on the wide arm of her chair and returned to the secretary.

"It's still your turn," he said when he saw that she had recovered.

"I think I forgot," she said. "No. Wait. I remember. I was wondering what you thought I might do."

"Do?"

"For work. We talked about it, remember? Or at least I did. I can't remain here forever, Dr. Monroe. That was never part of the plan."

"I wasn't aware there was a plan."

"Don't you think I should have one?"

"Too much has been made of them," he said. "Like roofs."

Rhyne's smile was a trifle uneven as she tried to decide if he was mocking her. "I need money. I couldn't even buy a stick of licorice at Morrison's."

"Whitley bought you some, didn't she?"

"Yes. She bought me cherry and lemon drops, too."

"But that's not the point, is it?"

"No. I don't want to be beholden. I should have work."

Cole leaned forward and set his elbows on the desk. "All right. But it's too important a decision to be discussing at this hour." He checked his pocket watch. "It's four-thirty. I don't know if that makes it too early or too late, but it's definitely wrong."

She nodded. "In the morning, then. *Later* in the morning." Rhyne eased her feet out from under her and stood. She dragged the shawl with her. "Good night, Dr. Monroe."

"Good night, Miss Abbot."

Hearing herself addressed in that manner was also a first, but this time Rhyne didn't laugh.

Whitley slathered butter on one half of a warm biscuit, then waggled her knife at Rhyne who was sitting opposite her at the dining room table. She ignored her brother's

181

reproving look. "I know what you can do," she said. She bit into her biscuit then held up one finger as she chewed, manners warring with the urgency to make her disclosure. Swallowing, she said, "The Miner Key."

Rhyne and Cole both stared at her.

"It's a good idea," she said defensively. "Mr. Martin is always looking for entertaining acts. And Molly told me that Rhyne used to perform there when she was my age, even younger. Molly never saw a show because she was too young, but her parents remember the Abbot Family Players and told her that Rhyne was excellent as Juliet. She could give readings and do short scenes." She set her knife down and regarded Rhyne earnestly. "Can you sing? It would be even better if you had a sweet voice or could play an instrument. Mr. Martin could fill the saloon every night if you sang 'My Old Kentucky Home.' "

Cole forestalled Whitley from taking another bite of biscuit by placing one hand over her wrist. "That was highly entertaining, Whitley. Perhaps Rudy Martin will hire you."

Whitley rolled her eyes at Rhyne. "That means no. Did you understand that? Sometimes Cole isn't easy to follow, but that means no. For both of us."

Rhyne objected to the idea that Cole could make this decision for her, but she didn't argue the principle because she happened to agree with the outcome. "It's all right," she said. "I don't want to be on stage again. I never liked performing."

"Really?" asked Whitley. "Why not?"

Rhyne shrugged. She used her fork to push some scrambled eggs around on her plate. "Everyone stares."

"But they pay to do it. People stare at me all the time, and I can't collect a cent."

Cole had a strip of bacon halfway to his mouth. His motion was arrested by Whitley's disclosure. "Here, Whitley? They're staring at you here?"

"Not now," she said. "And no one was ever mean about it, not like the girls at Miss Starcher's. You can't stop people from looking and wondering, Cole. I'm not ashamed of my scars. I wish you wouldn't make me be."

Flushing, Cole set the bacon strip back on his plate. He was aware of Rhyne watching him, but was more concerned by what Whitley saw. "What shames me," he said quietly, "is that I've given you reason — any reason at all — to believe what you just said."

Rhyne's gaze swiveled to the fine webbing of scars on the back of Whitley's hands. Where her skin was pulled taut, it was unnaturally smooth and shiny. The color was so pale in places as to be alabaster; elsewhere it was pink, edging toward red. Rhyne knew the scars went at least as far as the middle of Whitley's forearms because she'd seen Cole's sister with the cuffs of her blouse turned up, but if there was more extensive injury it was concealed by her clothes.

Whitley fiddled with her half-eaten biscuit. "I had reason to think it would be different in Reidsville. It's not New York, after all. When we first arrived, you allowed me to explore on my own now and again, but that's changed. You won't permit me to leave the house alone under any circumstances. You escort me to school or make me walk with the Hammond twins even if I want to be by myself. It is surprisingly easy to believe that you worry what people will say about me." She stopped idly turning the biscuit and raised her hands so the backs of them were visible to Cole. "Or say about my disfigurement."

Except for a heart stutter, Cole did not flinch. "You misunderstand, Whitley. My decision not to allow you to roam at will has nothing whatsoever to do with your scars." He indicated with his index finger that she should lower her hands. "There are other considerations."

Whitley sat back and folded her arms, tucking her hands from sight. She ignored Cole's disapproving stare. "He thinks I am being dramatic," she told Rhyne. "And yet he insists he will not seriously consider a career on the stage for me."

Cole shook his head. "Do not engage Miss

Abbot in our disagreement."

"Miss Abbot?" She glanced from Rhyne to her brother and back to Rhyne again. "You are Miss Abbot now?"

"I am Rhyne."

"Well, that is a relief. I cannot keep up with the changes in my brother since he made your acquaintance."

Cole had an urge to stuff Whitley's biscuit in her mouth. He quashed that impulse and settled for reminding her of her responsibilities. "Your breakfast, please, Whitley. You'll be late for school."

Sighing heavily, she shoveled eggs onto her fork. "It is a trial being your sister, Cole. Judge Wentworth is still in town, you know, and I might put my case before him." She addressed Rhyne. "Are there female lawyers, do you think?"

"I don't know."

"There should be."

Cole drew the napkin off his lap and wiped his mouth. "That, at least, is something worth pursuing, Whitley. If you speak to the judge, speak to him about that. Tell him you cut your teeth putting your arguments before your brother. If he has any sisters, he'll appreciate how effective that can be."

Whitley grinned. "That is an excellent suggestion, Coleridge. I shall take it under advisement." Her smile faded when she heard the knock at the front door. She slumped in

185

her chair. "That's the twins."

Cole pointed toward the hallway. "Go. Take your biscuit."

Whitley did what Cole had restrained himself from doing: she stuffed the biscuit in her mouth. Mumbling an apology for rushing off, she shot up from her chair and hurried from the dining room.

"Don't allow her to fool you," Cole said when she was gone. "She'd much rather have Dot and Digger Hammond walk her to school than me."

Rhyne pushed her plate away. With Whitley gone, there was no reason to pretend she had an appetite. "Why *don't* you let her go anywhere by herself?"

"She distracts herself. Everything is interesting to her, and she doesn't particularly like the classroom. I'm not sure she'd arrive without an escort."

"That's school." Rhyne knew her chin was up; she heard the edge of challenge in her voice. "What about other places? Why can't she be distracted on her way to Morrison's, for instance? What does it matter if she goes to the bakery by way of Wickham's Leather Goods?"

"I don't approve of her wandering around on her own."

"But you let her do it when you first came to town. Whitley said that and you didn't disagree. She's right. Something changed."

Cole placed his napkin on the table. "This doesn't really concern you."

"I think it might. I think you're afraid that what happened to me could happen to Whitley."

"Can't it?"

Rhyne fell silent. She didn't know how to answer that question. She rubbed the underside of her chin, an affectation that she'd often employed as Runt. Some habits of deep thinking were difficult to break.

Cole watched her internal struggle play out on her face. She chewed on the inside of her cheek and furrowed her brow. Her slate gray eyes clouded. "It's all right, Rhyne. You don't have to answer, but please don't think I'll let you take Whitley's side on this. I have to do what I believe is best."

Rhyne nodded jerkily. She brushed crumbs from the table into the palm of her hand and started to gather utensils.

"Leave them," said Cole. "For now. There's something I *would* like an answer to."

She set her knife, fork, and spoon down carefully and brought her head up. "What?"

"Sometime last week — I don't remember when precisely — Whitley mentioned that you'd never asked her about her scars. She assumed I told you how she got them, and I allowed her to think that was the case. She doesn't mind if I do tell someone, but she knows that I generally let her speak for

187

herself. So my question is this: why *haven't* you asked her?"

Rhyne's eyebrows lifted in a perfect arc above her eyes. "When someone asked me improper questions, I jammed my fist in their nose." She ran her index finger along the bridge of hers. "You noticed right off that mine's been broken a time or two. I didn't figure to have it set again."

"Whitley wouldn't have punched you."

"Well, I don't know why not. Folks need to discipline their prying. Sometimes it just takes waiting a thing out. It's like trying to coax a hatchling from its nest. It'll happen when it happens."

It wasn't that Cole disagreed, only that he thought that she wasn't being completely forthcoming. "Then you weren't concerned about *quid pro quo?*"

Rhyne's mouth curled to one side at his use of the Latin phrase. "There you go again. I know what it means, but if you want to keep talking like that, I suggest you invite Wyatt Cooper to play cards. Besides being the sheriff, he's a lawyer, and he can *quid* your *pro quo* and raise you a *habeas corpus.*"

Rhyne actually rocked back in her chair when Cole gave a shout of laughter. She watched him closely, suspicious of this sudden change in his humor. "What did I say?"

Cole required a moment to compose himself before he could answer. "I'm not certain

I can even explain it," he said. "You have a talent for turning a phrase that can snap me to attention."

"Well, then, soldier. At ease. You almost pushed me and the chair over." She reached for her utensils again, and this time Cole didn't stop her. She gathered his things, then Whitley's, and balanced the whole of it in her arms as she started for the kitchen. Just outside of his reach, she paused and pivoted on her heels to face him. "I did understand what you meant, though. And you're right. I might have asked your sister what happened to her if I'd thought she wouldn't ask the same of me. Something for something."

Whitley came out of the schoolhouse swinging the strap that held her books together. She came close to clobbering Digger Hammond in the back of the head when the arc of her books went wide. Digger was oblivious because he was playing shoulder tag with his friends, but Dot saw what nearly came to pass and gave Whitley a quelling glance. Whitley offered an apologetic smile that she didn't mean in the least. She would have rather been bumping shoulders with Digger than trying to match Dot's sashay.

Whitley forgot all about the sway in her step when she saw Rhyne waiting for her at the perimeter of the schoolyard. She barreled right through Digger and his friends, ignor-

189

ing their protests, and ran straight at Rhyne.

"Whoa, girl." Rhyne put out a hand. "I didn't bring a bridle."

Whitley giggled. "We hardly spent any time outdoors today, and Mr. Cassidy frowns on us older girls running around. He thinks we're chasing boys. *I* don't, but I can't say that he's wrong about some of the others."

"Is that so?" Rhyne looked over the trio of boys coming toward them. "Are those the ones they chase?"

Whitley glanced back. "Some of them. Digger Hammond. Ben Martin. Tom Morrison. A few have to stay behind to clean slates." She added confidentially. "They got in trouble for tripping the girls."

Rhyne watched the progress of the trio and put her hand on Whitley's elbow to encourage her to fall in step.

"Hey, Runt! That really you?"

Rhyne recognized that it was Tom Morrison calling after her. He had the same nasal quality to his voice as his mother.

"Let's go," Whitley whispered. Now she was the one doing the surreptitious tugging. "They'll just be stupid."

"Runt!" Tom called again. "Wait up!"

Setting her jaw, Rhyne shook off Whitley's hand and turned to face Tom Morrison. The boy was at least eight years her junior but more than a head taller. Except for the unfortunate nasal whine, Tom took after his father. Thin, verging on skinny, he had angular features and broad, bony shoulders that he hadn't grown into.

"Hello, Tom." She nodded at his friends. "Boys."

Ben Martin squinted at her. "You sound different."

"Really? I don't recall that we ever traded words."

Ben thrust his thick hand forward. "Ben Martin. My pa owns the Miner Key. I saw you go in there a time or two. Heard you ask for whiskey."

Rhyne shook his hand. She felt him test her grip, and she gave it back in equal measure.

"Damn," Ben said, withdrawing his hand. Pride kept him from shaking it out. "I think it's really him."

"I told you," Digger said. He shifted his weight uncomfortably and stole a glance at Whitley. "The doc lives right next door. I seen Runt plenty of times going in and out with Whitley."

"I *saw*," said Whitley. "*Seen* requires a helper. I *have* seen."

Rhyne almost laughed as all three boys turned to stare at Whitley, their jaws slack. She asked for it, Rhyne thought, carrying on like her professor brother. "C'mon, Whitley. We should be going." Without thinking, she raised her hand to her forehead.

Tom nudged Ben with his bony elbow. "Did

you see that? Runt was gonna tip his hat at us. Real polite-like." He looked pointedly at Rhyne. "That's a *bonnet,*" he said slowly. "Bon-net. You don't tip one of those."

"You must be confused somethin' awful," Ben said. "Is it true you shot your balls off?"

Whitley's mouth formed a perfect O. She stamped the ground with one foot and set her arms akimbo. "Ben Martin. That's a terrible thing to say. Take it back."

Ben shook his head. "What? I didn't mean anything by it. It's just a question. It's what I've heard some folks saying."

"You're making that up," Whitley said. "The only folks saying it are you and Tom and Digger."

"Not me," Digger said. "I mean, not *I.*"

"You don't even know what balls are," Tom said at the same time.

Rhyne was aware that a crowd of students was gathering around them. All ages and both sexes were represented in the circle. She made out the youngest to be about six and the oldest was a seventeen year old that she recognized as one of Will Beatty's nieces. She wondered if she could drag Whitley away or if the girl meant to dig in her heels.

"I do so know," Whitley said.

Apparently it was to be heel-digging. Rhyne sighed.

"Well?" Tom pushed his chin out, challenging her. "Go on. Tell everyone. What are they,

Miss Knows-So-Much?"

Whitley swung her tethered books at his head and knocked him sideways. Tom stumbled, fell, then scrambled to his feet. He put his head down and charged at Whitley. Rhyne put out her foot, and he went sprawling. Ignoring the spontaneous cries of pleasure from the spectators, she put Whitley behind her and stared down Ben and Digger.

Digger surrendered easily and began to back away. There never was any real fight in him, Rhyne knew. If she understood the nature of the glances he darted at Whitley, he was probably a little sweet on her. Ben Martin, however, looked as though he wanted to assist his fallen friend, or at least make a show of it.

"Now that's not right," Ben said. "All the advantages are on your side because we're not allowed to hit girls."

"Just see if you can, Ben Martin," Whitley said over Rhyne's shoulder. "I'll hit you with my McGuffey's *Reader.* It's not good for anything else."

"You say that, but you're standing behind her. Him. The *he-she.*" He grinned so widely that his dumpling cheeks forced his eyes into slits. "The *freak,*" he said. "Like you."

Whitley dropped the book strap and shoved Rhyne hard enough to move her sideways. She went after Ben with arms flailing, shiny knuckles bared, her thumbs tucked into her fists. The circle expanded to make room for the combatants. Rhyne put her foot down on Tom's hand as he started to rise and winced as Ben drove his shoulder into Whitley's mid-section.

"Don't you dare move," Rhyne told Tom. She pressed on his hand just enough for him to know that she meant it, then she circled behind Ben, grabbed him by the wrist, and jerked his arm behind his back. He was heavier by eighty or so pounds, but Rhyne had leverage and experience wrestling her brothers to the ground. While Rhyne held Ben, Whitley got in a solid punch, giving Ben a sharp upper cut that knocked his teeth together. Rhyne wasn't surprised when Whitley's grunt of pain was a match for Ben's.

Rhyne's skirt and petticoats hampered her movements, but not so much that she couldn't find the sweet spots at the back of Ben's knees and make him buckle. She released him quickly so he couldn't pull her down with him. After that, it was easy. She jerked the ribbon from her bonnet and used it to tie his wrists behind his back, then returned to Tom and jammed the bonnet on his head.

She was flushed, satisfied, and only a bit out of breath when she looked up and saw Wyatt Cooper had joined the circle. He stood much taller than the tallest student and towered over the little ones. They'd stepped back from him, all of them looking up, most of them with expressions that were frozen somewhere between guilty and admiring. His attention, though, was all for her and Whitley Monroe.

"Maybe you both should come with me," he said calmly, giving them a nod. "I'll walk with you for a spell. Whitley, get your books. Boys, I want to believe you're done now. Don't disappoint me." He turned and started walking, clearly expecting that they would follow.

They did. Whitley grabbed her books off the ground and trotted after him. Rhyne paused to brush herself off and give Tom and Ben a warning stare they would remember. Whitley's classmates hurriedly made an opening for her.

Rhyne easily caught up to Whitley and the sheriff. Whitley was hanging her head as she walked, but Wyatt wasn't giving her any attention for it. "He isn't taking us to jail, Whitley," she said.

"No. That would be better. He's walking us *home*."

Rhyne looked past Whitley to Wyatt's implacable profile. "Are you?"

"I sure am."

"Oh."

Rhyne felt like hanging her head. "How's your hand, Whitley?"

"Feels like it's broken."

"Let me see." She raised Whitley's right hand and looked it over. "Make a fist."

Whitley did, grimacing slightly.

"You're fine, but you're lucky. You could have broken your thumb by tucking it in your hand that way. When you make a fist to hit somebody, your thumb goes on the outside." She demonstrated first, then arranged Whitley's hand correctly. "There. That's the way you do it."

Whitley examined her fist and held it up for Wyatt to see. "Is she right?"

"She is."

"That's good to know. Thank you, Rhyne."

They walked in silence after that. Whitley tried to slow the pace as they approached the house, but Wyatt arched an eyebrow at her and she didn't fall back again. They didn't enter the house by the side entrance. That was for the use of Cole's patients. Wyatt ushered them in the front door and indicated they should have a seat in the parlor.

"I'll see how busy Dr. Monroe is," he told them. "Maybe he won't have a patient and you won't have to wait too long. I always thought that waiting was the worst."

Whitley agreed. She cupped her hand to partially cover her mouth and whispered to Rhyne. "I wish he would take us to jail."

Rhyne saw Wyatt pause ever so briefly as he was walking out the door and knew Whitley had been overheard. What she couldn't know

196

was if Wyatt was smiling.

Cole wasn't.

Out of the corner of her eye, Rhyne watched Whitley for clues as to what she might expect. Wyatt was gone. She'd seen him walk in front of the house as he headed back to his office, so she knew he'd left by the side door. What followed had been a terrible quiet, and Whitley predicted they would not get any dinner.

"At least Sheriff Cooper feeds people in his jail," Whitley had said. "I know because Molly Showalter told me that her Johnny delivers meals from Longabach's sometimes."

Rhyne realized that Whitley thought they would share the same punishment, but Rhyne knew she was the grown up, even if Whitley seemed to have forgotten, and Cole's censure would be a different thing when it was turned on her. When he came in, she surreptitiously nudged Whitley to lift her head and look her brother in the eye.

Cole approached the divan where Rhyne and Whitley sat and stopped within a few feet of it. "The sheriff says there was a fight. I'd like to have your version of what happened. Whitley, you first."

Rhyne watched her swallow hard, but to her credit she kept her head up and her eyes forward, and gave a good accounting of events. She only left out that Ben Martin had called her a freak, but Rhyne thought she understood the omission: Whitley was trying to protect her brother.

"Is that about right, Rhyne?" Cole asked.

"I remember it pretty much the same."

Cole nodded shortly. "Let me see your hand, Whitley."

She dutifully held it up, flexing her fingers and working her thumb to show there was no lasting injury.

"Wyatt told me that Rhyne showed you how to make a fist for fighting. Show me." He watched her make a proper fist. "All right. Why don't you both go up and dress for dinner? We're going to the Commodore tonight."

CHAPTER 6

"I cannot recall when I last ate so much," Whitley said when she stepped onto the sidewalk in front of the hotel. "I believe the Commodore has served me the finest meal I have ever had. The veal cutlet was extraordinarily tender. And, oh, the almond cake . . . goodness, that made my mouth very happy." She stopped walking to put her hands on her midriff and push her belly out. Her corset prevented her from making a display of her gluttony. She hurried to catch up to Cole and Rhyne. Darting around them, she pivoted and began walking backward. She patted her belly. "Look. I will explode when I remove my corset. I think it will be worth it, although I shall be very sorry to leave you both with the unpleasant chore of cleaning up my guts."

Cole cast his eyes momentarily heavenward. "Turn around, Whitley, before you fall and break your neck." Even as he said it, Whitley caught her heel on the uneven boards of the sidewalk and started to tumble.

Rhyne and Cole leaped forward simultaneously to grab her flailing arms. Cole managed to get her by the elbow. Rhyne caught her wrist. They jerked Whitley upright and set her firmly on her feet.

"Flibbertigibbet," Rhyne said, not unkindly. "Are you all right?"

Whitley nodded, avoided Cole's stern look, and fell into step beside them. "It was a good meal, though, wasn't it? Thank you, Cole."

"You're welcome." He glanced sideways at Rhyne. Except to answer the few questions that Whitley put to her, she had been quiet throughout dinner. Cole thought her expression then had been bemused. Watching her now, the impression remained. "Did the Commodore meet your expectations, Miss Abbot?"

Rhyne was pressed out of her reverie by Whitley's nudge. "What?" she asked vaguely. "I mean, pardon?"

"Cole asked if the hotel met your expectations." Whitley looked past Rhyne to her brother. "Maybe she didn't have any, Cole. Not everyone does, you know. Some people just like to be surprised."

Cole gave her a wry look. "Could I hear Miss Abbot say whether she's one of those people?"

Whitley nodded. "If she wants to answer."

Rhyne laid a restraining hand on each of their forearms. "I never saw two chickens peck at each other the way you two do." Shaking her head, she released them. "Now, about the Commodore . . . I liked it just fine. I never ate tomato bisque before. I didn't know it was soup until Mary Evans put in it front of me. I had my mouth set for some kind of fancy French biscuit, but the soup was all right, and it didn't sit heavy in my stomach like the chowder at Longabach's."

"You probably had more room for your salad right off," Whitley said. "I wish I'd had the bisque instead of the potato soup. I was pushing at my stays after the first course."

Cole reached around Rhyne's shoulders and tugged on Whitley's braid. Her mouth snapped shut. "Go on," Cole said to Rhyne. "What else?"

"Well, I knew it would be elegant. I saw some of the things they were carrying into the place when it was being built. Marble sinks. Brass fittings. Carved headboards. But I didn't imagine the dining room would be a jungle. Why do you suppose Sir Nigel brought in all those plants? Some of those ferns were as tall as you."

"Potted plants are popular in the better restaurants back east," said Cole. He didn't have another explanation for it. Everything about the Commodore, from its burnished walnut wainscoting to the fine linen tablecloths, suggested to Cole that the owner had built his hotel with the fashionable houses in

New York and Paris in mind. Nigel Penny-worth had come over to their table and introduced himself, paying extravagant compliments to Whitley and only slightly less effusive ones to Rhyne. In spite of a score of years spent living in the United States, the majority of them in Reidsville, the English émigré had not acquired the flat vowels of his neighbors. His accent made Whitley hang on every word. Rhyne, contrarily, did not seem impressed.

"What did you think of Sir Nigel?" he asked.

"Oh, 'e's a proper blow'ard wot don't know 'is Cockney from 'is West End." She abandoned the working accent for the one of privilege that Nigel affected. "One must tolerate him, however, because he is so agreeably amusing. It's all the potted plants, don't you know."

Cole and Whitley stopped in their tracks, while Rhyne continued as though she were unaware of leaving them behind. Whitley was grinning when she caught up. Cole's faint smile was more thoughtful.

"How did you do that?" Whitley asked.

"She studied for the stage," Cole reminded his sister. And, he suspected, Rhyne was a gifted mimic. "Did Judah teach you?"

Rhyne nodded but offered no other information. She hoped that would be the last Judah's name was mentioned. She had not even asked the sheriff if he had been out to see her father and was relieved that Wyatt hadn't seen fit to raise the subject.

"He must have been a very fine actor," said Whitley. "Our father was a general in the Union Army, which is not nearly as entertaining as trodding the boards, but a worthy career all the same."

Rhyne covered her mouth with her fist and repressed an urge to laugh with a polite cough. "I didn't know that," she said when she could speak again.

Cole was glad to be turning the corner toward home. There was no longer any sidewalk and hardly anyone about. Whitley was free to move ahead of them again and chatter away safely outside of Cole's reach.

"Thaddeus B. Monroe," Whitley said. "The 'B' is for Braxton, the same as Cole's middle name. I'm a 'B', too. But it's Brookes. That was our mother's maiden name. She volunteered in the wards for wounded soldiers during the war. Father told me he didn't try to stop her, that he knew the limits of his command. I always thought that was very clever of him. He graduated from West Point, you know, and that is no easy thing to do. Cole was accepted there, but he hated it and got permission to leave. Isn't that right, Cole? Father said it was because Cole was more like our mother, that his calling was healing, not soldiering. I am not convinced, though,

203

because Father never saw Coleridge stand up to Dr. Erwin. If he had, he'd have known Cole was a fighter, too."

They reached the house and Whitley trotted up the steps to the front door. She waved gaily to Digger Hammond who was sitting on his porch trying to make whistling sounds with a broad blade of grass. "Walk with you to school tomorrow," she called to him.

He fumbled with the makeshift whistle and smiled widely at her, revealing a sizable gap between his front teeth. "Sure. That'd be fine. I mean, I'd like that. Maybe Dot will be sick or sleep in or something."

Cole and Rhyne exchanged amused glances as Whitley nodded enthusiastically before she disappeared into the house.

"I suppose there are no hard feelings," Cole said.

"His mistake was being with the other two boys. I don't think that will happen again." She climbed the steps beside Cole. "How long you figure it'll take him to realize he's got a better whistle with that gap in his teeth than he does with that sorry blade of grass?"

Chuckling, Cole just shook his head and ushered Rhyne into the house. Whitley was already at the top of the stairs, and she paused to wait for Rhyne. Cole touched Rhyne lightly on the elbow. "I'd like to speak with you before you go up," he said. "Do you mind?"

Rhyne was puzzled, mostly by the gravity of his invitation, but she didn't hesitate. "No. Of course not." She called up to Whitley. "Go on. I'll be up in a little while."

"Holler for me if he asks you to go to the woodshed."

Cole's tone reflected all the suffering of Job. "We're going to the parlor, Whitley. And, anyway, you've never been to the woodshed for anything but wood, so don't pretend you have experience beyond that." He watched Whitley turn the corner and said in an aside to Rhyne. "She hardly goes for wood, either."

The parlor felt considerably more inviting to Rhyne than it had when the sheriff had instructed her and Whitley to wait there. She waited by the divan, uncertain if she was supposed to sit or not. Cole had gone straight to the drinks cabinet and removed a decanter of whiskey.

"Would you like a glass?" he asked. "There's sherry, if you'd prefer it."

"Now, how would I know if I favored sherry when I've never had it before?"

His mouth compressed into a thin line as he realized his error. "I suppose Runt Abbot never asked for a sherry in the Miner Key."

"That's right." Her gaze dropped to the open interior of the cabinet. "I bet Sir Nigel drinks it."

Cole ignored her disparaging tone and spoke to the hesitant curiosity he glimpsed in her eyes. "It's often served at dinner parties. Men and women drink it."

"We already had dinner."

"There's no getting around that." He poured himself two fingers of whiskey while he waited her out.

"I don't really like whiskey," she said finally. "But I don't think that's because I'm a girl."

"I'm sure it's not."

"I always wondered about that. Judah and my brothers had a taste for it. Leastways, I don't think they were pretending same as I was."

Cole set the stopper back in the decanter. "Last chance," he said, raising his glass a fraction.

"The sherry," she said quickly. "I'd like to try it."

"Good for you, Miss Abbot. Tomato bisque and Spanish wine in the same evening." He rooted in the cabinet to find the appropriate glass and then poured her a good measure. He carried it over to her. "Won't you sit? Tell me what you think."

Rhyne lowered herself to the divan. She stared at the delicately stemmed glass in her hand but didn't drink. "How much do I swallow?"

He hadn't even thought to tell her not to knock it back like a shot at the Miner Key's bar. "Sip it," he told her. He moved to the comfortable armchair and sat. "It is a compliment to how well you inhabit that gown that accounts for the lapses in my memory. I found it especially difficult to see Runt Abbot this evening."

She squirmed and took something bigger than a sip for her first taste. It was pleasant, especially at the back of her throat where whiskey always burned. "Keep your eyes on my nose. That should help you see Runt."

Cole's smile hinted at his regret. "I think I may have given you the wrong impression by ever mentioning your nose. The slight asymmetry does not make it unattractive."

"You mean crooked don't make it ugly."

"Well, yes, I suppose that's what I meant." He paused, regarding her suspiciously over the rim of his glass. "Amused?"

"You tickle me sometimes: 'The slight asymmetry does not make it unattractive.'"

Cole had been right: Rhyne *was* a gifted mimic. She had perfectly captured his tone and cadence. Even the deeper pitch of her voice was amazingly accurate. "May I try?"

"Certainly."

He cleared his throat. "'Crooked don't make it ugly.'" He didn't need Rhyne's hoot of laughter to know he'd performed badly. "I sounded like a screech owl."

"I don't know about that, but you made the mistake most men do when they're trying to imitate a woman's voice. You reached for the high notes. You can't be a soprano. What you want to do is soften your voice, make it more like a whisper."

"I don't think I'll try again, thank you." The experiment had made his throat a little raw. He took a sip of whiskey and let it slide smoothly back. "It's a handsome nose, Rhyne. That's what I should have said. Better than delicate because it gives your face character."

"I think everyone agrees that I have plenty of that."

"Don't turn away from a compliment. Just say, 'How kind you are to say so,' and be done with it. That way you acknowledge the giver and don't pass judgment on the remark. You can decide what you think about it later."

"How kind you are to say so."

Cole's eyebrows drew together as he tried to place the voice that he'd just heard. "Was that Rachel Cooper?"

"I thought the words sounded better coming from her." She rolled the stem of her glass between her fingers as Cole shook his head and tried to appear unaffected. She'd seen the same look of repressed amusement when he dealt with Whitley, but she also knew there was a line that made him dangerous when crossed. "What did you want to speak to me about?"

"Yes, that. I have been thinking how I might broach the subject since this afternoon, but the idea of it has been percolating much longer." Because she merely stared at him, he plunged ahead. "This is about the management of this house, my sister, and your desire for employment. It occurs to me that by hiring you as our housekeeper, we could arrive at a solution that would satisfy all of us."

"Housekeeper," Rhyne said, turning that over in her mind. "I don't know, Dr. Monroe. I was thinking that maybe I could put food in front of people at the Commodore, like Mary Evans did for us tonight. You put down extra money for her. I saw it. That probably comes in handy."

Cole had no idea if she was amusing herself at his expense again, literally. "I would pay you a significantly better wage than Sir Nigel."

"But I bet there'd be cooking."

He nodded. "You've been doing that now. Do you imagine I can't tell the difference between your cooking and Whitley's?"

"Now, don't go telling her you noticed. Anyway, she helped and she's coming along."

"*That's* what I mean." He set his glass down and leaned forward. "Before Whitley and I left New York we had a housekeeper *and* a cook. I was spending long hours at St. John's and Whitley was often left alone with them. Perhaps I should have insisted that she return to boarding school, but it wasn't in me to force her for my convenience. There were problems there, not unlike what she faced today."

"So Sheriff Cooper did tell you. I wondered."

"He told me. And he told me about the vile teasing that you were subjected to." He waved aside whatever comment hovered on the tip of her tongue and went on. "Neither Mrs. Abernathy nor Mrs. Green could abide Whitley. She wore them out. Three tutors, also. She is irrepressible, even unruly at times, but it is not in me to try to quash her spirit. When we came here — her idea, incidently — she argued her way into being permitted to manage our home. Even though I easily can afford to hire help, she does not want me to engage anyone to assume the responsibilities or even to assist her. As a result, Miss Abbot, the household accounts are indecipherable, my shirts are scorched, and I've only had bread that's risen above the loaf pan since you arrived. I cannot find my bootjack. I've had to replace my razor strop. Twice. As a mercy to me, and on pain of death, she stays out of my surgery and the library. That affords me two areas, at least, where I have been able to retain some semblance of order."

"You make a compelling argument yourself."

"As I said, the idea has been percolating." He regarded her with a faintly crooked smile. "Which reminds me . . . Whitley brews excellent coffee on Thursdays and Sundays. I cannot explain what happens on other mornings."

"She reuses the grounds," Rhyne told him. "It is a matter of economy, she says. On Thursdays and Sundays she uses fresh." Rhyne shrugged. "Thriftiness is indeed next to godliness." She watched Cole sigh heavily and reach for his glass. "I know. But I don't have a heart stony enough to correct her."

"Sometimes I think she says things like that just to get a reaction."

"I'm sure of it. She adores you. She always begs your notice."

"Do you see how it is, then? Without help, I'm afraid she will wear me out as well."

"You'd send her away?"

"I don't know. We have a pact, but I'm not certain I will be able to do my part. If her attention to her studies is not improved, we agreed that she would return to Amelia Starcher's Seminary. I would have to stay here to honor my contract with the town."

"How is she doing?"

"Poorly, I'm afraid. I think she's testing my resolve."

"You're already surrounded by Indians if you only think that's what she's doing. You better pray for the cavalry."

Cole was glad he didn't have a mouthful of whiskey. "I *am* praying for the cavalry."

"Me? You think that's me?"

He nodded. He set his glass aside again and

ticked off the proof on his fingers. "Companion. Mentor. Tutor. Housekeeper. Cook. Manager. Accountant. That makes you the cavalry. Have I missed anything?"

"Just how much you're going to pay me."

"You'll do it?"

"The pay?"

Cole named the salary. "Plus room and board." He waited, but she offered no reaction. "It's fair, I think."

Her mouth curled to one side as she considered it. "How much do you suppose they charge to let a room at the boardinghouse?"

"I don't know. Why do you ask?"

One of her eyebrows kicked up. "I know I'm ignorant about town living, but I didn't sprout full grown from the cabbage patch this morning. I've about run out my welcome here. I need to find my own place, Dr. Monroe, whether you hire me on or not."

"I don't see why. There's enough room here. It doesn't make sense to change an arrangement that we've managed thus far."

She hesitated. "I don't know. It won't feel like I'm on my own."

"You're not supposed to be on your own. Single women don't take rooms in the boardinghouse. The hotel would be a better accommodation, but even with the generous wage you could earn here, you'd spend most of it on your room. Thriftiness, remember?" He saw that coaxed a small smile out of

Rhyne, but he could tell she wasn't convinced. "Is there someone you'd like to advise you?"

Rhyne hadn't considered that she could ask someone else. She was used to making her own decisions. "Maybe Mrs. Cooper could set me straight. She came to town alone a few years back. Lived in the same house she and the sheriff live in now." She worried the inside of her lip. "The house was ready for her when she got here and she moved right in. She never lived anywhere else."

"I didn't realize." He regarded Rhyne shrewdly. "Is it respectability that concerns you? Is that what you were alluding to when you spoke about town living and cabbage patches?"

Rhyne finished her sherry. "I guess that's right. Respectability's got something to do with it. Folks might not like you letting me stay here. You have to think about their good opinion. Whitley told me how your contract with the town works. That committee can boot you right out at the end of a year, and it got me considering that I might be an excuse someone could use if they were leaning that way. I'm used to people not thinking much of Runt Abbot, and that dustup at the schoolyard kind of proves my point."

Cole had no liking at all for what she was saying or where it was headed. She was concerned about his reputation, not her own.

"They're just boys, Rhyne. You said so your-self."

"Of course they are, but apples don't fall far from their trees, do they? There's talk behind my back, and there will be talk behind yours. For me, I don't care so much, but you've got more than your fine reputation to consider." She held his gaze, her expression frank, and said quietly, "You have to consider Whitley."

Cole was raising the covers to slip into bed when he heard distinctive footfalls in the hallway. The same board creaked that always creaked when Whitley was skulking on the other side of the door. He crossed his bed-room with considerably more quiet.

Whitley gave a wild start when Cole opened the door. She would have fallen back against the far wall if he hadn't caught her by the wrist and dragged her into his room.

"Why are you still awake?" He closed the door. "And why are you sneaking around?"

"I'm awake because I want to know what she said," she whispered. "And I'm sneaking because that's what you do if you don't want someone to hear you."

He thought it best not to tell her about the warped board that invariably gave her pres-ence away. Better to know where she was than where she was not.

"Well?" she demanded. "What did she say?

Is she going to stay?"

"She's undecided." He took the lamp from Whitley's hand before she dropped it in her excitement and placed it on the dresser top. "Take that blanket on the trunk and wrap it around you. Why are your feet bare? Where are your slippers?"

Whitley went for the blanket and ignored him about the slippers. She crawled onto the bed at the foot and crossed her legs tailor-fashion, pulling the woolen blanket around her shoulders. She impatiently swatted at some flyaway strands of her unruly hair. "What do you mean she's undecided? How can that be?"

"It happens that she has a mind of her own, Whitley." Cole returned to the bed, pulled back the covers, and climbed in. He sat with his back against the headboard and drew his knees toward his chest.

"Of course she has a mind of her own," she scoffed. "Whose else would she have?"

"She actually thinks with it," he said, tapping the side of his head and giving her a pointed look.

Whitley did not allow herself to be sidetracked, which was proof, she could have told him, that she could think, too. "What were her objections?"

"You and me. She doesn't want to live here."

"I don't understand."

"She thinks her presence will tarnish us. Miss Abbot is concerned that living here could be used by the committee as a reason to push me out at the end of the contract year, regardless of whether I want to stay. She also made the point that you would suffer for your friendship with her. Her opinion on both counts is heavily weighted by this afternoon's altercation."

"Well, that is just silly. You will not abide your decisions being subject to committee rule. And what do I care about suffering for a friendship? It sounds noble. It is just the sort of decent gesture that our parents would want us to make."

It was true, Cole thought. The apple really didn't fall far from the tree. "You are certain, Whitley? You're right that I don't care for myself, but Miss Abbot's right when she says I need to be concerned for you."

"As long as I don't have to begin addressing her as Miss Abbot, I'm certain."

"She's not saying no to the position," Cole said. "At least not yet. She talked about taking a room at the boardinghouse."

Whitley screwed up her nose. Her freckles momentarily bonded. "Runt could stay there, but Rhyne shouldn't."

"I explained that. It's confusing for her." He told Whitley about Rachel Cooper living on her own when she came to town. "I suggested to Miss Abbot that she speak to Mrs.

216

Cooper. We'll have to wait and see."

Her cheeks puffed as she blew out a lungful of air. Wait-and-see was her least favorite activity. "Is there anything I can do?"

"Go to bed, Whitley."

"But —"

"Bed."

Rachel Cooper set the silver tea service on a side table and poured two cups of tea from the pot. "Sugar?" she asked Rhyne.

"Please, Ma'am."

Rachel arched an eyebrow. "I thought we were long past that. You must call me Rachel."

Rhyne nodded. She surreptitiously observed Rachel's graceful, economical movements as she finished pouring and added the sugar. Her hands turned delicately as she lifted the cups. Rhyne took hers and held it carefully in her lap, conscious of Rachel's eyes on her.

Belatedly, Rachel realized she was staring. "Forgive me. I'm admiring my own handiwork, I'm afraid. I chose the particular shade of gray because it is a match for your eyes. The dress suits you, or perhaps it's that you suit the dress. I can never decide which is more complimentary." She waved a hand airily. "It doesn't matter. You are looking very fine, Rhyne."

"How kind you are to say so."

Rachel blinked. That response was unexpected. Behind the rim of her cup, she smiled. "What can I do for you?" she asked. "Not that I am ungrateful for your company. Indeed, it is a pleasant diversion from laying out a new pattern, but I don't consider it likely that you came simply to pass the time with me."

"No, ma'am. Rachel. No, I didn't." Afraid that she would spill her tea, she didn't try to lift the cup. "Dr. Monroe made a proposal last night." She watched Rachel's smooth brow wrinkle like linen. Wondering at the reaction, she reviewed her words. "Oh! You think . . . oh, that's comical . . . he didn't . . ." She steadied the cup and saucer as she began to laugh. "He didn't *propose* to me. He made a proposal. It's not the same thing at all." She suddenly remembered herself. "It doesn't flatter him much that you'd think it, but I reckon it's a compliment to me, so it is kind of you to mistake the matter."

Rachel replaced her cup and saucer on the tray and sat back as if pushed by a physical force. She felt as though she had to catch her breath. "Start at the beginning," she said finally. "I think I'm ready."

Rhyne shared the important details of her conversation with Cole. "I'd like to accept his offer of hire, but I don't know if it's proper that I live there. I wonder how it might change folks' mind about the Monroes if I stay with them. The sheriff probably told you

218

what happened at the school. That sort of thing might happen again, and I have to tell you, it's not all that easy to square off in one of these dresses." The pitch of voice changed slightly, as did her intonation. "Not that I am ungrateful for what you've done. Indeed, it is a pleasant diversion from wearing trousers, but I don't consider it likely that I can win many fights in a dress."

Rachel's mouth opened fractionally. It required a moment to register what she'd just heard: her own voice coming back at her, repeating words almost identical to ones she'd spoken earlier. "Is that me?" she asked. "Do I sound like that? My goodness, it was, wasn't it? It was *exactly* me. How did you do that?"

That wasn't a question that Rhyne could really answer. The truth was, she didn't know, and on this occasion she hadn't been entirely conscious of doing it. "I meant no offense," she said quickly. "I wasn't mocking you."

Rachel leaned forward and bridged the distance between her and Rhyne by placing her fingertips on the back of Rhyne's hand. "No, don't distress yourself. I didn't think for a moment that you were mocking. I think you're trying to learn. It's astonishing, really." She gently nudged Rhyne's saucer, encouraging her to drink some tea, then she sat back again and gathered her wits.

"As I understand it, the essential duty of all

of the positions for which Dr. Monroe wants to employ you is teaching. He obviously sees something in you that makes him believe you will be able to guide his sister. The way I hear you describe it, I think he does not merely want a housekeeper, or a cook, or a tutor, or any of the other things you mentioned. He wants someone who will gently take Whitley in hand."

"I've gentled horses before, but I don't think Dr. Monroe knows that."

"Maybe he senses it. People can, you know. That's why they bought animals from you. You gentle horses. Some people break them."

"That's just an expression. It doesn't mean they really break them." She fell silent as Rachel merely continued to stare at her. "He did say he didn't want to quash her spirit."

"See?"

"But what about associating myself so closely with them? Living there, and all. What about that? I'm not bedridden now. I haven't been for a long time. It was different when I was the doc's patient, but I held my own yesterday. Folks are going to know I'm fit."

"Indeed." Rachel's smile was wry. "Let's put that aside. Tell me, are you comfortable there? Do you feel safe? Are you treated well?"

"Yes. Yes to all of that. It was hard at first. You know, to accept so much do-goodin'. Whitley didn't know what to do 'cept fuss and talk at me. And Dr. Monroe, well, he'd done what he could out at the cabin. They pushed and prodded some, though not with any of those instruments the doc has in his bag."

"There's a small mercy."

"That's what I thought, and on account of them being so kind to me, I thought I should maybe make a like effort."

"You shouldn't accept the offer because you're grateful, Rhyne. You're going to work very hard for that salary."

"Sure, by doin' mostly the same things I did for Judah. He didn't pay me. Hell, most times he didn't let me sit at the table with him. The Monroes invite me to share their meals all the time. They don't even ask anymore; they just expect it."

Rachel hardly knew whether to weep or laugh. "The doctor and his sister have excellent manners."

Rhyne grinned. "Don't they just?"

Rachel chuckled. "What do you want from me, Rhyne?"

"Direction, I think. I'm not good with advice; mostly I ignore it. But I'd be a fool not to take direction."

"It's forward."

"Pardon?"

"The direction is forward," said Rachel. "Stop looking over your shoulder. Stop looking for trouble. You can't prevent people from thinking what they will, but really, Rhyne,

221

your view of the town isn't one I share. My experience in Reidsville has been that the gossip is generally harmless, people look out for one another, and once there's something new to talk about, the last new thing fades away. The philosophy is live and let live."

"Judah wasn't much for town," Rhyne said. "Before I was born he lived here with my ma and my brothers. The house is still here. Randy showed it to me. I don't know why he moved out, but he did, and I came along, my mother died, and we just made do where we were. He revived the Abbot Family Players when he saw I could learn my lines and take a part, but he thought the town didn't properly appreciate his talent."

"Perhaps they didn't."

Rhyne leaned in to share a confidence. "Between you and me, Rachel, I don't know what would have been enough."

"I see. So it was like that."

"It was."

Cole walked out with his last patient of the day to find Rhyne waiting for him. She was perched on the edge of one of the room's two ladder-back chairs, her hands folded in her lap, her spine holding her narrow frame in its most proper carriage. The posture suggested to him that she had just returned from visiting Rachel Cooper and that she had been paying attention to every nuance of Rachel's bearing.

"Hey, Runt," Ned Beaumont said as he hobbled past her. "Heard you got the best of the Morrison boy yesterday. Rudy's kid, too. Can't say I'm surprised. You always could scrap real good."

"How kind you are to say so."

Cole's steps faltered as he jerked his head around to look at Rhyne. She gave him a pleasant, butter-wouldn't-melt-smile, and waved good-bye to Mr. Beaumont. Cole watched Ned get safely down the steps before he shut the door and turned to Rhyne. "How kind you are to say so?"

Rhyne watched him shake his head, but there was no mistaking the glimmer of a smile that changed the shape of his mouth. "I spoke to Mrs. Cooper."

"And?"

"I accept the position."

"And?"

"And your offer to bunk here."

"I don't believe I said 'bunk,' but I take your meaning."

She stood and thrust her hand at Cole. "Shake, then. We have a deal."

He stared at her hand, then extended his own. He met her eyes. "Shake."

Rhyne pumped his hand. "I reckon I'll find Whitley so we can start dinner."

He nodded. She left.

They pretended the current in their hand-shake hadn't been real.

Whitley heaved a sigh hard enough to flutter the papers in front of her. "It can't possibly be important to know this," she said, jabbing a finger at the list in front of her.

"You haven't tried. Let's just go through it once and see how many you already know." She took the study paper away from Whitley. "Start with Aurora."

"Goddess of the dawn."

"Bacchus."

"God of wine."

"Ceres."

"Goddess of the earth, grain, and harvest."

"You're a fraud, Whitley Brookes Monroe. Cupid."

"God of love."

"Diana."

"Goddess of the hunt."

"Janus."

"Do you think my brother's handsome?"

"What?"

"I heard Dot Hammond tell Susan Walker that Cole was handsome. I wondered if you thought he was."

"Not as handsome as, say, Janus."

"God of new beginnings. Symbolized by two faces. That's like Dot Hammond. Two-faced. I thought she was my friend, but all she wants to talk about is Cole."

Rhyne folded the list of Roman deities in half and tucked it between the pages of Whitley's reader. "You know all of this. Why do you pretend to be what you're not?"

She shrugged. "Why did you? You were pretending, weren't you? I mean it's not true that you used to be a boy."

"Oh, Lord." She leveled Whitley with a narrow-eyed glance and gave her Runt Abbot's husky voice. "We're not gonna talk about my balls again, are we?"

Whitley's own voice rose a full octave. "Do you *have* them?"

"Do you even know what they are?"

"I do, but I'm not saying."

"Uh-huh."

Whitley grabbed Rhyne's wrist. "Come here, I'll show you."

Rhyne resisted Whitley's attempt to pull her to her feet. She used her own intonation. "I don't know. I don't think it's a good idea." Nothing to do with balls and Whitley could possibly be a good idea. She regretted the lapse in judgment that made her utter the words in the first place.

"Come with me. Please?" When Rhyne remained firmly in her seat, Whitley threw up her hands. "Oh, very well. I'll be right back. Don't leave." She fairly sprinted out of the dining room and skidded into the hallway. The clink of glass beakers and test tubes alerted her to Cole's presence in the surgery.

She tiptoed past the door and slipped into the library. It only took her a moment to find what she was looking for. Tucking it under her arm, she beat a retreat back to the dining room. Rhyne was precisely where she left her, but not looking particularly happy about being there.

Whitley set the book on the table in front of Rhyne and sidled up to her chair. She reached over and opened the book, thumbing through the pages quickly. Familiarity with the volume helped her find what she was looking for without difficulty. She flattened the pages to reveal the twin illustrations of a naked male, the left side a frontal view, the right, the profile perspective. "There," she said, pressing her finger to the figure's groin. "That's what the boys call balls." She turned several more pages, uninterested in illustrations of the gastro-intestinal, circulatory, and nervous systems, and went directly to reproduction. Here the groin area was revealed in minute detail, much of it from the inside.

"See. There's a sac. And the balls are in the sac. They're really testicles and the sac is a scrotum, but you'll never hear Tom and Ben use those words. They think they know so much." She rolled her eyes. "Boys."

Rhyne slammed the book closed, nearly trapping Whitley's fingers between the pages. "Take it away," she said. "Put it back exactly where you found it and don't remove it from

226

the library again. Don't remove it from the *shelf* again."

Startled by the edge of anxiety in Rhyne's tone, Whitley blinked widely. She accepted the book when Rhyne thrust it at her, but she stood rooted to the floor. "It's all right, Rhyne. Really."

"Take it."

Whitley turned and fled.

And ran headlong into Cole.

"Careful," he said, embracing her to take the force of the collision on himself. "What is this?" He placed his hands on her shoulders and drew back to examine her face. "Tears? What's wrong, Whit?"

She ducked her head.

"Oh, no. No hiding, Whit. Tell me."

Whitley twisted her shoulders in an attempt to remove Cole's hands.

"Where is Miss Abbot?" He looked past his sister to the entrance to the dining room. When his attention returned to Whitley, he noticed the book under her arm. "What do you have there? And do not tell me it is a book because I can plainly see that it is."

Her response was to press her lips tightly together.

Cole sighed. "Go," he said. He released her shoulders and stepped to the side. As she darted past, he plucked the book from under her arm. Cole thought she might try to wrestle it from him, but she barely paused.

She was halfway up the stairs before he reached the dining room.

Rhyne was gathering Whitley's papers, slate, and schoolbooks when Cole stepped into the room. She had heard the skirmish in the hallway, but didn't know Cole had recovered his book until she glanced up and saw him cradling it in his arm. A fine tremor made her fingers clumsy as she attempted to square off the papers.

Cole did not speak immediately. He observed Rhyne first, noting her pale features, the almost bloodless lips, the slight quiver of her fingertips. Her narrow shoulders were hunched, set forward protectively, and the effect was to make her appear more vulnerable, not less.

As soon as he stepped toward the table, she backed away. He stopped and regarded her questioningly. She merely stared back, her eyes troubled, her entire demeanor uncertain and unsteady. Cole spoke the five words guaranteed to get her back up. "Are you afraid of me?"

Rhyne straightened her shoulders and lifted her chin. Her stare was feral.

"No," he said. "I don't suppose you are." He held up the book, reading the title for the first time. "*Burnside's Illustrated Anatomy.* Is this the source of everyone's distress?"

"I am not distressed."

That was clearly untrue, but Cole did not

press. "Whitley's not talking, either." He placed the book on the table and looked up in time to see Rhyne staring at it with distaste. "So it is the book. I imagine Whitley took it from the library. Was there a question? Something she wanted to reference?"

Rhyne held on tightly to the items in her arms, conscious of feeling protected by the small barrier they provided. "It's my fault. I let her provoke me into challenging her. She went after the book to prove she knew something that I didn't think she did. Turns out, she did know."

Cole waited for more to follow, but Rhyne seemed to believe her explanation of events sufficed. "That's all?"

She shrugged. "That's the gist of it."

He very much doubted that. "If Whitley proved her point, why is she upset?"

"You'll have to ask her."

"I'm asking *you*. Explain it to me." He pushed the book across the table. "Better still. Show me."

Torn between bravado and surrender, Rhyne bit hard into her lower lip. She tasted blood. "Maybe this isn't a good idea."

"What?"

"Working for you."

Frustrated, Cole thrust a hand through his hair. "I didn't imagine Whitley could get the better of you this quickly. Mrs. Abernathy and Mrs. Green lasted considerably longer."

"She didn't get the better of me."

"That's not how I see it. You're ready to leave, or did I mistake your meaning?" When she said nothing, he went on. "No, I didn't think so. By my reckoning, you haven't earned a full week's pay. What has it been since we exchanged that handshake? Four days? Five?" Cole knew the answer almost to the minute, but he wanted to press her.

"Five days."

"Is that what your word is worth?"

Rhyne slammed the books and slate on the table. The loose papers skittered across the polished surface. She picked up *Burnside's Illustrated Anatomy* and pitched it at Cole's chest. Her accuracy was as good with a book as it was with a rifle, and she caught him squarely in the breastbone.

"Find it yourself."

Cole took the shortest route to reach her. He launched himself *across* the table. The direction of the assault was so unexpected that Rhyne momentarily froze. That indecision cost her dearly. Cole caught her by the waist and used his own momentum to force her back against the wall. Before she could catch her breath, he changed his grip and pinned her wrists level with her shoulders.

He held himself still, aware of nothing so much as the roar of blood in his ears and thudding of his heart. He took measured breaths and waited for calm. Slowly, so slowly that he was hardly conscious of the movement, his head dipped forward until it rested against Rhyne's brow. He listened to her breathing now, not his own. Quick, shallow sips of air revealed her wariness. She was alert, not paralyzed by fear, and Cole could only imagine that she was waiting for an opportunity to strike or flee.

It fell to him to make certain she made the right choice.

He lifted his head but continued to lean forward, pressing her wrists to the wall with minimal effort. He turned his hips slightly, giving her his flank to avoid a knee to the groin.

"Are we agreed that you struck first?"

The answered hovered on Rhyne's lips, but in the end, she only nodded.

"For the life of me," Cole said, "I cannot decide if you expect me to try to beat you bloody because you're Runt Abbot, or dismiss you from your employment because you're Rhyne."

She swallowed hard. "Why not both?"

Cole found her question intriguing. It wasn't issued as a challenge, but put to him out of real confusion. "Because there is no sense in it. Neither response resolves anything. Doing both would be . . ." He paused, searching for a word to describe the folly she was inviting.

"Like using a sieve to fill a leaky bucket?"

He stared at her. "Yes," he said after a long moment. "*Exactly* like that." He eased his hold on her wrists but didn't release her. She didn't attempt to test his grip. "Are we done, Miss Abbot?"

"Yes."

He let go and pivoted to the side, giving her ample room to walk past him. Rhyne's hands fell to her side, but she didn't push away from the wall. She stared straight ahead, concentrating on her breathing, waiting for her heartbeat to quiet. Cole glanced at the book Rhyne had pitched at him. Lying unopened on the floor, *Burnside's Illustrated Anatomy* looked harmless enough, certainly not capable of provoking so much in the way of emotion and conflict. He left Rhyne's side and went to pick it up.

"Go on to bed," he said, laying the book on the table. "It's late." He saw her uncertainty. Her eyes darted from him to the book then back to him. He didn't miss the effort it required for her to peel herself away from the wall.

Rhyne straightened and smoothed the material of her gown over her midriff. Taking a steadying breath, she rounded the table. "One hundred eighteen and one hundred nineteen."

He barely heard her, and what she was telling him didn't immediately register. She was gone from the room when it came to him.

Cole pulled out a chair but only to rest his knee on the seat as he turned the book toward him. He opened it and used his index finger to carefully turn the pages. The ones he was looking for were creased at the corners, suggesting they had been visited more than once and were probably dog-eared for easy reference.

Cole spent no time at all studying the drawings. Closing the book, he sat down slowly and tried to recreate the scene between his sister and Rhyne in his mind. He had no doubt that the illustrations fascinated Whitley, and it was easy to imagine her sneaking in to the library to satisfy her curiosity. It was not so different than Johnny Winslow comparing parts with his siblings.

Rhyne's response to the drawings was more complicated. She admitted provoking Whitley in some manner, so she would have felt responsibility for the book being removed, and perhaps concern about what he would have to say. But Cole believed that her reaction was more visceral than cerebral. He remembered the fine tremor in her hands, the hunching of her shoulders, and finally, the stillness in her features that could not mask her aversion.

Confronted with the same pictures, Runt Abbot would have snapped his suspenders and spit, perhaps engaged in some ribald humor that made him one of the boys. But

Rhyne was no longer afforded the same protections, and it was Rhyne who had been violated.

And now violated again.

234

CHAPTER 7

Pounding at the side door made all three of them put down their forks. Cole's chair scraped the floor as he pushed back from the table. "I'll see who it is."

Rhyne could see that Whitley wanted to follow. She encouraged her to stay seated with a small negative shake of her head. Whitley hesitated, then surrendered. Neither of them resumed eating.

Cole only returned long enough to tell them that he would be leaving. "There's been an accident at the mine. That's Will Beatty at the door. He's going to take me out to the site. Don't wait up for me."

Whitley turned around in her chair and called after him, "I could help, Cole!" When there was no response, she started to rise.

"Don't trouble your brother," Rhyne said. She pointed to the seat of the chair, indicating that Whitley should occupy it.

Whitley sat again, this time even more reluctantly than the last. "I wouldn't be in

235

the way. I know how to help Cole."

"I'm sure you do. Did Cole teach you, or was it something you learned from your mother? I believe you told me she cared for wounded soldiers."

"That's right, but Mama never stopped volunteering in the hospitals. She wouldn't let me go with her, but she always talked about what she did there. Cole never did. Mama mostly went to St. John's, same as Cole. St. John of God is a teaching hospital. You know what that is, don't you?"

"Not really."

Whitley shrugged. "Well, it's associated with the university where Cole studied, and lots of things he had to learn were taught right there at St. John's. He watched surgeries and autopsies and followed the doctors around on the ward when they diagnosed and treated the patients."

"Autopsies? What's that?"

"Cutting up dead people."

Rhyne frowned. "Now why would you want to do that?"

"*I* wouldn't, but my mother said the doctors do it to learn what killed the patient. Cole says it's mostly doctors that kill the patients, but Dr. Erwin didn't want to hear that."

"Who is Dr. Erwin?"

Whitley didn't answer immediately, distracted by the sound of the side door slamming shut and the hurried tread of Cole and that no-account Beatty boy on the steps. She pushed her plate away, no longer willing to pretend an interest in her dinner. She picked up the dangling thread of conversation without a prompt from Rhyne. "Dr. Erwin is in charge at St. John's. He's very important, but not as important as he thinks he is. That's what Mama used to say."

Whitley's voice dropped to confidential tones. "She didn't care for Dr. Erwin. Same as Cole. Where they disagreed, though, was about Caroline Erwin. Cole liked her enough to ask her to marry him, but Mama never warmed to her — not that anyone outside the family would have even known. It was a very private matter."

"Dr. Monroe is married?" asked Rhyne.

"No. He *was* engaged. Caroline ended it not long after Mama died, but that's because Cole thought it would be better that way. If she hadn't, he would have. He said it was because he couldn't be what she wanted him to be, but I think it was because of me."

Rhyne regarded Whitley suspiciously. "How much did your brother actually tell you, and how much did you learn listening at doors?"

Whitley did not pretend to be insulted. "I'd never know anything if it weren't for closed doors. Cole says I'm incorrigible. I had to look it up. It means I'm —"

"I know what it means. And he's right."

Rhyne pushed some peas into her potatoes and took a forkful of both. "Why do you think the engagement ended because of you?"

In answer, Whitley held up her hands so that Rhyne had a clear view of her scars. "He blames himself. After the accident, he did not like to leave me alone. I cannot say that I minded. I was afraid. Sometimes I still am, but I think you know that."

"I do, but I don't know why."

"Neither do I," she said, slumping back in her chair. "Confusing, isn't it?"

Rhyne nodded. Her gaze dropped to Whitley's hands resting on the edge of the table. "Do you blame your brother?"

"No. What happened was entirely my fault, but Cole believes he should have better understood my nature and taken precautions." She waited for Rhyne to ask the question. When none came, she sighed. She could better resist the application of thumbscrews than silence. The latter was true torture. "Very well, if you must know . . ." Whitley pretended she didn't see Rhyne's brief smile. "Our home in New York had a carriage house in the back that Mama allowed Cole to make over for his own use. He created a laboratory there. I didn't — don't — understand most of what he did there, but I know that what he was studying opposed Dr. Erwin's teachings. It was one source of their conflict. I suppose you can imagine that Caroline Erwin was the other."

"Did your mother tell you that?"

"She confided in her friends. I was at the door, remember?"

"It's a wonder one side of your head isn't flat."

Whitley grinned and placed a hand protectively over her right ear. "It's a wonder, isn't it?" When she'd coaxed a faint smile from Rhyne, she let her hand fall to her lap and continued in a more serious vein. "Mama fell sick suddenly. Pneumonia. It was complicated, Cole said, by disease she carried with her from the hospital. That was always his argument against our mother going there. It was the same one Papa used when he was alive, and it had the same effect. Which is to say it had no effect at all. She could not be kept away from good works. She called it an obligation of privilege."

Whitley fiddled with her unused spoon, turning it over and over in her hand. "I was twelve when she died. She didn't make Cole and me promise to look after each other; it was just understood. Cole and Caroline delayed their wedding. I can't be sure, but I think that was Cole's idea. He had to make so many difficult choices with his time. There was the hospital, his studies, the estate attorney, his fiancée, and me. Something — or someone — was always demanding his attention." She tapped the tip of her nose with the bowl of the spoon. "You probably will not believe it, but I was the least demanding."

But not the least needy, Rhyne thought. "Cole probably required a lot of looking after."

"See? *You* understand." She set the spoon down. "He worked such long hours. If he wasn't at the hospital or studying, then he was in his laboratory. He saw Caroline less, slept less, ate less. He always made time for me, but I liked it better when I could do things for him. It felt like a contribution, not a chore, and it seemed to me that I was honoring my mother and her good works."

Whitley's gaze fell to her plate. She stared at it until the delicate red poppies blurred, then she blinked and looked up to find Rhyne watching her. There was no coercion in Rhyne's candid stare, but Whitley realized how much she wanted to talk about *that* night.

"Cole left the house much as he did this evening," she said. "Like his hair was on fire. On that occasion he was rushing to meet Caroline at a charity ball. Her father was going to be honored, and the entire affair was arranged by the Howells, a family of considerable influence in society. Mrs. Abernathy and Mrs. Green — they were our hou—"

"I know who they are," said Rhyne.

"Oh. Well, they retired for the evening and

left me to do the same. When I was readying for bed, I saw that Cole had left a lamp burning in the carriage house. I didn't go there often — Cole doesn't like interruptions — but I knew that an unattended lamp posed a danger to his experiments and the chemicals he kept on the shelves. It was a warm night and only a short walk to the carriage house, so I didn't concern myself with putting on a robe. I knew there was a chance I wouldn't be able to get in because Cole kept it locked, but I thought I might find an open window or a key above the door. I looked for both and found neither. I only tried the door as a last resort."

She shrugged as if this were of no consequence. "It opened."

Rhyne wanted to wince. She was aware of desiring a different ending to Whitley's story than the one she was about to hear.

"I might have taken the lamp and left," said Whitley, "but you know that I did not. Cole left things in such a disarray that I could not help but want to clean up after him. In my mind I imagined how pleased he would be with my efforts, and Mama would have done as much for him, I was sure of it."

Whitley picked up her glass of water and rocked it back and forth. "There were half a dozen beakers just about this size crowded beside the sink. All of them had water in them so I emptied them into the water that was already in the sink. I swept, cleared the table, straightened the shelves, and then I went back to wash the beakers. The sink was deep and the water came up to my elbows when I dipped my arms in."

She set the glass beside her plate and held out her hands and wrists to study them. "I don't really remember what happened after that. Cole had to explain it to me."

"I reckon you'll have to explain it to me."

"Do you know what vitriol is?"

"I never heard of such a thing."

"That's the old alchemy name for sulfuric acid. I learned all about it afterward. That's what was in the beakers. It would have been worse for me if there hadn't been any water in the sink, but that diluted it some. Still, you can see what acid does to the skin. I fainted, but Cole doesn't think I fell to the floor right away. He thinks I tipped forward and got hung up on the edge of the sink before I dropped. Since there was no one around to see what happened or wash me off, the acid just kept burning. Most people think it was a fire, but it wasn't. Sometimes I say it was because they understand it better. Not everyone can understand vitriol."

"What made you think I could?"

"Because I've seen you studying some of Cole's books. Not *that* one," she added, just to be clear that she knew *Burnside's Illustrated Anatomy* never left the shelf. "I think you'll go learn all about it the same as I did."

Rhyne's smile was appreciative. "I suppose I will. Was it Dr. Monroe that found you?"

"You can call him Cole, you know."

"Did Mrs. Abernathy call him that?" asked Rhyne. "Did Mrs. Green?" She watched Whitley roll her eyes. Cole's sister never quite admitted defeat, but she did at least recognize the futility of further discussion.

"Yes, *Cole* found me. He arrived home hours later. It was his custom to look in on me before he retired. That night was no different, and when he saw I wasn't in my bed . . ." She lifted her hands helplessly.

"He must have been frantic."

"I don't like thinking about it," Whitley said quietly. "It makes my stomach all uncomfortable, like I'm going to —" She stopped herself. "The lamp in the carriage house was almost out of oil by then, but there was enough of a glow for Cole to see. He forgot that he left it burning, so he guessed that's where I had to be. It didn't take him long to understand what happened once he found me. He tended to my burns before he carried me back to the house, and he hardly left my bedside after that. Caroline finally convinced him to hire someone to care for me, change the dressings, and help with the therapy. Later, when I was better, she suggested Amelia Starcher's Seminary."

"It must have been difficult for your brother

243

to send you away."

"He only did it because he convinced himself it was right and proper." She shrugged. "And it wasn't so terrible."

"Whitley. I know you disliked it there."

"I *despised* it, but that doesn't mean something good didn't come of it."

"Oh?"

Whitley could not rein in her smug smile. "Cole convinced Caroline to end their engagement. I know it was because she didn't support his decision to take me out of school. I didn't have to listen at a door to learn that. Some things are easy to figure out even if you're only fourteen, which is how old I was by then. Besides, she talked about me as if I wasn't in the room with her, or worse, as if I couldn't understand."

"She didn't appreciate that your guile was the equal of her own."

"No, she did not. Wait. What do you mean by that?"

"Just that I think you had something to do with the broken engagement."

"Now how would I have done that? I was only fourteen."

Rhyne laughed. "You can't have it both ways. One minute you're braggin' that you're fourteen like you're going on forty, and the next you want me to believe you're fourteen like you're going on four. You're about as slippery as rainwater and as cagey as an old

244

fox." She pointed her fork at Whitley. "But I like you just fine for it."

"How kind you are to say so."

Rhyne grinned and resumed eating, not at all concerned that her food had grown cold.

"Put him on the table," Cole directed as he led the way into his surgery. He began lighting lamps and setting out his instruments.

"You're not going to take my leg, are you, Doc?" It was the question Ezra Reilly had been asking since he awoke from the blast that had knocked him twenty feet down the mountain. No one, not his four litter-bearers, or Cole, was answering it any longer. The truth was, no one knew if the leg could be saved. The early reassurances no longer seemed sincere, especially after Cole refused to give them. Ezra's leg was grotesquely twisted above the knee. The thigh was swollen to twice its size because of the fracture.

"You fellas got all the cord, didn't ya?" asked Ezra. "Shoulda been no reason for the spark to jump like that. Must be something wrong with the fuse."

"Someone got it all," Will reassured him. "Everyone knows you're real careful with the explosives. Wyatt's got everyone looking through the debris for what might have caused the dynamite to fire early."

"It's the cord, I'm tellin' you." He closed his eyes and moaned softly as his leg was jostled. He missed the exchange of glances around him, the ones that guiltily wished he would just pass out. "Goddamn, but it hurts. You got somethin' for me, Doc? Maybe some whiskey? This is no time to be stingy."

George Barkley put a restraining hand on Ezra's shoulder. "Quiet yourself, Ezra. The doc's sure to have something better than whiskey. Ain't that right, Dr. Monroe?"

Cole turned away from where he was preparing the vaporizing mask. "Another moment."

Will Beatty asked, "Should I go find his wife, Doc?"

"That's probably a good idea, Will." He remembered Will's story about having to keep a bucket in his lap while Doc Diggins performed surgery on Sheriff Cooper. It was better to have him out of the room.

Ezra shook his head violently. "Don't want her here! Let her be. Don't want her to see me like this."

"Virginia will turn every woman in town on me if I don't bring her here," Will said, backing away from the table. "Won't take me but a few minutes." He was gone before Ezra could make another protest.

Cole went to the sink and began to wash his hands. "Any of you men ever assist in a surgery?"

George Barkley looked at Eugene Hammond who looked at John Cromwell. George

246

spoke for all of them. "Nope."

"I require a volunteer."

"I'll do it."

All three men pivoted sharply in the direction of the door. Ezra craned his neck to see who had spoken. The effort made him groan and his head fell back.

"Is that Runt?" he wanted to know.

George and Eugene parted so Ezra could see. "Sure is," George said.

Rhyne ignored the men and went straight to Cole's side. "I can help. I'll do whatever you tell me."

"That's the best offer I've had." He glanced back at the others. "Show them where they can wait. Tell Whitley to make coffee for them. I don't mind if they want a whiskey to go with it."

Rhyne thought they might argue, but when she turned and pointed toward the door they began filing out. She knew it wasn't anything she'd done that made them compliant. Coleridge Monroe fairly radiated authority, confidence, and the urgency of action, a commander in his own right, at least in this theater of operations.

"I'll be right back," she told Cole. She laid her hand gently across Ezra's brow as she passed him on her way to find Whitley.

They emerged from the surgery two hours later. Cole's apron, the sleeves of his shirt, even the tips of his shoes showed evidence of the bloody trial. Rhyne stayed back, slightly to one side, and let him talk to the men and lone woman that had crowded into the waiting area.

"There was a compound fracture of the femur . . . the thigh bone," he said. "I was able to set it, but he'll probably have a limp. That's the good news." His pause was slight. "I was unable to save his hand. Ezra never understood how badly it was injured. He had enormous pain in his leg, but almost none in his hand. I'm sorry. I stopped the bleeding, cauterized the wound, but there was nothing to save but a —" His gaze fell on Virginia Reilly, a pale, blue-eyed woman with softly rounded features that gave no hint that she grasped the enormity of what he was telling her. He amended what he had been about to say. "There was nothing to save."

Virginia nodded shakily. "Right or left?"

"His left hand."

"I suppose that's something," she said. "Odd, how it happens. He's right-handed."

Pastor Duun laid his hand on Virginia's shoulder. "He's going to live. There's God's blessing. And there'll always be something for him to do at the mine, one-handed or two."

"There will never be two again." Virginia's laugh was a trifle hysterical. "Were you thinking I'd go back to whorin', Pastor, if my man couldn't work?"

"Now, Virginia," Duun said calmly. "Don't put words in my mouth. I wasn't thinking anything of the kind."

Virginia Reilly shook off Duun's hand, not feeling at all charitable toward him or his god at the moment. "May I see my husband, Dr. Monroe?"

"Of course. He's still sleeping."

Rhyne stepped aside to let Virginia pass and then followed her to Ezra's side. Behind her she heard the door close and knew that Cole remained with the other men. "It's all right if you want to talk to him," Rhyne said. "Softly like. It might begin to rouse him."

"Then he'll be in pain," whispered Virginia. "I don't want that. How pale his sweet face is. Did the doctor bleed him?"

Rhyne shook her head. "He doesn't hold with that, he says. Besides, there was a lot of blood lost because of the injury."

Virginia pointed to the large swath of bandages around her husband's left wrist. "Are you certain his hand isn't in there? There's so much gauze."

"It's not. But Dr. Monroe was careful to leave enough skin to pull over the stump. That will help it heal properly. And his stitches are as elegant as Mrs. Cooper's. You won't find any fault there."

"What do you know about it?"

Rhyne ignored the challenge in Virginia's

voice. "Dr. Monroe talked to me about what he was doing the whole time. It's how they did things back at the New York hospital. It helped him concentrate."

Virginia bent her head and turned her cheek so she could feel Ezra's gentle breathing on her face. She stayed that way for a full minute before she straightened. "When can I take him home?"

"I don't know. Not tonight for sure. Maybe tomorrow. You'll have to ask the doctor."

Virginia nodded. "George said you volunteered to help right off. None of them had the stomach for it."

"One of them would have done it if I hadn't been around. It was just hard for them, being there and all when Ezra got hurt."

"Will went back out to the site. No one's sure what went wrong. Ezra's always real careful when he's settin' charges."

"I heard John say that. The others agreed."

"Real careful," Virginia repeated softly.

"I'll go talk to Dr. Monroe." She watched Virginia to see if the other woman even heard her. There was acknowledgment in the slight bow of Virginia's head. Rhyne left her alone with her husband.

Ezra Reilly left the surgery late the following afternoon, carried home by his fellow miners with Cole directing the transport. Cole promised Virginia that he would come by as often as he thought necessary to change Ezra's bandages and see to the splint. He gave her laudanum for her husband's pain and told her he'd show her how to wrap the bandages once Ezra began to heal.

Cole went to see Ezra after dinner and returned to find Rhyne on her hands and knees in the surgery, scrubbing blood off the hardwood floor. "What are you doing?"

"And you with all that fancy schoolin'," she scoffed.

"All right. A better inquiry is *why* are you doing it."

It still seemed like a nonsensical question to Rhyne. She wrung out the rag in her hand and sat up on her knees. "There were bloody footprints all over the floor before I mopped it the first time. Now it needs a good scrubbing."

"Leave it. I just hired Digger to clean up. He was happy to oblige me, probably because he thinks he'll catch a glimpse of Whitley."

"You trust Digger in here?"

"I'm not going anywhere. He can work around me, and everything's put up that he could get into." He held out his hand to Rhyne. "Let me help you."

Rhyne dropped the rag into the bucket and gave him her hand. He drew her to her feet so quickly that she almost fell into him. She caught herself by placing her free hand on his shoulder.

Cole didn't release her hand immediately. He stared at her upturned face and watched the rise of a soft pink color in her cheeks. She held his gaze, her gray eyes wide and wary. She was poised slightly forward on tiptoe, her mouth lifted so that with very little effort he might claim it. His eyes dropped to those lips, their shape defined now by the dark and narrow space between them. He felt a vibration travel the length of her, and had it been capable of sound he would have heard something as delicate and sweet as a plucked violin string.

She drew a shallow breath. It brought him closer.

Cole wanted to believe Rhyne understood there was an invitation in her raised mouth, in the parted lips, in the way she sipped the air. Her anticipation was palpable. So was her apprehension.

He stepped back, putting himself away from her, and released her hand. She dropped to her heels and no longer had any use for his shoulder. He resisted the urge to glance at the clock on the shelf behind him, but he saw Rhyne's eyes dart in that direction.

Cole wondered if she was looking for confirmation that, indeed, time had not stopped; it only seemed that it had.

Rhyne smoothed her apron over her midriff and offered a brief parting smile as she picked up the bucket. "I need to check on Whitley.

She's supposed to be writing an essay."

Nodding, Cole stepped aside to let her pass. His eyes followed her until she disappeared in the hallway. He remained rooted to the floor a few moments longer, then slowly shook his head. Amused by the wanderings of his mind, rather than concerned by them, Cole began preparing slides for the microscope while he waited for Digger Hammond to arrive.

Rhyne carefully counted out the coins as she placed them in Mr. Porter's large palm. She appreciated his patience while she dug in her change purse for another five-cent piece. "One dollar and thirty-five cents."

"And I thank you, Miss Abbot." Douglas Porter placed the money in a coffee tin that he took from the china cupboard. Once he returned the tin, he picked up the basket of laundered clothes on the kitchen table and passed it into Rhyne's open arms. "Maggie says I'm supposed to remind you that one of our boys could bring this around when the laundry's done. That'd save you walking the length of town with it. Plenty of folks do it that way."

"I don't mind. Not today. Sun's out." The recently laundered clothes in her arms still smelled of fresh air. "Give Mrs. Porter my best. And thank her for the extra care she gives Dr. Monroe's shirts. Whitley says he's fussy, but I think she's forgetting that she always scorched them."

"I'll tell her." He reached around Rhyne and opened the door for her. "Ever since he treated my wife's chilblains Maggie thinks the sun rises and sets by the doc's word. I guess there are a lot of folks comin' around to that thinking. Especially after he done what he did for Ezra."

"That's good to know," said Rhyne. Ezra was still bedridden because of his leg, but his stump was healing well and he didn't complain much about pain in a hand that was no longer there. Virginia was caring for him almost exclusively, with Cole dropping by to visit every three or four days. "I'll be sure to tell Dr. Monroe that Mrs. Porter's chilblains aren't troubling her."

Rhyne stepped onto the porch and was aware of Mr. Porter following her. He was a broad, sturdily built man. His cheerful face and gregarious nature were like opposing forces to the strength of his powerful arms and chest. She'd seen his wife and children swallowed whole by his good-natured embrace, and for no good reason that she could think of, she was always afraid that the same would be turned on her.

Where Runt Abbot would have stayed his ground, Rhyne took a step back. Even with the large basket of clothes between them, she was unable to keep herself from doing so. "I reckon I'll be seeing you, Mr. Porter."

He stopped basking in the sunshine and nodded at Rhyne. "Good day to you, Miss Abbot. Have a care that you don't stumble." He watched her cross the sidewalk. "Peculiar girl." Then he went back inside.

Whitley looked up from her slate, a nub of chalk between her fingers. Rhyne was absently polishing a silver spoon — the same one she'd been polishing the last time Whitley glanced at her. Whitley finished solving the quadratic equation on her slate before she set down the chalk. The equation was one that Cole gave her when she told him she'd completed every one of Mr. Cassidy's boring long division problems. He called it an assignment, but she knew a euphemism when she heard it. This was punishment. The problem she couldn't quite solve, however, was reconciling herself to the fact that she was enjoying it.

"Do you think I'm peculiar?" she asked Rhyne.

Rhyne stopped polishing. Her slight frown put a crease between her eyebrows. "What prompted that question?"

Whitley sighed. "I must be, otherwise you'd have answered 'no' right off."

"No. No, not at all. It's just that Mr. Porter said the same thing about me this afternoon."

"To your face?"

"No, as I was walking away. I'm sure he

didn't mean for me to hear him. He wasn't talking to anyone. He said, 'peculiar girl,' like I was some sort of puzzle that he couldn't quite figure out."

"Oh, well that isn't too bad, then."

"Isn't it?"

"No. It makes you interesting. Intriguing, I think is a better word."

"You don't think he will try to hug me, do you?"

Whitley laughed. "No. He wouldn't do that. Did it seem as though he might?"

"He always looks on the *verge* of it."

"That's how Digger looks at me," Whitley confided. "Like he's on the *verge* of kissing me. What do you suppose stops him?"

"A finely honed sense of self-preservation," Cole said as he walked into the room. "The next time he's on the *verge* I want to know about it." He sat down beside Whitley and drew her slate toward him. "How long did this take you?"

"Two minutes," she said. "Maybe less. I don't know. I wasn't gawking at the clock, and anyway, why is it important? No, don't answer. I don't *care* if it's important. I want to know why I should tell you if Digger's thinking about kissing me."

"He's always thinking about it." Cole used his handkerchief to erase the slate. He ignored Whitley's heavy sigh when he picked up the chalk and wrote another equation for her. "I

256

only want to know when he's at the tipping point."

Whitley accepted the slate and the chalk. "I don't see why. If you ask me, Coleridge, wanting to know Digger's tipsy point makes you downright peculiar." She started working on the equation. "And you shouldn't get your heart set on me telling you. You can give me quadratics until I choke on chalk dust and it won't persuade me to confess."

Cole glanced across the table at Rhyne. She was studying the spoon in her hand for smudges, but it was the faintly bemused smile curving her lips that let him know what really held her attention. He looked back at Whitley, watched her hand fairly fly across the slate as she scribbled out the solution to the problem. "Witch," he said affectionately, slipping an arm over the back of her chair. "It's not even a struggle for you, is it?"

"No, but you have succeeded in convincing me that I am the very definition of peculiar. And I don't thank you, Coleridge. No, I do not." She returned the slate to him. "Another, please. I am oddly fascinated by the idea that there are two solutions to every problem."

"Here. This one will require the use of a formula." He wrote it out for her at the top of the slate then presented the problem. "Chew on that for a while." He wiped chalk dust off his hand. "And please find a bigger piece of chalk." When Whitley ran off to get another stick, Cole addressed Rhyne. "What about you, Miss Abbot? What makes you peculiar?"

She frowned. "Just how long were you standing in the hallway?"

"Not long enough to hear anything bad about myself. And if you are thinking of comparing me to Whitley, remember that my sister is incapable of exercising the same restraint."

"I've learned. She's had her feelings hurt by comments never meant for her ears."

"I know, but I'm surprised you do. She must have been talking to you about Caroline Erwin."

Rhyne nodded. "Do you mind?"

"Not at all. She told you I was engaged?"

"Yes." She rubbed a tarnished thumbprint from the bowl of the spoon. "Are there regrets?"

"No. Not on my side. I doubt that Miss Erwin harbors any."

"But you loved her."

"Did Whitley tell you that?"

"No, but isn't that why —" She stopped. "I don't know very much about it, really. About why people marry, I mean, and why they don't. Othello strangled his wife. Romeo and Juliet were . . . well, I'm sure I don't understand them. Lady Macbeth ruined her husband with her ambition."

"The tragedies confuse a simple premise,

don't they?"

"What simple premise?"

"That people marry because they find someone they can imagine sharing their life with. Love is part of it, an important part, especially in the beginning, but there must also be admiration and respect, a willingness to act in concert, and an appreciation that sometimes one must act alone. There are mutual interests and separate ones. I've always thought of it as a dance. A complicated one. Missteps. Miscues. But in the end, I am convinced if they both hear the same music, it's a satisfying arrangement."

"Did you and Miss Erwin ever hear the same music?"

Cole winced. He rarely waxed poetic and here was further proof of why he should never indulge. "If we did," he said, "it was never at the same time."

"But you're sure people do, aren't you? You said you were convinced."

Wishing he could turn the conversation, Cole nonetheless answered her. "I've never forgotten the first time I saw my parents waltz. Whether it is accurate or not, that is the image I hold in my mind when I think of marriage. I suppose you could say that watching them dance shaped my beliefs."

Standing just out of sight in the hallway, Whitley thought she should probably go in and rescue her brother, but first she had to swipe at the wash of tears stinging her eyes.

Rhyne woke abruptly when she heard the door to her room swing open. She pushed herself up, threw off the covers, and was waiting for the intruder with her rifle raised and cocked.

"Jesus, Joseph, and Mary," Cole muttered under his breath. He had come very close to clutching his heart. "Put that thing away. Didn't I tell you not to point it at me again?"

Rhyne lowered the rifle and set it so it wouldn't fire by mistake. "What do you want? Is it Whitley? Is something wrong?"

"Whitley's fine. She knows I'm leaving. Sarah Ann Beatty's in labor. Mrs. Best is with her, but Jack Beatty came for me because the midwife can't turn the baby."

Nodding, Rhyne stooped and slid the Winchester under her bed. "I'll look out for Whitley."

"Thank you." He backed out of the room and would have closed the door if Rhyne hadn't rushed forward and put a restraining hand on the knob. "What is it?"

She didn't have an answer, didn't understand the urgency that had pushed her toward the door in the first place. She hovered there a moment longer, staring at him, wondering at the strain that showed in his features, then she nodded once and allowed the door to close quietly.

Cole had not yet left the house when Rhyne ushered Whitley inside her room. "The left side," she said, infusing her tone with more weariness than she actually felt. The ruse was necessary to prevent Whitley from talking her ear off when what she wanted was quiet, if not precisely sleep. "I'm on the right."

It was close to dawn before Rhyne was able to ease herself out of bed without rousing Whitley. She carried a shawl and slippers and gave Whitley one last over-the-shoulder glance before she left. The floor was cold even where rugs covered it. After tiptoeing down the stairs, Rhyne stepped into her slippers and threw the shawl around her shoulders. In the kitchen, she checked to make certain the grate was free of ashes before she started a new fire. By the time Whitley had to rise for school, Rhyne wanted to have two loaves of bread in the oven and porridge on the stove.

She was punching out the wheat dough after its second rise when she heard the door to Cole's office open. When no one called out, she realized it was Cole returning. She had already determined that she wouldn't search for him. If all had gone well at the Beattys, he would find her. If it hadn't, he would also find her. It no longer seemed odd that he sought her out. For him to do otherwise would trouble her now.

She knew the moment he came to stand at the threshold of the kitchen. Concentrating on shaping the dough into two loaves of equal size, Rhyne didn't lift her head. She did not mind that he watched her work and felt no pressure to hurry or to give him her attention. Perhaps he found watching the activity as calming as she found performing it. She set each loaf in a pan prepared with grease and brushed them both with milk before she slipped them into the oven. Turning around, she wiped her hands on her apron, and looked at Cole for the first time.

Everything she didn't want to know was there on his face.

"I'm so sorry," she said quietly.

He nodded, wearily rubbing the underside of his chin. He pushed away from the doorjamb and drew out a chair. As was often his habit, he spun it on one leg until it faced the table backward. He straddled it and sat, resting his arms along the back rail.

"There's coffee," she said.

"Please."

Rhyne prepared a cup for him and set it under his nose. He thanked her with a brief glance, but he didn't say anything. She began clearing the table.

"Leave it," he said.

"All right." Rhyne laid the rolling pin on the floured breadboard and sat before he had to tell her it was what he wanted. She brushed back a wayward lock of hair and tucked it behind her ear.

Cole watched her streak her hair with flour and didn't say a word. It was easy to imagine how she would look sitting across a table from him in thirty years. In spite of the long night behind him, and the rigors of the day ahead, he felt his mouth twitch, and because he believed she could not possibly appreciate the wandering of his mind, Cole raised his cup and hid his smile from her.

When he set the cup down again, he was ready to tell her everything. "Sarah Ann was already eighteen hours into labor when Mrs. Best realized the baby had turned. She knows the dangers of a breech presentation. Certainly she has more experience with them than I do, but nothing she tried worked. When she couldn't turn the baby, she sent Jack for me."

Cole paused, turning his cup around but not lifting it to drink. "I don't know what they thought I could do." He shook his head. "No, I do know. They thought I could save her and the baby." His short laugh held no humor. "As though Sarah and her child had just slipped underwater and all I had to do was extend a line."

Rhyne wanted to offer her hand. Uncertain if it was the right thing to do, or if it would be welcome, she sat on it instead.

"Do you remember the equations Whitley was doing after dinner?" he asked.

Rhyne nodded. "The ones with two solutions."

"Yes. One negative. One positive. And they're both right. There was nothing like that at the Beattys' tonight. I told Jack that I might be able to save the baby, but not Sarah Ann. I couldn't promise him that I could do it, only that I *might* be able to. He wouldn't let me cut his wife. She begged him; she wanted the baby to have a chance. He couldn't do it, and I lost them both."

"I'm sorry, Cole." There was an unfamiliar ache at the back of her throat, another behind her eyes. "So sorry."

Watching tears hover on the rim of Rhyne's lower lashes, Cole suddenly realized he'd never known her to cry. The monogrammed handkerchief she pulled from her apron pocket was the one he'd given her, but she had it in her possession because of laughter, not grief. Was she remembering the loss of her own baby? he wondered. Mourning for Sarah Ann whom she knew or a child that she never would? Did she hurt for Jack Beatty? Understand Mrs. Best's sorrow?

Then he knew. Her heart ached for *him*.

He stood, circled the table, and drew Rhyne to her feet. "I'm going to put my arms around you," he said quietly. "This is for me. I need it."

She nodded faintly. It was comfort that she wanted to give him. Her eyes never left his.

Cole slipped his arms around her waist and rested them at the small of her back. "You can do the same."

But she couldn't. Her arms hung at her side. She crumpled the handkerchief in one fist and worked it convulsively.

"See?" he said. "The tears are gone."

Rhyne blinked. Her long lashes spiked. Her smile was watery. "I won't say it's because I'm afraid."

"I know." He could feel the fine tremor of her body beneath his palms.

"Tell me about the baby," she said.

"A boy. Small and perfect. It only seemed that he was sleeping. Jack named him Edward James. That was what Sarah wanted if it was a boy. It was her father's name."

"And Sarah Ann?"

"She held Jack. He crawled into the bed with her, and she held him like the baby she never would. I remember she kept stroking his cheek. Mrs. Best and I left them alone. When we heard Jack moving off the bed, we knew she was gone."

Rhyne pressed her lips tightly together as pain pierced her heart. The wound was ragged and deep, and radiated wide from the very center of her soul. She was unaware of how profound her sorrow was until she heard herself speak in a voice she barely recognized as her own.

"I killed my mama, too."

Rhyne would have wrested herself away from Cole, but he held her fast and pulled her closer. He raised one hand to cradle the back of her head and pressed her cheek in the curve of his neck and shoulder. Her body jerked with sobs. The effort she made to control her breathing only made it worse. Her slender frame was so tight with tension that he thought she would break.

Cole pressed his mouth against her hair. He spoke to her, whispering words that had no real meaning but still offered sweet comfort in their cadence and repetition. The impact was gradual, measured in the fractional softening of the breaths she took and the longer intervals between them. There were no new tears, only the tracking of old ones. Tension slipped away, hurried off by a shudder that left her unable to stand without his support.

He felt her quiet. When she leaned against him, the weight of her seemed as nothing. Where his palm cradled her head he was aware of the fine texture of her hair. It was still unfashionably short, a little ragged at the nape where she tended to brush it away from her neck, but there was no mistaking that this was a woman's crowning glory. Thick and curling at the ends, he only had to pass his fingers through it once to raise the fragrance of lavender soap.

His hand slid lower to cup the slender stem

of her neck. He felt her pulse under his fingers. His thumb made a pass from her chin to the hollow of her throat and rested there.

There was no moment that he consciously stopped talking and began kissing her. His mouth grazed her ear, her temple. He brushed her forehead, then the space between her dark eyebrows. Her cheek was still damp with tears. He found the corner of her mouth. Her lips parted around a shallow breath and he covered them with his own.

There was tenderness. There was need. His mouth moved over hers, delicately at first, sipping, tasting, then with greedy purpose. Her lips were damp, pliant, and parted just that much to allow the tip of his tongue to make a sweep between them.

Her breath hitched. He caught his own.

His mouth came back to hers. He sucked on her lower lip, nibbled on the upper one. His tongue bumped against the ridge of her teeth and passed over the soft underside of her lip.

A chair scraped the floor as Cole kicked it out of the way. He backed Rhyne against the table. The hand he'd used to support her moved to her waist, and he inched closer, finding that small space she'd made for him between her legs.

He brushed aside the hair that fell softly against her neck. He lowered his head. His lips grazed what he had uncovered. Her skin was smooth and warm, the scent of her inviting him to linger.

She turned her head, exposing the long line of her throat. He put his mouth to her skin and sucked. Her hum of pleasure vibrated against his lips. His hand at her waist slid lower until it rested against her hip. With almost no effort on his part, she came to sit on the edge of the table.

He abandoned the warmth of her neck to return to her mouth. He kissed her again. Then again. Deeply. Hungrily. Need welled up inside him, powerful and prevailing, impossible to ignore.

But not impossible to control.

He lifted his head and waited for the unsteadiness of his own breathing to pass. His eyes were closed, but he did not doubt that she was watching him, or that her gaze would be wide and wary. Opening his eyes, he gently cupped her face in both his hands and met her stare.

"I imagine you regret leaving your rifle behind," he whispered.

Rhyne did not respond.

Cole sighed unevenly. "I shouldn't have said that. I'm sorry." He let his hands fall away and plowed his hair with one of them. "Are you all right?" His eyes roamed over her, pausing once when they came to the small bruise on her neck, lingering there the way his mouth had. "Christ. You have to say something, Rhyne."

She raised one hand to her mouth and touched her lips with her fingertips. They felt vaguely swollen, but the shape of them was unchanged. The pressure she applied was light, like his first kisses, and she had the sense of his mouth moving over hers.

She lowered her hand and slid to the floor when Cole took a step back. She held on to the edge of the table on either side of her and tested the strength of her legs. It would not have surprised her if she'd been as wobbly as a foal, but why that would be true was more difficult to understand. She wasn't injured, and that was the only point of reference she had for the weakness in her legs.

That left the kiss. The kisses. He'd done it so many times she didn't know how to distinguish one from the other. Some made her heart race. Some made it stop. It was exactly what her heart did when she was afraid, but fear was nothing at all like what she felt. At least she didn't think it was. It was hard to know when she was unused to admitting that anything scared her.

Rhyne patted down her apron to find her handkerchief before she saw that it was lying in a crumpled ball on the floor. She used the back of her hand to brush at her cheeks and swipe at her eyes. She sniffed once. That was all it took to put practical matters in front of her. "I should check the bread."

Cole didn't put his hands on her, but he did block her path to the stove. "Oh, no," he said, shaking his head. "You have to say something that makes sense. I watched you put the loaves in. They're not close to being done."

"I like to visit them."

"I swear, Rhyne, I —"

She held up a hand, palm out. "I don't take kindly to bullying, Dr. Monroe."

"I wasn't b—"

"You were, but we'll let it rest. As to the other, we should let it rest as well, only I doubt that either one of us can do that. So I'm working up to asking you the thing that's mostly weighing on my mind."

Cole waited.

Rhyne's chin lifted a notch and she screwed her courage to the sticking place. "I've been wonderin' why you stopped."

CHAPTER 8

Ann Marie Easter called the meeting of the Reidsville Physician Search Committee to order. After Gracie Showalter led them in prayer and Rachel Cooper reviewed their purpose, the first order of business was to evaluate Dr. Monroe's performance as the end of six months neared.

Alice Cassidy, the schoolmaster's wife, began as she always did. "Well, it's likely to fall on deaf ears, but I can say without fear of lightning striking me that his sister is a firecracker."

The eight other members of the committee merely traded glances.

Alice frowned. "Shall I interpret your silence as unanimous agreement?"

"You should interpret it as having fallen on deaf ears," said Rose Beatty. "Really, Alice, can't you let it pass unremarked even once? Everyone knows about the fight in the schoolyard. That was months ago and hardly worth a comment then. Besides, what's wrong with being a firecracker?" She smiled widely and gave her head a flirty toss. Her heavy fall of coal black hair rippled down her back. "That no-account Beatty boy likes it just fine."

"Now, don't go inviting trouble, Roseanne," Estella Longabach said. "Light that fuse of yours at home where it's appreciated."

Ann Marie tapped her gavel against the table. The linen tablecloth muted the sound, but the place settings bobbled and water stirred in the goblets. She questioned whether meeting in one of the Commodore's private rooms was a good idea. Sir Nigel had regarded her gavel with great suspicion, and she felt compelled to promise that she wouldn't smash his imported china.

"Ladies, please. May we go on? Who has something to report regarding the *doctor's* performance?"

Rachel Cooper spoke up. "I think we can all agree that he's proved his competency many times over. There was that awful explosion at the mine, Margaret Porter's chilblains — for which she offered this committee a testimonial — the usual colds and minor injuries, Sid Walker's rheumatism, the outbreak of chicken pox in the Morrison and Wheeler families, and Ned Beaumont's unhappy encounter with a mule. Those are the things we know about. We are fortunate that so many people have sought one of us out and shared their experiences with the doctor. My own experience with Dr. Monroe is that he's discreet."

There was a general murmur of agreement among the ladies.

"What about Sarah Ann Beatty?" Gracie Showalter asked.

"I think the question we must ask ourselves," said Rachel, "is whether the outcome would have been any different if Doc Diggins was here."

The women turned as one to Rose. She was only a Beatty by marriage, but the family was not represented in any other manner.

"You all know that Jack and Will are cousins. That makes them about as close as brothers in other families. Jack's still grieving hard, mostly because he's wondering if he'd have his child if he'd let Dr. Monroe cut Sarah Ann. He plainly tortures himself with what he can't know. I can't see that that's any fault of the doc's." She picked up her goblet and tapped her manicured nails against the glass before she sipped from it. "I also have to say, since Rachel forgot to mention it, that Dr. Monroe has been very good to the girls at Miss Adele's place. And he doesn't expect anything in trade the way Doc Diggins did from time to time."

"That's because he has Runt Abbot living with him," Alice Cassidy said. "He doesn't have to dally at Miss Adele's when he can diddle at home."

Rose's ebony eyebrows made a feline arch toward her widow's peak. "That never stopped your husband."

Alice Cassidy's face flushed. "You take that back, Rose Beatty."

Rose could have said that she took it *on* her back, but she didn't relish the idea of Alice throwing something at her. Besides, it wasn't true. Thomas Cassidy never set foot in the house when she was the madam, and she doubted that anything about that had changed under Miss Adele's management.

"I take it back," Rose said calmly. She left it up to Alice to decide if she was sincere.

Mrs. Duun gently inserted herself into the uncomfortable silence that followed. The pastor's wife was a quiet, well-spoken woman with more than a trace of her native Norwegian accent still firmly in place. "Julia Hammond is a friend of mine, and I don't believe she would object to me sharing her observations. You know, of course, that Mrs. Hammond lives next door to the doctor. She tells me that Miss Abbot — I prefer to call her Miss Abbot — rarely leaves the house except on the doctor's business or to accompany Miss Monroe somewhere. I think we know that to be true. Dr. Monroe spends long hours in his surgery, often late into the evening. Mrs. Hammond can see the lamps burning. She says that Miss Abbot works equally hard, but that cannot surprise anyone at this table as we are all aware that Judah Abbot was difficult and demanding. These are things we know; all else is speculation." Her gaze swiveled to Alice Cassidy and offered a gentle reproof. "I move that we declare the first half-year with Dr. Monroe a success and order our luncheon."

"Second," Rachel Cooper said quickly. Under the table she set her hand hard on Rose's knee.

Ann Marie called for a vote. Mrs. Duun's motion passed without any further discussion or dissent. They agreed the luncheon was a success.

"Have you ever seen so much snow?" Whitley turned away from the window to glance back at Rhyne. "I suppose the answer is 'yes.' "

Rhyne didn't look up from the book she was reading. "Since you know I've lived all my life in these mountains, I thought you could figure it out for yourself."

Whitley sighed mournfully. "I'm at sixes and sevens. That's what my mother would say. It means I don't know what to do with myself."

As that was not significantly different from Whitley's usual manner, Rhyne simply ignored her.

Looking around the library, Whitley's eyes settled on Cole's writing desk. "I shall compose a letter."

"What an enterprising idea," Rhyne said absently.

Whitley made herself comfortable in Cole's chair. She found the footstool with her toes and nudged it into position under her heels. Opening the lid, she rooted through the contents looking for a clean sheet of paper. Since she didn't particularly *want* to begin a letter, she wasn't terribly disappointed when she didn't find any paper.

Deciding that Cole's notebooks were probably more interesting than anything she could have written, she opened one and began to read.

It only took her a few minutes to correct her assumption. There was nothing in the notebook to hold her interest. Most of what Cole recorded was in words she couldn't understand and code she could not decipher. She recognized the names of a few chemicals, sulfuric acid being chief among them, but phrases like *in vitro* and *bacillus* meant nothing to her. Even the drawings left her uninspired. She could appreciate Cole's careful renderings of what he saw under his microscope, and his stippling was so precise that it gave the tiny squigglers a dimensional effect, but even then they were not worthy of her undivided attention.

She wondered why they commanded so much of Cole's time.

Whitley returned the notebook to the desk.

276

She dropped her elbows hard on the lid and supported her chin on the backs of her hands. "Why don't you and my brother speak any-more?"

Rhyne turned the page. "We speak."

"No, you don't. Not the way you used to."

"Whitley, your brother and I talk all the time." Uncertain that she could remain composed, Rhyne didn't dare look up even though Whitley had all of her attention now. "What about that letter you were going to write?"

"I don't want to do that. Besides, my great-aunt owes me a letter."

"I seem to recall that you are not finished embroidering your initials on the handker-chiefs you bought."

"One is enough. I shall go mad if I have to do the others."

Rhyne sympathized. Fine needlework was a distasteful activity. "There is always Jules Verne." For a moment, Rhyne thought she had diverted Whitley, but when she darted a look in her direction, Whitley was shaking her head and the smile she was displaying did not bode well.

"You're too polite," Whitley said. "Both of you. It's not natural. That's what I meant when I said you don't speak the way you used to."

Rhyne was forced to close her book and set it aside. "There is nothing unnatural about being polite."

"*Too* polite, I said. There's a difference, and you shouldn't pretend you don't know what I mean."

"Why aren't you having this discussion with your brother?"

"Because he's in the surgery. He's *always* in the surgery."

"That's not true."

"Pardon me. He's with his patients or he's in the surgery. He's avoiding you, so he has to avoid me, too. It isn't fair, Rhyne. *I* didn't do anything."

Rhyne tried to see her way past Whitley's argument, but couldn't find a response that would get her there. Whitley was right about all of it. "Would it be better if I left?" asked Rhyne.

"Left? You mean now? You would go to your room?"

"No. I mean find another place to live."

"And let Coleridge win? Why would you want to do that?"

"There's no contest, Whitley. I'd leave because you're so plainly unhappy. That's what *I've* noticed."

"My brother hasn't."

Rhyne sighed softly. "I can't speak for him."

"That's because you don't speak *to* him." Whitley raised her head and threw up her hands. "Is it because he kissed you? Because if it was, I don't understand. It seemed as though you were kissing him back. Was I wrong? Didn't you want him to kiss you?"

Rhyne stood quickly. "This is definitely a conversation you should be having with your brother. I can't talk to you about it. I'm sorry, Whitley. Excuse me. I'm going to start dinner."

Watching her go, Whitley shook her head. Kissing didn't seem so complicated when she and Digger did it.

Rhyne gave Whitley several opportunities after dinner to approach Cole. She had to admit that Cole's disposition did not invite conversation, but Whitley rarely took her brother's mood into account when she had something to say. Rhyne was forced to conclude that Whitley wasn't going to broach the same subject with Cole that she had with her.

That left it to Rhyne to beard the lion.

She took her time tidying the kitchen. It had the desired effect of hurrying Whitley off to bed. Rhyne dried her hands on a towel, removed her apron, and went to find Cole.

He was bent over his microscope when she entered the surgery. She waited for him to finish the drawing he was making before she spoke. As soon as he lifted his pencil, she stated her business.

"I want to talk to you about Whitley."

Cole rubbed his forehead. "Can it wait?"

"I wouldn't be here if I thought it could."

He swiveled sideways on his stool and laid his pencil down. "Very well. What is it?"

"She knows that something's not right."

"A particular something?" he asked wearily.

Rhyne pointed to him, then to herself. "She says we're too polite."

"Whitley's not stupid. We're so polite it makes my teeth ache."

"I know. Mine, too."

"All right. Do you have a suggestion? Because I don't. I don't know how to go back to what was." He rubbed his eyes with the heels of his hands. "What time is it?"

Rhyne looked at the clock. "Half-past nine." She took in his rumpled appearance in a single glance. His hair was deeply furrowed by one too many passes of his hand. Pale violet shadows underscored his eyes. He'd rolled up the sleeves of his shirt to just below his elbows. One of his suspenders had slipped off his shoulder, and he'd kicked free of both shoes. His heels were propped on the lowest rung of the stool.

She walked up to him and laid her hand against the side of his face.

"Don't," he whispered. But he didn't remove his cheek from her palm. "We agreed."

"You said I wasn't ready. I never agreed."

"You were repulsed by an illustration in a *book*, Rhyne. Of course you're not ready."

Her thumb made a pass across his cheekbone. "You're putting the cart before the horse. The way I remember it, we were just kissing."

"There is no *just* kissing."

Rhyne let her fingertips graze his face, his neck, then come to rest on his shoulder. "Now, see, that's a lie right there. What parts you had in your mind that were going to happen *didn't* happen, so it was just kissing. I'd like to try it again, maybe figure out what to do with my hands this time."

Cole took her by the wrist and removed her hand from his shoulder. "I think you've figured it out." He let her go. It only troubled him that he felt the loss so keenly.

"Did you think I didn't like you kissing me?" She leaned her hip against the table and folded her arms under her breasts. "Is that why you stopped?"

"I told you why I stopped."

"Because if you didn't right then, you didn't know if you could."

"That's right."

"I think you could." Her head tipped to one side as she studied his face. "You have the nose for it."

"What does *that* mean?"

"It's noble, remember? You're fashioned to do what's proper. Now, if it was crooked like mine . . ." She shrugged. "You'd be inclined toward the indecent."

Cole stared at her. "You know that's absurd, don't you?"

Rhyne's mouth flattened momentarily. "Of course I know." She glanced around for the other stool that she knew was in the room and saw it had been pushed under the table. She pulled it out and sat. "It's as absurd as the argument you've been making."

"I don't agree."

"No, you wouldn't." She folded her hands in her lap and inclined her head toward him. "You're good at healing. It seems like the whole town knows it. When I'm out, people stop me and tell me what you did for them. It takes me twice as long to get back sometimes because of the talk. It's all about what you do for others. The morning that you stood in the kitchen after Sarah Ann and her baby died, I saw how it tore you up. I meant to give you ease, only I couldn't, not the way I wanted to, not when I needed the very same myself."

Rhyne pressed her hands together. She inhaled slowly, trying to calm her hammering heart. "You're right to suppose there are things I don't understand — plenty of them, I reckon — but I *know* there ought not to be shame for needing each other. You're the first person that ever held me, except for those that held me down. That counts for something. The way I see it, we were stealing comfort that morning, and it's nothing either one of us should feel sorry for."

Rhyne straightened her shoulders and

separated her bloodless fingers. She smoothed her dress over her knees. "Whitley saw us in the kitchen," she said. "Saw us kissing. And now she sees us going so far out of our way to be mannerly that we might as well live across town. She says it isn't fair, and she's right. You hole up in here like your face is on a wanted poster and Whitley and I are the law. Your sister doesn't deserve to be treated as if she's the enemy. If avoiding me means you have to avoid her, then we've come around to one of those problems with only one solution. I'll have to leave."

She stood. "You think about it. Let me know what you decide."

Rhyne completed all the rituals of readying herself for bed in spite of knowing she was too out of sorts to sleep. At sixes and sevens, Whitley would have said, and Whitley's mother before that. Had Mr. Shakespeare penned it even earlier? Chaucer?

She thought of all the books in Cole's library. Could she find the answer there? It was a better use of her time than wondering if tonight was her last evening in this house. The thought had been turning over in her mind so frequently that her head was a regular whirligig.

Rhyne's flannel nightgown was inadequate protection for the chill that penetrated the house at night. At this time of year no one ever allowed the fire in the stoves to go out, but keeping them lighted required attention and effort. Although it was not her primary reason for going downstairs, Rhyne took time to add coals to the kitchen stove and the one in the surgery. The library's stove required no additional fuel. She warmed her hands and backside before she began searching the shelves.

The book she eventually pulled down was not the reference she sought. *Burnside's Illustrated Anatomy* was heavier than she remembered. Her arms sagged a little with the weight of it, and she wondered how she'd manage to pitch it so accurately that Cole couldn't avoid the blow. Anger, she reckoned, was what primed the pump. She raised the book experimentally and realized she'd have difficulty tossing it as far as the chair that was only a few feet away.

It made sense, she supposed, that Runt Abbot won so many fights. He had . . . *she* had . . . spent most of her life being purely pissed. It was hard trying not to feel that way now.

Rhyne dragged the heavy shawl from the back of the chair and pulled it around her shoulders as she sat. She was wearing thick woolen socks, but she still lifted her feet off the floor and tucked her legs to one side. She rubbed her hands together to generate enough heat in her fingers so she could turn the pages.

Inhaling deeply, she carefully opened the book to page one hundred eighteen.

There was a pressure deep in her chest as she stared at the naked figure on the page. Letting out a long breath only relieved a fraction of the ache. Was it revulsion that made her want to look away? It was merely a drawing. It wasn't as if it could hurt her. Why wasn't she as openly curious as Whitley? She really had never had the opportunity to study a man before, not this way, not without fear of ridicule or retaliation.

She didn't know how long she had been studying the illustrations before Cole walked in, but she didn't pretend she was so absorbed in the book that she didn't hear him. Her smile was faintly crooked, but it wasn't guilty.

"I came to check on the stove," he said. "I saw your light."

She nodded. "The stove's fine."

"Do you mind?" He rubbed his hands, indicating he wanted to warm them at the stove.

Rhyne waved him on. "The wind's picked up."

"It woke me." It would have been truer to say it kept him awake since he hadn't been asleep, but even that was not the entire truth. Wrestling with the problem she'd put before him was the full accounting of why he couldn't find any rest. He held his palms out to the stove, his back partially presented to Rhyne. "You took the Burnside down."

"I did. I'm learning the proper names. I wonder if my brothers knew they had a penis. Instead of pecker, I mean. Or a cock. They called it that some—"

Looking back over his shoulder, Cole stopped her with a single raised eyebrow. "Instead of a rainspout, perhaps?"

She flushed, surprised he remembered. "That's when I was young."

Cole turned around and clasped his hands behind his back. "How old were you when you realized you weren't like your brothers?"

"Five, or thereabouts. We were tramping through the woods, and they had a call of nature. I tried to do the same as them because the privy was so far away. They couldn't run back to the cabin fast enough to tell Judah that I'd been capitated."

"Capitated?"

She shrugged. "They probably said castrated, but that's the way I remember it. I also remember how hard Judah took his strap to me for what he called 'showin' off my girl parts.'" She saw Cole wince. "I suppose you never had a strap put to your backside."

"No. My father delivered stern lectures about responsibility and duty."

Rhyne winced. "It sounds painful, but I reckon it's what you get used to."

"I reckon it is," he said quietly.

Rhyne closed the book and set it on the table beside her. She nestled her cold fingertips in the folds of her flannel nightgown.

"You're freezing," said Cole.

"Hardly."

"Come over here and stand."

She shook her head.

"But you're shivering."

She merely watched him, waiting.

"Could you be more stubborn?"

This time one corner of Rhyne's mouth curled upward. "Could you?"

Cole closed the distance between them so quickly that Rhyne had no time to catch her breath. It was just as well. He would have taken it away. Grasping her upper arms, he lifted her out of the chair. She couldn't quite get her legs under her and she fell into him. He found her mouth while she was still trying to find her breath. His lips ground against hers. The heat that he'd abandoned at the stove was replaced by one that was entirely more satisfying.

Rhyne's hands found their way between their bodies, and she clutched the lapels of his dressing gown. She felt her toes graze the carpet as she was lifted again. He turned both of them, putting his back to the chair. She held on, her eyes closed, and gave herself over to a kiss that made her shiver more violently than when she'd been cold.

The hot suck of his mouth held her fast.

His tongue pressed against her lips, her teeth, and finally speared her. The tip of it tickled the roof of her mouth. She pushed back, tentatively at first, then with more confidence, tasting him in a like manner. She caught the flavor of baking soda and peppermint and a hint of . . . *sherry?* The memory of tasting it for the first time came back to her pleasantly, but this was better.

He changed the slant of his head, and she followed his lead. His mouth was hot, humid, his lips faintly damp from the sweep of her tongue. She flicked his upper lip. His groan startled her, caused her to hesitate, but he didn't raise his head and she didn't turn aside. The moment passed, and her heart resumed its strong, steady beat.

The first that she knew he was no longer holding her upright was when she felt his fingers in her hair. She wished desperately that it were longer for him, long enough to wind around his hand or be crushed in his fist. He ruffled it and tugged lightly on the curling ends. He pressed his fingertips against her scalp, cupping her head in his palms.

His mouth moved away from her lips. He kissed her cheeks, her temples, the corners of her eyes. He caught the tip of one earlobe between his teeth and nibbled. She thought she might have whimpered, but she wasn't sure. He kissed the space between her eyebrows and then the crooked bridge of her

288

nose. He wouldn't let her avoid that last kiss. "Shh," he whispered. "I like it."

It was sleight-of-hand that put her in his lap. Nothing else explained it. One moment she was standing on his toes, and in the next he was completely under her. She still clung to the lapels of his robe. They remained her point of reference when everything else was shifting.

What shifted next was his hand. Rhyne felt it slip under the shawl and come to rest close to her heart. He had to know how hard it was thumping.

"Feel mine," he said.

She stared at him dumbly.

"Go on. Feel mine."

Rhyne would only allow herself to release one lapel. She uncurled her fingers slowly, stretching them just a bit before she slid her palm under Cole's robe and laid it flat over his heart. It beat against his chest as if it were looking for a way out.

"The same as mine," she said.

He nodded. He touched his forehead to hers. "Are we stealing comfort now, Rhyne?" When she didn't answer, he said, "What do you want?"

"This is . . . nice."

"It is." He removed his hand from under the shawl and laid it over hers. "Has no one really held you before?"

"No one that I can remember," she whispered. "Only you."

Cole drew her down so her head rested against the curve of his neck and shoulder. "I never thanked you properly for assisting in the surgery."

"With Ezra? That was months ago."

"Then I'm months late."

"But you did thank me," she said. "That very night."

"Not as I should have." He turned his head and kissed the crown of hers. "I still have books back in New York. Fundamental subjects mostly. Biology. Chemistry. But they'll help you understand the things you keep pulling down from my shelves. I'm sending for them tomorrow. I want you to have them. You can burn them in the stove if you like, but I hope you'll make better use of them."

"Books of my own? They would be mine?"

Cole nodded. "You have a hungry mind, Rhyne. I think it's been starved far too long."

Her head came up so suddenly that she heard her neck crack. "Oh, it has. It *has*." She let go of his lapel and wrested her other hand from under his. She cupped his face, held it still so she could look hard into his eyes, and then she kissed him on his perfectly formed mouth.

It wasn't a mannerly kiss. It was a deeply carnal one. Everything she learned from him, she gave back, and it was different still because she was in charge. She teased him with her lips and tongue and pushed her fingertips into his thick thatch of hair. She riffled it at the nape, back and forth with her index finger as if she were turning over cards. His skin was warm, scented by the soap he used after leaving the surgery. She buried her face against his neck. Her nostrils flared as she breathed him in.

Her kisses were long and slow and deep. She did not think beyond what was now. She took his hand and moved it to her heart. She held it there until she was ready, then she lifted it so that it covered her breast. The heat of his palm slowly penetrated the flannel. Her breast swelled. The tip of it became a hard nub.

When she released his hand, he didn't paw her.

Cole watched Rhyne closely as she lifted her head. His hand remained exactly where she put it. She breathed in slowly as though she were testing her own mettle. Her pupils were dilated, her eyelids heavy. Her mouth was parted. The tip of her pink tongue touched her upper lip. There was no mistaking her arousal. There was also no mistaking his.

He couldn't begin to count the ways that wanting her was wrong. He doubted that the sum of all those things could persuade him to give her up. She fascinated and frustrated him, often in equal measure, on occasion at the same time. She was tender with Whitley, tough when she had to be, and her own vulnerability terrified him.

He'd missed her these last few months. His self-imposed exile to the surgery had denied him countless opportunities to be in her company, to watch her gain confidence as Rhyne Abbot but never fully abandon Runt. She still struggled with the trimmings of being a woman. The ivory combs that Whitley picked out for her wouldn't stay in her hair. The corsets were too confining, the heeled shoes barely comfortable. She still wasn't used to wearing gowns, although she inhabited them handsomely. He knew that sometimes she wore trousers underneath her skirts instead of petticoats. He never said a word.

"Can you feel me, Rhyne?"

She nodded. His erection pressed against her thigh. "That's your penis. It means tail."

He removed his hand from her breast and raised it to his mouth. He cleared his throat in time to keep from choking on laughter. "So it is."

Rhyne stared at him. "That's right, isn't it? It means tail."

"Yes."

"Then why do you want to laugh?"

Her direct question sobered him. "I don't. Believe me, I don't." He touched her mouth with his fingertips, tracing the shape of it.

His darkening eyes searched hers. "What do you want?"

She wished he hadn't asked. "You know I'm not a virgin."

He took her wrists and gave them a small shake. "I also know you're not a whore. You've never talked about what happened to you."

"And I won't now. Don't ruin it." She put her mouth within a hairsbreadth of his. "Kiss me."

Their lips brushed once. Twice. Clung. Cole opened his dressing gown and lifted her hands to his chest. He directed her fingers to the buttons on his union suit. She opened three before her hands slipped under the material and lay next to his skin. At the same time, she rubbed against him experimentally. His cock pulsed hard and heavy against her hip. His hands only tightened marginally on her wrists.

Rhyne felt the stirring of her own blood. She shook off his hands and spread her fingers across his chest. She traced the lines of his collarbones and learned the breadth of his shoulders. His skin was warm and smooth. She dragged her fingertips through the mat of red gold hair. She heard his breath hitch and felt the hesitation of his heartbeat.

There was a wildness in her that Cole did not try to restrain. There was also innocence that he could not preserve. Without any guidance from him, she found her own way to straddling his lap. Her nightdress bunched just above her knees as she settled herself on his thighs. They fit snugly in the chair.

She leaned into him, brushing against his chest with her breasts. She did it again, then again, and it wasn't enough until she took his hands and laid them over her breasts and felt her nipples pucker in the heart of his palms. She untied the ribbon that gathered the neckline of her nightgown. The shawl slipped off her shoulders, and she never felt the loss of heat as Cole's hands slipped inside the gaping neckline and cupped her breasts.

She shivered, but it wasn't the same as being cold.

He lifted his head and found her mouth. Each time he kissed her he thought of more. He wanted *more*.

"I can stop now," he whispered against her lips. His voice was a harsh rasp, almost unrecognizable to him. "I can still . . ."

The shake of her head was nearly imperceptible, and she spoke so quietly the words merely hovered at her lips. "Heal me."

He simply stared.

"Heal me."

The touch of his mouth on hers was infinitely gentle.

She let him help her with the rest of the buttons on his union suit because her fingers were no longer as steady as they had been.

He rearranged her bunched nightgown so it spread around them and palmed her bare buttocks. Watching her, he urged her up to her knees. He ran his hands along the backs of her thighs, then around the front, and finally settled on her hips. He exerted the slightest pressure with his fingertips, but it was enough for her to know what he wanted and what she should do.

Just as Rhyne began to lower herself, Cole took his erection in hand and thrust forward. He knew the moment she felt the head of it between her thighs. Her hesitation cost him dearly. The pounding of the pulse in his neck was nothing compared to the beat of blood in his cock. He moved the hand on her hip to the small of her back and tilted her hips. She surprised him by reaching under her gown and finding him with her hand. He removed his own, took her by the hips again, and waited for her to seat herself.

It was not easy for her. He thought it might even have been painful. She'd been aroused, but not ready. Not wholly. Not for this. But after that first hesitation, she didn't pause again until he was fully inside her. That was when she slid her arms around his shoulders and buried her face against his neck.

His hips twitched, but it was the only movement he made. He put his arms around her, held her close, and let her quiet. She took quick and shallow breaths at first. He felt the soft expulsion of every one of them.

"Stay there," he said quietly. "Just like that. I'm going to touch you."

His hands were at her back, sliding slowly up and down her spine. His lips were brushing her ear. She could feel the tension in his thighs alongside hers. And between them . . . *there* . . . it was impossible to imagine he could touch her more deeply.

Until he did. His fingertips made a pass between her thighs, separating the moist lips and rubbing the kernel of flesh that nestled there. Her entire body jerked from the current of pleasure that ran through it. When he did it again, her head came up. The next caress made her heart seize. The breath she craved lodged at the back of her throat.

Her hips shifted. She rubbed against his hand. She lifted, fell. The pressure inside her eased while another one built. She lifted again and this time when she fell it was into nature's own rhythm.

Closing her eyes, she gave herself up to it.

Cole watched Rhyne's pleasure build and felt his own rise with it. There was tension in her features but it wasn't something to be afraid of, rather it was something to embrace. Her chin came up, exposing the line of her neck, the intriguing hollow of her throat. The movement of her small breasts captivated him. The aureoles puckered and the nipples scraped the fabric of her gown. He pushed aside her neckline and waited a heartbeat for her to rise. Pulling her closer, he flicked her nipple with the tip of his tongue. On her next pass, he captured her breast with his mouth.

Rhyne dug her fingers into Cole's shoulders. She bit down on her own lip to keep from whimpering. The hot suck of his mouth tugged deeply, mysteriously on her womb. His lips circled her with heat; his mouth was a brand. Her hips jerked faster. She rode him harder. The spark between her thighs became a licking flame that teased her with its elusive, graceful dance.

When the fire turned liquid and chased blood through her veins, Rhyne finally cried out.

Cole threw his head back and grasped Rhyne by the waist as he pumped his hips. It was only moments before the shudder he felt under his fingertips became the shudder he felt under his skin. She didn't so much collapse against him as melt. Cole understood. It was easier to imagine himself as a puddle at the foot of the chair instead of sitting in it.

He breathed deeply and exhaled slowly. She was still contracting around him. A second wave a pleasure went through him, merely an echo of the first, but still strong enough to make him close his eyes and set his hands firmly on her hips. "Don't move," he whispered.

"I didn't."

"Don't move."

She felt them then, contractions deep inside her, ones she wasn't even sure she could control. When she tried, the effect was the opposite of what she'd hoped for. He grimaced and pressed his fingertips harder against her skin as another shiver came and went. The pleasure was so acute that it cut closer to pain.

"Jesus," he said under his breath. He opened his eyes to find her staring at him. The corners of his mouth lifted slowly, but the smile was a shade regretful. He cupped her chin. His thumb touched her lower lip. "Are you all right?"

She nodded. "I didn't expect . . ."

"Neither did I."

"Did I hurt you?"

The question surprised a low chuckle from him. "No." He kissed her. "No, not at all. Did it seem to you that you had?"

She touched his face. His features were relaxed now but she remembered how rigidly he'd held his jaw, how quickly the muscle had jumped in his cheek. Tension hadn't been confined to his body. She had seen it in the set of his mouth and the tight lines at the corners of his eyes.

"Yes," she said. "It did."

"Then I'm sorry for it, but I swear you didn't hurt me. The very opposite in fact."

"You told me not to move."

"Ahh. That. Inklings of pleasure, I'm afraid. I didn't want to stir them again."

"Inklings."

Cole slipped his hand under her breast and rolled her nipple between his thumb and forefinger.

Rhyne gasped. He barely touched her, yet pleasure snapped every one of her nerves. Her body went rigid and then her hips jerked involuntarily.

"Inklings," Cole said, letting his hand drop away. He rested it on her naked thigh.

She required a moment to come back into her skin. "Damn." It was an expression of wonderment, not a curse.

Cole's lips twitched. Of course she would say damn. "Let me help you up."

"I can move now?"

"I hope so. I can't say the same for myself."

Heat caressed her cheeks, and her eyes darted away. Using the wide arms of the chair to brace herself, she let Cole lift her. She scrambled backward off his lap and spun around while he made himself decent. She fiddled with the ribbon in her neckline to close the gap in her gown. The discarded shawl was under her feet. She picked it up and swung it around her shoulders.

"Are your parts covered?" she asked.

"I thought you were learning their proper names."

She sighed. "Yes or no?"

"Yes."

Rhyne pivoted to face him again. She hadn't expected to find him standing. It wasn't in her nature to back away so she angled her head. "I'm feeling like I do when there're too many forks at my plate."

Cole nodded. Overwhelmed. Uncertain. Awkward. "It's no different for me."

"You're kind to say so."

Cole caught her arm when she started to go. "Rhyne. Wait. I mean it. This . . ." He searched for a word to describe what had happened between them and failed to find one. "*This* is outside my experience, too. Did you imagine it wasn't?"

"I tried not to think about it."

"Would you rather it were different?"

"Yes. No." She shrugged helplessly. "I don't know. It seems as though one of us should be able to make an exit."

"I think you're confusing exit with escape." He drew her closer and slipped his arms under hers and around her back. He pressed his lips to the crown of her tousled hair. "We're going to exit together, Rhyne. We're going to my bedroom, and I'm going to take care of you."

"I don't need a doctor."

Cole suddenly remembered a conversation between Rachel and Wyatt Cooper from months earlier. They had been sitting around the table in Rhyne's cabin, and Rachel had extracted a promise from her husband to forget he was the sheriff for a while. Cole recalled with clarity his own reaction to that promise. He hadn't been able to imagine the circumstances that would make him act in a similar way. He'd thought then that it would be like shedding his skin. He felt exactly the same way about it now, but the prospect didn't cause him to hesitate.

"I'll leave him at the door," he said. "I promise."

And like that, it was done.

Rhyne sat on the edge of Cole's bed. After months as his housekeeper, she had more than a passing familiarity with his room. She changed the sheets weekly, dusted the chest of drawers, arranged his shaving kit and hairbrush beside the washstand. She knew that he liked things ordered, so she was careful to fold his clothes neatly and place his footstool twenty-six inches from the chair by the stove. She filled the porcelain pitcher with fresh water daily and made certain his razor was as sharp as his scalpels. She could have recited the exact contents of his armoire.

It was no more or less than she'd done for her father.

He had a fancy silk dressing screen that he'd brought from New York. Whitley had one, too. It made her suspect that the Monroe family employed more than a housekeeper and a cook. There probably had been maids and a valet, someone whose job it was to turn out the doctor and his sister so they were fit for their high society, someone who handed clothes around the screen and assisted with buttons and laces when they were asked.

Cole was behind that screen now. It didn't matter that she couldn't see him properly. The occasional splash of water in the basin let her know he was attending to himself. She heard him open the window at his back, toss the water, then pour more into the basin. The screen fluttered as a wintry blast swirled into the room. The painted dragons on the panels filled their bellies with air, but Cole slammed the window closed before they could breathe fire.

Rhyne stole the blanket from the trunk at the foot of his bed and wrapped it around her. When Cole stepped out from behind the screen and gestured for her to come forward, she dragged the blanket with her.

"Don't you have a robe?" he asked.

"I'd be wearing it, wouldn't I?" She was sorry for the words as much as the way she said them. "I'm all prickly," she said.

"I noticed." He stepped aside so she could get behind the screen. "Everything you need is there."

"I have soap and water in my own room. I could do this there."

"But you don't have a screen, and therefore

no privacy."

She waved him off. "I'd have plenty of privacy because I'd be alone."

"You wouldn't be, though." He picked up a towel that had been warming beside the stove and laid it over the screen. "And I think that would have made you uncomfortable."

The water in the basin was very cold. She soaked her cloth quickly and rung it out, then she raised her nightgown to complete her ablutions. The blanket fell off her shoulders, but she stood on it to keep her feet warm while she finished.

"Is there blood?" Cole asked from the bed.

Rhyne poked her head around the screen. "I thought you left the doctor outside."

"It's not a doctor's question. It's a . . ." He hardly had to think — the word came easily to his lips. "It's a lover's question."

Rhyne ducked back, dropped the wash-cloth, and bent over the basin to splash her face. Suddenly the water did not seem cold enough.

"Rhyne?"

She straightened, bracing herself on the edge of the washstand. She glanced at the cloth hanging over the lip of the basin. "There's no blood." Unlike before. Before there had been blood.

"Are you finished?"

She nodded, realized he couldn't hear that, and answered him. "I'm done."

From his angle at the bed, Cole could see that she'd lost the blanket. "Then come here. And bring the blanket with you."

Rhyne stepped over it and stooped to pick it up. Her head swam. She put her hands down to steady herself.

"Are you all right?"

She heard the concern in his voice. "Fine. I'm fine." Straightening slowly, she pulled the blanket with her. She was holding it in her arms when she stepped around the screen.

"You're pale. Come here."

Although she wasn't afraid, she was glad when he didn't advance on her. "I'm fine. Really." She approached the bed and let him take the blanket from her arms. He put it around her shoulders and used it to inch her closer until she was standing between his splayed legs. "If you try to take my temperature, I swear I'll take a poke at you."

He believed her and told her so. That seemed to satisfy her. "Would you like to sit down?"

She looked at the space on the bed beside him, then over at the chair by the stove. "Homer wrote about choosing between Scylla and Charybdis. I reckon this is one of those times."

Cole chuckled as she tugged the blanket out of his hands and sat beside him. "So which one am I?"

She merely cast him a sideways glance and

allowed him to choose for himself. "Why am I still here?" she asked. "Aren't you done caring for me?"

"I think you know we have to talk."

"We could have done that downstairs."

"No, we couldn't. Not with you trying so hard to escape."

"I still am."

"Whitley's down the hall. Sleeping, I hope. If not, there's a creaking floorboard outside my room that alerts me when she's up. I need to know that we can talk privately, Rhyne. You want that, too, don't you?"

Cornered, she nodded.

"Good." He hooked his heels on the bed frame and made a steeple with his hands. "I want you to marry me."

She frowned deeply. Her head still felt a little thick. She rubbed her temples and tried to clear it.

"I want you to marry me," he repeated. "I should have said it earlier. I should have told you it would be the cost of being together. You could have decided then if you were willing to accept the terms." He bowed his head and stared at his steepled fingers. "I should have made sure you understood. I'm sorry that I didn't, Rhyne. I'm sorry that you didn't know."

Rhyne let his words wash over and wondered what he expected her to say. He hadn't asked her a proper question. He only put the thing before her and told her he was sorry. She couldn't think of a single reason that he'd want to tie himself to Runt Abbot. If she were as mean-spirited as she wanted to be, she'd drag him in front of the parson in the morning. He'd know sorry then. He'd know sorry to the soles of his shoes, and it would serve him right.

"Do you suppose it's the fornicatin' that's made you squirrelly?"

CHAPTER 9

"Why do you do that?" asked Cole.

"Do what?" But Rhyne knew what he was asking, and she felt small for pretending otherwise. Cole knew, too, because he didn't say anything, and the pressure of his silence built until it was a weight on her chest. "Runt Abbot is who I am," she said quietly. "I thought you needed to be reminded. And your brain *is* addled if you think I'm going to marry you. I just didn't know any other way to say it. I was going to tell you to go to hell."

"You understand there could be consequences?"

"I suppose you mean a child."

"That's only one of them, but we can start there. What would you do?"

Rhyne was unaware of her arms protectively slipping around her abdomen. "I don't know. I don't think I could pass it off to Mrs. Cooper."

Cole pushed his hand through his hair. "Well, hallelujah for that."

Rhyne's head snapped sideways, and she stared at him. "What did you hope to hear? You're making me say things out loud when I can barely think."

He conceded that she had a point, although he didn't share that with her. "I have to consider Whitley," he said, trying a different tack.

"She's another consequence?"

"I think so. She'll figure it out, Rhyne. She always does, and she'll have certain expectations."

"Same as yours, I bet."

"I'd be very surprised if they were any different."

Forlorn, Rhyne stared at the floor. "She'll never understand why I won't marry you."

"Probably not, since I don't understand it myself."

"It's a damn fool notion," she said. "That's why."

"I know you think so."

Rhyne pulled the blanket tighter around her shoulders, but not because she was cold. "I guess Whitley'll have to be disappointed in me."

"She'll be disappointed in both of us."

"I don't see how."

"She knows better than to assign all the blame to you."

"I think you're wrong. She didn't like it when she thought you were going to marry

308

Miss Erwin."

"Whitley didn't like Caroline. For that matter, neither did my mother. Did she tell you that?"

Uncomfortable with sharing Whitley's confidences, Rhyne nodded reluctantly.

"They tolerated her, but they never embraced her." Cole tried to catch Rhyne's eye, but she wouldn't look in his direction. Her gaze remained firmly fixed on the patterned rug. "The comparison of you to Caroline doesn't work at all."

Rhyne was certain of that. Caroline Erwin knew what to do with the little fork. She probably wore silk drawers and owned a robe. Maybe more than one. And she didn't have hair, she had *tresses*. Long blond tresses that held combs inlaid with turquoise and mother-of-pearl. It was also likely that her nose was as straight as a compass needle. Rhyne didn't care for her much, but she couldn't fault Cole's eye for beauty.

Rhyne also knew it was true that neither Whitley's judgment, nor that of her mother's, was influenced in any great measure by Caroline Erwin's appearance. The things that had the ability to erode Rhyne's confidence would have been taken for granted by Mrs. Monroe and her daughter. Their society was filled with young women who could navigate their way as gracefully and as assuredly as Miss Erwin.

"What was she like?" asked Rhyne. This, at least, was a marginally more comfortable subject — for her.

Cole didn't answer immediately. "I suppose that depends on whether I tell you about the woman I fell in love with or the one that I forced to end our engagement."

"Tell me about both."

He dropped his feet to the floor and stood, then he went to the stove and added some coals from the scuttle. When he returned to the bed, he pulled back the covers and got under them, resting his back against the headboard and drawing up his knees. He didn't invite Rhyne to join him.

"The first time I saw her," he said, "was at a dinner that her father held for all the student doctors at St. John's. Dr. Erwin was a widower and he had pressed Caroline to act as our hostess. She effortlessly held the attention of every gentleman at the table, so much so that her father had to save his welcoming remarks until cigars and port were served."

"Why did that make a difference?" asked Rhyne.

"Naturally, Caroline had to excuse herself after dinner."

"Oh." *Naturally.* There were so many conventions that Rhyne realized she still did not understand. "Did she notice you?"

"That's a very good question. I thought she

did. She said she did. But that was one of her talents. She didn't merely command attention; she gave it as well. She had the ability to make every person she spoke to feel as if they were the most important person in the room. She cast a very wide net."

"More like a spell," Rhyne muttered. "Sorry." She hadn't meant him to hear her comment, but when he chuckled she felt duty bound to apologize.

"You're not wrong," he told her. "It was a spell. She was astute. Clever. Accomplished. She held very firm opinions and was fearless about voicing them. I didn't understand then that there was nothing radical in her thinking, that her ideas were largely identical to those of her father. It was only that she could make them sound fresh. I thought she was an original. My mother thought she was an excellent reproduction."

Rhyne thought that she'd have liked Cole's mother. She was less certain that the reverse would be true. Rhyne scooted backward on the bed, wrestling with the blanket as she went. When she'd finally positioned herself so she could see Cole, she crossed her legs in front of her and set her elbows on her knees.

"Should I go on?" asked Cole.

"What? Yes. Please. I'm comfortable now."

Cole's fingers curled tightly in the folds of the blankets. It kept him from giving in to the urge to push Rhyne flat on her back and

311

kiss her until they were both breathless. Fornicating *had* made him squirrelly.

"I have to explain to you about Caroline's father. Dr. Erwin is the head of surgery at St. John's. He's an influential and respected physician, and he has a sharp intellect. He earned the position because of those things. I will never say otherwise. What I will say, and have said publicly, is that time stopped when he took over."

"Time stopped? What do you mean?"

"He taught what he understood, but he discouraged experimentation of new techniques or discussion of theory. He read the journals and dismissed their conclusions. He ridiculed thinking that attempted to challenge his. He was brilliant at what he knew, at what he could teach, but in the new position he remade himself as God. He made himself omnipotent."

"He didn't like you."

"That is putting it kindly. Whitley would say he was afraid of me. Perhaps even jealous. I'm not saying that I agree with her, but it's true that Dr. Erwin and I rarely saw things in the same light. He had no tolerance for my research and discredited my work. He found ways to keep me out of the hospital's laboratory by assigning me patients that should have gone to less experienced doctors by that time."

"Why didn't you leave?"

Cole did not have to think about it. "Caroline. That's the simplest answer. You should understand that she wasn't fundamentally rebellious. I suspect the only time she acted in opposition to her father's wishes was when she agreed to marry me. It was odd, but once she did that, she began to try to remake me in her father's image. I might have seen it sooner, but my mother died and I inherited the responsibility for my sister's welfare. There was so much to do between settling the estate and working, I didn't have a great deal of time for either of the women in my life. I didn't even understand that they didn't like each other."

He regarded Rhyne frankly. "Whitley said she told you about the accident that burned her hands."

"Yes, she did."

"I'm always curious about the particular version. Did she mention, for instance, that I was gone from the house that night?"

"Yes. To a charity affair, I believe. Honoring Dr. Erwin."

"Did she tell you that she knew I was going?"

"Yes."

"I thought so."

"You mean she didn't know?"

"No. I lied to her. I told her I'd be at home, working in the carriage house if she needed me. Caroline was desperate for me to attend the gala. She said it would help heal the breach between her father and me. She wanted to be on my arm that night, and I couldn't say no to her. She was very persuasive — another of her talents."

"So you lied to Whitley."

"There were servants in the house. I told myself I wasn't really leaving her alone." His smile was no smile at all, but a grim line that spoke to regret and contempt for his actions. "In my haste to get ready, I forgot about the lamp I'd left burning in the carriage house."

"That's the light Whitley saw from her window."

"No. Not exactly. What Whitley saw was fire licking at the windows. A small animal . . . a stray cat . . . perhaps a rat . . . is most likely to blame for overturning the lamp. What Whitley didn't see was me trying to put the fire out. It never occurred to her that I wasn't anywhere around. She knew I'd told her I'd be in the carriage house, and the only explanation that came to her for me letting the fire grow was that I must have fallen asleep inside."

Rhyne felt her heart begin to slam against her chest. She stared at him, saying nothing.

"Whitley didn't hesitate. She didn't call for help, and she didn't tell anyone she was leaving the house. To my lasting regret, not only did I leave a lighted lamp unattended, but I also neglected to lock the door. I know she flew into the room with no thought for herself. Sometimes when I close my eyes . . ." He paused, shook his head. "She beat at the flames with an old rug that was lying by the door. She didn't even realize I wasn't in there yet, maybe if she had she would have just gotten out. Instead, once she'd gotten the fire down to where it was only smoldering, she started throwing water on it. There were all types of chemicals on the shelves. There were beakers of acid beside the sink."

"Sulfuric. Vitriol."

"She told you that, did she? Well, there were other things besides that, but that's the one that stays with her. She tossed them all into the sink. I think she meant to dip the bucket in so she'd have a decent amount to toss on the fire. That's what I imagine. She doesn't really remember much about what happened next. I know the chemicals reacted to release noxious gases, and I know she fainted. She fell forward into the sink long enough to cause the burns you saw, then she lay on the ground until the fire caught again and our caretaker noticed it. He went in, found Whitley, and carried her outside. The carriage house burnt to the ground, but the pumper trucks arrived in time to save the neighbor's home and ours.

"Mrs. Abernathy knew where I was. She sent William, our caretaker, around to the hotel where the gala was being held. I left as soon as I received the message. Caroline came with me. She stayed for the first twenty-four hours, maybe longer. I don't really know. Like Whitley, there are things I don't quite remember."

"It's better that way," she said gently. "At least I think so."

Cole didn't disagree. "It was different with Caroline after that. It happened so gradually that I didn't notice at first, but I have to tell you that what altered was my perspective. Caroline remained as she ever was. I think I mentioned that she was persuasive, but it's just as true that I no longer knew my own mind. I'd failed Whitley. I didn't trust myself to know what was best. I sent her away to that seminary. Caroline was so certain it would be good for her. It wasn't. They would have tried to turn her out in Caroline's like-ness, if you can imagine that."

The thought of it curled his mouth. This time it was a real smile, faint, but apprecia-tive. "Whitley knows something about resist-ing those kinds of efforts. She wore them out. All of them."

"She said you took her out of the school."

"I did. I can also tell you honestly that I don't know how much longer they would have let her stay."

"Then the threat to send her back . . . ?"

"A threat, mostly. Don't misunderstand. There are other schools."

"Uh-huh."

Cole tried not to be moved by Rhyne's ironic smile or the mischief in her eyes, but he was immune to neither. Not knowing if she would accept the overture or not, he held out his hand.

Rhyne did not try to argue with herself about it. She just went. He would have lifted the covers for her, but she didn't allow him to do that. She did accept his hand and let him pull her closer. She sat back against the headboard beside him and tucked the blanket loosely around her. Their shoulders touched, and under the blanket, she sought out his hand and laid hers against it. His fingers closed over hers.

"Caroline was unhappy with my decision to bring Whitley back. She viewed my sister as a constant distraction to what was important: my career, our engagement, and her father's legacy. I'm not certain of the exact order, but I finally understood that there was no place for Whitley in her life. She worried about Whitley's future, but when I pressed to understand the nature of her concern, I realized that what she was afraid of was that Whitley would not make a good marriage, or worse, that my sister would attract the sort of notorious suitors that come around when there's a fortune to be had."

"Whitley has money?"

"God, no. Not yet. She's what is properly

called an heiress. My parents set up a trust that will be hers when she's twenty-five."

"Does she know?"

"Yes."

"She never breathed a word."

"I'm not sure that she ever thinks about it."

"*I'd* think about it," said Rhyne. "A lot."

Cole squeezed her hand. "Caroline did. There were generations of money in her family, most of it from shipping enterprises. Her father broke from the Erwin tradition when he became a physician. They were certainly well off, but not as rich as members of the larger family. Caroline saw marriage to me as a way to put the balance back."

"You have money?"

"In addition to what the town pays me? Yes." He turned his head to study her profile. She appeared deep in thought. "Are you reconsidering marrying me?"

Rhyne shook her head. "But I am going to ask you for a raise."

Cole's head knocked against the headboard as he started with laughter.

"Shh. You're going to wake Whitley."

"Maybe I should."

Rhyne refused to be baited. "Was there a last straw for you and Miss Erwin? You know, something that made you know for certain that you couldn't marry her?"

"Oddly enough, it was at a dinner party, this one hosted by another physician from

318

the hospital. Caroline accompanied me. Her father could not attend. I listened to her as attentively as every other person at the table that evening, but what I heard was her father's voice. It was as if he were holding court. I knew then that she would never be happy allowing me to make my own way. I would have to follow in her father's steps exactly. There could be no deviation. I understood then that I didn't love her any longer because I finally knew her, and I realized she couldn't love me because she would never know who I am. I was a long time reaching those conclusions, but ending the engagement was the proper course to take."

Cole waited for Rhyne to comment, but she remained silent, letting her head fall back a few degrees and closing her eyes. Her hand stayed in his. He had no idea what she was thinking, and her silence lasted so long that he thought she might have fallen asleep.

"Why did you come here?" she whispered. Her voice was reedy, the pitch unsteady. "What's Reidsville got except that it isn't New York? You could have gone most anywhere. From the things I read, New York's so big I bet you could have lost yourself in it. And if not there, there's plenty of places like it. Boston. Philadelphia. Even Chicago, if you don't mind the smell of the slaughterhouses. I don't understand why you came here and took it upon yourself to be so damn interfering. Doc Diggins played cards and tended to people that needed him. He didn't go out of his way to look after people that didn't ask nothin' of him."

Cole decided that Rhyne must have been holding on to that for a long time. He waited until he was sure she'd run out of steam. "When you say 'damn interfering,' can I assume you're referring to the fact that I offered you employment?"

"Employment's the least of it. You want me to marry you. That kind of meddling could put a busybody like Alice Cassidy to shame."

"I don't agree."

"Well, you wouldn't, would you? It's your idea."

"Do you wish our paths had never crossed?"

"Just about every other day."

"And on the in-between days?"

"I think of all your kindnesses."

"It must be confusing."

She opened her eyes and stared at the raised pattern of roses and vines on the far wall. After a while the intricate design on the flock paper made her eyes swim. "It puts powerful knots in my stomach."

He nodded. He was more than a little familiar with them himself. "Do you remember that I told you it was Whitley's idea to come here?"

"Is it true? Or some version of the truth?"

Cole supposed he deserved that. "It's true.

I was still at St. John's. I didn't want to leave as a reaction to ending the engagement. It was important to me to think it through. Whitley, you might have noticed, tends to be more impatient. She saw the search committee's advertisement in the *Times* and answered it. I didn't know anything about it until I received their reply along with a contract. I didn't immediately accept the offer, but the idea of living in a place where no one knew us, well, that was appealing, and I knew Whitley wanted to be out of society. Had she still been in New York, she would have made her coming out a few months ago. It didn't matter that every girl there would have worn satin gloves that reached their elbows. Whitley knew the kinds of comments that she could expect. Things like: *"Fashion is always about deception, dear. How fortunate you are that your brother can afford to buy you so many elegant gloves."*

"Was that Caroline?" asked Rhyne.

"Yes."

"You pitched your voice better that time."

"I remembered what you said: whisper."

Rhyne smiled faintly, still absorbing all that he'd told her. "Miss Erwin is spiteful, I think."

That was probably putting it too kindly, Cole thought, but he agreed with her assessment. "I had a letter recently from a colleague in New York. He wrote that Caroline is engaged again, this time to a physician specializing in disorders of the heart and lungs."

"Did it stir regrets?"

"Not one."

Rhyne's nod was barely perceptible. She slid down the headboard a few inches, just enough so that when she leaned sideways, her head rested on Cole's shoulder. "In the morning," she said, "when you think about tonight, will it stir regrets?"

Cole blew out a deep breath. "You load a question like a six-shooter."

"I suppose I do. You don't have to answer. It wasn't fair."

"What would you say?"

She didn't stir as she turned the matter over in her mind. "I regret that I was selfish," she said finally. "I didn't consider your honor, or that you'd feel so bound by it that you'd want me to marry you. I can't account for all the feelings that welled up inside when you put your mouth on me, but I know how purely stubborn I can be, and I wanted more of what you were givin'. You chase away the darkness, and I got real greedy for some light."

Cole was glad she was at ease with silence. His chest was uncomfortably tight, and the constriction in his throat barely allowed him to breathe, let alone speak.

The lamp on the bedside table grew dim as the oil wicked away. Shadows flickered across the flock paper, then were still. The coals in the stove needed replenishing, but neither of them moved to tend to the fire.

In time, they slept.

Cole wasn't particularly surprised to find himself alone when he woke, just disappointed. He recognized the sounds of early morning activity: pots banging in the kitchen; Whitley's hurried descent down the stairs; the exchange of greetings; and realized he'd slept much later than was his habit.

By the time he arrived at the dining room table, Whitley and Rhyne were almost done with their breakfast.

"He rises!" Whitley said, pointing her knife at him. A dollop of orange marmalade dropped on her plate, narrowly missing the tablecloth. She scooped it up with her finger and plopped it in her mouth. "I told Rhyne it was all right to let you sleep late because you *never* do, and you've been looking so peaked lately that I was *sure* you needed sleep to recover your color and remove those sadly abused bags from under your eyes. Do you see, Rhyne? I was right. Coleridge is looking fine, and I think his disposition is improved."

Cole dropped a kiss on Whitley's proffered cheek. Straightening, he touched his tongue to the corner of his mouth. "I believe that's a spot of marmalade you have there, Whit. Good morning, Miss Abbot."

"Good morning."

Cole pulled out his chair at the head of the table and sat. "I looked out my window and saw we were blanketed with another foot of snow. Does that explain why the only sunshine we'll see today is in your face?"

"Rhyne says I can stay home. Didn't you, Rhyne?"

"I did," she said. She glanced at Cole. "The wind's still blowing a lot of snow around. There will be drifts as tall as Whitley. It's not safe. Mr. Cassidy won't open the school."

"Well, you would know." He uncovered a serving plate of scrambled eggs and helped himself. There was toast and crisp strips of bacon under another dome. "The marmalade, please." Whitley slid it across the table. He spread some on one triangle of toast and turned his pointed gaze on his sister. "Bags under my eyes? Medical bags, I hope."

She giggled. "Of course."

"So what is the plan for today?"

Her face sagged. "You're talking about schoolwork, I suppose."

"Not necessarily. Just something to occupy you."

Rhyne spoke up. "I was thinking that Whitley could help me. I have some recipes that I've scribbled on bits of paper here and there. Whitley's got such an elegant script, it seemed to me that she could write things down so I could read them plainly." She looked at Whitley. "That's after we finish the regular chores, you understand. If you're here, there's no reason you can't give me a hand."

"There's our plan," said Whitley, beaming at her brother. "What's yours?"

"I have to go to the telegraph office and send a wire about getting some books, then there are patients to call on." He picked up a forkful of eggs, ignoring their surprised stares. He imagined they both thought he'd be spending the day in the surgery bent over his microscope. "Mrs. Ferris has a troubling cold in her chest. John and Eleanor Best's youngest boy has the whooping cough. Ezra told me his stump's been giving him some pain. I told him to come see me, but he shouldn't expose his arm on a day like today."

"You shouldn't go out either," Rhyne said. "You don't really understand what can happen. You can lose your way going from here to the woodshed."

"I'm not discounting the danger," he said. "But I made promises. This is what I do. I'll be careful."

And there was no arguing with that.

Rhyne and Whitley spent the day attending to household tasks. They ate lunch in the kitchen, and Rhyne showed Whitley the scraps of paper where she'd recorded the recipes. She baked an applesauce cake that she would serve after dinner while Whitley copied the recipes in her beautifully refined style. They each found reasons to go to the parlor to check the clock on the mantel. Sometimes less than a half hour passed between visits.

They settled in the library while the dinner roast cooked. Neither made an effort at small talk. Rhyne found Whitley's quiet alarming. It seemed to her that Cole's sister had passed through worry and arrived at dread. She didn't know what assurances she could offer Whitley, not when she wasn't feeling them herself. Whitley would see straight to her own concern; she probably already had.

"Would it help to sit at the window?" she asked.

Whitley shook her head. "It's already too dark. I wouldn't be able to see him. Why isn't there a moon tonight, Rhyne? A fingernail of moon would help him find his way home."

"Lamps are burning all over town. We have one in every window. He can't mistake this house."

"What if he's lying in a drift? You said they'd be as tall as me."

"Then it's a good thing your brother's taller, isn't it?"

Whitley jumped to her feet and began to pace the room. "Why'd he have to be a doctor anyway? He could have been a soldier."

"I don't see how that would ease your mind."

"At least he'd have a gun," she said. "He's

a fine shot, did you know that? He was the best with a rifle in his class at the Point. Papa said he was admired for it, not just by the other cadets, but the commanders, too. Instead of staying with his rifle, he gave it up to walk straight into sickness. There's no weapon for that. He sits with people who have the croup and the measles and fevers so hot they can scald a person's brain, and he can't shoot at any of it."

Tears flooded her eyes, and she pushed at them with the heels of her hands. "Our mama died because she visited the sick wards. The poorest people go there, Rhyne. It's the only way they can see a doctor, and most of the time they wait until they're so sick they have to be carried in. I don't blame them. They're afraid, and it's an awful place. Sometimes their own family won't visit them there, but our mother went because she said no one should die alone. She sat at their bedside to give people peace of mind and she caught her own death."

Rhyne sat back in her chair. Stunned, she stared at Whitley. "Does your brother know how you feel?"

"No! No, and you can't tell him. Promise me that you won't tell him."

There was no mistaking Whitley's very real horror at the prospect of being unmasked. "But, Whitley, it grieves you."

"It doesn't matter. If he knew, it would be

327

awful for him. He would feel as though he should give it up." She held up her hands, showing the backs of them to Rhyne. "Because of these. He blames himself, and I don't know if anything will ever change that. I can't put him in a position where he believes he has to choose between the two things he loves best in all the world."

"Oh, Whitley." She stood and opened her arms, inviting someone into them for the first time. She had no idea what she would do if the overture was refused, but it didn't come to that. Whitley launched herself at Rhyne and threw her arms likewise around her.

So much was plain to Rhyne now. She understood what prompted Whitley to answer the *Times'* advertisement. Cole was probably not wrong that his sister wanted to be gone from New York society, but that told only half the tale. She wanted him in a safe place, away from the hospital, away from the crowded wards that had killed their mother. Whitley was still trying to save him.

"You must be the very best sister," Rhyne whispered against Whitley's ear. "I wonder if he knows that."

Whitley sniffed. "He does. I tell him regularly."

Rhyne smiled. She stroked Whitley's hair while she blinked away her own tears.

It was this scene that Cole interrupted as he parted the library doors. Startled, Rhyne and Whitley stepped away from each other and stared at him. There was a dusting of snow in his copper hair and ruddy, wind-blown color in his cheeks. Bits of ice at the hem of his trousers melted and dripped on the floor. The tips of his boots were wet. He still seemed to be in possession of a complete set of fingers and toes. In fact, he looked rather pleased with himself.

Arm in arm, their shoulders braced as if for battle, Whitley and Rhyne marched past him as if he weren't there.

"I hope you intend to explain it to me," Cole said later that evening. He accepted the cup of hot cocoa that Rhyne brought to him in the surgery. "It was extraordinarily quiet at dinner this evening." He pushed out a stool for her and invited her to sit. "Has Whitley gone to bed?"

"Yes."

"She didn't say good night. She usually does."

"She will tomorrow. Whitley doesn't hold a grudge for long."

"I know she's angry at me. What I don't understand is why."

"She was worried about you." After a moment, she added, "We both were."

"Then I thought you would have been glad to see me."

Rhyne shrugged. "I suppose we had to

329

know you were all right before we could allow ourselves to get properly riled."

Cole lifted a single eyebrow. "I'm not sure that even makes sense."

"It does from where I'm sitting."

"A woman's mind is a considerable mystery."

She liked the sound of that. "That's what I have, don't I? A woman's mind."

He saw that it pleased her. "You do." He sipped his cocoa. "Have you given any thought to the arrangement I offered yesterday?"

All day. What she said was, "No. I gave you my answer."

Cole nodded and offered no pressure to change her mind. He pushed aside a tray of test tubes and another of glass slides to give him room to set his cup and saucer on the table. "I saw Wyatt Cooper today. He was in his office. I stopped in to say hello."

"Did you talk Latin or speak like regular folks?"

"Like regular folks, I expect. I asked him if he was able to make his usual Thursday rounds. I know sometimes he stops in to see the outliers." He watched Rhyne carefully for some reaction, but she gave nothing away. "He told me the snow wasn't a problem until he headed back. It didn't keep him from visiting Judah."

"Of course it didn't."

He waited, but she didn't ask. "Your father still has the younger Beaufort boy helping him out. Wyatt says Danny's kept the place from falling down around Judah's head."

"Danny's a hard worker. He helped me with the horses now and again so he knows his way around the place."

"Well, it seems to be working out." Cole tapped his cup with his index finger. "Wyatt asked me if you ever saw Judah around town. I told him I didn't know. You never mentioned it."

"I haven't."

"But you'd tell me if you did, wouldn't you?"

"Maybe. I don't know. Is it important?" She frowned at him. "Why are you talking about Judah?"

"Wyatt believes he's been around."

"He's allowed, isn't he? No one's put up a fence to keep him out."

"No, but the sheriff seems to think that he has no reason for being here. What supplies he needed, Danny got for him before hard winter set in. If there's something else that comes up, Will or Wyatt will take it to him. He hasn't asked for anything."

"I don't understand." She could feel her agitation growing and tried to quell it. "Has someone seen him or not?"

"No one can say for sure. Wyatt's had a couple of reports of someone that might or might not be Judah coming into town late at night. Will said that Sid Walker saw someone passing on the outskirts of the open mine. It could have been Judah, but Sid couldn't swear to it. Except for his brief stay in the jail, I understand that it's been a long time since the good citizens of Reidsville rubbed elbows with your father."

"That's the way Judah wanted it."

"Can you think of something that would bring him around?"

"No. I think people are mistaken."

Cole considered that. It was what he and Wyatt wanted to believe. "You're probably right, but as soon as there's a break in the weather, I'm going out to see him."

Rhyne's stomach roiled. "Leave him be. He'll put a bullet through you. Don't think that he won't. His fingers might be a little stiff, but his vision's keen."

"Wyatt said he asked for me."

"Does that seem right to you? Did the sheriff say that Judah was sickly?"

"He said he was favoring his left side more than usual."

"Well, that should tell Wyatt that it isn't Judah coming into town."

"I thought of that, too." So had Wyatt. They hadn't dismissed the idea that Judah was laying a trap. "I won't be going alone, Rhyne. Will or Wyatt will accompany me."

"You better take the sheriff because Judah

definitely won't spare that no-account Beatty boy."

"All right."

Rhyne stood. "I'm going to bed before I get all riled up again."

Cole let her go, but he suspected it was already too late for that.

Rhyne stared at her reflection in the vanity mirror. She fiddled with a lock of hair that kept slipping out from behind her ear. In a fit of frustration, she spit on her hand, twisted the lock into submission, and tucked it in place. "I'd spit on you, too, Coleridge Monroe," she whispered, "if I thought it'd tame your cussed ornery ways."

She pushed at her brush so that it skittered across the top of the vanity and banged against the mirror. She had a powerful urge to hit something with her fist. It felt as if she was losing her mind . . . her *woman's* mind. The image in the mirror didn't help her. It was like staring at a stranger.

Rhyne turned around on the tuffet and put her back to the mirror. She hugged herself, not because she was cold but because she needed the comfort. When Judah got her this peeved, she'd take her Winchester and go out for a spell. Sometimes she'd stay out all night. Sometimes she'd come back and sleep under the porch.

She had her Winchester, but it was an awfully cold night for contemplating sleeping outdoors. And what would she do with her rifle in town? Sheriff Cooper frowned on folks carrying loaded weapons. There was even some kind of ordinance against it. She'd end up bunking in the jail.

It was not completely unappealing.

"Squirrelly," she murmured under her breath.

She stretched her legs toward the stove and wiggled her toes. The woolen socks were as thick as mittens. She could track through the house without a sound, as stealthy as a fox hunting in the dead of night.

Rhyne rose and ignored the invitation of the turned down covers on her bed in favor of the ones she knew she'd find in Cole's room. She was careful to step around the floorboard that would have announced her presence outside his door.

Except for the orange glow through the stove's grate, his room was dark. She allowed her eyes a moment to adjust before she crossed to his bedside. He was turned away from her, toward the middle of the bed, and he didn't stir the entire time she stood there.

Rhyne went around the bed, skirted the trunk at the foot, and came up on the other side. She'd been wrong that there would be an invitation, but it didn't deter her. She'd come to the place where she could find her mind again, the woman's mind that eluded her when he was too long out of her sight.

Raising the covers, Rhyne carefully maneuvered herself onto the bed. She unfolded along the length of it, then inched backward until she could feel the heat of his body. She listened to his breathing, and the steadiness of it was its own comfort. Reaching behind her, she found his hand and eased it around her waist. The slight curve of his body allowed her to fit her bottom neatly in the pocket of his groin. Only then did she release the breath she'd been holding.

At her back, Cole smiled. Holding Rhyne meant that sleep was finally within his grasp.

It was the warmth that made her so reluctant to leave his bed. A sliver of rosy light defined the edges of the curtains. The sun was not properly up, and she craved a few more minutes of the peace she'd found in Cole's bed. She'd already determined that escape would not be as easy as entering had been. Sometime during the night their positions had changed, and now she was on her back with Cole resting one of his knees across her thighs.

There was also the matter of his hand cradling her breast. If his thumb moved even a fraction, it would caress her nipple. To her astonishment, she'd no sooner thought it than her nipple became a bud that thrust against the fabric of her nightgown. She blinked. His thumb hadn't moved at all, but her breathing had quickened.

Slowly, she slid her hand along her side until it was within inches of her breast. She walked her fingertips up the curve but stopped short of reaching the peak. Raising her hand a fraction, she let her fingers hover a moment before she extended a single nail and dragged it across her nipple. The small burst of pleasure made her eyes widen.

"Let me do that for you."

Cole's voice was husky, thick with sleep and wanting. It touched off a current of heat in Rhyne that ran all the way to her toes. She let her hand fall back to the bed and kept her eyes on his. When she spoke, it was merely a thread of sound. "All right."

Cole moved his thumb precisely as she'd imagined. Pleasure radiated across her skin, and she felt her breast swell in the cup of his hand. He'd moved closer, though she didn't know how that was possible. His breath was warm against her ear, and she realized they were sharing a single pillow. His thumb made another lazy pass across her breast. Several long moments passed before it came again. She held herself very still, her breath lodged firmly in her throat in anticipation of another pulse of pleasure.

When his thumb didn't so much as twitch, she turned her head to the side to look at Cole. His face was largely in shadow, but she could tell he was watching her. She put her fingertips to his mouth to sense the shape of it. The curve was so slight that she could have been convinced she'd imagined it. The gleam in his eye, however, was no trick of the firelight.

"You haven't fallen back to sleep," she said.

"Hardly."

She laid her hand over his at her breast. He resisted her small effort to move him. "Then what are you doing?"

"Anticipating."

Her lips parted on the first sound of her question and then she was silenced by his mouth. His kiss was as maddening as his touch had been. His mouth advanced and retreated as if he were engaged in a campaign and kissing her was a strategy. When he captured her mouth, it was to pleasure himself with deep, drugging kisses that made Rhyne glad that she was lying down. There was a moment's respite when he lifted his head to catch his breath, but he used that time to plan his next foray, this one a perfect raid on her senses.

He dropped kisses on the corner of her mouth, her jaw, and the tender hollow at her temple. His lips traced the sensitive cord in her neck. At her shoulder, he pushed aside her gown and put his mouth against her skin. The ribbon that held her nightdress fast disappeared into his hand and then his hand disappeared under the gown. This time when his thumb passed over her nipple, it was flesh to her flesh.

He created a steady pulse of pleasure that continued to throb in her breast long after he'd moved on. His knee pushed between her thighs. The barrier of her nightgown frustrated him. His lips tickled her throat, then moved to her chin. Finally, they hovered just above her mouth. She tried to nudge his lips with hers, but he held himself just out of her reach.

"Lift your gown." He turned more fully onto his side and removed his knee from between her legs.

Rhyne's fingers were curled into the sheet on either side of her. They remained there as if frozen. Under the covers, Cole slid the heel of his hand from where it rested between her breasts all the way to the juncture of her thighs. The heat from his hand as it passed over her flat belly seemed to thaw Rhyne's fingers. She dug them into the folds of her flannel gown and began taking handfuls of the material until she felt the hem brush the tops of her thighs. She closed her eyes as Cole's fingers dipped between her legs.

He leaned over her. "You haven't fallen back to sleep, have you?"

"Hardly."

"Then what are you doing?"

"Anticipating."

He kissed her. Slowly. Deeply. Then his fingers began to move.

Rhyne thought about the things that she had come to savor: a clear, cool night when stars were falling out of the heavens; nuzzling the neck of a horse she'd finally gentled; being the one left standing when the fighting was done. And this. If she didn't count those moments when he simply held her in his arms, what Cole was doing to her now was easily at the forefront of everything.

Between halting breaths, she told him so.

He made a sound that might have been a chuckle or might have meant he was choking. She didn't especially care. She told him that, too.

Cole quieted her with his mouth. It helped to quell his smile.

She was damp against his fingertips. He stroked her until she was wet. He watched her arch her neck and felt the rise of tension in her arms and legs. Her hips rose and fell. He drew back the hood of her clitoris and slid his finger over it. Her heels dug into the mattress, and she twisted as she lifted off the bed. Her lips parted. She sucked in a draught of air, held it, and sucked in another.

He whispered against her ear. "Let it out. It's all right. I want to hear you."

It was tempting. He tempted her. But if she gave in, it was a certainty that she'd wake the dead. Whitley was just sleeping down the hall.

Rhyne clamped her teeth together and the only sound she surrendered whistled sharply between her teeth.

"Mule-headed." Even to his own ears it sounded suspiciously like an endearment.

Rhyne fell back on the bed. Her limbs were as thick and heavy as molasses. She was so liquid and lethargic that she could imagine pleasure rippling her skin. She felt Cole's hand leave her thighs and come to rest at the curve of her waist. Her breathing slowed, and she opened her eyes. She stared at the ceiling.

There was considerably more light in the room than there had been when she woke. Cole's face was no longer in shadow. She did not have to guess that the slim smile hovering on his lips was a satisfied one. "Why are you looking at me like that?"

"Like what?"

"Like you've been into the cream."

If anything his smile deepened. "Haven't I?" He thoroughly enjoyed watching the tide of rosy color that washed over her face. The elbow she jabbed into his abdomen did not make him enjoy it less.

"You tried to trick me," she said. She removed his hand from her side and pushed at her nightgown.

Cole turned on his back and cradled his head in his palms. He let Rhyne rearrange her gown and shift the blankets until they were as high as her neck. "Shutting the barn door? Isn't it too late?"

"You think so? The way I figure it, that horse hasn't been ridden yet." She quickly rolled on her side, clamped a hand over his mouth, and muffled what surely would have been a shout of laughter. "Stop that! You're going to bring Whitley down on us." She waited for the rumble in his chest to subside and could admit to herself that she was a little sorry when it was gone. She tentatively lifted her hand, waiting to see if she could trust him.

"I don't think you'd mind at all if that floorboard started to creak," she said.

He took her wrist and moved her hand out of the way. "I'd mind," he said. "A little."

"You were hoping I'd bring her running."

"How's that?"

"When you said you wanted to hear me."

"You're wrong. I merely wanted to hear you. You're so quiet. I wasn't thinking of the likely consequences just then."

Rhyne wasn't sure that she believed him. She raised herself on one elbow and studied his features. He looked remarkably sincere. "I have to leave," she said.

"I know. Go on. I'm not going to try to make you change your mind."

Rhyne slipped out of the room as quietly as she'd come, relieved by what he'd said at the end. She knew he could have done it.

CHAPTER 10

She came to him the following night and the one after that. She slept in her own bed on Saturday because she didn't think she could face Pastor Duun in the morning, and on Sunday night Cole was called away when Teddy Easter developed an earache that fevered him. That was the evening Whitley came looking for comfort and crawled into her bed and stayed there. Rhyne didn't begrudge Whitley the solace she sought, even when she heard Cole come in by the side door and climb the stairs to his room.

On Monday night she returned to his bed and all the rest of that week. Sometimes he was awake and made space for her. Sometimes he slept and she found her own place beside him. If she wanted to talk, he obliged her, answering her questions about his childhood, his family, the singular moments he recalled as a cadet. If she only wanted his arms around her, he never objected. She liked feeling his breath ruffle the fine hairs at the nape of her neck and the light caress of his palm along her forearm.

And if what she wanted was to feel star-bursts of pleasure skitter across her skin, he gave her that too, then maddened her by asking for nothing in return. He let her know every joy for herself and wanted none of it turned about. If she searched for him with her hands, he firmly removed them. If she was too insistent with her mouth, he broke off the kiss. Even when she was brazen in her need to have him inside her, he avoided that end.

He steeped her in pleasure and filled her with emptiness.

Rhyne thought she might go mad.

"I'm not climbing in your bed tonight," she told him, slipping into his room.

Cole glanced up from his book. "I know. It's Saturday."

She shut the door and leaned against it. "That's not the reason."

"All right." He continued reading.

Rhyne stayed where she was and waited for him to realize she wasn't leaving.

"You're still here," he said, looking up. He turned the page, but didn't return to it. "Is something wrong?"

She was tempted to throw up her hands and repeat his words, but in a less friendly and inquiring tone. She kept her hands where they were and walked over to the chair and sat. "Why don't you read over here?"

"Is that what you came here to ask?"

"No, but now I want to know. You have a chair and a footstool, a table for a lamp if you'd like, and the warmth from the stove, yet you're reading in bed."

"And if I fall asleep, I'm where I want to be."

Rhyne nudged the footstool closer and dropped her heels on it. She studied him a moment, but he merely returned her inquiring gaze. "I know what you're doing."

"I thought I was reading. Or at least making the attempt. Is there something else?"

He was doing it now, pretending he didn't know. How was she supposed to explain that to him without sounding like a lunatic? "It's what you're *not* doing."

"I have to put the book down." He closed it and set it on the table. "Now, is it something I'm doing or something I'm not?"

"It's both. And stop laughing at me. I know you are."

He hadn't made a sound, but that didn't mean he wasn't guilty. "Do you want me to apologize?"

"Why? You wouldn't mean it."

"I still thought I should make the gesture."

Rhyne snorted and turned her head away.

"Tell me what it is, Rhyne," said Cole.

She heard gravity in his voice that hadn't been there before. She stared at the stove because looking at him made her go queer in the head. "I don't like the way you're twisting me up inside," she said quietly. "It's a regular Gordian knot in there. You know what that is?"

"I do."

"I figured you probably did. There will always be that gap between us. I only learned about it while I was helping Whitley study Alexander the Great."

"You think there's a gap?"

"Sure there is, and don't insult me by pretending otherwise. I know there's times that I'm foolish, but I don't think I'm a fool." She laid her hands over her stomach as it began to churn. "See? I'm all twisted again, and you don't own a scalpel that's sharp enough to cut through it."

Rhyne braced herself and turned back to look at him. "I never feel much like a woman except when you're holding me. I've never made the acquaintance of my own body until you introduced us. Mostly, I was ashamed, and I carried that feeling around long before I met up with . . ." The acrid taste of bile rose in her throat. She swallowed hard and amended what she had been going to say. "Long before what was done to me was done to me. You understand that? It's hard to be plainer."

"I understand."

She nodded and continued. "So when I

come in here and you put your fingers in my hair like it was some kind of fancy silk, and you kiss me like you're sucking the sweetness from a berry, well, it's the shamefulness that you wash away. It'd be hard to let Pastor Duun catch a glimpse of me from his pulpit on Sunday morning after spending Saturday night with you, but that's because he'll see all the way to my shameless heart. I don't want to feel bad about what feels so good."

Rhyne tilted her face and regarded Cole from slate gray eyes that were suddenly plaintive. "You keep denying yourself what you give so generously to me, and it's not right. In fact, it's selfish."

"Rhyne."

"No." She shook her head. "No, you're not allowed to say my name like that, like maybe you're trying to reason with a child. You've got me so churned up I'm liable to turn to butter. If you're doing it because you think I might have a disease on account of me not being a virgin, then you need to tell me that."

Cole pushed his hand through his hair. "Jesus, Rhyne."

She ignored him. "If you're doing it because you're afraid you might put a baby in me, then I expect there's something you can do to see that it doesn't happen, you being a doctor and all."

He stopped holding his head in his hand and gave her a withering look.

"But if you think what you're doing is going to hitch me to your wagon, you need to visit Adele Brownlee's fancy house and choose another filly."

Cole threw off the covers and crossed the cold floor in three long strides. He grasped Rhyne by the elbows and pulled her to her feet. Before she could form a protest, he swung her up in his arms and carried her over to the bed. He dropped her on it unceremoniously and then turned away.

From the bed, Rhyne watched Cole fling open his armoire and take out a shirt, trousers, a vest, and his jacket. He tossed all of it over one shoulder, shoved the armoire closed, and stalked to the door.

She pushed herself up on her elbows. "Where are you going?"

"Miss Adele's," he said. "To see a madam about a horse."

"Why, Dr. Monroe, I own that this is a pleasure." Adele opened the front door wide enough to let him in. "Here, step in a little more, would you? Ain't none of us that bite. The only nip is the one that's in the air, and I'd prefer you leave it outside."

She looked around and motioned to Susan Fry. "Susan. You come here and take the doctor's hat and coat while I fix him a drink. What will you have, Doctor? I've got some

347

real Kentucky bourbon if you have a taste for it."

"Bourbon would be fine." He let Susan brush snow off his shoulders before she removed his coat. He beat his hat against his thigh to clear the dusting and gave it over. Susan smiled coyly as she took it. Yellow ringlets as tight as springs framed her face and bounced when she bobbed her head. Cole knew the color was not her own, and he was fairly certain the same was true of most of the springlets. He returned her smile without committing himself and followed Adele into the parlor to find that drink.

Raymona Preston was sitting at the piano fingering the keys. She hummed a tune instead of playing one. Her silky robe was mostly open, revealing a chemise and pantalets. She wore black kid boots and stockings that matched the pink roses on her robe. "Hey, Dr. Monroe," she said as he passed.

Cole recognized the man sitting next to her on the bench as the town's wheelwright. With his heavily muscled shoulders and broad back, Ed Kennedy dwarfed Raymona, but Cole noticed it was Ed that sat at the edge of the bench to make sure there was room for the lady.

Cole went over to the sideboard were Adele was standing. She was delicately featured with a narrow face and leaf-green eyes that were tilted exotically. Her fiery red hair was tamed in a smooth coil at the back of her head. She wore emerald earrings and a pearl choker with a silverplate inlay that was engraved with her initials. Her satin gown looked as if it had come from a Paris salon, but Cole suspected the design and construction was all Mrs. Cooper's doing.

"You're looking very well," Cole said, taking his drink.

"I've had better compliments," she said, "but at least I know you mean it sincerely." She leaned her head toward him and spoke confidentially. "Now, who can I get for you tonight? Raymona's taken, but Susan's free. Some of the other girls will be finishing up directly. Nora's in the kitchen fixin' a plate of gingerbread cakes, but I know she'd love to show you off on her arm."

"If you don't mind, Adele, I'd just like to sit for a while. Take my drink over there. Maybe listen to Raymona play."

Adele put her hand on his arm and invited him to laugh with her. "Darlin', Raymona can't play two notes together that don't sound like they're having an argument. That's why she's hummin'. Maybe in a little while she'll sing something. Ed likes that and she's got a pretty voice. If he doesn't take her upstairs for a solo, there's no reason you can't enjoy it, too." She pointed him in the direction of the far corner of the room. "Go on. Settle yourself in. I won't let the girls bother you until you tell me otherwise."

Cole thanked her and crossed the parlor to the two empty leather chairs in the darkest part of the room. At first he thought the chairs were situated to invite conversation between patrons — this brothel's version of a gentleman's club — but after he was seated and realized that what the angle really did was encourage him to take in all of the room at once, he understood the chairs were for men who found their pleasure in watching.

Well, Cole decided, he had engendered very little in the way of gossip since arriving in Reidsville. Perhaps it was time. He sat back, sipped his drink, and enjoyed the view.

"They're quite something, aren't they? Prettiest girls in one place outside of a sheik's harem."

Cole jerked upright, realizing he'd nodded off. His tumbler was still a quarter full of bourbon. He glanced down at himself to make certain he'd drunk what wasn't there and not spilled it.

"Susan. Nora. How about one of you gals refilling the doctor's glass?"

Neither the booming voice nor the looming shadow belonged to Adele Brownlee. Cole rubbed his eyes with his thumb and forefinger and looked up, comprehending at last what had interrupted his sleep.

It was Susan who hurried over with the bourbon. "Adele says we were supposed to just let him sleep, Judge. Now you gone and woke him up." She topped off Cole's glass and did the same for the judge when he held his out. "Why don't you come over and sit by me? We can look at those stereographic pictures together."

The judge waved her off. She pouted prettily, but she didn't argue. "She didn't really want to look at pictures with me," he told Cole. "I've been upstairs once tonight. Doubt there's any pictures in their collection that would provoke me to climb those steps again." He looked Cole over, head to foot. "You're the new Doc Diggins, aren't you?"

Cole stood and offered his hand. "Coleridge Monroe."

"Elijah Wentworth." He pointed to the chair beside Cole. "May I?"

"Please." Cole sat after he saw Wentworth made himself comfortable. "You're the circuit judge."

"That's right. I've been traveling these parts for twenty years. Lord, it's twenty-five now. I wish you hadn't made me think of that."

"Sorry."

Wentworth dismissed the apology. "Bah! What can you do? The alternative's death, so counting up the years is better all the way around."

Cole agreed. "It's hard to believe you have so many years on the bench." It wasn't flattery that made him say it. The judge still had a thick head of dark hair. The threads of silver he did have were almost entirely isolated to his temples, lending him a distinguished air, not an aging one. His beard was neatly clipped and only lightly salted with silver. He carried himself well, shoulders back and head erect. There was no evidence of curvature of the spine. He was of average height with a narrow frame that Cole suspected had only recently begun to spread at the middle. Putting aside the fact that they were meeting for the first time in a brothel, each of them with a drink in their hand, it was Cole's opinion the judge was not a man of many vices or indulgences. His features showed no dissipation, and in fact, remained largely unlined. He had a friendly smile and gray eyes that hinted at deep thinking and consideration. Those two characteristics explained better than any how Elijah Wentworth had been elected to his office again and again.

"Are you on the stump now?" asked Cole.

"Next election's two years away. Haven't decided if I'm going to run again, but then I almost always think that. I was hoping for a federal appointment after we declared statehood, but Grant couldn't find his way out of a bottle long enough to remember there were favors owed." He shrugged. "If it's going to happen, it'll be under this new president."

"I take it you endorsed Cleveland."

Elijah Wentworth laughed. "Between you

and me, I did everything but raise my robes and do a fan kick." He settled back in his chair and crossed his legs. "He'll take office in March, and then we'll see."

"Well, good luck to you."

"We'll see," the judge said again. He sipped his drink. "So how do you find Reidsville? You've been here long enough to have an opinion. What is it?"

Cole did not have to think about his answer. "I've been struck almost from the first by its self-sufficiency. Most everything a person needs for a comfortable life is already here, and what isn't, is brought into town on the Calico in very short order. Naturally there are other places that can make similar claims, but they're almost always cities of a certain size. The scale of this town's industry and prosperity seems out of proportion to its population."

"You know they're mostly miners, don't you? Sure, there are folks that operate businesses, but they exist because of the miners. One way or another, everyone serves at their will and pleasure."

Cole was very aware that his contract made him one of those people. "Yes, but I never hear anyone talk about a new strike. Most of what my patients tell me is that one mine after another seems to be playing out."

"They would know," said Wentworth. "Gold and silver lodes are hard to come by."

Cole shrugged. "I'm not familiar with their operation. The only time I was at one of the active mines was when I was called out after an accident."

"Ezra Reilly."

"That's right."

"You did real well by him. I heard it from Wyatt and Will."

"It depends on your perspective, I suppose. I wanted to save his hand."

"I imagine Ezra feels the same. Still, that doesn't mean you didn't give your best."

Cole smiled faintly. "You're kind to say so."

Both men fell silent. Raymona Preston was singing at the piano, her slim shoulder listing against Ed Kennedy's brawny one. Her lilting voice carried to the back of the room. When Cole looked over at the judge, his eyes were closed. Cole thought it would be a mistake to suppose the older man was sleeping, and he was proved right when Wentworth suddenly spoke.

"I understand that Runt Abbot's living with you," he said quietly. "Did I hear right? You took her in as a housekeeper?"

"Yes, it's true. She prefers Rhyne now."

"Does she? That's something. Her mother'd be pleased, I shouldn't wonder."

Cole felt the hairs on the back of his neck prickle. "You knew Miss Abbot's mother?"

"Miss Abbot?" The judge smiled faintly and kept his eyes closed. Raymona's tender

354

melody washed over him. "Guess I never thought there'd come a day when that would be Runt's appellation. Took me quite a spell to reconcile what I was hearing with what I thought I knew, but then I've spent half my life listening to lawyers so I sorted through it eventually." He raised his glass, sipped. "You asked me about her mother, though, didn't you? Delia Abbot was the first woman I saw when I came to Reidsville. I wasn't a judge then, just a lawyer looking to take on a few cases, and I stopped in the Miner Key. The stage wasn't much back then — Rudy's made it bigger since the old days — but I don't think I really noticed."

He held up one hand and made a pinching motion with his thumb and index finger. "In the blink of an eye, the world got that small because all I could see in it was Delia Abbot. She was Lady Macbeth that night. It was the first time I understood what poor Macbeth faced. I'd have killed for her, too."

Cole wasn't sure if the judge was talking about Lady Macbeth or Delia Abbot. "You said she'd be pleased. You knew her maiden name was Rhyne?"

"I did. I knew how she spelled it, too. But I don't suppose that matters. Runt was always . . . well, he was Runt." He opened his eyes and looked sideways at Cole. "I saw her once. Miss Abbot, I mean. She was carrying a basket of laundered clothes from the Porter place. That no-account Beatty boy pointed her out, but for me that was merely a confirmation. What struck me was how much she looked like Delia. I'd never seen any resemblance before. The small terror that was Runt Abbot never put me in mind of anyone but Judah. I guess that made her every bit the actress that her mother was."

"Did you ever see Miss Abbot on stage?"

"No. I was never in town when she performed. That's the nature of traveling the circuit. There're things you're bound to miss somewhere."

"Miss Abbot doesn't know very much about her mother," said Cole. "I suspect she'd appreciate hearing what you could tell her."

"Oh, I don't know that I have anything to say that she hasn't heard."

"No one's ever mentioned that you were in love with Delia Abbot."

Elijah Wentworth chuckled. "Me and just about every other young buck. Judah couldn't beat us off with his stick."

"He carried it then?"

"He always carried it."

"Tell me about him. What do you remember?"

The judge rolled his tumbler between his palms. "I didn't know him well. No one did as far as I could tell. He lived in town then, but he kept to himself. Delia and the two

356

boys stayed close. I had the impression that Judah insisted on it. You have to understand that I fell in love with Delia the moment I saw her. It was already too late for me by the time I learned she was married, which, I believe, was before she ended her soliloquy."

"You were struck hard."

"Felled like a giant oak. There was no hope of picking myself back up after that. I could only lumber along." He grinned, satisfied with his pun even while Cole groaned softly. "Forgive me. I can't always restrain myself." He held up his drink, stopping Cole from directing him to the point. "I know. You were asking about Judah. Because he was so private, there's nothing I know about him for a fact that didn't come from Delia. She told me once that Judah tried his hand at a number of things before he arrived at performing. They met in Philadelphia. Both of them were employed in the same household. If she told me the family's name, I don't recall it now. I take it they had some social standing. It was important to her that I knew that, though I don't know why."

"There's social standing in being the employee of a prominent family," Cole said. "At least among others in the same set of circumstances. She was trying to tell you that she and Judah came from that world."

"She was a lady's maid to the daughter, and he was a cook."

"Those are desired positions. Important ones. Do you know what happened?"

"I know he didn't work there very long. A few months, I think. It's hard to remember. There was some kind of to-do and he left. I always assumed it was his temperament. It's said about cooks, isn't it? They're temperamental."

"I've heard it said about actors as well."

Wentworth nodded. "Perhaps that's what attracted Judah to those crafts. Delia left the family soon after Judah. He was ten years her senior and about as reliable as a broken watch, but God help her, she loved him. She was too young to know her own mind, just fourteen herself when she married him, but it happens like that sometimes. He labored on the railroad for a while, took odd jobs that came up, and tried his hand at cooking now and again as they moved west. He was a self-educated man. Read everything he could get his hands on, Delia told me. He collected books the way some people collect lint. She admired that about him, but I believe it cost her as time went on."

"How so?"

"She had an idea of who he was that didn't quite fit the facts."

"Did he abuse her?"

"I never saw a mark."

Cole recognized that it wasn't precisely an answer to his question, but he let it pass. He could sense the judge becoming more reticent, even cagey, with his remarks. "How did they come to Reidsville?"

"Mining. Judah fell in with a few men who did some prospecting, and the way I heard it is that they just arrived one day and settled in. This was a couple of years before the war began. As far as I know, Judah never tried to join up. The fellows that brought him to town did, though, and they're long gone now."

"I had the impression that Judah and Delia had been performing before they arrived."

"They were, but it didn't put much money in their pockets. That's how Judah came to be a miner." The judge finished his drink and raised it to get Susan's attention. "That didn't last long. Once he worked out an arrangement with Rudy's father at the saloon, he gave up going to the mines. They did all right. All that reading came in handy. He wrote some of his own plays from the books he had, and the people here never tired of the classics."

Susan bounced over and refilled his glass. "I think you're going to need an escort to the Commodore tonight, Judge."

"Don't you sass, Susan. I guess I can find my way over there just fine."

She hugged the cut-glass decanter to her bosom after Cole refused another round. "If you say so, but I'm plainly skeptical."

He laughed and sent her on her way, then

he turned slightly and touched his glass to Cole's. "To reminiscences."

"After two bourbons, I would have said 'to memories.' "

"Three," the judge corrected him. "I had one when I came in. This is number four."

"Then I am triply impressed."

Wentworth stared at his glass, his eyebrows slightly arched. "Actually, so am I."

Cole gave him a moment to pick up the thread of their conversation.

"Judah was talented," the judge said. "At least he seemed so to me. I can tell you, though, without fear of contradiction from those that remember, that the real draw to the saloon on those evenings was Delia. The whiskey and Rudy's father's special brew ran a close second and third."

"Did Judah know?"

"I think he did. The applause told the story. He received his due from the crowd. The boys, too. They were maybe eight and ten when I saw them perform — nothing then like the hellions they became after Delia passed. As I said, they were all well received. But Delia? At the end of her performances it took minutes for the dust to settle. The miners could whoop it up. Stomp their feet. Drum their glasses against the tables. Clapping was about the quietest thing they did. Yes, I think Judah knew very well how everyone felt about his wife."

"Did that have anything to do with why he moved out of town?"

"I can't say."

Cole watched the judge turn the tumbler in his hand. *Can't* or *won't*, he wanted to ask. "Does anyone know?"

"What's Runt say?"

"Miss Abbot says Judah never really talked about it." Wentworth made a sound at the back of his throat that might have been surprise or merely thoughtfulness. Cole went on. "She only knows the house where she used to live because her brothers showed her. If they knew why Judah packed up the family and moved to his valley, they never said."

"Then maybe it's only Judah that can answer that question."

"I'm going out to see him when the weather breaks," said Cole, watching the judge closely. "I just might ask him."

"You do that," Wentworth said, eyeing him shrewdly. "And watch your back. If I didn't impress upon you that Judah guards his privacy, then it's a good thing I sit behind the bench and no longer have to argue in front of it."

"Wyatt's coming with me."

"Then tell him I said to watch *his* back. Judah's never cared much for the law."

"Or lawyers?"

"Or lawyers," he said. "That makes Wyatt doubly unwelcome."

Cole was sure the judge knew he hadn't been referring to Wyatt. He let it pass. Sometimes not driving home a point made one. He finished his drink. "I'd like you to come to dinner some evening this week. How long will you be in town?"

"Sadly, this is my last night. I'm boarding the Admiral in the morning, which is why you find me here tonight. I have a trial to preside over in Clear Creek County the day after that."

"Well, perhaps the next time you're in town, you'll let me know. The invitation stands."

"Thank you."

Cole stood, setting down his empty glass. "There's just one more thing I'd like to ask you."

Elijah looked up inquiringly. "Yes?"

"Do you know of any women lawyers?"

"So," Cole said, linking his arm with Whitley's as they walked home from church, "the judge told me about Myra Bradwell. She and her husband, who was also an attorney, helped Mrs. Lincoln with her petition to be removed from the asylum where her son put her."

"Really?" Whitley asked. "Did you hear that, Rhyne? There *are* women arguing for money."

To Cole's way of thinking it was a perfect

362

evolutionary adaptation, but he hadn't reached his thirtieth year by actually saying things like that out loud. He waited to hear Rhyne's response. Out of the corner of his eye he saw her murmur something that Whitley heard but that he missed.

"It's a considerable challenge, Whitley," he said. "Most of the women that his honor named came to his attention because of the suits they filed to be permitted to join the bar and practice law on their own. Mrs. Bradwell was denied that right in Illinois."

"But why?"

He noticed that Rhyne was staring straight ahead, but he suspected she was attending to the conversation. "I invited the judge to dine with us some evening when he's returned to town to take questions like that. I warned you'd make him answer for every slight, but that he shouldn't take it personally. I was relieved to learn he has three sisters and understood my warning."

Whitley nudged him with her elbow. "He's going to think I have no manners."

"*I* think you have no manners. He's going to think you're charming."

She beamed. "It will be very nice to have company. Don't you think so, Rhyne? We can have cream of pea soup and broiled mutton, and I can make graham pudding or perhaps scalloped apples. Do you think the judge will like my scalloped apples? Cole always compliments me for them."

"I think you're getting ahead of yourself," Rhyne said. "We don't know when he's coming, or even if he will."

"I think he will. Don't you, Cole? It was a sincere invitation, wasn't it? You did not merely say it in passing."

"It was sincere," he said, "but Rhyne's correct. You're getting ahead of yourself."

"That's what planning is, isn't it?"

Rhyne and Cole exchanged amused glances, then Rhyne remembered that she was trying to avoid Cole and looked quickly away.

Whitley missed that brief communication and continued discussing the menu and the reasons for planning it now. Cole and Rhyne let her go and made all the right murmurs at the appropriate times, but the glance they shared left them each unsettled and lacking any plan of their own to put it to rights.

"You're certain, Doctor?" Rachel Cooper sat on the edge of the examining table and regarded Cole Monroe anxiously. Her legs dangled over the side until Cole moved a footstool under them.

"I'm certain," he said, scribbling some notes in his log.

"How far along am I?"

He smiled. "You probably know that better than I do, but from what you've told me and what I could learn from the examination of your cervix, I'd say you are just shy of four months. Does that sound about right to you?"

She nodded, still afraid to hope. She laid her palms flat against her midriff. "Will I carry it until the end?"

Cole hesitated. "I know what you want me to say, Rachel, but I can't predict what will happen. I can only tell you that there's no reason for me to suspect you'll have any trouble. You're fit and healthy. Rickets is the scourge of a woman's bones and her ability to bear children. That's not a problem for you. Barring trauma or disease, I believe you'll be fine."

He put the book away. "Now, tell me why you came here. I would have gone to your home to do the examination. You suspected what I would find, so why not do it where you'd be more comfortable?"

"My husband doesn't know yet. I didn't want to hint at it until you confirmed it for me. If I'd asked you to the house, he would have guessed. Coming here, well, I can tell him I brought samples for Rhyne to look at." She pointed to the swatches of fabric she'd placed on the unoccupied stool. "And I did, so it isn't an untruth."

"Well, he won't learn about it from me, but you'll tell him tonight, won't you? He's escorting me to Judah's place tomorrow. It'd be hard to keep a secret like that the whole way."

"I'm going to his office right after I show Rhyne the samples. I imagine you'll know I spoke to him because he won't be able to peel the grin off his face."

Rhyne did not follow her usual routine after Whitley left for school. She ignored all the chores facing her for the day and set about attacking the one that couldn't be put off. She was pleasant to the people she passed on her way to Joe Redmond's livery in spite of the fact that she simply wanted to growl at them.

She managed small talk with Joe and paid up what she owed him for boarding her horse, then she walked Twist out of the stable and led him up the alley back to the house. After hitching the gelding to a post at the back porch, she went up to her room and took her rifle from under the bed.

She always tended to it, so it was cleaned and ready for her. She kept the cartridges in the bottom of the chest of drawers under some scented paper that Whitley gave her. Rhyne was never sure whom she was supposed to write, but she appreciated the gift, and it made her box of ammunition smell like lilacs.

She stripped off her skirt and tucked her tailored shirt into the brushed corduroy trousers that Rachel Cooper made for her. It didn't take her much time to unlace her shoes and replace them with a pair of comfortable boots. She had to twist her hair into a knot and hold it at the back of her head with one hand while she jammed her hat on with the other. When had her hair gotten so long?

Hoisting the Winchester under her arm, Rhyne stood back from the vanity until she could see most of herself reflected in the mirror. She didn't look exactly like Runt Abbot any longer, but she was confident she could still ride and shoot like him.

Cole's first thought when he saw Judah Abbot again was that the man had aged considerably. His iron gray beard was growing in whiter and the creases at the corners of his eyes were more defined. His perpetually tight frown made the parenthetical crescents on either side of his mouth look like crevices. Cole noticed the most dramatic change when he examined Judah's hands. The lightly callused palms were gone. These hands belonged to a man who was laboring.

"Are you wearing gloves when you're working, Mr. Abbot? This wound in the heel of your left hand doesn't seem to be healing well."

"Damn splinter felt as big as a railroad spike," Judah said. "I thought it was going to go all the way through my hand."

Wyatt drummed his fingers lightly against the tabletop. "So you weren't wearing gloves."

"Well, I'm getting to that. I'd just taken them off to set the fuse. There's a stump I wanted gone and I —"

"You used explosives to get rid of a stump?" Cole glanced at Wyatt for confirmation that this could possibly be true. When Wyatt merely shrugged, Cole asked Judah, "Had it offended you?"

"It was there. I didn't want it to be. That's offense enough." He regarded Cole with eyes that had gone frosty. "And don't step on my lines again."

"He means you interrupted him," said Wyatt.

Cole gave him a sardonic glance, but didn't comment and set about cleansing the partially healed wound instead. He found three slivers still lodged in Judah's flesh that he removed with tweezers. Pus oozed from deep inside. Cole squeezed it out until Judah's blood ran clean and then he bandaged the hand.

When he finished, he went to the pump in the kitchen and washed his hands. He carried back the coffee pot and a cup and put them in front of Wyatt. "To give you something to do besides playing percussion."

Wyatt looked down at his hand and caught his fingers in the act of more idle drumming. "Sorry. Didn't realize." He delivered the apology absently, and he was grinning while he said it.

Cole merely shook his head, but he couldn't blame Wyatt for wanting to get back to town and his wife. Rachel had been right. Her husband was nearly stupid with the news that he was going to be a father.

Having marginally settled Wyatt, Cole turned his attention back to Judah. "I want to know about the problem that brought me out here. Wyatt said you were favoring your left side and complaining of some weakness. I need you to get up and show me. You can use your stick if you like."

Judah hesitated. It was Cole's mildly skeptical gaze that finally brought him to his feet. "I can't say that I approve of your manner, Dr. Monroe. You're a mite arrogant for my tastes."

"Walk over to the bookshelves and back."

"Superior," Judah muttered, but he did as directed.

Cole observed his gait carefully and noted the listing to the right and the drag and drop in Judah's left foot. When Judah returned, Cole indicated that he should sit. Judah lifted his walking stick threateningly, but Cole seized it and Judah stumbled and fell awkwardly back in his rocker.

Wyatt left the table to take the stick from Cole and put it out of the reach of both men. "What are you thinking, Judah? Let Dr. Monroe do his work."

"He's not respectful."

"And naturally your plan is to beat that into him." Wyatt sighed heavily and set the stick on the table. "That makes about as much sense as using dynamite to get rid of a stump. Judah, sometimes I could beat you with this myself and call it a very good day." He sat down and picked up his coffee cup. "Go on, Cole."

Cole hunkered down in front of Judah and held up his right hand, palm out. "I want you to push against my hand as hard as you can. This is your opportunity to knock me on my ass." He noted the gleam in Judah's eye and knew that was exactly what the older man hoped would happen.

Judah leaned forward and put out his hand to meet Cole's. He shoved hard while Cole pushed back. He was able to force Cole to shift his feet to keep his balance, but his strength wasn't sufficient to make him topple.

"Good," said Cole. "Now your other hand."

When Cole raised his left hand, Judah applied himself again. This time, though, he couldn't move Cole even a fraction of an inch, and it was Cole who pushed him back in his chair.

"All right. Now, let's try it again, but this time use your right foot." Cole lifted his hands and allowed Judah to place his heel in the cup of his palms. With this attempt, Judah's strength and leverage was enough to set Cole on his backside. "That's good, sir." He rose back to his haunches and put out his hands again. "The left foot."

Judah pushed, but Cole remained precisely where he was.

"Harder," Cole said.

Judah's grimace did not improve the outcome. His foot dropped heavily to the floor when Cole let it go.

Cole stood, brushed off his hands, and studied Judah's face closely. "Recite something for me," he said. "A favorite passage. Anything."

Judah gave it a moment's thought, then he spoke as if before an audience. " 'For Brutus, as you know, was Caesar's angel: Judge, O you gods, how dearly Caesar loved him! This was the most unkindest cut of all; for when the noble Caesar saw him stab, ingratitude, more strong than traitors' arms, quite vanquish'd him: then burst his mighty heart.' "

"Well chosen," said Cole. The irony Judah hoped to affect was not lost on him, but he made no further comment about the passage. "Your speech is faintly impaired," he said. "Is it better or worse than it has been?"

Judah offered a surly, tight-lipped smile. "What did they teach you at your fancy school, Doctor? I'd have to talk to myself to know that, and I haven't jumped off that cliff yet."

Wyatt said, "I didn't notice it on my last visit. That's been a little over a month now."

Cole nodded and addressed Judah again. "Your arm and leg . . . were they better or worse when Wyatt was here?"

"That makes some sense, at least. They were better."

"Memory loss?"

"Not that I remember."

Wyatt gave him an ironic glance. "Very amusing, Judah."

Cole ignored Judah's chuckle. It was obvious that his patient enjoyed poking at them, with or without his stick. He slid out a chair at the table and sat, then he took the log out of his satchel and made a few notes.

Judah craned his neck. "What are you writing there?"

"I'm simply recording your symptoms and complaints so I can refer to them the next time I see you."

"When's that going to be?"

Cole looked up. "Let me be frank, Mr. Abbot, it appears you suffered a mild stroke. Your presentation is not entirely consistent with the diagnosis, but I am not familiar with another possibility to explain the unilateral weakness. Your memory appears to be intact, and you haven't lost the facility to laugh at your own jokes. There is something to be said for humor, in whatever manner it presents itself."

"Is that right?"

"It is." He finished documenting his observations and closed the book. "If you lived in town, I would want to see you weekly to measure your progress, but that's not going to happen with you being here. If the weather holds — and Wyatt says that's not likely — I could come out again in a month. It's possible it will be as long as six or eight weeks before I'll see you again. You should arrange for Danny Beaufort to drop by more often, even if you don't need him for chores. That's just a precaution in the event you require assistance."

"What's Beaufort going to do? The boy can't find his toes when he's wearing socks."

"I don't know what he can do, Mr. Abbot, but at least you won't be alone." Cole snapped his satchel closed. "Is there anything else?"

Judah looked him over, his pale blue eyes narrowing slightly. "I reckon you think you're better than me."

"And I don't suppose there's anything I could say or do that would change your opinion, so I won't lose any sleep over it." He started to rise, but Judah gestured at him to sit back in his chair.

"What's lit a fire under you?" asked Judah. He darted a glance at Wyatt. "You, too, Sheriff. Usually I can't get rid of you, but today I can plainly see that I am persona non grata. Where's the harm of sitting a spell? Don't you always tell me what's going on somewhere or other, even if I don't want to hear it? Well, today, I do."

"There's not much to tell, Judah. Everyone's been —"

Judah held him off with a raised hand. "There's some currant cake under a bowl in the kitchen. You and Dr. Monroe help yourselves to it. I should have offered it when I saw you didn't have any biscuits or tarts for me."

Wyatt and Cole exchanged baffled glances.

"Well, go on," Judah said. "It isn't proper to refuse now, is it?"

"I'll get it," said Cole. He rose and went to the kitchen while Wyatt began relating what passed for news in Reidsville. When Cole uncovered the cake, he saw that a quarter of it was gone. Cole had to admit that it made Judah's uncharacteristic offer a little more agreeable. He quickly cut and plated three slices and carried them back. He gave Judah a plate first and observed him eagerly taking his first bite.

"You've always had a sweet tooth?" asked Cole, passing a plate to Wyatt and then sitting down again.

"Born with it, I expect." He stabbed his fork in Wyatt's direction. "Can't you eat and talk at the same time?"

Wyatt cut off a bite and continued his

recitation.

The dirty windows made it difficult to see into the cabin and forced Rhyne to walk right up to them. Even she was not so adept a tracker that she could cross the porch without being heard, so she ignored the windows at the front and went around to the small one at the back where she could look into the kitchen. It would have been surprising to see someone there, but she knew she could find an angle that would allow her to see farther into the cabin. By tilting her head this way and that, she was able to make out that it was Wyatt's back she was seeing at the table and that Cole was sitting across from him. Because Judah's chair was off to the side, he was not visible.

There was very little in the way of movement. Cole's satchel was on the table and it looked as though it might be closed, which meant that either he'd completed his examination or that it had not yet begun. Given the time he and Wyatt had already been in the cabin, she suspected it was the former.

So why were they still sitting at the table? Judah tolerated Wyatt, but only just, and Rhyne couldn't imagine that her father had anything but contempt for Coleridge Monroe. It didn't make sense that they were overstaying a welcome that was never all that welcoming.

Pressing her face even closer, Rhyne saw Wyatt's head turn toward Judah and realized the sheriff was talking to her father. She wished he would scoot his chair to the side so she could see what Cole was doing. It was impossible to know if he was contributing to the conversation.

Frustrated, Rhyne stepped back and considered what she might do. The window she had not yet tried was the one in Judah's room, and she would only be able to see into the main part of the cabin if her father's door was open. That seemed unlikely to her, but she had no other choice.

Staying close to the cabin's walls, she skirted the perimeter until she was outside Judah's room. She used the sleeve of her jacket to rub out a smear of dirt that was on her side of the window, then shaded her eyes from the sunlight and peered in.

The open door gave Rhyne her first glimpse of her father in more than six months. She had avoided thinking what it would be like to see him again so she was unprepared for how deeply it would affect her. What she understood about the kind of love that could exist between a parent and child she had gleaned from stories in the Old Testament and novels of Dickens and Alcott, and it had no relevance in the life she knew with Judah. Still, Rhyne allowed that it would be a lie to pretend there wasn't a bond, and an even bigger lie to pretend it wasn't twisting her insides now.

She didn't have time to reflect on what it meant or how to differentiate it from the knot she felt when she was around Cole. What she saw through the window put every other consideration out of her mind because watching Wyatt lift a fork to his mouth made her afraid she had arrived too late.

Rhyne didn't worry any longer about being heard. She ran around to the front of the cabin and hopped up on the porch. She announced herself at the same time that she threw open the door. That foresight saved her from staring down the barrel of Wyatt Cooper's Peacemaker. He was coming out of his chair and already drawing on her when she crossed the threshold.

"Dammit to hell, Rhyne," Wyatt said, holstering his weapon. "I might have killed you. Jesus. What were you thinking?"

The interruption had also pushed Cole to his feet. He stared at Rhyne and talked right over Wyatt. "What in God's name are you doing here? Dammit, Rhyne. What were you thinking?"

Judah was the only one who kept his seat, but he also joined the chorus. "Out of my sight, whore! You're not wanted here! What were you thinking?"

Rhyne kept her Winchester pointed at the ground. She ignored her father entirely while her eyes wandered from Cole's face, to Wyatt's gun, and finally came to rest on the cake crumbs on their plates. It was only then that she settled her full attention on Judah and hoisted the Winchester so that it pointed at her father's chest.

"If either one of them dies from your poison, Judah Abbot, you remember that you saw my rifle now because I'm not going to show it to you again. You'll never know where the shot comes from that's goin' to kill you."

CHAPTER 11

"Are you boys all right back there?"

The *boys* exchanged glances and didn't answer.

Rhyne looked at them over her shoulder. Neither Cole nor Wyatt appeared in danger of slipping from their saddle, but they also had not regained their healthy color. "Not much in the mood to talk?" She shrugged. "I reckon I wouldn't feel like it either. You're probably all cramped up from heaving."

That was something of an understatement. Their retching had been so violent that even now, almost an hour after leaving the cabin, it hurt to draw a deep breath. The fact that Rhyne was enjoying herself at their expense did not incline them to be sociable. They suffered her gentle nudging because they figured they probably owed her.

It wasn't possible to know for a certainty that Judah had poisoned them, but Rhyne's conviction was so powerful that not acting on it would have been foolish. While Rhyne held her rifle on Judah, Cole prepared a purgative of ipecac syrup from his medical bag with a saltwater chaser. Maintaining his innocence, Judah refused to drink any part of the emetic, and merely shook his head at Cole and Wyatt when they did. As they stood on the porch heaving currant cake and what remained of their breakfast over the side, Judah's booming laughter nearly drowned out the sound of their retching.

Cole took what was left of the currant cake, wrapped it in a kerchief, and placed it in his satchel, while Wyatt promised Judah that if they could prove poisoning, he would be back to arrest him. Judah was unimpressed and unconcerned.

"I ate the cake the same as you," he reminded them. "But thank you kindly for the entertainment." He was still chuckling when they filed out.

As the trail widened so they could ride three abreast, Rhyne slowed Twist to allow Cole and Wyatt to catch up to her. They drew up on either side and matched her pace.

All trace of humor was absent from Rhyne's features now. "I was afraid you wouldn't believe me," she said. "I didn't know what I was going to do if that happened."

Cole said nothing, but Wyatt couldn't let it pass. "I have to be honest, Rhyne. I don't know if I do believe what you were saying, but there was never any doubt in my mind that you believed it. It seemed best to err on the side of trusting you."

"I'm telling the truth. You should have taken him in and saved yourself the trouble of riding out again."

"It's a matter of evidence," said Wyatt. "I couldn't very well jail him for hospitality, now could I? He has a compelling argument: he ate the cake."

"Doesn't matter," said Rhyne. "He's like a snake."

Cole ducked his head to miss a low hanging branch. "What does that mean?"

"Some snakes have poison in them, and it doesn't bother them a whit, but just let one bite you, and . . ." She shrugged. "That's how my brothers explained it to me."

Wyatt adjusted the brim of his hat. "Rusty and Randy were known for some tall tales, Rhyne. Judah's mean as a snake, but that doesn't make him one. Sounds as though your brothers wanted to scare you." He looked over at Rhyne, but she was staring straight ahead. If her brothers' stories had frightened her, Wyatt didn't expect her to admit it. "And don't forget, Judah didn't bite us."

"Just the same," she said, "he tried to poison you. You'll see."

Wyatt looked over Rhyne's head at Cole. "Is she right? Will you be able to show me something?"

Cole felt Rhyne's gaze join Wyatt's. "This isn't what either of you want to hear, but the answer is I don't know. If we'd found something in the cabin that he might have used, it would be easier. But since the search gave us nothing, what I can tell you depends on the type of poison, how much is in the cake, and whether or not I can extract it."

Rhyne snorted. "That's too many complications. There's a nest of mice in the woodshed. Feed it to one of them. A dead mouse is evidence that people can understand."

"She has a point," said Wyatt.

"I intended to start there, but you need to understand that it's not conclusive," Cole told them. "If the mouse dies, there can be reasons for it that have nothing at all to do with eating the cake. If the mouse lives, it doesn't prove that there's no poison, but suggests the possibility that the mouse is indifferent to it."

"It'll die," Rhyne said. "I know it'll die."

Whitley carefully lifted the book that was serving as a lid on the mouse box. "Cake's gone again," she announced. "I do believe Mr. Willoughby is fatter and happier for it. Still, poor thing. He wants to be out in society."

Rhyne sighed. "I wish you hadn't named him." She made a sweep across the shelves in Cole's surgery with a feather duster. "I feel

382

guilty for wishing him dead."

Cole looked up from his microscope. "Whitley, put the book back. If Willoughby escapes, I cannot speak to what will happen to you."

"Oh, it must be very bad if you cannot say what it is in front of Rhyne." At his reproachful glance, she replaced *Sense and Sensibility.* "May I at least peek at the others?"

"A peek."

There were two other boxes. Mr. Knightley resided under *Emma* and Mr. Darcy under *Pride and Prejudice.* Whitley's contribution to the experiment underway in Cole's surgery was to give the mice their literary prisons. It was also her idea to feed Willoughby the cake. If a mouse had to be sacrificed for science, she told them, then it must be Willoughby because he broke Marianne Dashwood's heart.

Cole did not care what his sister's reasons were, but he did wonder if he'd have ever learned that she was reading Austen without these experiments. It seemed unlikely. Whitley enjoyed confounding him.

"Mr. Knightley is resting," Whitley whispered, setting the book back. She looked in the last box. "And Mr. Darcy is composing a letter to dear Elizabeth Bennet." She giggled when her brother and Rhyne both turned to stare at her. "I merely wanted to see if you were paying attention."

"Well, we are," said Cole. "And you deserve

much less of it."

Whitley ignored his dismissal and slid onto the stool across the table from him instead. "It's been three days."

"Yes?"

"And Mr. Willoughby hasn't died of currant cake yet. I really think we should let all of them go." She cast Rhyne a guilty glance. "I'm sorry. I am, truly. But it does seem a bit cruel, don't you think? Ghoulish, too. If Willoughby had died right away, that would have been tolerable. Now it will be tragic."

"Really, Whitley?" Cole's right eyebrow arched a fraction. "Tragic? Just how well do you know Willoughby?"

Her mouth twitched. "All right. It will *not* be tragic."

Rhyne stopped dusting and approached the table. "Whitley's right. We should let them go. The cake you put aside for Willoughby is almost gone and he's showing no signs of sickness. Maybe it's exactly as you said and mice are indifferent to Judah's poison."

"I also said there might be no poison," he reminded her. "You have to consider that you were wrong."

"I'm not wrong."

Cole could find no indication that she was prepared to back down from her position. "Then my methods are inadequate to prove you're right." He pushed back from the table. "I'm sorry, Rhyne, but there's nothing I can

384

find that supports your contention. Wyatt and I can be grateful that you arrived when you did, and that will have to satisfy."

"Would you do it again?"

"Do what again?"

"Eat something Judah gave you."

"No." He saw she was only partially mollified and prepared himself for her next question.

"And if you ate something and only realized afterward that he'd made it, would you give yourself a dose of that syrup?"

Since the mere thought of taking the ipecac made his stomach curdle, he considered that it probably wouldn't be necessary, however, he knew what Rhyne needed to hear from him. "I'd take it again," he said. "On your word alone, I'd take it again."

Whitley, who had been following the conversation closely, added her support. "I'd take it, Rhyne. I'd heave like a drunken sailor for you."

"Good lord, Whit," said Cole.

Rhyne's eyes swiveled to Whitley's in sympathy. "I don't expect Judah's ever going to offer you a plate of anything, but it's good to know that you're prepared." She tickled Whitley's arm with the feather duster. "Go visit the bread. I need to speak with your brother."

Whitley sighed, slid off the stool, and headed toward the door. On the point of leaving, she paused for the last word. "His name is *Cole.*"

Shaking his head, Cole watched her go. "She's right, you know. It wouldn't hurt."

Rhyne ignored the overture. She did not want to insert intimacy into their conversation. "What will you tell Wyatt?"

"The same as I told you: the truth. There's no evidence that will allow him to bring Judah in. If you're worried what will happen the next time Wyatt goes out there, I think you can trust him not to eat or drink anything. You made an impression, Rhyne. It will last."

"Do you think so?" She wanted to be hopeful, but uncertainty laced her tone. "People never much cared what Runt Abbot had to say."

"Are you sure that's true? Or is it that Runt Abbot didn't have much to say?"

"Maybe that," she admitted. "Maybe a little bit of both."

Cole nodded. He turned on the stool so he was facing her and held out his hand. She put the feather duster down and let him draw her between his legs. "I'm sorry about Willoughby."

"Not nearly as much as me and Marianne Dashwood."

Chuckling, he slipped his hands around her waist and clasped them together at the small of her back above her bustle. "I had no idea about Miss Dashwood. Was Jane Austen your idea?"

"No. I never heard of her. Judah only had books written by men. Mrs. Cooper brought them by. I began reading *Emma,* but all that girl's meddling put me in mind of Whitley so I passed it along. If there was a lesson to be learned, I think she missed it."

"Or pretended to," said Cole. "Still, she appears to have read them all, so that's something." He watched a faint smile touch Rhyne's mouth. Too quickly, it disappeared. He regretted that more than he regretted Mr. Willoughby's continued existence. His eyes drifted downward to her abdomen. "Tell me about the knot. How is it?"

"Still Gordian."

Cole wasn't surprised. Since returning from Judah's, Rhyne appeared as if she were always on the precipice of being ill. "Is there something I can do?" he asked. Then he remembered the accusation she leveled at him a week ago. "Or something I can *not* do." He'd hoped to tease a smile from her again and was disappointed that he failed.

Rhyne glanced sideways at the three medical bags sitting on top of the cabinet. "I don't suppose there's anything in one of them for me."

"I don't suppose there is."

She fell silent. The lump in her throat forced her to swallow hard before she could talk. "I thought you were going to die."

Cole watched her beautiful gray eyes brighten with tears. For once, she didn't seem embarrassed by their appearance. She didn't swipe at them or try to blink them back. She allowed them simply to hover on the rim of her lashes. Even when they spilled over, she didn't touch her face.

"I was afraid," she said. "More afraid than when I thought I was dying."

He knew what that admission cost her. "I had no idea," he said. "About either time."

Her nod was almost imperceptible. "I told Mrs. Cooper about the first, but not this last. I was worried sick about Wyatt, but it wasn't nearly the same as how I felt about you. I didn't think she'd want to know that."

"I imagine she'd understand."

"Really?"

He nodded. His hands tightened a fraction. "But I'm curious. What do you suppose accounts for the difference?"

She frowned. Tears welled again. "I don't know."

Cole did not let her see that her answer disappointed him. He only had to see the forlornness in her eyes to appreciate that she was telling him the truth. She *didn't* know. She wasn't ready.

"I haven't changed my mind," he said. "Have you?" When she didn't answer, but simply looked at him, Cole realized he was holding his breath. He let it out slowly. "Rhyne?"

"I need to think."

He was encouraged that this was a different answer than the ones that came before. "Is there someone you want to talk to?"

"Not this time."

"All right."

"Are you going to speak to Whitley?"

He was truly bewildered. "About what? You haven't said that you will marry me."

"If I agree, Whitley still would have to approve."

"Like hell."

She flinched. "How can you say that?"

"She's my *sister*, Rhyne. I will listen to her opinion, but she can have nothing to say that will alter my decision — or yours."

"Your happiness is important to her."

"As hers is to me."

"What I mean is, she'll have to believe that this marriage will make you happy."

"Of course she'll believe it. Why wouldn't she?"

Because it might not be true. Rhyne kept the troublesome thought to herself. She gently removed herself from Cole's embrace and took a step back so she was out of his reach.

He wanted to ask if he could expect her to come to his bed this evening, but he restrained himself. She hadn't been in his room except to change the sheets and put away his clothes since the night he went to Miss Adele's. If it hadn't been for the trip out to see Judah, Cole wasn't sure she'd be talking to him yet. In his mind, the surest way to keep her from returning to his bed was to raise the subject. As he was hardly in a position to dictate more terms, he cautioned himself again to wait her out.

"I need to get dinner started," she said.

Cole let her go. Truly, he thought, was there any other choice?

Rhyne sat with her back to the other patrons in the Commodore's dining room. She sipped her tea and ignored the low-pitched conversations going on behind her. There was a time when she would have assumed she was the subject of every one of those discussions, but that had gradually changed. Oddly enough, as she became surer of herself, she also came to realize that folks had better things to talk about than what she was doing. She no longer went looking for a nose to put out of joint to match her own.

"May I join you?"

Rhyne looked up to find Rose Beatty standing beside her table. "Yes, of course."

"You don't have to say that to be mannerly," said Rose. "I won't take it as a slight."

"No. I mean it."

Rose swung her skirts to the side and sat. She motioned to one of the waiters and placed her order. When he was gone, she confided to Rhyne. "I only stopped in because I wanted to be alone. Sometimes there's no better way to do it than with other people around." She frowned as she removed her gloves. "Did that make any sense at all?"

"It did to me."

"Good. Because there's days I only understand about half of what I'm saying. If Will doesn't catch the other half, there's no help for us."

Rhyne's heart felt a little lighter than it had before Rose joined her. She hadn't realized how close she'd been to being purely miserable.

Rose put a hand on her forearm. "Drink your tea. Don't wait on my account. Yours will grow cold by the time mine arrives." She glanced around the room. As it was after luncheon and well before dinner, not many of the tables were occupied. "Mostly men up from Denver for the gambling," she said, returning her attention to Rhyne. "But you probably noticed that."

Rhyne nodded but didn't offer an opinion.

"They come for the high stakes games at the Miner Key," said Rose. "Everyone thinks they're a card sharp until they get in a game with the locals." She sighed and regarded Rhyne's profile. "Enough of that. I heard about what you did out at your pa's for Wyatt and the doctor. I thought I should tell you it's appreciated. The sheriff's been my friend for a lot of years. I know you'd have done the same if it had been Will who'd gone along. And I don't think you'll find anyone with a bad word to say about Dr. Monroe. Even Sid Walker's stopped complaining."

"I didn't realize that everyone knew. About what happened at Judah's, I mean."

"I won't take that as an insult, since I don't believe you meant it that way, but you should know by now that I'm *not* everyone. Oh, no. No apology. I said you didn't intend an insult, didn't I?" Rose's tea arrived. She added cream and sugar to her cup and sipped. "I know what went on because that no-account Beatty boy told me, and he knows because Wyatt had to tell him. Rachel knows, of course, but that's it. End of the trail."

That wasn't so bad, Rhyne decided. "Did your husband tell you that Willoughby didn't die?"

"Who's Willoughby?"

"The mouse that gorged himself on currant cake. Whitley named him."

"Oh. Well then, yes. I did hear the mouse lived. Doesn't change anything in my eyes. You did what you thought was right. That counts for something. Counts for a lot, actually."

Rhyne nodded slowly, thinking perhaps that it did. "May I ask you something personal?"

Intrigued, Rose stared at Rhyne over the

rim of her teacup. "Ask away. We'll see if I answer."

"Did you ever think you'd be someone's wife?"

Rose's eyes narrowed. "Are you asking because I was a whore?"

"No. Well, yes. Maybe I am. That changes things for a woman, doesn't it? If she's a whore, I mean. What makes a man want a woman like that?"

Rose blew out a deep breath. "Now I understand how you won all those fights, Runt. You don't hold anything back." She put up a hand. "Don't go all apologetic on me again. I can't stand that. Honesty's more refreshing and wherever these questions are coming from, I'm guessing they're going straight through your heart. Is that about right?"

Afraid she would begin to cry, Rhyne only nodded.

"All right." She waved the waiter over and asked for some whiskey for their tea. "Medicinal. Dr. Monroe will tell you that." She inched her chair closer to Rhyne. "I guess you have to decide what kind of woman you are," she said. "That's different from the kind of woman *other* people think you are. It's that simple, and it's that hard. Mostly it's about not letting folks beat you down. For me, it's been easier here in Reidsville than it was in other places, but even some of the women who came before me and married miners years ago can forget themselves. They'd like to pass judgment on me or the girls still working at Miss Adele's if we let them."

The whiskey came and Rose took the bottle from the waiter when he started to pour. "I'll take care of this," she said, winking at him. "Put it on my bill." When he was gone, she poured a finger's worth into her cup and a little bit more than that into Rhyne's. She set the bottle between them. "You asked me if I ever thought I'd be someone's wife, and the answer is 'yes.' I thought it would happen for me the same way it did for my mother, although maybe not so many times. I had a lot of fathers growing up, Rhyne."

Rose caught Rhyne's eye to make certain she understood. "When I was older and already whoring, I put it aside, not because I didn't want to be married, but because my thinking was still a little crooked. When I came into my own and stood up for myself, that's when I knew some man would be damn lucky to have me in his life and not just in his bed. That no-account Beatty boy might have even realized it before I did. He waited me out, came by and played the piano for me, and he never asked me upstairs. Did you know that?"

Rhyne shook her head.

"Well, it's true. So what makes a man want a woman like me?" Rose smiled slyly and

394

tapped her temple. "The good sense to know that I'm the best thing that ever happened to him." She paused, sipping her tea and watching Rhyne out of the corner of her eye. "Drink your tea. You'll know your mind a little better after the whiskey softens it up."

Cole thought he'd seen his last patient when he said goodbye to Mrs. Easter and her eldest boy. He was preparing to extinguish the lamps in the surgery when he heard the side door open. He recognized Will Beatty's voice immediately. "I'm in here," he called. "Come in."

"Rose is with me," Will said, appearing in the doorway. "She's got something to tell you." He motioned behind him, encouraging his wife to step forward.

Since Cole's experience with Rose Beatty was that she was anything but reticent, her reluctance intrigued him. He tried to peer around Will's shoulder. "Is she ill?"

Will grinned so widely that his dimples carved deep crescents on either side of his mouth. "Oh, she's just fine. A little too fine for my tastes this time of day, it not being quite the dinner hour and all, but I reckon I can handle that. C'mon, Rose. The doctor's waiting." Will leaned against the doorjamb and crossed his arms, making just enough room for Rose to slip past him.

Her bright, but somewhat vacant glance

was all Cole had to see. "She's been drinking, Will."

"Don't I know it."

Rose held up her hand to get Cole's attention. "I'm here, Dr. Monroe. You and Will should be careful about talking as if I weren't."

"You're right. Come in, both of you. What can I do for you?"

Still grinning, Will looked at his wife. "You tell him."

Pressing her generous mouth into a thin line, Rose cast a disapproving glance at that no-account Beatty boy. Damn, but if that didn't make him chuckle. She had a feeling she was a little more worse for wear than she'd first thought.

"It's about Rhyne," she said to Cole. "I saw her in the Commodore dining room earlier this afternoon and we shared a table and some conversation."

"And about half a bottle of Sir Nigel's best whiskey," Will said, unable to help himself. He pretended he didn't see Rose's attempt to sneer at him. Her lips weren't quite working together.

"Medicinal," Rose said. "We drank it in our tea with cream and sugar."

"Waste of good whiskey," said Will, "if you ask me."

Cole was inclined to agree. "Where's Miss Abbot?"

"Well, that's what I've come to tell you." She smiled pleasantly at her husband when he put a hand at her back to steady her. "Thank you, dear."

"Miss Abbot?" Cole asked again when Rose merely stared at him. "Your table companion, Rose?"

"Oh. Yes. Rhyne. She's still at the hotel, you see. I really thought that was best, and Sir Nigel agreed with me. He had an empty suite so he put her in there. I paid him for it, the whole thing being more or less my fault."

"More," said Will. "Definitely more."

Rose's features were set earnestly as she pleaded her case to Cole. "I didn't know she couldn't hold her liquor. She's Runt Abbot, for goodness sake. Runt Abbot. He used to walk right into Rudy's place and order at the bar. I *saw* him . . . her . . . them. How was I supposed to know?"

Cole was hard-pressed to keep from laughing. It helped to avoid catching Will's eye. "Well, now you do. Is she all right?"

Rose's brow furrowed as she gave the question the deepest consideration. "Doesn't have a head for drink," she said at last. "Doesn't have the stomach for it, either."

"I see." That caused Cole to sober. "She was sick?"

"Mmm."

Will steadied Rose again. "Nigel sent someone round to get me after they got

Rhyne up to her room. I told Rose that she had to come here and explain to you what happened. If you decide you want to go see Rhyne, Rose and —"

"I most certainly want to see Miss Abbot," Cole said, interrupting.

"I thought you might," said Will. "Whitley can come with us. Spend the night if she likes. I know how it looks right now, but Rose'll be —" He stopped because Cole was already nodding his head, agreeing to the arrangement. "Glad that's settled. I'll put up a sign; let folks that might come by know where they can find you. You go on. It's Suite 200. Better take a change of clothes and maybe some headache powders. You're going to need them."

Will's last piece of advice was sufficiently ambiguous, prompting Cole to pack a small valise with not only what might benefit Rhyne, but what he could use as well.

Nigel Pennyworth was expecting Cole and discreetly passed the key along. Cole required no assistance finding the suite. He did ask for dinner to be sent up in an hour and also for disturbances to be limited to emergencies. Sir Nigel assured him that he would arrange for both.

Cole did not try to be particularly quiet when he entered the suite. The small sitting room was empty. He let the valise thump to the floor beside the chaise longue and listened for the sound of movement in the adjoining bedroom. There was none.

Shaking his head, he opened the connecting door and looked in on Rhyne. She was lying close to the edge of the bed, one bare arm dangling over the side, the other pushed under the pillow. He suspected that when Rose left Rhyne, the blankets had been neatly tucked around her. Since then, Rhyne had fought a lively battle with them. They were bunched around her waist and tangled between her legs. One of her calves was completely uncovered, although she had managed to keep her feet buried.

Rhyne's green-and-white checked dress was lying over the back of one of the chairs near the stove. Her corset and petticoat were folded on top of one wide arm while her cloak was draped across the other. The bustle and velvet hat rested on the chair's plump cushion. Rhyne's shoes were under the chair.

Surveying the throne of neatly arranged garments, Cole realized that either Rose was not quite as inebriated as she appeared or that no-account Beatty boy had offered more assistance than he let on. He hoped it was the former but suspected it was the latter.

After he'd unpacked the valise and straightened the covers around Rhyne once again, he returned to the sitting room, found a current copy of Artie Showalter's weekly paper and stretched out on the chaise to read. When dinner arrived, he ate alone at the small table and put enough aside for Rhyne in the event she had an appetite for something other than tea and toast.

From time to time he checked on her. The basin on the floor beside the bed remained unused. Recalling what Rose told him earlier, Cole imagined that one bout of kneeling over the bowl had been enough to empty Rhyne's stomach. He eventually removed the basin and put it in the bathing room.

The Commodore hotel had amenities that many people in Reidsville did not yet have in their homes. The luxury of Sir Nigel's palace was well known beyond the town and attracted gamblers who had a taste for the fine life and the curious who wanted to experience it just once. Hot and cold running water, dark walnut cabinets, marble sinks, and polished brass fixtures made the bathing room as decadent a place as one could find in town, and the ball-and-claw footed tub was the room's most self-indulgent feature.

Cole didn't try to resist the tub's siren call. He closed the door and began stripping off his clothes.

Rhyne woke with a powerful thirst. The sound of running water only made it worse. Driven by her need, she wrestled with the covers until she was free of them, and then

400

she slid out of bed. The room tilted as soon as she stood. She grabbed for the night table and held it until she got her bearings.

Getting the floor to stay level was only the first part of her problem. Several long, disorienting moments passed before Rhyne could identify her surroundings. Once she did, she remembered everything that explained why she was here.

"Oh, God," she murmured, aware that she was wearing a chemise, drawers, and stockings and that every other article of clothing was decorating an armchair. "I swear, Rose Beatty . . ." She let the thought trail off because it was incoherently formed at best. Revenge needed to be carefully planned, and she was in no condition to do that now.

Sawdust tasted better than what she had in her mouth. She tried to lick her parched lips and discovered her tongue was as dry and gritty as sandpaper. Running water drew her attention again. She tested her steadiness by releasing the table and taking a step back. When she was confident that the initial wave of dizziness had passed, Rhyne went to find the source of the water.

It didn't occur to her to knock. She remembered quite clearly that Rose had gone, or rather that Will had taken her away. Rhyne felt heat in her cheeks just thinking about it. She pushed the door open, went straight to the sink, and thrust her cupped hands under the cold-water tap. She stood frozen in that posture — her head bent heavily forward, her eyes closed — for some time before she realized her palms were not overflowing with clear, cool water. In fact, they remained dry as a dust bowl.

Raising her head slowly, Rhyne opened her eyes. There was a moment where she caught her reflection in the gilt mirror above the sink, but what captured and held her attention was what she saw over her left shoulder.

Whipping around so quickly that the room tilted again, Rhyne braced herself against the sink. She stared, her mouth slightly agape, as Coleridge Monroe calmly sat up in the tub and turned off both faucets. He smiled, gave her a casual salute to acknowledge her presence, and then lay comfortably back against the curved end of the tub and slid down until water lapped at his shoulders.

Rhyne felt her knees sag. Lamplight infused the water so that it lay like gold leaf across his shoulders and throat. If it weren't for the fact that his breathing was steadier than hers, Rhyne could easily have been convinced that he'd known the touch of King Midas.

"Hell and damnation, Cole," she whispered.

One of his eyebrows kicked up, not because she'd sworn, but because she'd called him Cole. "It's about time," he said, reaching for a bar of soap.

Rhyne didn't immediately understand what

he was referring to. When realization came, she threw up her hands. "That's what you have to say?" She didn't give him an opportunity to answer what was essentially a rhetorical question. "What are you doing here?"

He flicked the water with one hand and held up the soap in the other. "Isn't it evident? In fact, it's more obvious than what you're doing here." He pointed to the footstool beside the tub where he'd placed several towels. "Put the towels over there and sit down. You're listing like a ship in a storm."

Rhyne looked down at herself. It was true. "I need water." She gave him her back while she searched for a glass. Finding one, she filled and drank from it three times before her thirst was satisfied. After filling it a fourth time, she approached the tub but did not go so close that she could see under the water. She used one foot to drag the stool closer and set the towels where Cole could reach them. When she sat down, she did not quite reach Cole's eye level.

She offered a trifle lopsided smile. "Mrs. Beatty ladled whiskey in my tea."

"So she told me. Medicinal, I believe, was the explanation for it."

"That's what she said."

"Were you feeling poorly?"

Rhyne mocked herself with a short, ironic chuckle. "Not as poorly as I feel now." When she fell quiet she saw that Cole was still waiting for something that passed as an explanation. "I suppose you'd say that I had thoughts that needed sorting," she said finally. "I was on my way home from Maggie Porter's and just kind of wandered into the Commodore. I had enough money for a cup of tea and a scone, but I only ordered the tea. I don't know how long I sat there before Rose came in. Until she arrived, I'd mostly been sitting, not thinking or sorting. It was better after she sat down. I didn't know I wanted company, and then she was there, and I realized that I did."

She watched Cole turn over the bar of soap in his hands. She didn't think he realized he was doing it. All of his attention was for her. She basked in it the way he basked in the warm yellow lamplight, and she knew without a doubt that she was the more golden for it.

"Rose Beatty is probably the last person I'd have thought to go to with the troubles in my head, so it's good that she came to me. Turns out, she knows a powerful lot about the kinds of things I was thinking. And that was before we got liberal with the whiskey. After that, she plucked thoughts from my mind like they were weeds and she was clearing space for a garden."

Cole tempered his smile. "Is that right?"

Rhyne nodded. She took a sip of water to wet her lips and then raised the glass to her left temple and held it there. "Rose might have cleared too much ground for a first planting."

Cole took pity on her. "I brought some headache powders. They're in my bag in the bedroom."

She didn't have the wherewithal to do more than murmur her thanks. She used the lip of the tub to help her slowly lever herself to her feet, and then she shuffled into the bedroom to find his satchel, keeping the glass of cool water pressed against her temple the entire time.

When she returned, the glass was drained and granules of bitter salicylate dotted her upper lip. She rinsed her mouth at the sink, scrubbed her face, and pushed damp fingers through her hair to tame the dark, unruly curls. Behind her, she watched Cole dip below the surface of the water to remove soap from his hair. When he came up, he threw off water like a puppy before he reached for a towel.

Rhyne sat down again and held out her hand for the damp towel when Cole was finished with it. He eliminated spiky tufts of copper hair by smoothing them with his palms. Rhyne's own fingers itched to plow the same field, but she squeezed water out of the towel instead.

"It will take some time for the medicine to work," Cole told her.

"I know."

"Perhaps you should lie down."

She looked longingly at the tub. "I'd like to bathe."

"You can join me. It's as big as a pond."

"I think I'll wait." If he was disappointed, Rhyne had no hint of it. For herself, she was a little disappointed that he didn't insist. She watched Cole stretch. The tub was not quite of a size to accommodate his length. His kneecaps broke the surface when the soles of his feet rested against the far side. "Aren't you getting cold?" she asked hopefully.

In answer, Cole sat up and leaned forward, reaching simultaneously for the plug and the hot-water faucet. There was a gurgle when he pulled the plug, but that sound soon disappeared as hot water rushed out of the tap. He reset the plug, let the water run a little longer, and then turned it off. Afterward, he settled back and closed his eyes. He wasn't terribly surprised when Rhyne threw the damp towel at his head.

"Folks around here tend to think you've got pretty, city manners," said Rhyne. "You sure have them fooled."

Cole removed the towel and dropped it over the side of the tub. His arm remained extended toward Rhyne. He turned his hand, palm up, and curled his fingers ever so slightly. His mouth curled ever so slightly as well. His hand invited her. His mouth invited trouble.

Rhyne put her hand in his and was drawn off the stool more by his smile than the infinitesimal tug of his fingers. She rose to her feet, took a step forward, and then climbed into the tub. Heedless of the fact that she was still wearing stockings, drawers, and a chemise, Rhyne lowered herself into the water so that she was facing him. Reaching behind her, she pulled the plug to drain just enough water to keep it from spilling over the sides.

Rhyne rested her forearms on the lip of the tub and allowed Cole to draw her feet toward him until her calves rested on his thighs. Beneath the water, his fingers were busy removing her stockings. She blushed when he carelessly tossed them away and one of them clung to the flock paper.

Cole glanced at it. "I wonder what will become of your drawers."

Rhyne slapped at his hands when he began tugging on the lacy hem of her drawers, but only succeeded in stinging her eyes with soapy water. He used the distraction to his advantage. Her drawers did not cling wetly to the wall, but they did drape rather coyly over the side of the sink.

"Tell me about your headache," he said. His hands caressed her from ankle to knee and back again. He did it several more times before she finally answered him.

"It's gone."

Cole nodded, satisfied by her surprise. The steamy bath, the heat rising in her blood, and the novelty of this particular distraction probably had more of a palliative effect than the headache powders.

"Good," he said. With just a touch here and there, a nudge, a tug, a caress, Cole managed to turn Rhyne so that she was cradled against him, her back flush to his chest, her hips resting between his open thighs. There was tension at first; he felt it along the length of her spine and in the awkwardness of her hands on his knees. Gradually it eased as she grew more comfortable with the position and the gentle lapping of water against her skin each time they stirred.

"Is it late?" she asked. "It was dark when I woke. I never thought to look at the time."

"It can't be eight yet."

She nodded, relieved. "Where's Whitley?"

"Will and Rose whisked her away. It remains to be seen if that was a mistake."

Rhyne turned her head to try to look at him, but he put his hands lightly on either side of her and straightened her out. That didn't stop her from asking, "What were you thinking?"

"Of you," he said quietly. "I was thinking of you."

She closed her eyes. It was as if his voice

had slipped between the water and her skin. She was enveloped by it, safely cradled and cherished. The feelings were unfamiliar to her, but where she would have sought to escape them this morning, she fought now to keep them close to her heart.

"I deserve you," she whispered. A tear leaked from under her lashes. "It's one of the things I didn't understand." Her voice was as thin and fragile as a thread of glass. "But here's the other, and it was harder to reckon. I'm worth deserving, too."

Cole started to say something, but she raised a hand over her shoulder and lightly placed her fingertips against his lips.

"If you don't know it yet, I'm hopeful it'll come to you by and by. That no-account Beatty figured it out about Rose when she was still whoring, so I'm fairly confident that you'll —"

Rhyne was crying in earnest now, although she wasn't entirely certain why, and then Cole was turning her in his arms and kissing her face, kissing all of her face, so that no matter how the room tilted, the singular touch of his mouth set everything straight again.

"You're deserving," Cole said against the mouth. He said it again at her ear and ruffled the fine hair at her temples. He whispered it against her cheek, tickling her skin with his breath and lips, then punctuated it with a

409

flick of his tongue. "Did you really think I didn't know?"

He wouldn't let her speak. He needed her mouth under his, and he kissed her long and slow and deep. She made tiny whimpering sounds at the back of her throat that were nothing at all like her sobs. He could feel their vibration against his palm when he touched her neck.

Water rippled around them; some of it slipped over the side. Rhyne's skin glowed with dewy wetness and the transparent color of the lamplight. Cole sipped from the curve of her neck. He pushed damp, dark tendrils of her hair aside and kissed her behind the ear. She moaned softly, caught him by the back of his neck and held him there, her nails making crescent impressions on his flesh. She would have slipped under his skin if she could have found a way in.

He stripped away her wet chemise and flung it away. Neither of them looked to see where it fell. They were aware of what was different this time. Always before there had been something between them: her night-gown, his union suit, the blankets they shared. Mostly, too, there had been darkness. Now they were naked in a pool of liquid light, their bodies sleek and slippery and glowing.

She crawled over him, straddled his thighs. Rising, she cupped her breasts and offered them. Her fingers stroked his damp hair as he sucked. Fire ignited along filaments that connected muscle and tendon and sinew. She felt heat in her fingertips, at the back of her throat, and as deep as her womb. With each tug of his mouth she understood better that her body was exquisitely fashioned to give and receive pleasure. She was aware of the thickness of her blood, the heaviness in her limbs, and contrarily, a perfect lightness of feeling. She was glad of his hands on her hips. He held her down as nothing else could have.

The broad planes of his body intrigued her. His shoulders were smooth and taut. She traced the rigid line of his collarbones with her fingertips and then flattened her hands against his chest. She stroked his arms and felt his corded muscles shift beneath her palms. When her thumbs tripped lightly over his shoulder blades, she heard him draw a ragged breath.

The sound of it stirred her.

Rhyne closed her eyes. He drew back and she knew he was watching her. She let him, unembarrassed by anything that he might see in her face. Whatever it was that held his interest, he'd put it there. She smiled as Cole caught her by the waist and lowered her enough to bring her mouth within a hairsbreadth of his.

He nudged her lips. They parted for him, and when the tip of her tongue peeped out, he closed the gap and drew it into his mouth.

It was a deliciously sensual kiss, swirling heat and sweet fire. She moaned softly, and he took the sound and kept it for himself. He was hard against her belly. She tilted her hips forward, rubbed, wanting more now. Wanting him.

When she would have found him with her hands, he stopped her, taking her by the wrists and raising her hands to his chest. He began to lift his head, but her lips clung to his. The shape of his mouth changed. He smiled, kissed her again, and when he drew away he was still smiling.

Rhyne slipped one hand out of his hold and touched his lips. "I reckon you have about the prettiest mouth I've ever seen."

Cole blew gently against her fingertips. "Is that so?"

"Mmm. It's even prettier when you're smiling."

"Then I'm glad you give me so many reasons to do it."

She traced the line of his nose. "*This* is still a proboscis."

"It certainly is."

"Noble, though."

Cole was not feeling particularly noble. He recaptured the wrist that was doing all the exploring. "I want to take you to bed."

Rhyne nodded.

Her agreement didn't assure him that she understood. "That means we have to get out of the water."

"Of course."

"I was hoping we could do that together."

"All right."

He searched her face. "You're certain?"

Rhyne's breathing quickened. "You're fixing to show off your boy parts, aren't you?"

Cole touched her forehead with his. "It's come to that, yes."

She said nothing for a moment, and then, "Take me to bed."

They untangled first. Cole released her, and Rhyne used the sides of the tub to lever herself away. Their eyes held; neither of them moved.

"I'm ready," she reminded him. "I promise you." And to prove it, she pulled the plug.

It was as bold an invitation as Cole had ever received, and the last vestige of hesitation vanished. Wresting the plug from Rhyne's fingers, he pitched it toward the sink before she changed her mind. He heaved himself out of the water and extended a hand to Rhyne.

She absently accepted his hand and let herself be drawn to her feet. Her stare never wavered from his erection. It was difficult to reconcile its size with the fact that she'd once taken all of it inside her. "It's as big as a stallion's."

That comment moved Cole to look down at himself. "No, but you're kind to say so."

He placed two fingers under her chin and tilted her face toward him. "You need to watch where you're going." Letting her go, he stepped out of the tub and grabbed the towels. He placed one in Rhyne's hands and dried himself with the other. When he was finished, she was still standing in the tub. The water had drained, but she was dripping, and the towel was mostly a damp ball of linen clutched in her fist.

Cole could see that the cold was prickling her skin. He took the towel back and briskly rubbed her down. He stopped when a measure of color returned to her complexion. "Better?" he asked, tossing the towel aside.

"Much." She expected that he would help her out of the tub, but she wasn't prepared for him to swing her into his arms. "What are you —"

His raised eyebrow silenced her.

Rhyne slipped her arms around his neck and recalled the last time he carried her to bed. On that occasion, he'd dropped her like she was a sack of snakes and then went off to find better company at Miss Adele's. Staring up into Cole's darkening eyes, she had no fear that was going to happen tonight.

CHAPTER 12

He laid her on the bed and followed her down. Between quick, darting kisses they tugged at the blankets until they were warmly cocooned. They paused then to catch their breath, but only briefly. The pull each felt for the other was too intense to be ignored for long.

Cole nudged Rhyne's thighs apart. She raised one knee as he moved between her legs. In spite of what she said she wanted, regardless that she believed she was ready, Rhyne felt herself tense in anticipation of being held immobile by his weight. Cole felt it too. He leaned over, supporting himself on his forearms, and brushed her lips with his.

"You know there can be pleasure," he whispered. "Tell me you remember that."

Her fingertips alighted on his shoulders as softly as butterflies. "I remember."

"Say my name."

"Coleridge."

He smiled. "Then you know everything

that's important for now."

Rhyne supposed that she did. He certainly made her feel that way. Her lips parted, inviting his kiss, and then her thighs parted, inviting the rest of him.

He'd held back so often and so long, that Cole was afraid it would be over even as it began. Biting back a groan, he thrust into her. Rhyne immediately made him her captive. Her arms and legs closed around him, and, *there,* where she held him so intimately, the honeyed walls of her vagina contracted. His cock pulsed, and the quickening beat of his blood was hers to control.

Of course it was. She owned his heart.

Rhyne watched Cole's pupils steal the color from his eyes. She imagined she could see her reflection in the dark pools that were more proof of his wanting. It was an agony for him: desiring her, and desiring not to hurt her. His skin was stretched taut over his cheekbones and the line of his mouth was more grimace than grin.

"You know there can be pleasure," she whispered.

It was enough. He rocked her hard, pushing her back but not down. She met his thrusts so there could be no doubt that it was what she wanted, too. Their bodies moved in almost violent concert, warriors circling, clashing, falling back. They fought without exchanging a single blow, although there were marks to prove there had been combat.

Her nails pressed deeply into his taut shoulders. Using only his mouth, he left his brand on the curve of her breast. She set her teeth against his earlobe and nipped. He clutched a handful of her hair while he plundered her mouth.

Pleasure rode on the back of hunger. Every pressured touch, every hurried caress, fed a need that had been too long denied. With her lips and tongue and fingertips, Rhyne urged Cole to take his release, but it was the deep, throaty cries of her own pleasure that pushed him from the precipice.

Sated, they lay still while their breathing quieted and their heartbeats slowed. Neither spoke. Words would have been an intrusion just then.

Rhyne did more than tolerate Cole's weight. For the brief time that he lay covering her, she found comfort in it. As far back as she could remember she'd never looked to anyone for protection, yet she was certain that what she felt in these moments was protected. The sense that she was cherished squeezed her heart.

Cole raised himself on his elbows long enough to kiss Rhyne on the mouth, and then rolled onto his back. She immediately closed the gap between them by securing herself to his side like ivy. He made a cradle for her head against his shoulder and drew her arm across his chest.

"I don't want to leave," she whispered. "Ever."

He stroked her arm. "We have the suite for the night."

"That's not close to forever."

He murmured his agreement against the crown of her dark hair.

Rhyne closed her eyes. "When do you reckon you'll be talking to Pastor Duun?"

"About twelve hours from now." He felt her start of surprise. "Did you really think I'd give you an opportunity to change your mind?"

"My mind's set."

"I'm glad to hear it."

"I was thinking about yours."

"Mine? I thought I was clear about what I wanted."

Rhyne tilted her head to look at him. "You don't know everything."

Cole understood she wasn't speaking in generalities. "I'll know when you tell me," he said. "I can wait."

She sighed. "You make it sound simple. It's a lot more complicated in my head."

He didn't doubt it for a moment. "Why don't you tell me about that?"

"You want to know why it's complicated?"

"That's right." He gave her arm a light squeeze. "I like puzzles, remember?"

She eased her head into the comfortable cradle he provided. "Well," she said, drawing out the single word as she thought about all the ones that needed to follow. "I'm thinking that there's things I know that you don't that could change your kind feelings toward me if I told you what they are, and I'm thinking that you still might want me to marry you in spite of no longer feeling kindly toward me because you hold so fast to your honor. I'm also thinking that what I tell you might make you feel obliged to tell someone else, and the consequences of that aren't so easy to figure, but you being possessed of a fine moral character that I mostly admire, you'll suppose that justice will beat ugly every time, even though I know for a fact that ugly wins its fair share of things.

"And there's my feelings for you that I'm considering. What I know about loving someone can't fill a thimble, but somehow I have it in my mind that it will be worse than the worst beating I ever took if you tell me to leave, and maybe only a little less than the worst if I leave before you tell me, so I'm weighing those things, one against the other, and wondering if telling you what you don't know favors the first or the second. Or maybe it doesn't favor either."

Rhyne drew in a breath and exhaled softly, her voice returning to a whisper. "Maybe telling is just honest and right. Maybe things need to be said because a person shouldn't hold on to ugly forever, no matter what might happen." Her short laugh was shaky and self-conscious. "And that's why it's complicated."

Cole held her just as he had throughout her slightly breathless recitation, his cheek resting against her hair, his hand stroking her forearm. He waited until he was certain she could hear him over the hammering of her own heart before he spoke. "Here's what I know that you don't," he said. "I love you."

Rhyne's heart tripped over itself. "I'm surely glad of it, but it doesn't make things less complicated."

"Then maybe this will: I think you killed the men that raped you."

In her mind she imagined herself bolting from the bed. The reality was that she was so startled that she couldn't move.

Cole was relieved when she didn't fling herself away, but he was aware that the distance between them now could not be measured by conventional means. "You don't have to say anything," he told her. "I'm not looking to you to make a confession or protest your innocence. Neither is required. Both are true."

She frowned. "I don't understand."

"I mean that confessing to murder doesn't always make you guilty, not in my eyes, probably not in the law's."

"See?" It was an accusation. "That's what I

meant about you being the kind of man that believes justice can beat ugly. It's not so nearly often enough."

"I know what you meant, but this time ugly *was* beaten. You shot them, and that was justice."

Rhyne hesitated. "Not that I'm admitting to anything, but if it was justice, it wasn't the law. I know that much."

Cole knew it too. "I don't feel at all obliged to tell anyone," he said. "Even if I had something more than my suspicions. It could be that a certain sheriff and no-account Beatty boy already have it figured out and have no intention of doing anything about it."

"What do you mean?"

Cole shrugged. "Will's the one that told me about a couple of men that he and Wyatt tracked into the mountains somewhere around your place."

"They've tracked a lot of men out that way."

"But not every miscreant is found dead at the end of the trail. In this case, one of them was shot in the head, the other in the privates."

"Sounds like a falling out."

"Sounds like," Cole repeated.

"Probably that's all it was."

"Probably." Cole's fingers threaded through hers. He squeezed lightly. "That shot to the privates, though . . ." He let the sentence hang. His lips brushed her hair. "Someone was purely pissed."

"Someone was."

Cole had it in his mind that calling on Pastor Duun would be the first order of the morning, but his own appetites took precedent, and then there was breakfast. The small round table in the sitting room was so laden with the food Rhyne had ordered from the kitchen that there was barely space for their plates and cutlery. He only raised an eyebrow when she began uncovering the dishes.

"I'm hungry," she said by way of explanation. "It wasn't decent what you did to me on an empty stomach."

Cole forked two flapjacks and put them on his plate. "That wasn't your stomach I heard growling." He managed to get his hand out of the way before she stabbed him with her fork. "Or was it?"

Rhyne's smile was inscrutable. She passed him the syrup after she drowned her pancakes.

Cole added a few crisp strips of bacon to his plate and a large spoonful of scrambled eggs. His stomach rumbled loudly as he reached for the coffee pot.

Rhyne laughed. She carved out a bite of pancake and put it in her mouth. The pancake melted away while maple syrup clung deliciously to her tongue. "Food of the gods," she said, cutting out another piece. She glanced up and found that Cole was staring at her mouth. She started to raise her napkin, but he reached across the table and stopped her.

"Let me." He gave her no time to consider what he was going to do. Rather than rising, he simply pushed the table out of the way and leaned across the space that separated them. He kissed her deeply, tasting sweetness that was more than the syrup on her lips and tongue. When he sat back, he pulled the table into position, and picked up his fork. "Never doubt it," he said, spearing a strip of bacon. "*That* is food of the gods."

She stared at him, a blush stealing over her face. "I stand corrected."

He smiled. "Eat up."

They both did, but the air was charged and the simple act of eating became foreplay. Their mouths were engaged in one activity while their minds were engaged in another. Even as they ate, their eyes drifted toward the bedroom. They thought about the rumpled covers, the musky scents of skin and sex, the pillow that he'd used to raise her hips when he took her from behind.

She saw his perfectly sculpted hand as it had been when it cupped her breast, and again when it slipped between her legs. She knew the shape of her own body by the molding of his palm, the gentle turn of his skilled fingers as he caressed her.

He saw delicate blue veins in the underside of her wrist and recalled the quickening of her pulse. He was reminded of all the ways she moved him and moved for him, how she responded to his touch, both subtle and demanding. Her curiosity excited him and made him cautious. Her trust, now given, seemed absolute, and there was nothing that he could imagine that she would not let him do. She'd said as much to him, and for that reason, he reined in his imagination.

Until he saw the syrup on her lips. That was when he decided there was really no reason he couldn't finish breakfast in bed.

Rhyne knew they were returning to the bedroom before Cole was on his feet. She saw it in the darkening of his eyes as they settled on her face, and she responded to the predatory watchfulness by pushing away from the table and standing. She reached for his hand. He reached for the syrup.

Rhyne never saw his sleight-of-hand. Stripped of her chemise and drawers and lying almost sideways across the bed, the first she knew that he had something in his hand was when he knelt between her open thighs and tipped his fist above her belly. She stared at the thin rivulet of syrup spilling from the center of his palm. He opened his hand to reveal the dainty china pitcher just as the first drop touched her belly. He heard her draw sharply on a breath and watched her skin retract.

He filled her navel and then drizzled the rest in a lacy pattern across her abdomen and around her breasts. Putting the pitcher aside, he studied his handiwork long enough to cause her to stir. He leaned forward, careful not to disturb the liquid lace. "What do you want?" he whispered. "Tell me what you want."

It was impossible for her to look away. She knew her eyes were a mirror of his, knew that they reflected his desire as much as they revealed her own. "Feed on me," she said. "I want you to feed on me."

Undone, Cole took her breast in his mouth and sucked. The pleasure of it was so finely honed that it made her whimper. Her breasts were tender, the aureoles rosy from the attention of his lips and fingertips throughout the long night. Her nipples were sensitive to a whisper. The hot and humid suck of his mouth was a firestorm.

She came the moment his lips closed around her other breast.

Cole gave her no time to catch her breath. He pulled her legs around him and thrust deeply inside her. She jerked, pulled him down by his shoulders, and arched her back, smearing his chest and abdomen with syrup. He paused just long enough to register the look of triumph in her eyes before he reclaimed all of it for himself.

After leaving Rhyne at the house, Cole went to Rose's to get Whitley. During the walk home, she peppered him with so many questions about Rhyne's health that they were already turning the corner to the house before he got in a word edgewise. "Stop, Whit," he said, taking her arm as she made to cross the street. "And let me have your valise. I'm tired of you banging it against my leg."

She handed it over. "It took you long enough to offer. I swear, Cole, your mind drifts more than snow in a blizzard." When he gaped at her, she giggled. "Digger said it first, only he was talking about me."

"Good for him." He ignored the saucy wrinkling of her nose and steered her away from the house. "Longabach's," he said. "Raisin pie."

Whitley was wearing her most fiercely anxious expression by the time they reached the restaurant. Estella showed them to a table away from the window and fussed a little over Whitley's unruly hair before she took their order. Whitley smiled bravely and felt her lower lip tremble. She stared at her folded hands after Mrs. Longabach tiptoed away.

"Whitley," said Cole. "Look at me." When she wouldn't raise her eyes, he didn't press. "I don't have any idea what's going through your mind right now."

"You're going to tell me something I don't want to hear. Something bad. Maybe that you're sending me back to Miss Starcher's." She risked a glimpse at him and found no confirmation of her worst fear. "Or maybe that we're *both* going back to New York." She shot him a second look, this one slightly sideways from under the fan of her fiery lashes. He was staring at her with the intensity he usually reserved for what appeared under the lens of his microscope. "Or maybe it's Rhyne that's leaving. Is that it? You're angry at her because she got drunk with Mrs. Beatty, and now she has to leave because you think I'll take up drink and be just like her." *That* got a reaction. "Well, maybe I will, and won't you be sorry? Is she packing her things? Is that why you brought me here? I want to see her." She started to get up, but Cole clamped a hand around her wrist and with just a look, ordered her back in her chair. Tears welled in Whitley's eyes. "I can't sit here. Not if she's leaving."

"She's *not* leaving."

"She's not?"

"No." Cole released Whitley's wrist and spoke only when he was certain she was firmly settled in her chair. "Rhyne is going to be my wife. Pastor Duun is going to marry us this afternoon." Sitting back, Cole regarded his sister with a certain amount of satisfaction. "So this is what it takes to make you speechless. I've always wondered."

It wasn't that Whitley didn't have anything to say. It was that she had a *hundred* things to say — all at once. A dam of words clogged her throat. She thought that must be the reason tears spilled so freely. She wasn't used to saying nothing. The frustration would likely kill her, and then she'd miss the wedding.

"All right," said Cole. "I have a few questions anyway. Why did you ask about Rhyne's health when you knew that drinking was the problem?"

Whitley took out a handkerchief and dabbed daintily at her eyes. "Because I didn't *want* you to know that I knew. It was so important to everyone that I shouldn't know the truth that the polite thing seemed to be to let you go on lying."

Cole blew out an uneasy breath and pushed a hand through his hair. "It serves me right, I suppose. What else do you know that you're not supposed to?"

She put her handkerchief away and merely stared at him.

"Well, thank you for that. I want you to promise that you'll never tell me."

Smiling, Whitley crossed her heart. She saw Mrs. Longabach approaching. "Our pie's here. Wedding talk has restored my appetite."

"Wedding?" asked Estella, setting their

plates down. "Who's getting married?"

Whitley ignored Cole's nudge under the table. She beamed at Mrs. Longabach. "My brother and Rhyne Abbot are getting hitched. That's right, isn't it? That's what you say here? Getting hitched."

"We do, and isn't that some kind of good news?" Her thin face was transformed by a broad smile as she looked Whitley over. "And I reckon you look about as happy now as someone can and still call it decent. My, oh my. Wait until I tell Henry. He suspicioned it some time ago." She handed them each a fork. "When's the wedding, Doctor? I'd be happy to put out a spread."

"Thank you, but we're getting married this afternoon. Pastor Duun already agreed. I couldn't ask you do something on such short notice."

Estella Longabach pursed her lips. "Humph. Sounds to me as if I was going to get *no* notice. I'm not saying there's a right way do things, Dr. Monroe, but there sure is a wrong way. What you're fixin' to do is, well, I can't say exactly since there's a pair of pink and pretty ears sitting right here."

Whitley preened, complimented by Estella's reference to her ears as both pink and pretty. She only smiled more deeply when Cole scowled at her.

"Miss Abbot and I agreed that there would only be the pastor and his wife present, and

429

Whitley, of course, to give Miss Abbot away."

Whitley managed to keep herself from bouncing out of her chair. "Really, Cole? I'm to have a part?"

He nodded. "Rhyne insisted."

"You'll need another witness," Estella said. "Whitley's not old enough to stand up for you. Who's that going to be?"

"I'm sure Pastor Duun has thought of that."

"And I'm sure he hasn't. Who would he ask without offending someone he didn't? The same goes for you. Anyone you invite is going to lord it over the rest of us, and won't that just set folks talking?"

"The people here don't strike me that way."

Whitley felt compelled to offer her opinion. "People are mostly the same everywhere. Just scratch them a little. You'll see. I think you should listen to Mrs. Longabach. She knows this town a lot better than we do."

Whitley was sorry for her interference when she saw Rhyne's face pale as she described the conversation with Estella Longabach. Her eyes pleaded with Cole to make it right.

Cole took Rhyne's hands and warmed them between his. "I didn't agree," he told her. "Whitley should have said that right away. It doesn't matter to me if Estella's correct about everything. We're getting married this afternoon." He watched some color return to Rhyne's complexion, but her eyes were still too wide and watchful and the expression in them was pained.

Whitley scooted the tuffet she was sitting on closer to the sofa where Cole and Rhyne were sharing the same end. "I didn't know it was you," she said to Rhyne. "I thought Cole was the one that didn't want the attention. I thought he wasn't being fair to you. Caroline Erwin asked for every kind of persnickety thing, and I could tell he wished she'd stop talking about ribbons and engravings and silver filigree, but he let her go on and on because he just can't help being decent."

"Did you think I suddenly *could* help myself?" Cole asked dryly.

"Maybe I did. I don't know." She shrugged. "I suppose I thought Rhyne would do whatever you wanted. I didn't realize you were doing it for her."

"Did it ever occur to you that it's what we both want?"

"Are you doing it for me?" asked Rhyne at the same time. That brought two pairs of green eyes swiveling in her direction. "Well, are you?"

This was ground that called for careful treading, and Cole wished he were the skilled diplomat his father had been. "I love you, Rhyne, and I'm proud and humbled that you're willing to marry me. I would show you off to the entire town because I can't help but be cast in a better light when you're at

431

my side. I think we —"

Rhyne gave him a sharp look. "Folks already see a halo around your head. The light doesn't get better than that."

Whitley leaned forward. "She's right, Cole. And I'm not certain about the part where you said you were humbled, although it was very prettily said."

Out of the corner of his eye, Cole saw Rhyne nodding in agreement. He pinned Whitley back with a sharp, reproving glance, and then turned to Rhyne. "I wanted you to marry me weeks ago, so I can't think of a single reason why it shouldn't happen today. I *am* that selfish. That doesn't mean I don't want to celebrate our marriage. I'm also that proud. I'd fill the church with as many people as could be there by three o'clock if you could tolerate it. Not having them there is no kind of sacrifice for me, Rhyne. Not having you be my wife at nightfall is."

Before Rhyne could respond, he turned to Whitley. "And if a man isn't humbled by your acceptance of his proposal, then he doesn't think enough of you. Show him the door at once."

Cole released Rhyne's hands and sat back. He slid an arm along the couch behind her shoulders. Almost immediately she settled into his offered embrace. When she looked up at him, he saw just a hint of contentment in her smile. The fullness of it was there in her eyes.

Fascinated, Whitley looked from her brother to Rhyne and back again. Being a witness was infinitely better than being an eavesdropper. She kept it to herself in the event Cole had not already gauged her avid interest.

"I wouldn't mind if Rachel Cooper was there," Rhyne said at last. "I could stand that."

Cole nodded. "She *is* responsible for us meeting when we did."

"And there's the sheriff to consider."

"That's right. Wyatt insisted that I go out to the cabin."

Rhyne pressed her index finger under her chin as she continued to think. "That no-account Beatty boy escorted you."

"He did. He also found you."

"We can't *not* ask him to be there. I never had a problem with Will."

"That's what he says."

Rhyne pursed her mouth to one side. "Rose should come. She helped me think straight."

Whitley nodded wisely. "Whiskey does that." That earned her a glare from her brother and a frown from Rhyne. She held up her hands in a gesture of innocence. "Just something I heard."

Amused, Rhyne simply shook her head. "Is there anyone else?"

He ticked off the people whose name she'd

mentioned. "That's four in addition to Mrs. Duun."

"Well, I reckon that'll do. I've played cards with more people than that at a table. Seems like I should be able to have them there."

Cole squeezed her shoulder lightly. "You're sure?"

"I'll know come three o'clock."

Whitley frowned. "There's something I don't understand. You used to perform on stage in front of everyone that could squeeze into the Miner Key, and now it seems as if . . ." She shrugged helplessly. "I don't know how it seems exactly. Are you afraid, Rhyne? Is that why you don't want hardly anyone there?"

Rhyne placed her hand on Cole's knee to keep him from interrupting. "Performing is pretending, Whitley. Sometimes it's being someone you're not. Sometimes it's about believing in someone you could be. There's never been much difference for me whether I was on stage or just living my life. Pretending is how I got by. There're still some days, even after all this time of being with you and Cole, that I'm not used to my own skin. I don't know what I'd do if folks came to gawk at me trading vows with your brother. Runt Abbot's hard to shake. Could be I'd do something that would shame us all."

Her fingers tightened on Cole's knee. "You asked me if I was afraid, and the truth is that

I am. Embarrassing you and Cole is what scares me. The fewer people there to witness it, the better off we'll be."

Whitley blinked and fumbled for her handkerchief. "There's nothing that you could do that would embarrass me."

"Then you need to raise your standards."

"No, I don't," she said stoutly, swiping at her eyes. "Tell her, Cole. Tell her that she can't shame us." She used her handkerchief to wave him off when he would have spoken. "Never mind. It's because you're decent, just like my brother. And decent people don't do shameful things. Manners and such are learned, but decency, that's bred in the bone, leastways that's what my father said, and I believe him."

"My father is Judah Abbot," Rhyne said gently.

"Doesn't matter. It doesn't mean it was bred in *his* bones. It could be that it was passed along by your mother, right there in her womb when you were only a seedling. Isn't that right, Cole? Like hair color and whether a person has blue eyes or brown. Cole, tell her about that man and the garden peas." She stood. "He can explain it all to you. I was only half listening when he explained it to me, but I think I got the gist of it." She started for the door.

"Hold up, Whit," said Cole. He couldn't decide if he was relieved or aggravated that she was abandoning him. "Where are you go-ing?"

"I have to pick out the proper dress, don't I?"

"There's time for that later. What I want you to do now is call on the Coopers and the Beattys and invite them to join us at the church at three o'clock."

"Me?" She pointed to herself. "I can go? Alone?"

"Yes. Don't disappointment me by taking the most circuitous route."

"Oh, I won't. Straight there. Straight back." She hurried over to the sofa, but the first generous hug was for Rhyne, not her brother. "Thank you. This is your doing. I don't know how exactly, but I know that it is." She threw her arms around Cole. "Thank you. You are an excellent brother."

He waited until Whitley was flying up the steps before he spoke. "I'm always excellent when she gets something she's wanted."

"She can't appreciate that telling her no sometimes makes you an excellent brother as well." Rhyne paused and gave him a frank look. "Do not confuse that with being an excellent husband."

He leaned over and did what he'd wanted to do since she'd joined him on the sofa. He kissed her. "No confusion."

Rhyne touched her lips as if she could seal the stamp of his mouth there. She smiled behind her fingertips. "Is Whitley right?" she asked. "Am I somehow responsible for her being allowed to go out alone?"

"You tried to tell me once before that it was safe for her to be out, or as safe as it can be for any young woman. I know now what you left unsaid."

"It's still unsaid," she reminded him.

"But understood."

"You know Whitley will dawdle."

"Also understood. It's in her nature to be curious." He glanced at the bookshelves. "Bred in the bone, perhaps. Like decency." His eyes found the slim volume on genetics tucked between Darwin's *On the Origin of Species by Natural Selection* and *The Descent of Man.* Cole knew Whitley's fingerprints would be all over them, just as they were all over *Burnside's Illustrated Anatomy.* "It's an interesting idea that she has about decency. I don't know if her hypothesis would hold up to scientific scrutiny, but I like the way she thinks about things."

"She said it was what your father told her."

"He might have. I don't know. I can imagine him saying it." He smiled. "I can imagine Whitley doing something that provoked him to say it."

Rhyne raised her legs and folded them to the side, positioning herself in that way tucked her closer against Cole. She watched him stretch his legs and felt the tension ease out of his taut frame. They sat there as if the clock wasn't ticking behind them, as if they had nowhere to be in five hours. It felt right, and neither of them stirred.

"We could have a social after," Rhyne said, mulling it over even as she spoke. "Not today. Today is for us. But later, maybe Saturday. That'd be enough time for Estella to do a spread like she said she would. We could ask folks to bring a little dish to help her out. We could ask Sir Nigel, too. He'd want to show off the Commodore's fine cooking. There'd be dancing. I bet that no-account Beatty boy would play the piano. They've got one in the saloon. Ned Beaumont plays a banjo and there'd be Doug Porter and Abe Dishman to play fiddle."

Cole rested his cheek against her hair. "You'd want that?"

"It'd be a social. It wouldn't be just because we got married."

"It wouldn't?"

"No. It would be an end-of-winter social." She raised her eyes and stared out the window. Sunshine lightened the azure sky and made the frost flowers in the corner of every pane of glass glisten brightly. Snow clung to pine boughs and limned tree limbs shaved of their leaves since autumn. There were drifts leaning against the north face of the house and mounds of snow on either side of the porch steps and walkway. She didn't need Sid Walker to tell her that mountain spring was still a long way off. "A midwinter social, then. People need that."

"Have you ever been to one?"

She shook her head. "Not exactly." Rhyne wasn't looking at him, but she knew there was an eyebrow being raised in her direction. "Rusty and Randy went. They left the house after Judah was sleeping, and I followed them. They danced with all the girls and twirled each other around when the girls were taken. They both got drunk and carried on and got a good lickin' when they stumbled home in the middle of the night, but they told me later that it was worth it."

"What about you?"

"No one knew I was there. I watched everything from the roof of the fancy house. It had a trellis back then that made it easy to climb. It seemed to me that everyone had a fine time raising a ruckus."

Cole thought back to the dinner parties and opening night galas that he'd attended over the years. There'd been teas and luncheons and balls that went on well after midnight. He'd accepted invitations engraved in gold leaf, offered his hand to dozens of young women in need of a dance partner, and presented his card at the door when he called on them later. On Caroline's arm, he'd gone to christenings and farewell parties. He'd been present when her cousin made her debut, and he'd escorted her to the theater and to the races.

What he'd never done, he realized now, was raise a ruckus.

"I want to dance with you," he said.

She turned her head. "Now?"

"Always," he said. "I want to dance with you always."

Rhyne wore her finest dress, the one she kept at the back of her armoire because she couldn't bear to ruin it with water spots or flecks of mud. The batiste handkerchief dress had a closely fitting cuirass bodice and pleated draping. The sweep of the bustle was not pronounced and the clean, almost masculine tailoring did not allow for more ornamentation than lace cuffs at the wrist and ruching along the high neckline. The batiste was the color of cherry blossoms and complemented her ebony hair and slate gray eyes.

She was ready at two o'clock, or thought she was. Rose and Rachel arrived unexpectedly, sent Cole away, and cornered Rhyne in her bedroom. Rose trimmed and dressed her hair with combs decorated with seed pearls while Rachel used a light touch to apply rouge to her lips and cheeks. She brushed Rhyne's forehead and nose with powder and dabbed her wrists with perfume. Rose fussed with a pair of pearl earrings until she realized that Rhyne's lobes weren't pierced.

"I don't suppose there's anything to be done about that now," Rose said, eyeing Rhyne's reflection in the mirror. "Still, if we put a cape over your shoulders . . ."

"You're not drawing blood," Rachel said. "Goodness, look at her. I think she's overwhelmed."

Rhyne was, but it was because her heart was so full. She stared back at them, her eyes too big for her face, and didn't say a word.

"Of course she's overwhelmed," said Rose. "Yesterday she was trying to figure out why some man would want to marry her, and now she's about thirty minutes from putting herself in that same some man's hands."

"I think we know who 'some man' is, Rose." Rachel picked up one of Rhyne's hands and began to buff her nails. "You love him, don't you?" she asked, watching Rhyne closely. "Because that would be a good start."

Rhyne nodded.

Rose's fingers fluttered at the back of Rhyne's neck, arranging tendrils of hair that wouldn't stay in the combs. "He'd be a damn fool if he didn't return the sentiment," she said stoutly. She finished with Rhyne's hair and stepped back to survey what she and Rachel had wrought. "Exquisite."

Rachel gave Rhyne back her hand and took the other. "She's talking about you," she told Rhyne. "*You're* exquisite." She smiled when

Rhyne blushed. "I don't suppose you're accustomed to people complimenting your looks."

"No, Ma'am." Self-conscious, Rhyne touched the bridge of her nose with her fingertip.

"Ma'am?" asked Rachel. "Where did that come from?"

"Runt, I reckon. He comes out when my regular thoughts freeze."

"Now, that's handy," said Rose.

Rachel's look was quelling, but Rose only grinned. "I hardly remember my wedding day," Rachel said. "My first wedding day, that is. It wasn't in the church at all. Wyatt and I got married in his law office with Judge Wentworth saying what needed to be said. Sid Walker and Henry Longabach looked on. Every part of me was frozen. Do you feel something like that?"

"I do," said Rhyne.

"Keep those two words in your head," Rose told her. "You'll do fine. You won't need Runt at all."

As it happened, Rose Beatty was right. Even frozen, Rhyne remembered the important things. She repeated her words flawlessly, reciting each solemn promise with a gravity equal to Pastor Duun's. While the minister didn't seem to realize she'd captured his intonation and accent in her responses, Cole did, and when they turned to face the gathering as husband and wife for the first time, he didn't try to suppress his grin any longer. He bent Rhyne over his arm and kissed her until all the blood rushed to her head. There was stomping and clapping and hoots of laughter, and it echoed in Cole's ears long after they left the church.

He'd raised his first ruckus.

Saturday evening, the town turned out for the midwinter social. Organized by Mrs. Longabach with the able assistance of the Physician Search Committee, every sort of food appeared on the tables in the Commodore hotel, the Miner Key Saloon, and Miss Adele's. The three businesses were in spitting distance of one another, and with it being too cold to eat and dance out of doors, the committee looked to another solution that would accommodate the expected turnout.

It was Mrs. Cassidy who suggested that the feasting should be a progression. They would begin with soups and salads and breads in the Miner Key. The tables in the Commodore would hold hot dishes: vegetables, meat and fish, potatoes and noodles. Miss Adele's had room for desserts, which they all agreed was fitting. People could eat backward or forward or stay in one place and have their fill of whatever they liked. Liquor was available everywhere, but so was café noir and Russian tea.

The soups arrived in large tureens. Potato, cream of pea, vegetable, mushroom, and kornlet were the most popular, but there was a good deal of interest in Mrs. Easter's cream of celery and the iced bouillon soup provided by the Commodore chef. Fresh greens for salads were not available, but there were delicious offerings made with dried apples and nuts and clear sauces, some tart, some sweet. Cottage cheese was flavored with dollops of apple butter, and pickled string bean salads were arranged on plates with thinly sliced radishes all around. The breads were as varied as the soups. Tables seemed to sag under the weight of baskets of rolls and braided loaves.

It was the same in the Commodore. Fish and fowl, beef and mutton and pork, it was all there in a variety of sauces, braised and broiled, roasted and stewed. The potatoes were served whole or mashed or scalloped, and the noodles were seasoned with herbs and butter or swam in gravy. There were platters heaped with turnips, pickled cauliflower, and stewed tomatoes.

At Miss Adele's, trays of cakes, pies, and cookies covered every flat surface in both parlors and the dining room. Four flavors of ice cream, caramel sauce, and chopped walnuts, compliments of Sir Nigel, were available in the kitchen.

Rhyne held on to Cole's arm, too dazed by what she saw to even think about picking up a plate. "I've never seen the like."

Neither had Cole. At formal dinner parties, he was used to food coming in waves from the kitchen, prepared by cooks that remained largely invisible and carried to the table by servants that were wounded if they brought attention to themselves. This was a banquet, a feast of such immense proportion that it was difficult to comprehend.

Rhyne wore the dress she'd worn at their wedding. It wasn't her first choice, but Whitley convinced her that she'd bring more notice to herself by wearing something plain and everyday than by wearing her finest. It was a good argument, and when Rhyne walked into the Miner Key, she saw immediately that Whitley had known better than she. The miners in particular were turned out in their very best.

The men had brushed off their top hats and frock coats. They wore trousers that were checked and striped and often paired them with vests of opposing patterns. Their shirt fronts and band collars were pristine white, and their wives or mothers must have made sure they scrubbed under their nails because Rhyne often caught them admiring their hands as they lifted their drinks.

The women wore batiste and velvet and fine wool. A few wore silk with cashmere shawls.

The colors were all from nature's palette: moss green; apple blossom; poppy red. The jewelry was jet and ivory and pearl. Women daintily lifted their skirts to show off embroidered slippers and kid boots. Their hands fluttered to their hair to secure combs, or to their neck to make certain a favorite brooch was still in place.

Cole bent his head toward Rhyne and spoke so he couldn't be overheard by any of the score of people pressing in on them. "Would you rather be sitting on Miss Adele's roof?"

Smiling, Rhyne shook her head. "I like this view just fine."

"Good," he said, straightening and looking over the assembly. "You're the reason it's all happening."

"More like we're the excuse. I reckon just about everyone was pining to show off their finery."

"I don't know about that." He lifted his chin to indicate where the crowd was three deep at the soup table. Johnny Winslow looked distinctly uncomfortable. He was tugging on his stiff collar as though he needed to make room for his Adam's apple. The lovely Molly Showalter stood in front of him fussing with his shirt bib and chasing away his hand from his throat. She was smiling. He was suffering.

Rhyne watched Johnny and Molly for a moment, recognized the intimacy inherent in

Molly's quick and busy gestures. She turned to Cole and looked him over. She was not particularly surprised to find not so much as a loose thread or a hair out of place, but it was annoying because she had an itch to straighten something. He wore his single-breasted tailcoat with more ease than most of the men crowding the bar. His dress collar didn't appear to bother him in the least, and his black cravat was folded simply and fastened with a diamond stickpin. His silver-threaded silk vest fit him as comfortably as his own skin. His trousers were pressed flat, and his shoes were still as polished as when he put them on.

Rhyne sighed. As far as she could tell he was untouched by a single crease or dust mote. "It's not natural," she said.

Cole politely inclined his head toward her and pointed to his ear to indicate he hadn't heard her over the laughter and animated conversation all around.

Cupping her hand to her mouth, she raised herself on tiptoe and spoke into his ear. "You ought not to look so damn fine."

Cole grinned. He caught her by the wrist and at the waist and brought her flush against his chest, holding her steady on her toes. He was aware of a murmur of excitement around him. "I think they expect me to kiss you."

"You'll get wrinkled."

He regarded her oddly. "I have no idea what

you mean by that." Rhyne started to explain, but her parted lips presented the opportunity Cole was waiting for. He settled his mouth firmly over hers, and they both heard the swell of voices. It was a quick kiss, a stolen kiss, but it tempered the mood of the guests.

When Rhyne stepped back, she surveyed him again. Because the single hair that clung to the shoulder of his tailcoat was as black as the fabric, Rhyne almost didn't see it. Naturally, it was her hair. Coleridge Monroe did not crease, gather dust, nor apparently did he shed. Still, her smile was practically gleeful as she plucked the hair from his coat. With a little flourish, she smoothed over the material for good measure.

"Feel better?" he asked.

She nodded. "As a matter of fact, I do."

"Good. Let's see if we can get something to eat."

There was room enough for dancing in the saloon and the hotel and a sufficient number of musicians for both. People wandered from table to table among the three sites, eating and drinking their fill as they visited neighbors and congratulated the newlyweds, sometimes more than once. Eventually they divided themselves between the Miner Key and the Commodore when fiddlers and banjo players began tuning their instruments.

Will Beatty took his place at the piano in the saloon and played some scales to get a feel for the instrument. He grinned at Rose as she looked over the sheet music. "I know you favor songs with words," he told her. "But I got something I want to play for Cole and Rhyne. Wave them over here."

Rose raised her hand holding the sheet music and shook it to catch Cole's attention. She could barely see Rhyne for the press of people, but when Cole began to move, the crowd parted for him. It generally took a badge to make that happen and Rose was duly impressed. He had his hands on Rhyne's waist and was steering her forward.

Rose fanned Rhyne with the sheet music. The new bride was looking flushed and a little out of breath. "You can't keep kissing her every chance you get," she told Cole. "You're going to make her faint from good fortune."

Cole chuckled. "I wish that was the problem."

Rhyne put out a hand to stop Rose. "It's the crush."

That no-account Beatty boy swiveled around on the piano stool. "Too many people suckin' on the same air. That's what it is. Since there's no help for it, are you ready to dance? I figure there's still space enough to do that. I have a song picked out for you."

Cole looked at Rhyne. She was worrying her bottom lip and her eyes were mildly anxious. "We don't have to dance," he said.

"If you'd rather not."

"Oh, no. I want to."

Nothing in her expression indicated she was looking forward to it. He knew Will and Rose saw it, too. "Rhyne?"

"I *want* to," she insisted. Before she lost her nerve, she seized Cole's hand in one of hers and put her other hand on his shoulder. "You better start playing, Will."

That no-account Beatty boy didn't miss a beat. He signaled to the fiddlers to follow his cue and then his fingers were moving lightly across the keys and the first strains of Strauss's *Blue Danube* waltz lifted into the air.

Cole looked down at his wife. A tiny crease had appeared between her eyebrows, and her lips were moving faintly as she counted out the three-quarter time waiting for him to start. "I'm a fool," he whispered, "but follow me anyway."

She did. It seemed to Rhyne that her feet hardly touched the floor as he made her part of the waltz's lilting melody. After three turns, she even stopped counting and looked away from his diamond stickpin and into his eyes. She ventured a smile. The crowd faded, the room opened up, and for as long as the music played it was just the two of them moving as though they were one.

Cole didn't want to let her go. When the waltz ended, he would have liked to spirit her away. There was no one present that was going to allow that to happen, and he reluctantly gave Rhyne over to Henry Longabach as Will changed tunes. Cole invited Estella to dance. He took a turn with Rachel when Wyatt claimed Rhyne. It was Ann Marie Easter who warned him he'd be lucky to get another dance with his bride, and he knew she was right when Digger Hammond left Whitley's side long enough to partner Rhyne in one of the reels.

Rhyne laughed a trifle breathlessly as she was spun from Artie Showalter into another pair of arms. She expected to be twirled or tipped or taken up in a bear hug, but none of those things happened. Her new partner remained rooted to the floor, holding her almost at arm's length, steadying her when his immobility caused her to finally stumble.

"My God," Elijah Wentworth whispered. "You really are just like her."

Rhyne looked up into gray eyes not so very different from her own.

"Delia," the judge said. "You're Delia reborn."

CHAPTER 13

Cole pulled the stickpin from his neck cloth and placed it in the black lacquered box on top of the chest of drawers. Out of the corner of his eye, he watched Rhyne at the small vanity that they had moved together from her bedroom into the one they shared. She was sitting on the velvet tuffet with her back to the mirror and staring at nothing in particular on the far wall. Her fingers trailed idly along the buttons of her cuirass bodice, but she hadn't opened a single one thus far.

She'd been vaguely distracted since leaving the social and had started forcing a smile before that. He was the one that suggested leaving. Music and laughter followed them all the way home, and even now when he moved toward the window, he could hear Abe Dishman's energetic fiddling above the sound of chatter and song. He imagined it would be nearing dawn before the last of the revelers wandered home or fell asleep where they dropped.

"Whitley enjoyed herself this evening," said Cole. "I don't think she was without a partner all night. Even the Morrison boy asked her to dance, and I don't think Digger liked it." Rhyne nodded, but Cole wondered if it wasn't simply a response to the sound of his voice. She was still pensive. "Ned Beaumont told me that the Showalters took delivery of a two-headed calf yesterday."

"Mmm."

Cole shrugged out of his tailcoat, hung it in the armoire, and closed the door with just enough force to cause Rhyne to start. She turned her head and stared at him, her dark eyebrows drawn.

"Is something wrong?" she asked.

"I don't know. I just told you the Showalters have a two-headed calf and you took it in stride."

"You said that?"

He nodded.

"I'm sorry." Rhyne began to unbutton her bodice. "Did you notice that Whitley danced all night? Digger looked fit to be tied when the Morrison boy took a turn with her."

"You don't say."

She didn't miss his wry smile. "What?" she asked as she shimmied out of her dress.

"Rhyne, I said the very same thing to you moments ago."

"You did?"

"I did." He stooped to pick up her gown

when she stepped out of it. "Do you want to tell me what happened that you're so preoccupied? Will says I should assume I'm at fault, but you don't seem angry, just absent."

"You were talking to that no-account Beatty boy about me?"

"No," Cole said patiently. "Credit me with a little more sense than that, please. That was Will's advice to me after the wedding. He seemed to think it was important that I knew. Apparently it was something Wyatt passed on to him, and he set great store by it."

Rhyne rolled her eyes. She sat on the tuffet again to remove her shoes and stockings.

"Well?" asked Cole.

She didn't look at him. "Judge Wentworth told me I was my mother reborn."

Cole laid Rhyne's gown over the back of a chair. He hunkered down in front of her and helped her with her kid boots. She'd only managed to fumble with the laces.

"It was startling," she said. "He's never spoken to me before. I didn't know he even knew who I was, and then he says that. Why did he think he could say that to me?"

"Perhaps he thought he was complimenting you."

"It didn't seem like a compliment, and I didn't thank him for being kind enough to say so. It seemed like he couldn't help himself."

"Maybe he couldn't." Cole removed

Rhyne's boots and began to roll down her stockings.

"He stared at me, and kept on staring even when I stared back."

"Did you ask him how he knew your mother?"

Rhyne shook her head. "I wanted to. I wanted to in the worst way, but it wasn't the right place, not with the music swirling around my head and folks singing and drinking. It wouldn't have been right to talk about her there, not for me, and I don't think for the judge, either." She took her stockings from Cole's hands and clutched them in her lap. "I reckon I'm being fanciful, but it seemed to me that the judge wanted to pretend he was dancing with Delia."

"Maybe it's not a fancy." Cole wrestled with what he should tell Rhyne about his conversation with Elijah Wentworth at Miss Adele's, and whether he should mention it at all. At the time, he'd thought it was the judge's story to relate, that Rhyne needed to hear it firsthand, especially when Wentworth was on his way out of town and unavailable to answer any of her questions. Cole tried to imagine how she might react to his silence but saw the trap in that soon enough. The truth was, he couldn't let what she would do sway his decision either to continue his silence or break it.

He stood and went over to the bed to sit.

His cheeks puffed a little as he exhaled deeply. He was aware of Rhyne studying him, already alert to some shift in his manner that he hadn't quite contained.

"Do you recall that I invited the judge to dinner a while back?" he asked.

"Yes. You wanted Whitley to hear what he had to say about female lawyers."

"That's right." He pushed his fingers through his hair, ruffling it for the first time all evening. "But that was more of an after-thought, not the purpose." He continued his explanation, watching Rhyne's features still until they were as impenetrable as a mask. When he finished speaking, her knuckles showed whitely against the stockings. "You were hardly talking to me at the time because I'd gone to Miss Adele's, but that had noth-ing to do with why I didn't tell you. I thought it was his place, not mine."

"So you let him ambush me in public."

"Do you really believe that?"

Rhyne lowered her eyes and stared at her hands. She finally shook her head, shamed by her accusation.

"I never saw the judge tonight until he was dancing with you. I certainly didn't expect he'd lose himself that way. Had he been drinking?"

She shrugged. "He didn't smell for it, or at least no worse than anyone else." After a mo-ment, she looked at Cole again. "Do you think he really loved my mother? More than just as an admirer, I mean."

"I don't know. It's one of the things I hoped he would tell you privately. He sought me out, Rhyne. There was intent, I believe. He wanted to learn something about Delia's daughter."

"I never heard anyone say that he had a curiosity about me when I was Delia's son."

"Perhaps because he couldn't see the resemblance."

She considered that and admitted, "Runt *did* make it a practice to avoid the judge."

"Any specific reason?"

"General principle." She made a swipe at her cheek with her fingertips and then held them up for Cole to see. "Do you know it can still surprise me to discover they're clean? I don't suppose there's a reason the judge should have seen through Runt Abbot's grime when no one else did." More thoughtful now, she smoothed the stockings in her lap, folded them, and placed them on the vanity behind her. "Do you suppose he'll remember your invitation?"

"We can ask him again. It might be better if it comes from you."

She nodded. "I'll ask Whitley to help me compose a proper one." Her eyes brightened a fraction. "And I can finally use that scented paper she gave me. It'll smell real nice."

Gunpoint couldn't have persuaded Cole to

explain that scented paper was not used for dinner invitations, at least ones that weren't intended to be intimate. "I cannot speak for his honor," he said diplomatically, "but I'd appreciate one like that."

She got up and walked over to him. His legs parted immediately, making room for her between them. She put her hands on his shoulders while he settled his on her waist. "Maybe I'll send you one, too."

"That'd be fine."

"Could be it'd be for something besides dinner."

"Ah, then may I suggest that you compose it on your own?"

She chuckled. "Whatever ideas your sister gets, she won't be getting them from me."

Cole's mouth flattened. "Digger."

"More likely she's giving that boy ideas. They spent a lot of time at Miss Adele's tonight."

"The desserts were there."

"They certainly were."

"You don't think they —"

Rhyne placed a finger perpendicular to his lips. "No, I don't. I think they were gorging themselves on ice cream and caramel sauce, but it was worth mentioning just to see your face."

Toppling her back on the bed, Cole exacted his revenge in a way that satisfied them both.

■ ■ ■ ■

One week later, Judge Elijah Wentworth became the dinner guest of the Monroes. Whitley conducted herself with all the social graces she learned from her mother, and while she certainly did honor to the memory of Margaret Brookes Monroe, her demeanor was so correct that Cole spent a fair amount of time anticipating the onset of disaster. All that goodness unnerved him.

Whitley's behavior had the opposite effect on Rhyne. She began the meal unnerved and by following Whitley's example, found her ease as dinner progressed. At no point did Whitley allow the conversation to become awkward or veer into subjects that were better discussed privately. Rhyne had no idea if that was because Whitley was ignorant of what occurred at the social or if it was because she knew at least some part of it. Her experience with Cole's sister led her to believe there was every possibility it was the latter.

It was as Rhyne was clearing the table so she could serve dessert and coffee that she noticed Whitley's attention was flagging and that her interest seemed less than genuine. "Please excuse us, Judge, but I need Whitley's help in the kitchen."

Both men stood as Whitley dutifully rose to

assist Rhyne. She gathered the things that Rhyne couldn't carry and followed her into the hallway. As soon as they were in the kitchen, she hurried to put her dishes in the sink and then leaned over it.

Rhyne emptied her arms of platters and cutlery and went to stand beside Whitley. "What's wrong? You're flushed."

Whitley shook her head. "I don't know. I started to feel odd before we sat down. A little queasy and hot and —" She pushed Rhyne away and vomited violently into the sink.

Rhyne's initial reaction was to press one hand against her stomach and the other over her mouth to keep from retching. She gagged once before she managed to control the response. Breathing deeply, she stepped back to Whitley's side and placed her palm against the girl's back. She rubbed gently as Whitley's narrow frame shook with spasms. Even after Whitley emptied her entire dinner into the sink, she continued to heave.

Rhyne glanced behind her and down the hallway to see if Cole perhaps had heard and was on his way to lend assistance. The cavalry was not coming. She pumped water to rinse away the waste while Whitley leaned weakly against the sink. When Whitley's shudders subsided, she asked, "Will you take a glass of water?"

Whitley only nodded faintly. Her fingers were trembling when Rhyne thrust the glass into her hands.

Rhyne kept her palm just beneath the glass in the event Whitley lost her grip. "Just a few sips," she said. "Then rinse your mouth."

Whitley did as she was told. "I want to sit down."

"Of course." Rhyne took the glass away and pulled out a chair. She hovered until Whitley dropped into it. "I'm getting your brother."

"No!" Whitley surprised them both with the strength of the grip she put on Rhyne's arm. "No," she repeated more softly. "Don't tell him I was sick. It will ruin the evening."

"Whitley, you can't return to the table."

"Make an excuse for me. Tell him I have a headache. I do. It wouldn't be a lie."

"I can't do that."

"But the judge will leave."

"So we'll invite him again."

"But —" She stopped because she really was too weak to argue. Her shoulders sagged with the realization that she was defeated.

Rhyne took immediate advantage. "I'm getting Cole so he can help you to your room. I can't very well escort you past the dining room without him seeing us." She made certain Whitley was squarely in the chair before she left.

It was an animated conversation that she interrupted in the dining room. Both men looked up as she entered, the judge politely, Cole rather more curiously when he saw her

461

hands were empty. "Pardon me," she said, "but Whitley's taken ill suddenly. Cole, she needs to lie down. Will you make certain she manages the stairs?"

Cole rose to his feet, excusing himself at the same time. "I won't be long," he promised.

Judge Wentworth watched him go. He asked Rhyne, "Is there something I can do?"

She shook her head, her tongue suddenly cleaving to the roof of her mouth.

The judge stood, walked to Rhyne's chair at the foot of the table and pulled it out for her. "Please, won't you sit down?"

Rhyne hesitated. "I should —" Her eyes darted toward the hallway as she heard Whitley and Cole approaching. She took her seat to keep the judge's attention from wandering in that direction. Whitley deserved a dignified escape after her splendid performance at dinner. "Thank you," she said as Judge Wentworth pushed in her chair. Her gaze fell on the empty table. "I'm sorry. I didn't think to bring the cake and coffee." She started to rise, but he waved her back down and returned to his chair.

"There's no reason not to wait for Dr. Monroe," he said. "I'd have a hard time doing justice to your cake right now, although I certainly would make the effort. The meal was delicious, and I thank you for it."

Rhyne managed a weak smile. The judge

was studying her again, but at least this time his regard was thoughtful, not merely stunned.

"Did your father teach you to cook?"

All of Rhyne's earlier anxieties returned, and she had a renewed appreciation for Whitley's role as the gracious, conversational go-between. "My brothers taught me," she said. Her mouth was dry. She wished she'd remembered the coffee. "Judah never cooked except sometimes for himself. Mostly he barked orders if he wanted something done a particular way."

"So Rusty and Randy were your mentors." He made a sound at the back of his throat that registered his surprise. "I never thought those boys did much more than raise hell."

"They did that, too." She shrugged. "They weren't so bad when no one was around to watch them. Leastways, they could have been worse."

"I'll take your word for it." Wentworth rubbed his jaw with his knuckles. "I think I make you uncomfortable," he said. "I'm sorry for that."

Rhyne stopped fidgeting with the napkin she'd drawn into her lap, but it was pointless to pretend he was wrong about her discomfort. "You're the only one that's ever remarked that I look like her. I keep coming back to that in my mind."

The judge inclined his head sympathetically. "I can't speak for anyone else. I noticed it right off."

"Cole said you saw me before the social."

"Did he? I wondered if you knew we had talked. Forgive me, but I didn't want to raise that particular conversation if it was unknown to you."

Rhyne noticed the judge shifting slightly in his chair. His eyes, too, had drifted away from hers. "I think I've made you uncomfortable," she said, and unlike him, she did not apologize for it. "I know from Cole that you made his acquaintance at Miss Adele's."

Elijah Wentworth cleared his throat. "The doctor is forthright, I see."

"He is." She felt no need to explain that she'd only learned the entirety of their conversation a few evenings ago. "He said you saw me walking home from the Porters."

"That's right. Will Beatty pointed you out, but as I told your husband, I knew who you were the moment these old eyes fell on you."

"Why didn't you say something then?"

"Couldn't."

"Because you were with that no-account Beatty boy?"

"No. Because I couldn't speak." His slight smile was rife with self-mockery. "I don't rightly recall the rest of what Will and I were discussing. I know I said all the proper things because he never asked if I'd just been mule-kicked, but that's what happened. You walked

464

through my line of sight, and I got mule-kicked."

Rhyne didn't know what to say. She was relieved to hear Cole's footsteps on the stairs. Her attention turned briefly to the open doorway.

Cole paused on the threshold but didn't enter. "I need to get my bag."

Rhyne frowned. "What's wrong with —"

He held up his hand. "I'll only be a few more minutes." Then he disappeared.

Judge Wentworth offered an understanding and regretful smile. "I should leave."

"No. Please don't. That is the very last thing that Whitley would want. Really, she will be sad to learn that her illness sent you away prematurely."

"So," he drawled thoughtfully, "I'm staying because it's what young Whitley wants."

"Yes." Rhyne pressed her hands together in her lap and made her admission reluctantly. "And what I want."

"Very well."

Rhyne thought that perhaps he would speak to all her unasked questions, but he merely sat there waiting for her to take the lead. "I know almost nothing about my mother," she said at last. "Judah did not encourage us to talk about her."

"He forbid it, you mean."

"Yes. He forbid it. What was she like?"

"Like no one else," he said without having

465

to think about it. "Loyal comes to mind. Strong-headed, even stubborn. She didn't look like a woman with enough grit to make the journey from Philadelphia to Pittsburgh, yet she stuck by Judah all the way to Reidsville and then a bit beyond that. Except when she was commanding the stage, her manner was soft-spoken and gentle, but she always held herself proud. She wasn't easily riled, but your brothers could do it from time to time. Rusty, I think it was, lined his pockets with candy from Morrison's. Delia took him by the ear, marched him back to the emporium to make amends, and then brought him to me to learn what the law had to say about thieves."

"All that, and Judah still waiting for him at home." Rhyne shook her head, sympathizing. "Poor Rusty."

"I don't know that Delia ever told Judah. It didn't seem as though she intended to at the time. I had the sense that she protected your brothers from the hard edge of Judah's temper."

"Then I stand corrected. Rusty was a lucky ba—" She caught the pejorative on the tip of her tongue and swallowed it. "Boy," she said instead. "He was a lucky boy."

Humor briefly brightened Elijah Wentworth's gray eyes as he watched a wave of color come and go in Rhyne's cheeks. Sobering, he absently stroked his neatly clipped beard. "I don't suppose there was anyone protecting you from the same."

Rhyne shrugged. "No one ever took a lickin' for me, if that's what you mean."

"That's what I mean." He continued to regard her thoughtfully. "I noticed you generally refer to your father as Judah. Do you address him that way?"

"It's his name."

"So it is. Did he ask you to call him that?"

"I don't remember that he ever asked me *not* to. Truth is, I don't talk to him much. Never have. Mostly it's conversation about him." Her chin thrust forward a notch. "I suppose you think my mother wouldn't have approved."

"I know she wouldn't have. She was particular about matters of respect and deference. She believed manners defined the social order."

"A snob, then."

The judge was taken aback for a moment, and then he chuckled. "If she was, she had the good manners to keep it to herself."

Rhyne remembered what Whitley had said about breeding. "Was my mother a decent sort of person?"

"She was. Gracious. Forgiving to a fault."

"Kind?"

"Yes. Patient, too."

Rhyne considered all of that before she sighed heavily. "There's the proof that I *must* be my father's daughter. No one's ever won a wager depending on me to be patient."

"Don't forget that I said Delia was steadfast and willful, or that she had enough grit to polish some of Judah's rough edges."

"I don't recollect that you said it quite that way."

"Well, I'm saying it now."

"Did you love her, Judge?"

The bald question startled Elijah Wentworth. He blinked, looked away, and blinked again. Years of presiding over trials helped him gain his composure relatively quickly. "We all —" He stopped because Rhyne's forthright stare gave him no quarter. The easy answer was not the right answer, and after all this time, Rhyne deserved more than what was convenient or safe.

"Yes," he said. "I loved your mother. I wanted to marry her."

"She was already married."

"So she reminded me every time I proposed." His slight smile hinted at his regret. "Loyal, remember? I naively thought she would change her mind. I drew up documents for a divorce, and she was properly horrified that I would take those measures without her permission."

"Why did you?"

The judge folded his hands in his lap and tapped his thumbs together. "Your mother loved me, Rhyne. She told me so, and I

468

believed her. The fact that she wouldn't leave Judah was a complication, not an end. I hoped that time and what she felt for me would whittle away at her resolve."

"Stubborn," said Rhyne. "Seems you knew about that firsthand."

"Indeed. Judah didn't like Delia being out of his sight. It's probably the reason he didn't last long at mining. He needed to know what she was doing and to whom she was speaking."

"Apparently with justification."

He frowned, disappointed by her response. "I think you judge your mother too harshly, but I'm not going to try to persuade you to do otherwise."

"Did Judah know about you?"

"I think he did, yes." His pause was almost infinitesimal. "Eventually."

"Is that why he moved the family away?"

"I've always believed so."

"Did you see her before she died?"

"I saw her twice. Both times she was with your father. I never saw her alone. We never spoke again." His voice had become a trifle husky. "I've never been what you would call a permanent resident of Reidsville. I was in Denver when she died."

Rhyne wanted to know if he had sensed her mother was gone before he learned it for a fact. She held the question back, afraid that the answer to what might be a fancy in her

469

mind would break her heart.

"Delia had a brother," the judge said. "Did you know that?" When Rhyne shook her head, he went on. "A bit older, I believe. There's every chance that he's still alive. Franklin was his Christian name. She called him Frankie, but it was Franklin Benjamin Rhyne. A tribute, I suppose, to Philadelphia's most famous citizen."

Rhyne was intrigued but not optimistic. "I reckon there are a lot of folks that honored Mr. Franklin that way. Backward and forward."

"I couldn't say. I'd be pleased to make inquiries if you'd like."

"I don't recall my brothers ever mentioning such a person."

"Perhaps they didn't know."

"Do you think there might be other kin?"

"Anything is possible."

Rhyne appreciated his guarded response. "I think I'd like it just fine if you made those inquiries," she said presently. "As long as none of them are directed at Judah."

"That never crossed my mind."

She believed him. "Is it true my mother was employed by a family as a maid?"

"That's what she told me. A maid to the young lady of the house is how she described it."

"Perhaps her brother did similar work."

"That's one direction the inquiry will take."

"I could write to my brothers, at least to Randy because he's as close as Leadville. He might remember something that could be helpful, and he won't tell Judah."

"An excellent idea. I'll consider how I might proceed this ev—" The judge turned in his chair as Rhyne's attention was suddenly focused in the doorway behind him. No special cognitive powers were needed to see that Cole Monroe was concerned and that whatever he had to say was for his wife's ears alone. Elijah Wentworth stood, and this time no one stopped him.

"I'll see myself out," he said, nodding to both of them. "Don't trouble yourselves. Please give my regards to Miss Monroe and thank her for a most intriguing debate. I hope she is well soon." He briefly rested his hand on Cole's shoulder before he quietly took his leave.

Rhyne was on her feet as soon as she heard the front door close. "Say it quickly."

"Her temperature is one hundred two degrees and indications are that it will rise. She was sick again upstairs although there was only the water you gave her left in her stomach. I gave her some bicarbonate. It remains to be seen if she'll hold it down."

"Indications," Rhyne said, not liking the ominous sound of that word. "What does that mean?"

"She's begun to cough and is complaining

of a headache. The latter could have any number of causes, certainly the fever alone can explain it, but the cough is more troubling."

"She was coughing earlier today, but when I asked her about it, she said she'd breathed in too many of the seasonings we were using. She didn't cough at all during dinner."

"Too excited, I suspect. I attributed her flush to that as well."

"What does it mean? What's wrong with her?"

Cole knew what Rhyne wanted to know, but he wasn't prepared to share his diagnostic impression just yet, not when certainty eluded him. He took Rhyne's hands in his. "She would benefit from an alcohol bath. I wonder if you —"

"Of course I will," she said. "Whitley doesn't want you doing that sort of thing for her."

His chuckle was slightly forced. "So she said before she asked for you."

Rhyne was suddenly and uncomfortably aware that Cole was studying her. His regard was not that of a husband for his wife but of a doctor for his patient. She removed her hands from his. "I know what you're doing. You might have just asked me how I'm feeling."

"How are you feeling?"

"I'm well," she said, mildly exasperated. "You?"

"The same."

"Do you expect that's going to change for either of us as suddenly as it did for Whitley?"

"It could," said Cole, and hoped to God that he was wrong.

"Then there's nothing to be done about it now. Let me go to Whitley. *You* can wash dishes."

Cole was scrubbing the roaster, all but lost in thought, when he heard his name being called. He let the roaster go and turned away from the sink, shaking out his hands. His first thought was that it must have been Rhyne, but when he looked down the hallway, he saw Wyatt Cooper standing in the entry. He waved the sheriff forward and went to meet him halfway.

Without preamble, Wyatt said, "It's Will Beatty. I managed to get him home, but you need to come right away."

Cole called up to alert Rhyne that he was leaving and where he was going. She reminded him that he'd left one of his medical bags in Whitley's room. Cole quickly took the stairs, and Rhyne met him at the top with it. "Whitley?" he asked quietly.

"Sleeping. I'm going to stay with her." Rhyne handed him the bag. "Go on. We'll be fine."

He nodded, thanked her, and kissed her on the cheek she proffered. By the time he reached the bottom of the stairs, Wyatt had the front door open. "Wait," said Cole, reaching for his coat. "You haven't told me anything. I might need more than what's in this bag."

"He's burning up. We've been riding most of the day. Did a little target shooting. He never said a word about how bad he was feeling, but I could tell something wasn't right. He started coughing, for one thing, and he didn't begin the morning like that. Seemed like he might have had a sore throat, too. We had to stop a couple of —"

Cole held up his hand. He'd heard enough. He pushed his bag at Wyatt while he shrugged into his coat and got his hat. "Everything's there," he said, indicating that Wyatt could head out the door. "But I have to tell you, I was hoping to hear that no-account Beatty boy got himself shot."

Rose was laying a damp cloth over her husband's forehead when she heard Cole and Wyatt enter the house. She called to them to come up to the bedroom. After Wyatt had helped her get Will out of his sweat-drenched clothes, she'd sent him after Cole. Except to clean out the basin after Will vomited in it, she hadn't left his side.

Now she stepped away to let Cole have her

474

place by the bed.

"Hey, Doc," Will said weakly. "Told Rose to leave you be. I don't —" A paroxysm of hard coughing cut him off.

"It seems your wife knows better than you do," said Cole.

"No surprise there," Wyatt said dryly. He found Rose's hand and gave it a gentle squeeze.

Cole shook out his thermometer while he rolled back the blankets covering Will's right shoulder. He slipped the thermometer in Will's armpit and addressed Rose. "Wyatt told me Will vomited a couple of times on the trail. Has he done it since he's been here?"

"Once. Hard enough to make me think he'd pass his stomach through his mouth, but it was mostly water."

"Mostly?"

"A little on the pinkish side, I thought."

Cole nodded. He'd already set his features to give nothing away. He turned back to Will. "Did you wake up feeling poorly? Don't talk. Just nod or shake your head."

What Will did was shrug.

"All right," said Cole. "I take that to mean you didn't feel well but not so bad that you thought you should stay home. Is that about right." This time Will nodded. "You started coughing on the trail?" When Will nodded, Cole went on. "Before noon?" Again, a nod. "Loose bowels?" Will grimaced and his already flushed face took on an even ruddier hue.

"For goodness sake, Will Beatty," said Rose. "Tell the doctor what he wants to know."

Cole turned his head to look at Rose. "Maybe if you stepped out a moment." He thought she might object. She certainly drew in a deep enough breath to suggest she meant tell him what she thought of his suggestion, but then she exhaled slowly and nodded. Indicating that she was going to put on a kettle for tea, she left the room.

"Loose bowels?" asked Cole as soon as she was gone.

Will nodded and held up two fingers.

"Twice," Cole interpreted. "All right. Let me see how high your fever is." He removed the thermometer, read it, and then shook it out. "One hundred two point five." He soaked a small cotton pad in alcohol and wiped the instrument clean before returning it to his bag. "I need to look you over," he told Will. "Did Rose strip you down to your drawers?"

"She took it all." He turned on his side, drawing up his knees as another fit of coughing strained his lean and wiry frame. He was slightly out of breath when he finished, but that didn't stop him from adding, "My wife likes me naked."

At the foot of the bed, Wyatt rolled his eyes but couldn't quite keep from grinning. "I'm going downstairs to sit with Rose. Holler if you need me."

Cole nodded. He sat on the edge of the bed and gestured to Will to turn on his back. When Will was settled, Cole drew down the blankets and sheet as far as his waist. Will's abdomen was blotched by a light rash that appeared to be climbing toward his chest. "Did Rose remark on this?"

Will raised his head a fraction to look down at himself. The effort strained his features but his surprise was still visible. Dropping back, he shook his head.

Cole understood that meant the rash was a very recent symptom, appearing perhaps within the last hour. He got out his stethoscope and listened to Will's heart, and then helped him onto his side just long enough to take measure of his lungs.

Cole let the stethoscope dangle from his neck. He tapped Will's chest with his fingertips and then pressed more firmly against his abdomen. Liver. Stomach. Small and large intestines.

"Jesus, Doc!" Will groaned and tried to knock away Cole's hand as firm pressure was applied to his bowels. He managed to ask if Cole was trying to kill him before another bout of painful coughing stole his breath.

There was an empty glass on the bedside table. Cole picked it up and waited for the coughing to subside. "Don't swallow," he said quickly as Will quieted. He slid a hand under Will's head to help him raise it and put the glass to his lips. "Spit."

Will did. His saliva was tinged pink.

Cole put the glass aside and eased Will's head back on the pillow. He watched the deputy's eyes stray uneasily toward the glass. "Are you more comfortable on your side?" he asked. When Will indicated that he was, Cole assisted him getting into that position and rearranged the covers. He put the stethoscope away. "I'm going to mix some bicarbonate for you. That will ease your stomach distress. I'll speak to Rose about what she can do."

Will was still looking at the glass. "Is it consumption?" His gaze suddenly locked on Cole. "You can tell me, Doc. I want to know."

"It's not consumption, Will. I promise."

Only partially reassured, Will asked, "Then what is it?"

Cole picked up the glass as he got to his feet. He set it carefully in his bag so that it wouldn't tip. "I'll know in the morning. Rest for now. That's my best advice." He closed his satchel but remained a while longer at Will's side, waiting for some sign that the deputy meant to sleep. When Will shut his eyes, he left.

Wyatt and Rose simultaneously looked up from their tea when Cole entered the kitchen. Rose stood to get a cup for Cole, but he waved her back and set his bag on the table.

"Do you have bicarbonate?" he asked. "I have some if you don't."

"I have it here," she said.

"Good. Put a teaspoonful in a glass of water and get Will to drink it down. I'm going to stop at Caldwell's and ask Chet to make an infusion of peppermint, caraway, and fennel. That should help with the dyspepsia."

Rose was immediately hopeful. "That's all it is? Indigestion?"

"That's a symptom of what it is." Cole's glance strayed to Wyatt. "How are you feeling?"

He took a moment to do an inventory. "Fine, I guess."

"Good. The same question to you, Rose."

She paused just as Wyatt had. "I'm good."

Cole's shoulders relaxed a fraction. He asked Wyatt, "Did Rachel have any complaints this morning?"

"No." He frowned. "Why would she?"

Cole stood behind a vacant chair and braced his arms on the back rail. His nostrils flared slightly as he drew in a breath. "Whitley's ill," he said. "It seemed to come on suddenly, although she might have been hiding her distress because she wanted to entertain the judge this evening. Her symptoms are almost identical to Will's. She doesn't have the rash yet, but I suspect that will come."

Wyatt understood then. "Will and your

sister are just the first."

"That we know of," said Cole. "I'm afraid so."

Rose's fingers tightened on her teacup. She wished it was a whiskey bottle and thought she probably wasn't alone in wanting to make it so. "What can I do for Will?"

"Don't let him get dehydrated. I don't think the water's the problem, but boil it for now. Give him tea. Chamomile. Peppermint. Both are fine. I don't know if you'll get sick, Rose. If you're fine now, maybe you won't. It's hard to say, but you have to do things so that caring for Will doesn't make you sick. Don't share a glass. Don't use the same plate or utensils. When you change his linens, especially if he soils himself, separate that bedding from everything else. I beg you not to send it out to Maggie Porter for laundering. Wash it here in boiling water."

Cole made certain he had her full attention. "And wash your hands, Rose. Wash them before you cook, before you eat, and always, *always* after you care for Will. Do you understand?"

Wide-eyed, she nodded slowly.

"Good. It's because I lost that fight to Dr. Erwin at St. John of God that I'm here at all. I have just enough of my father in me to make losing again unacceptable." He picked up his bag. "You coming, Wyatt?"

The sheriff's chair scraped the floor as he

pushed it back. "I'll check on you later, Rose."

"No. You go home. Be with Rachel." Her smile was a trifle uneven. "Whatever's coming our way already proved it has no respect for the law." She didn't get up to escort the men out. When the front door closed, she pushed her cup aside, folded her hands and began to pray.

Outside, Wyatt stopped Cole before they reached the street. "Is it typhus?"

"Not typhus. Typhoid fever. It's an important distinction." Cole started walking again.

Wyatt caught up and fell in step beside him, matching his long stride. "Why didn't you tell Rose?"

"I haven't even told Rhyne. It's still suspicion not fact. I have some of Will's spit in a glass in my bag. I'm going to examine it under the microscope as soon as I get home. A stool sample would have been better." He didn't think he needed to explain that Whitley would provide one with marginally less outrage than that no-account Beatty boy. "I don't want to start a panic, Wyatt. There are always people that get sick because they expect to get sick. The fewer of them, the better. If I'm correct, and it *is* enteric fever, then the best hope for all of us is that I can identify the source."

"The source?" asked Wyatt. "Not the cause?"

"The cause is *Salmonella typhi.* The source might be water or food or —." He bit off what he'd been about to say, concerned that he was getting ahead of himself. "Maybe both," he said as if that had been his thought.

"Not vermin? Not filth?"

"No. That's typhus. Reidsville is hardly a breeding ground for that plague. City tenements. Immigrant ghettos. That's where you'll find that disease. The bacillus I'm speaking of was identified only four years ago. It's the subject of considerable study, and there's still the question of a vaccine. Something akin to what Jenner discovered for smallpox would be the hope."

"Your research?"

"No. I'm afraid not. I've studied it, of course, but not here. My research is as much chemical as it is biological. I'm formulating and evaluating stains that will show the presence of different types of bacteria. If I'm successful, it's a step that will further promote the acceptance of germ theory."

"Sounds like it might be important."

Cole smiled briefly. "It sounds like I told you more than you wanted to know."

Wyatt shook his head. "No. You didn't. This is about the town . . . about Rachel. I want to know everything. I don't like feeling helpless."

Neither did Cole. He stopped walking. When Wyatt turned, moonlight illuminated

482

the tin star on his coat. Cole looked at it and then glanced down at the leather bag in his hand. "We're both unarmed," he said after a moment. He hefted the bag. "There's no cure in here. There's no cure anywhere. If it's enteric fever, then it will have to run its course. That's weeks, Wyatt, not days. Some people will die. I can treat the symptoms, but I can't treat the disease."

Wyatt nodded heavily. "If Rachel . . ." He couldn't finish. He clenched his jaw and didn't try to speak again.

"If Rachel contracts the fever," Cole said quietly, "there's almost no chance that she'll keep the baby, or if she does, that it will be born alive. I'm sorry, Wyatt. That's what you wanted to know, wasn't it?"

"Yes." His lips barely moved around the word.

Cole suddenly remembered what Rachel told him in confidence. Wyatt had already lost a wife and an unborn child. The weight on the man's shoulders was visible in Cole's eyes. "Don't assume that she'll be one of the victims. You won't be able to think straight, and right now I'm depending on your ability to do just that. Until I know the source, you're going to have to enforce a quarantine on the town. No one in. No one out." Black humor asserted itself as he set out again. "You might have cause to strap on a gun for that."

"Find the source, Doc," Wyatt said darkly, "and I won't have to use it on you."

Rhyne and Wyatt sat quietly on stools in one corner of the surgery while Cole prepared glass slides for the microscope. He had collected his journals from the library and occasionally consulted his notes as he worked, fixing each sample to a slide with a small amount of water and then passing it over a flame. Afterward, he flooded the slides with crystal violet, allowing them to set a minute, rinsed them in water, and then flooded them with iodine. After another minute, he flooded them with acetone alcohol, and then tapped out ten seconds on his fingertips before he rinsed them again. He flooded them with the counterstain and waited another full minute before he rinsed them in water and carefully blotted each one dry. His concentration was absolute, and he forgot about his anxious audience once he began working.

The smear of Will's saliva was inconclusive. He tried several samples, isolating the blood cells for evidence of the obligate bacilli, but could not make out the distinctive rod shape that the stain was meant to help him see. He reviewed his methods and the publication of Hans Christian Gram's work, wondering if the fault lay in his preparation or the translation from the original.

He began again, this time with the smear

from Whitley's stool.

Watching Cole disappear into his science was a revelation to Rhyne. She knew he approached his work in a careful, serious manner, but what she was witness to now was extraordinary. His attention to every detail, and his ability to take such measured, painstaking steps in the face of a threatening crisis, filled her with awe. His face revealed nothing save for his absorption in the task at hand. There was an economy of motion that she found fascinating, the finely honed skill of a man used to manipulating objects unfamiliar to most people. He held thin glass slides up to the light and studied them as a jeweler might study the facets of a diamond. He put the slides over a flame without burning himself and immersed them in chemical baths without splashing a single drop.

She couldn't make bread without getting flour in her hair.

Rhyne's sigh was inaudible. She exchanged glances with Wyatt as Cole sat at his microscope again. Neither expended energy pretending to be hopeful. They waited.

They all felt the vibration from the beating someone was giving the house's side door. Looking up from his microscope, Cole forgot himself just long enough to allow his annoyance to show. He sucked in a breath, forced back his frustration, and started to rise.

Rhyne was already on her feet and heading

toward the entrance. "Stay where you are. Let me see what it's about."

Wyatt resumed leaning against the wall, his long legs stretched out from the stool. "We could get lucky," he said, folding his arms across his chest. "Maybe someone broke a bone."

But no one was that lucky. It was Ted Easter, and he was there about his youngest boy Alexander. Coughing. Sore throat. Fever. And a headache. "At least it's not Teddy this time," he told Rhyne after she asked him to wait a moment. "I don't think he could tolerate another ear infection. I know his mother can't."

Smiling wanly, she disappeared into the surgery and shut the doors behind her. Cole and Wyatt were waiting for her. "You heard?"

They both nodded.

"What do you want me to tell him?"

"That I'll be along directly," Cole said. "In the meantime, he should stop by Caldwell's and get the infusion I asked Chet to start preparing." He consulted his pocket watch. "Chet's probably still in his store working on it."

Rhyne's gaze dropped to the microscope. "Do you know yet?"

Cole shook his head.

Rhyne opened the pocket doors behind her and backed out of the room.

Wyatt stared at Cole. "Why didn't you tell her?"

"Because Ted Easter would have seen the dread in her eyes. She'd do better facing a couple of miscreants than a father whose son has typhoid fever."

CHAPTER 14

Rhyne took her time getting ready for bed, hoping that she'd hear Cole's light tread on the stairs before she turned back the covers. When he didn't come, she stood at the bedside and stared at the neat arrangement of pillows and smoothed over the quilt while debating what she should do. If she crawled into bed now, it would be the first time in their short marriage that he wasn't within minutes of following. She didn't like it, and she turned away, unable to bring herself to disturb the bedcovers.

After checking on Whitley one more time, Rhyne padded down the stairs in her nightgown, slippers, and shawl. She ignored the light coming from under the library doors in favor of going to the kitchen to warm some milk. She made enough for two cups and carried them to the library.

Cole was hunched over the writing desk, one hand supporting his head while he tapped out a slow, relentless tattoo on the book opened in front of him. He had removed his band collar and unbuttoned his shirt at the throat. He'd rolled his sleeves as far as his elbows, but the gesture had been an absent or a harried one because the right sleeve was fractionally shorter than the left. Runnels marked his thick hair where he'd pushed his fingers through it, and a muscle worked tirelessly in his cheek as he read. Most telling of his tension, she thought, were the long legs tucked under the chair, not stretched out in front of it.

She placed his milk on one corner of the desk and sat down in the armchair to sip hers. When he finally looked up, she smiled because his surprise was so evident.

"How long have you been there?" he asked.

She shrugged. "Not so long that your milk's gone cold."

His eyes strayed to the cup on his desk. "This will not help me stay awake."

"My intent exactly."

"Rhyne," he said, shaking his head. "I need to —"

"Come to bed," she finished for him. "You need to sleep. You would say the same to anyone else."

The fact that she was right did not improve his humor. "I need to put it in writing. It all has to be set down in the event that I become ill. You. Wyatt. Chet Caldwell. *Someone* has to know how to proceed if I can't."

"I'm sure you're right, but it seems to me that morning is soon enough to make that start. You're bleary-eyed now from staring into that microscope, and I reckon your brain is about tuckered out from puzzling. I don't know that I'd trust anything you put to paper."

Cole very deliberately pushed the book aside and picked up the cup. He brought it to his lips. "Satisfied?"

She ignored his sardonic tone. "I looked in on Whitley," she said. "She was sleeping, but I could tell she'd been tossing and turning. I rearranged the bedcovers to keep her from throwing them off."

"Thank you."

"There's no need to thank me for doing for Whitley. I love her, same as you, and I want her well again."

Cole nodded. "Children usually fare better with typhoid than adults do, especially older adults like Sid Walker or Will's parents. For someone as young as Alex Easter, the symptoms will probably be less severe. I think it's safe to expect fewer complications. Whitley, though, she's . . ."

Rhyne saw that he couldn't complete the thought. Perhaps she was wrong to encourage him to sleep. He would never go easily. She couldn't ply him with enough warm milk to make that happen, not when he was honor bound to care for every life the way he did for his sister's.

"Whitley's not quite child, not yet adult." Rhyne said what Cole couldn't. "It's hard to know how it will turn out, isn't it?"

Cole wrapped his hands tighter around the cup and merely nodded.

To distract him, Rhyne said, "Tell me about those little pink rods again. I heard what you said before, but it's not easy making sense of it. It doesn't seem right that something so small can put that no-account Beatty boy off his stride. And Whitley? I thought it would take something like another freight train to stop her in her tracks."

The image of Whitley as a full-steam-ahead locomotive was an apt one, and it briefly roused Cole's smile. He appreciated what Rhyne was trying to do, and she wasn't wrong that his thoughts needed diverting.

After Ted Easter departed and Rhyne returned to the surgery, Cole had explained what he'd found on the slide under his microscope. He'd allowed her to look for herself. Her fascination didn't surprise him; her doubt did. He had come to expect that she would accept him at his word on all things medical, but she'd questioned him like a true skeptic.

"You've had a splinter in your finger before, haven't you?" asked Cole. "A speck of dust in your eye?"

"Of course."

"It's an imperfect comparison, but consider the discomfort and irritation both cause. Your finger will throb; your eye will water. Neither the splinter nor the speck is alive, but imagine if they were. Imagine that unlike you, neither requires oxygen to live. That means they're able to thrive in places where none exists."

Rhyne pointed to herself. "Like inside me."

"Yes. And in the process of living and reproducing, the bacilli . . . that is, the rods, produce waste that irritates the host. Human beings appear to be the perfect host for *Salmonella typhi*. No one's yet shown that it exists in other animals." He watched Rhyne's eyebrows draw together as she considered what he'd said. There was comprehension this time, and he knew that the reason she'd failed to grasp the implications at first was because he'd explained it badly. "It requires time for the rods to —"

"Bacilli," she said. "You can say it now. I looked it up. It's from the Latin for staff or rod." She pitched her voice lower and evoked Runt Abbot. "I reckon doctors just gotta have their secret language."

Cole discovered he had the wherewithal to chuckle. He was glad to learn it. "The *bacilli*," he began again, "require time to do their damage. It can take a week or more for someone who's been infected to experience the first symptoms. There are people who've had the bacteria inside them for several months before they begin to feel sick."

"So a hostess can pass along the bacilli without even knowing she's sick."

"A host," Cole corrected. "But yes, that's often the case."

"That's why you were so particular that I wash up after caring for Whitley."

He nodded. "And before and after other things you do as well."

"I remember." There was a certain irony, she thought, that Runt Abbot had to surrender his life of grime. "Will we all get the fever?"

"No."

"How can you be sure?"

"First, it's unlikely that the entire town has been exposed. Contaminated water would be the way something like that could happen, but Wyatt tells me that every home doesn't have the same source. Some families have wells. Others tap into an underground spring. The Commodore has its own tower that feeds off a spring higher up. Second, even if everyone is exposed, there will always be some people who won't get sick. I don't know why. No one does. But it happens in every sort of outbreak. The human race would have died out long ago if it weren't for those among us who can make a stand. The germs are legion, Rhyne. I don't like to think how insignificant our numbers are compared to theirs."

"I like it better when I can see what I'm

fighting."

"You did see," he reminded her gently. "Most people will never have the same introduction."

Rhyne sighed softly. "Whitley was right. It would be safer if you could shoot at something."

Cole thought of his earlier conversation with Wyatt. "Whitley said that?"

"Something like that, yes." Rhyne hesitated, wondering if she dared break Whitley's confidences. "You have to be watchful, Cole, and care for yourself. I don't think you understand how she worries that you'll become a victim of someone else's illness. It's how she views your mother's death. It's why she can't sleep when you're called away. She understands your germ theory well enough to wish you were a soldier. Never doubt that Whitley's motivation to leave New York was to get you away from the hospital." Rhyne smiled ruefully. "She thought you'd be safer in Reidsville."

He closed his eyes a moment, rubbed them with his thumb and forefinger. "I didn't know," he said tiredly. "I didn't know."

"She begged me not to tell you. I suppose I've proven she can't trust me, but I thought you should know. She'll blame herself if you get sick. The way she'll see it is that it's mostly her fault that you're here."

"God, what a mess."

Rhyne stood and went to him. She stepped behind his chair and leaned forward to put her arms around him. Her cheek rested against his hair. "Come to bed, Coleridge."

His eyes strayed to the book he'd pushed aside and then to his cup. It was empty. So was he. Recognizing that this was one of those times it was better to take advice than give it, Cole slipped out of Rhyne's loose embrace and followed her to bed.

Neither of them was thinking about making love when they turned down the covers. It evolved without conscious thought, the expression of a mutual need for comfort and escape. She lay with her head in the crook of his arm, her hand making idle passes across his heart, and knew such a profound sense of rightness in the moment that she thought she might weep.

"I love you," she whispered, and turned her head to place her lips against his flesh. She felt his fingers thread in her hair and begin to sift it. Her skin prickled. He brushed the nape of her neck. She thought he was probably smiling. Beneath her palm, his heart beat faster.

In spite of that, her world slowed. His touch was gentle, every caress a cautious exploration. He lingered. His kisses lasted almost as long as forever. He turned her on her side. They spooned, the cleft of her bottom flush to his groin. He rubbed her arm from shoulder to wrist. His fingertips grazed the sensitive underside of her elbow. His breath stirred her hair.

He drew her hand behind her. It slipped between the press of their bodies. Her fingers circled his erection. She raised her leg a fraction to accommodate his entry. Their breathing quickened, but nothing else. Without exchanging a word, they held themselves still and found pleasure deepening in the pause. His breath was warm against her ear. He whispered what he would do to her, and then he did nothing. Anticipation became a physical response. Her nipples tightened. Her nostrils flared.

Although she had been expecting it, she jerked when he cupped her mons. His fingers parted her damp lips. He rubbed the hood of her clitoris and his caress was both gentle and insistent.

"Yes," she said. And again, "Yes." She moved her bottom against him, felt his thrust in response. "There. Just there."

He kissed her nape, found the curve where her shoulder met her neck and suckled her with the same slow, inexorable rhythm that was the coupling of their bodies. There was only Rhyne, the woman scent of her sex, her pliant flesh, the surrender of her throaty cries.

She touched his forearm, found the back of his hand and scored his skin from wrist to elbow with the same slow, incremental pressure that was the rising of their pleasure. There was only Cole, the rigid sex, his naked need, the assault of his mouth.

She shuddered, shattered. She barely caught her breath when she felt him do the same, his hoarse, guttural cry edged with something like desperation. His arm remained tight around her waist, keeping her close, keeping them joined.

They fell asleep like that. It was the first time.

Whitley's fevered cry roused Rhyne to groggy wakefulness. She recalled falling asleep in Cole's arms, but now he lay sprawled on his stomach in the middle of the bed while she was in danger of falling out of it. Before she could throw back the covers, she heard Whitley call out a second time.

Easing out of bed with more care than she'd crawled into it, Rhyne grabbed her shawl but didn't spend any time looking for her slippers. She spared a glance for Cole before she left the room and was reassured by his abrupt little snore.

Rhyne had left Whitley's door open and a lamp burning in the event she was needed. She saw Whitley's distress before she reached the bed. The girl was tangled in the sheet and quilts but largely uncovered by them. Even as Rhyne reached down to pull them off, Whitley moaned and shifted, throwing her leg out over the side of the bed and trapping the twisted sheet under her.

Rhyne felt the dampness of the sheet as soon as she touched it. Patting down the quilts, she discovered they were damp as well. She placed the back of her hand against Whitley's forehead just as she'd observed Cole doing. The heat shocked her.

She looked around to see if Cole had left his thermometer, but his bag was gone. The last time he'd taken Whitley's temperature it had been one hundred two degrees, and she suspected it might be even higher now. With an uneasy glance toward the hallway, Rhyne decided she would see to Whitley's immediate comfort and then wake Cole.

After stoking the fire in the stove to keep the room warm, she retrieved fresh linens from the hallway closet and began to remake the bed around Whitley. She stripped off Whitley's damp nightgown and tossed it on the floor with the discarded bedclothes, and then she wrestled Whitley into a clean, dry gown. By the time she finished, she was perspiring from the effort.

Rhyne sat at Whitley's side and gently sponged her face and neck. She opened the nightgown and laid the cool sponge against Whitley's throat. Slipping the sponge under the material, she ran it across her collarbones and upper chest.

"Mama?"

The plaintive note in Whitley's voice pierced Rhyne's heart. She smoothed Whitley's brow with her fingertips, pushing back damp tendrils of hair. "No, dearest. It's Rhyne."

"Rhyne."

"That's right."

Whitley opened her eyes and stared at Rhyne. "I want my mama."

"I know you do." She dipped the sponge in the basin and bathed Whitley's face again. "Everyone does." Rhyne could say it confidently even though she'd never known her mother's comforting touch. What she understood was the yearning for the care of someone who loved her.

"She sang to me."

Rhyne had to bend close to hear. Her hand stilled. She required a moment to collect herself before she could continue her ministrations. "I don't know any songs." In church, she mostly mouthed the words to pretend she was singing with the congregation. "Leastways not ones like your mama knew." Her brothers had taught her the words to exactly two songs, neither of them repeatable to a gently reared young woman. Even Rusty and Randy had had the good sense to warn her not to sing them around Judah, but oh! how enthusiastically the three of them had sung about the ladies from France and Nantucket.

Rhyne found herself unexpectedly moved

by the memory. She drew a steadying breath and offered a smile that wasn't entirely forced. "There's one," she said, calling it to mind suddenly. She didn't suppose it mattered that she wasn't certain of the tune; she knew the words.

"Sigh no more, ladies, sigh no more,
Men were deceivers ever,
One foot in sea and one on shore,
To one thing constant never:
Then sigh not so, but let them go,
And be you blithe and bonny,
Converting all your sounds of woe
Into Hey nonny, nonny.

Sing no more ditties, sing no mo,
Of dumps so dull and heavy;
The fraud of men was ever so,
Since summer first was leavy:
Then sigh not so, but let them go,
And be you blithe and bonny,
Converting all your sounds of woe
Into Hey nonny, nonny."

Standing in the hallway just outside Whitley's room, Cole listened to Rhyne's softly lilting melody. She didn't sing the words as much as speak them in a cadence that made her voice an instrument of music. She stirred the air with each tender measure in the same way she stirred his heart.

He waited until the last notes faded, and then he waited even longer. It was some time before either of them spoke, so long, in fact, that he thought Whitley had fallen asleep. His sister, though, was the one that broke the silence, and surprised him further by calling for him.

Cole went straight to Whitley's bedside and greeted his sister softly, "Hey nonny." He looked across the bed at Rhyne. "Nonny." He observed that Whitley managed to grin while Rhyne flushed predictably. In that moment, all was right in his world.

Whitley tugged on Cole's hand. "Sit."

He obliged her. "What's Rhyne doing here?" he asked his sister.

Whitley tilted her head toward him and confided in a whisper, "Much ado about nothing." A slim smile touched her lips as both Cole and Rhyne chuckled. She closed her eyes.

Cole's glance at Rhyne communicated his question.

"I heard her cry out," she said. "She was restless. The fever is . . ." She didn't finish because Cole could see for himself that it was worse. "I changed the linens and her night-dress. I bathed her skin."

He nodded. Whitley still held his hand and while she didn't speak, she did squeeze his fingers. "I'm not going anywhere, Whit. Neither is Rhyne." He saw her head move faintly against the pillow in acknowledgment. Her hold on him eased a fraction.

Rhyne gently brushed tendrils of hair from Whitley's fevered brow. She smoothed the blankets and caressed Whitley's cheek with the back of her fingers. Pushing embarrassment aside, she crooned softly,

"Then sigh not so, but let them go,
And be you blithe and bonny,
Converting all your sounds of woe
Into Hey nonny, nonny."

Long after exhaustion escorted Whitley to sleep, Cole and Rhyne remained at her side.

In the morning, Cole outlined his plan to Rhyne between bites of silver dollar pancakes and crisp bacon. "I need to start with water samples. I'm not confident anything will come of it, but water has to be eliminated as a possibility."

"How do you do that?"

"Provided Wyatt's not taken ill, I'm going to ask him to organize the collection for me. He could get a couple of men to help him. They'll have to draw water from a few specific sites such as the spring, the active mine, and the Commodore's tower. They'll also have to take some random samples."

"Ezra Reilly could help," Rhyne said. "I don't suppose that missing a hand would be too much of a hardship on an assignment like that. He'd want to help."

Cole liked the idea. "I'll mention it to Wyatt. I'm thinking that two dozen samples are about the limit of what I can do in a timely fashion. Chet Caldwell should be able to supply enough bottles. It would be a great help if you could sterilize and label them."

"Of course."

He nodded, took a swallow of hot coffee and grimaced as he burned his tongue. Ignoring Rhyne's admonishing glance, he went on. "It's difficult to know how many more people will be struck down today. I'm hoping it's less than ten but would not be astonished if it were upward of a score. Every one of them needs to be interviewed about what they've eaten and where they've eaten it, particularly the night of the town social. Obviously, the interviews should happen quickly because the course of the fever is such that by the third week, it will be difficult to gather any information at all."

Rhyne set down her fork, her appetite gone. "The social?" she asked. "Why that night?"

Cole regarded her curiously. He'd been certain she already suspected. "The timing of the illnesses," he said. "It's just been eight days since the population of Reidsville — or most of it — was in one place. The social is what connects young Alex Easter to Whitley to that no-account Beatty boy. Perhaps their paths crossed in some other way that involved food or drink, but it's difficult for me to imagine how it happened."

"The social was *my* idea." Rhyne thought she might be sick. She placed a hand over her stomach. "Everyone came together because of us."

"You aren't responsible," he said. "*We* are not responsible. The pink rods, remember? *They* are responsible. Some kind of outbreak was inevitable."

"But the celebration brought everyone together."

Cole had no argument for that. If the contagion wasn't in the water, then without the social, the fever might have been confined to a single family. Thinking about it that way, though, made him realize there was yet another step to be taken. "In addition to learning what people ate and drank, we need to know what everyone brought to the table."

Rhyne was only marginally relieved that Mrs. Longabach had expressly forbidden her to make a dish for her own reception. "Take an account from every family?" she asked. "How can that be accomplished?"

Cole considered the breadth of the problem. "Artie Showalter could post something about it in the paper. We could hang posters, asking people to report to the sheriff or to me."

"I don't know," she said. "Folks might be a

little reluctant to come forward if they think they're in trouble."

"No one's in trouble."

"But they don't know that. You could tell them, and they still might not believe it. I feel guilty, and I didn't take any food to the feast. Not everyone's going to understand about those germs, Cole, and people might be afraid to come forward regardless of what they know. How do you think Rachel Cooper would feel if she thought folks got sick or died from eating her applesauce? I bet even she'd think twice about telling people what she brought."

"We have to find the source, Rhyne. No matter where it leads."

"I know that, but there has to be a better way than the newspaper and reporting to the sheriff. That's a recipe for —" She stopped and rapidly tapped her index finger against her cheek as she thought. "Recipes," she said. "That's the way we'll do it. We'll invite everyone in town to contribute their recipe for what they brought to the social. I'll say I'm compiling a bride's first cookbook. That's something we can put in the paper. I could get Rachel to help me collect them. Not door-to-door," she said quickly when she saw Cole start to object. "We'd organize them as they came in. Compare them to a list of all the families in town."

Cole nodded slowly. "That could work."

"We'll get a better response," she promised. "Not everyone, I'm sure, but more than you'd get the other way."

"You're right." His mouth lifted at one corner. "And clever."

"How quickly will you need the information?"

"I needed it yesterday," he said. "I want it in ten days."

"Then I'll ask Mr. Showalter to mention that if people want their recipe to be included in my book, they'll have a week to bring it by. I'll send round a special invitation to Sir Nigel and Mrs. Longabach. Their businesses provided more than a single dish. I want to be certain I collect everything from them."

"Good."

"When you speak to Wyatt, will you ask Rachel if she'll help me?"

"I'll ask her, but Wyatt may not allow her to come because of Whitley."

"She can't get sick just by visiting. I won't let her go up to Whitley's room. And I won't extend the slightest hospitality. No food or drink in the event that I'm already sick."

"I'll let him know," he said wryly. Cole glanced at his plate. He'd eaten everything. "What should I make of the fact that you cooked for me?"

She held up her hands. "I all but boiled these," she said.

He stared at her reddened palms. "Rhyne.

You don't have to go to that extreme." He took one of her hands in his, examined it, and then raised her knuckles to his mouth and pressed his lips against them. "I feel quite safe in your hands," he said, releasing her. "There's aloe in the surgery. If you're going to scrub your skin raw, use it."

Rhyne's reply was lost in the banging at the side door. She and Cole exchanged glances.

He stood, checked his pocket watch. "And so it begins."

Cole's first opportunity to speak to Wyatt came just before noon. He'd already visited three families with at least one member ill, treated a visiting gambler at the Commodore, a miner at the boarding house, and stopped by the Easter and Beatty households to check on Alex and Will.

Wyatt was studying a map pinned to the wall of his office when Cole walked in. Ezra Reilly was at the sheriff's side, looking on. Neither man turned to acknowledge the interruption. Cole remained silent, turning his attention instead to the cluster of small brown bottles on top of Wyatt's desk. Many of them were already neatly labeled. A few had no markings. He picked one up, read the label, smiled faintly, and set it down again. It eased some of the tension pulling at his shoulders to be reminded that he wasn't in this battle alone. Rhyne had obviously been busy.

Wyatt pointed out something on the map to Ezra, and then turned away to address Cole. "We've made a good start, I think."

"It looks like it." He set his bag on Wyatt's desk beside the bottles. "I take it you've spoken to Rhyne."

He nodded. "I went by your place first thing, but you were already called away. Rhyne explained what you wanted me to do. Ezra was glad to help. He got the bottles from Caldwell's, and Rhyne sterilized them and marked them for us. We've been getting samples since then. Rachel spoke to Abe Dishman about stopping runs of the Admiral and No. 473. He didn't like it, but she's the owner. Nothing's going to travel on the Calico Spur until you give us the word. Abe will just tell everyone that there's a problem in Denver with both engines. It breaks his heart to say it because he takes such pride in a smooth operation, but the lie's necessary to hold people for a while, help stem the panic."

Cole told him about the new cases.

Wyatt whistled softly, rubbed the back of his neck. "Do you want to take the bottles we already filled? We only have a half dozen or so left."

"I'll take them." He opened his bag and began carefully setting the labeled bottles inside. "Did Rhyne tell you about collecting recipes?"

"She did. She asked me about Rachel helping her. I told her I'd think about it, but I have to be honest: I have no intention of mentioning it to my wife."

"I understand. In your place, I'd probably do the same."

"Yes, well, maybe you can tell Rachel that when you see her, because I'll be damned if she didn't show up while I was bringing the bottles by and volunteered to help Rhyne. I think Rhyne knew how I really felt, and to her credit, she tried to discourage Rachel, but my wife sniffed that out in no time at all. It seems she understands this germ theory of yours better than I do, and I *saw* the bastards on your slide. She's not afraid. I'm the one that's terrified for her."

"I'll talk to her," Cole assured him.

"She reminded me that she didn't eat very much at the social. I didn't notice that night, but she said she was feeling out of sorts, not enough to want to stay home, but enough that she didn't have much of an appetite. Seeing all that food made her nauseated, she said."

"If I'm right, that could make a difference. Did she tell you what she ate?"

"Vegetable soup. I remember that. And I think she said she had a roll and some of the stewed tomatoes."

"Salads? Ice cream? The consommé?"

He shook his head. "Nothing like that. She still isn't used to our winters. This time of year, she doesn't eat anything that doesn't warm her up."

"Good. Those bastards, as you called them, are killed by heat."

Ezra turned away from the map and regarded Cole. There was a pallor to his complexion that hadn't been there moments earlier. "You said ice cream?"

Seeing Ezra's face, Cole wished he'd said nothing. "How much of it did you eat, Ezra?"

"Not me. Virginia. She loves it. I reckon she had two scoops. Maybe three, she had such a hankerin'."

"It might not be the ice cream," said Cole. "I only mentioned it as an example." He realized he'd relieved one man and set another to worrying. "Should be going." He hefted his bag. "Bring the rest of the bottles by as soon as you're finished. I'll start examining these right away."

There was a lull for several days with only one new illness coming to Cole's attention. He was still busy with people already infected, but his primary purpose in visiting them was not to provide respite, but to make certain other family members were taking precautions to prevent the spread.

Whitley developed the telltale rose spots on her lower abdomen and her fever remained dangerously high. Rhyne sat with her, reading, while Cole employed all the techniques he knew to study the water samples. Concerned that he was predisposed to believe the samples would be free of *typhi,* he made a second slide from every bottle and asked Rhyne to lend her eye to the task.

Finding nothing was good news. That's what he told Rhyne as he dropped, bleary-eyed, into bed one night. Rhyne lay awake for a long time after he slept, stroking his hair with her fingertips, reassured by the gentle sound of his breathing.

Rhyne's request for recipes appeared in the paper, and she had seven of them delivered before dinner. It was an impressive beginning. Rachel Cooper visited Estella Longabach and Sir Nigel, presenting them with Rhyne's scented invitation to have their recipes included in her cookbook, and graciously turned down their offers to dine.

More recipes came in the next day and the day after that. Sid Walker took ill. So did Virginia Reilly. Sir Nigel sent for Cole when two more of his guests showed signs of the sickness. It was a housekeeper the following day, and then Sir Nigel that needed attention later that night. The fever took a vicious hold on the young so that by the end of the week there was hardly a family with children who didn't have at least one that was slow and sluggish with the first symptoms.

Rhyne and Rachel pressed on with their collection. The responses dwindled, not so much because people were reluctant to participate, but because many of them were caring for someone who was ill, or ill themselves. People stayed indoors. Those that ventured out were cautious. The trains didn't run. Folks made do with what they had. The miners kept at their work, but they were solemn gangs that walked to and from the mines. Businesses closed early. A few closed entirely when the owners or a family member became too ill to work. Cole did his best to educate the town about the fever, but there were too many skeptics and not enough hours to convince them.

No one wanted to hear typhoid. It was seldom mentioned above a whisper.

Rhyne and Rachel were working at the dining room table, scraps of paper scattered all over the surface, when Wyatt poked his head in the doorway. "Are you about ready to come home?" he asked his wife.

Rachel sat back in her chair, pressing her hands to the small of her back. "I am," she said. "Rhyne and I were just finishing."

Wyatt cocked an eyebrow at her. "Find anything?"

She shook her head. "Still working at it. Tomorrow, maybe."

Rhyne gave her full marks for trying to sound hopeful. She asked Wyatt, "Did you come in the front or the side?"

"The side. Cole was sleeping in the surgery. Slumped over beside that microscope. Sorry to say that I woke him. He looks like he could use the sleep."

Rhyne nodded, but she didn't comment. It was true for all of them. "Did you stop in to see Will Beatty today?"

"I did. I'm not sure he knew I was there. What about Whitley?"

"The same." She straightened some papers in front of her. "How's Rose?"

"She's all right. Glad she doesn't have any signs of the fever so she can take care of Will, and halfway to killing him for being sick instead of her."

Rachel and Rhyne smiled appreciatively. It sounded *exactly* like Rose.

Rhyne glanced toward the hallway to see if Cole had followed Wyatt. When she didn't see him, she asked quietly, "Have you been out of town at all?"

He knew what she meant. "Yesterday was the first chance I had to ride out. I got around to everyone."

"Judah?"

"Even Judah. Full of piss and vinegar because the doctor wasn't with me like he promised. He showed me the hand that Cole patched up for him. It looked fine to me." He put his hand on his wife's shoulder and rubbed gently as he continued to address

Rhyne. "I didn't see him at the social, if that's what you were thinking. Turns out none of the outliers came in."

"That's what makes them outliers, dear," said Rachel. She turned her neck a little to give him better access to the taut muscles there. "Oh, yes. That spot. Right . . . there."

Wyatt grinned. Rhyne blushed. Rachel was oblivious to everything but getting the kink out of her neck.

"Were you worried about him?" asked Wyatt.

Rhyne hardly knew how to answer that. "A little, maybe. I'm not sure. I didn't like not knowing, I suppose. You say he's fine?"

"About as fine as he ever is."

She hesitated. "Did he ask about me?"

Now it was Wyatt that hesitated. He stopped massaging Rachel's shoulder.

"You can tell me," said Rhyne. "I wouldn't have asked if I didn't want to know. I don't expect much."

"No, Rhyne, he didn't ask."

She nodded, straightened a few more papers, and then nodded again. "Well, like I said, I don't expect much." She stood. "If you don't mind seeing yourselves out, I should go check on Cole."

When Rhyne was gone, Wyatt slid Rachel's chair away from the table and helped her to her feet. He was aware of her searching his face and didn't like the knowing look in her eye.

"Why did you lie to her?" she asked. "Because I know you did. What did Judah say that you couldn't repeat?"

Caught, Wyatt's cheeks puffed a little as he exhaled. "I told him what I told everyone else about what was happening in town. Cole wanted me to. He hoped it would be enough to keep them away for now. Most of them had a lot of questions. Judah had only one: 'Is she dead yet?' "

Rhyne took Cole by the hand and led him out of the surgery and up to their bedroom. "Sleep," she ordered him, pointing to the bed. "At least for a little while." She accepted the fact that he didn't argue as proof of his deep fatigue. "I'll warm some soup so it will be ready when you come back down." She snapped a spare quilt over him when he lay on top of the other covers. Bending, she smoothed his hair and kissed his brow. He was asleep before she let herself out of the room.

Rhyne warmed broth and bread for Whitley and carried it upstairs on a wooden tray. It was becoming a considerable challenge to get her to eat or drink, but Cole had impressed upon everyone who cared for the sick that dehydration would unnecessarily complicate the illness. The complications, he reminded them, were what killed.

Rhyne set the tray down and touched Whitley on the shoulder. The girl's eyelashes fluttered briefly and then closed. "I have something for you," said Rhyne. "Wake up. Let me see that you're in there." Rhyne thought she saw a faint smile tug at Whitley's lips, but then she also knew how much she wanted to believe it was so. She shook Whitley with a little more force. "There you are." Whitley's green eyes were glassy and vaguely unfocused, but at least they were open. "Let me help you sit up."

Rhyne had to do the lion's share of the work just to get Whitley into a reclining position where her head was a little higher than her shoulders. It required two additional pillows and some cursing.

"Runt Abbot," said Whitley.

"That's right." Rhyne sat on the bed beside her. "Runt still has a few things to say, mostly cuss words." Now she was sure she saw the corners of Whitley's mouth lift. "Sometimes swearing is what's called for." She broke off a small chunk of bread, dipped it in the beef broth, and held it close to Whitley's lips. A droplet of broth fell, and as soon as Whitley opened her mouth to lick it away, Rhyne pushed in the bread. Whitley wrinkled her nose but didn't spit it out.

"Let's see if we can go on that way," Rhyne said. "Puts me in mind of a mama bird feeding her fledglings." She took another piece of bread and sopped it in the broth. Whitley took it, dutifully opening her mouth when Rhyne's hand drew near. "Digger's been asking after you. I see him nearly every day when he's doing his outside chores." His sister was sick with the fever, but Digger hadn't succumbed. The vagaries of the *typhi* were something Rhyne thought she would never understand. Digger swore to Cole that neither Whitley nor his twin had eaten anything he hadn't. He'd made a full accounting of their gluttony that night, and when Rhyne saw Cole's notes she remarked it might have been simpler to ask the boy what they *hadn't* eaten. It remained to be seen if he would sicken at some later time, or if as Cole suspected now, he would escape unscathed.

"He sure is sweet on you," Rhyne told Whitley. "I think he lies in wait for me just so he can ask how you're doing. Your brother would beat him away with a broom if he could, but I like him. He doesn't help in the surgery any longer. His mother's afraid to let him, though what she thinks he might come by here and not at home is a mystery to me. She's a silly woman. Well-meaning, I think, but silly as a custard pie with no crust."

She pushed another broth-soaked bite of bread between Whitley's lips and continued chattering in the same vein, distracting her until every last morsel and bit of broth was gone.

Once Whitley fell back to sleep, Rhyne returned to the kitchen and put heartier soup on the stove to heat for dinner. She'd give Cole another half hour, she decided, before she woke him. He wouldn't thank her for letting him sleep the evening away, not when he'd promised Miss Adele that he would call on the fancy house tonight. One of the girls had fainted dead away in the kitchen, another hadn't been able to rise from her bed, both signs that they'd probably been suffering in silence for days — and quite possibly passing the contagion along.

Sitting at the dining room table while the soup simmered, Rhyne swept all the recipes she'd collected into a single pile. When Rachel and she had begun, they separated food by location. Salads and soups at the Miner Key. Main courses in the Commodore. Desserts at Miss Adele's. They'd also made a list of the dishes they remembered seeing that weren't included among the recipes and placed the name of each on a small card and put it in the appropriate category.

Perhaps, Rhyne thought, if she reorganized them in a different manner, she'd see something she hadn't before. She'd been so certain she would have something to give Cole that she felt the heaviness of her failure as a real weight on her shoulders. She stared at the

518

pile in front of her and blew out a breath hard enough to scatter some of the scraps of paper.

She picked up the one that had floated closest to the edge of the table and read it: *Cream of Celery* by Mrs. Theodore Easter. It seemed an unlikely candidate. Cole and she had both had a little of it. She found her list of foods that people who were sick reported eating. Ann Marie's soup was on the list. It could mean something, she supposed, or nothing at all.

She remembered Cole explaining to her that cold foods were more suspect than hot ones. That information barely allowed her to eliminate anything because baked goods like cookies, rolls, and bread could be touched by unclean hands after they came out of the oven. She was only able to place a few recipes to one side.

Rhyne began separating food by the amount of heat ideally used in preparing it. A dish of boiled potatoes seemed straightforward enough to put in the column marked hot, but then she wondered about the butter that had been added afterward. She slid the recipe into the column she thought of as uncertain. The meat dishes were particularly bothersome. She suspected the stews had been thoroughly cooked, but could not help but doubt that the same could be said for the poultry or fish or the beef. The number of recipes and food in the uncertain column began to grow along with Rhyne's discouragement.

The only category that did not strain her confidence was the one she'd made for the cold and raw foods. She put the iced bouillon there, the consommés, the ice cream as well as their chopped nut toppings. She thought about how the foods might have been handled in preparation and added the dried apple salads and deviled eggs. She placed every frosted cake in this column and foods that had been made more attractive with raw garnishes. She quickly rearranged some of the recipes, eliminating foods that were unlikely to have been touched after they were cooked.

Excited that she may have narrowed her search, Rhyne looked at the list of the sick and tried to find the common threads. After a time with no success, words blurred. Rhyne folded her arms on the edge of the table and set her head against them. A few minutes, she thought, and then she would try again. Only a few.

Her nose twitched. She breathed in the aroma of steaming vegetable soup. She could taste the moist fragrance of beef swimming in broth with corn, carrots, beans, and barley as it came to rest on her tongue. She opened an eye, stared at the bowl sitting just beyond her nose, and then darted a look upward to see Cole standing beside her.

He made no attempt to hide his concern.

"You could have taken a nap with me." He touched her cheek with the back of his hand and ignored the face she made. "You don't look as if you can hold your head up."

Of course she rose to the challenge, lifting her head and straightening her shoulders, and then graced him with a smug smile.

Cole merely shook his head and ordered her to eat.

Rhyne raised an eyebrow at him. She carefully unfolded her napkin and smoothed it across her lap, taking her time in spite of the fact that her mouth was watering.

Cole sat at the head of the table at a right angle to Rhyne. He snapped his napkin open and tucked one corner into the collar of his shirt. When Rhyne looked at him in surprise, he said, "You're too busy to do more laundry. I thought I'd try to keep my shirts reasonably clean."

Rhyne continued to stare at him.

"What?" he asked, looking down at himself. "Have I already spilled something?"

"My heart," she said feelingly. "All over you."

He glanced up. Her eyes were luminous. He thought it was possible that she loved him more in this moment than she had on their wedding day. Clean shirts and consideration. It was better advice than that no-account Beatty boy had given him.

Rhyne's vaguely loopy smile didn't fade

until she picked up her spoon and began eating. "Was Whitley still sleeping when you came downstairs?"

He nodded. "I saw she had fresh water at her bedside. Has she already eaten?"

"Bread soaked in beef broth. I tried to get her to drink, but she wasn't cooperative."

"I'll try later. She seems to be able to tolerate the peppermint tea." He waved his hand across the table to indicate the scraps of paper and cards. "There's been some change since the last time I looked in on you and Rachel. Did you find something?"

"No. I decided to study it all again but differently this time."

"And?"

She sighed. "And how do I know that Mrs. Porter thoroughly cooked her lamb or that what was cooked wasn't handled afterward by hands that weren't clean."

"I see your point."

"I keep thinking about the children."

"What about them?"

"Have you noticed that there's more children ill than adults?"

"Do you have the list?" His features revealed his confusion as he extended his hand in Rhyne's direction. "Let me see it. That doesn't sound quite right."

Rhyne found it under her bowl and gave it to him. "I probably explained it poorly," she said. "What I mean is that if you consider the number of children in Reidsville compared to the number of the adults, the children appear too often on the list. Shouldn't it be about the same?"

Cole put down his spoon and picked up the pencil that Rhyne had been using. He made a tic beside each child's name and saw immediately that she was correct. Children were disproportionately represented. He rubbed the underside of his jaw as he considered how that might occur.

"It could be that the list fails to capture all the sick adults." While he was thinking of it, he added the names of Adele Brownlee's ill girls. Though not certain, it was probable that both Susan Fry and Raymona Preston had come down with typhoid. "People are a lot more likely to seek help for their children than they are for themselves. If Sir Nigel hadn't taken it upon himself to report his sick guests, we might not know about them. And look at Adele's girls. They tried to hide it until they just gave out. There might be others as well."

"You told me that the symptoms were less severe in children."

"That's right. But I didn't say they were less susceptible to the bacteria. The truth is, I don't know. Looking at this list, it would be easy to conclude that they're *more* susceptible, but that would be hasty, I believe."

"Look at the things they ate," Rhyne said.

"Pastries, cakes, cookies, ice cream."

"An overindulgence on the sweets at Miss Adele's."

"That's right."

"There are adults on this list that swear they were never inside her place."

Rhyne nodded. "I can't account for the women or the single men, but it seems possible that the married men might not have been strictly honest. That's the sort of thing men hide from their wives, isn't it? Men besides you, that is. Judge Wentworth remarked that you were forthright for telling me you met him at the whorehouse."

Amused, Cole set the list aside and regarded Rhyne. "Can I expect that you will find ways to mention that particular night for the remainder of our lives?"

"Oh, I hope so."

"What is it that you imagine I did there that evening?"

"I can't know, of course, but I've always supposed you sat in one corner of the parlor drinking bourbon from a crystal tumbler while Raymona sang and Susan chattered. At least that's what I'd like to believe you were doing until the judge joined you. He probably had your attention for a time, and then you left."

"Mm. Fascinating. Other women might imagine something more . . ." He paused, searching for the right description. "More provoking and carnal."

"I imagine that, too," she confessed. "But you're never with Miss Adele or one of her girls when I do." Smiling coolly, she plucked the list from table and searched it again.

Cole returned to his soup. He considered asking how she knew that he hadn't gone upstairs at Miss Adele's, but he decided he liked not knowing just as well. He had his own imaginings, and one of his favorites was Rhyne confronting the madam. The threat of a broken nose might have been involved.

"What are you thinking?" he asked as he watched her glancing between the list in her hand and recipes and foods that she'd put into the column closest to her. "Those are the raw items?"

She nodded distractedly. "And dishes best served cold," she said. "Like revenge."

CHAPTER 15

They stared at each other.

Cole broke the charged silence. He spoke quietly, intently, "Revenge is a dish best served cold."

"I don't believe it," Rhyne whispered. But she knew it was more accurate to say that she didn't want to believe it. "He wouldn't have. He *couldn't* have."

"All right," said Cole. "Let's review your lists to see *if* it's possible. We don't need to concern ourselves with how it might have been done just yet."

Rhyne pushed her half-eaten bowl of soup away and tossed her crumpled napkin beside it. She arranged the cards that showed all the cold dishes and raw foods so Cole could see them as well. "The letter at the bottom of each one indicates where the food was served. Rachel and I began organizing that way. *M* for the Miner Key and so on." She turned one over. "We wrote who provided the dish on the back. We didn't want to speculate about who might have contributed to the outbreak as we worked. It made us too heartsick to think about it." Now it just made her sick. "Some women wrote their names as part of the recipe. Here, for instance: *Julia Hammond's Hot Water Sponge Cake.* Isn't that just like her? There was no help for that."

"I see. Why is sponge cake in your cold pile?"

"Because it was sliced up on the platter and drizzled with sugar glaze. It seemed to me that Mrs. Hammond was likely to have touched every piece."

"Did anyone on your list of the sick eat her sponge cake?"

Rhyne ran her finger down the list. "Only a few."

"Very well. Let's put it to the side as unlikely but possible. Besides the fact that you and I have been in the Hammond house and know that Julia would scrub the shine off the sun if she could, one hot water sponge cake wouldn't have infected so many people. Did she make other dishes?"

"No. Just the one."

Cole looked over the cards again. "How many of these were provided by Longabach's restaurant?"

Rhyne lifted the corner of each recipe to see the writing on the back. "There are three here. Estella prepared more than that, though. The others are either in the soup or entrée piles." Frowning, Rhyne shook her head. "Estella and Henry have been serving folks good food for a lot of years. It doesn't make sense that there'd suddenly be a problem."

"Johnny Winslow works for them. He told me Estella lets him cook now and again."

"You've lived here long enough to answer this question: Do you imagine she lets him do anything when she's not standing over him?"

"No," he said. "I don't imagine that she does." His brief smile vanished, and he regarded Rhyne gravely. "You understand that by defending your neighbors you're narrowing the list of suspects."

"I know." Her eyes left his. She stared blindly at the cards. "I know."

Cole gave her a few more moments to absorb the consequences before he said, "Let's look at the food provided by the hotel."

Rhyne drew in a shallow breath, nodded, and then began turning cards over. "The iced bouillon. One of the apple walnut salads. The pickled beans with the garnish of radishes. Sand tarts. All of the ice cream, nuts, and caramel sauce."

Cole gently removed the patient list from Rhyne's hand. Halfway through her search, her fingers had begun to tremble. She understood very well that the variety and quantity of dishes offered by the Commodore meant more people would have sampled them. "What about the hot dishes? You may as well turn over those rocks."

Rhyne swept the entrée cards toward her and turned them all over at once. She separated out the hotel's offerings and then gave them to Cole without looking.

"The roast lamb with mint jelly. Chicken and dumplings. The braised beef and roasted potatoes." He tossed the recipes back in the pile. These cooked dishes were unlikely contributors to the outbreak. "Sir Nigel was certainly generous."

"It's not his fault," said Rhyne.

"I agree." Cole leaned back in his chair and looked at his wife. She had no fight in her. She wasn't angry; she was defeated. It was a terrible thing to see. "It's not your fault, either."

She darted a sideways glance at him. "No? Explain that to all the folks suffering right now. Try explaining it to their families."

"We're one of those families," he said gently. "No one in this house blames you."

Now Rhyne's gaze lifted toward the ceiling, her mind's eye seeing beyond it to the room above where Whitley lay. She groped for her napkin and quickly pressed it against her eyes.

"You're not responsible," he said again.

"I've *always* been responsible." She fisted the napkin, her knuckles turning white. "Always."

"We're getting ahead of ourselves. We don't know with certainty that he did anything."

Rhyne scowled at him. "Don't pretend what *is,* isn't. We know. The puzzle that's left is how he did it." She stared at the damning evidence in front of Cole until her eyes blurred a second time. She forgot about the napkin in her hand and swiped at the tears with her fingertips. Embarrassed by what she still thought of as a woman's frailty, she turned her head away so Cole couldn't see her and tried to summon Runt Abbot.

The hell of it was, somewhere inside her he was crying too.

"Tell me what you're thinking, Rhyne." She was so long in answering that he thought she wouldn't. When she did, he hurt for her.

"I don't know that I ever understood how much he despised me. It seems plenty clear now. I suppose it always was to other folks, but I must have been fitted with blinders at birth. Nothing else accounts for not seeing it for myself."

"He was all you knew, Rhyne. All you had."

She shrugged. "I should have known better."

"You should have *had* better. Do you understand what I'm saying? I can't speak to what he did for your brothers, but he was no father to you."

Rhyne shook her head. "That's not true," she said quietly. She turned to look at Cole again, her eyes clear, her features composed again. "He wasn't a father like yours, like most people's, I expect, but he kept a roof over our heads, took work when he had to, and he read to us. Read to us a lot, mostly things that were hard to understand at first, but he had a fine voice and it wasn't the worst thing that he liked the sound of it. I didn't go to school, but you know I didn't grow up ignorant. That was mostly Judah's doing. He could have raised me to be as stupid as a stump, but he didn't. Maybe he thinks I owe him for that. Could be I do."

Cole didn't know what to say, and because there was nothing to be gained taking an opposing view, he kept silent.

"I don't love him," she said. "But I can't quite bring myself to a place where I can hate him. It must seem strange to you, what with you knowing what he did to me. And I'm sure not telling you that I understand it myself, but it's just not inside me to feel that way toward him. Could be what I'm afraid of is showing all that ugly."

The expression in her slate gray eyes grew troubled. She pressed her lips together, worried the underside. "It doesn't mean I couldn't kill him, though. I could. It surprises me a little that I can say it, but not so much as it probably surprises you. There're folks that are going to die. You said it would happen, and I believe you. I figure you should know I could kill him for that. It wouldn't be for hate; it'd be for justice."

Cole put out his hand and covered hers with it. "Don't think about that."

Now it was her turn for silence. She didn't tell him that she couldn't think about anything else. She'd already said too much of what was on her mind. Managing no better than a wan smile, she removed her hand from under his and drew it to her side.

Cole regarded his extended hand before slowly retracting it. "We still don't know how," he said.

"He got himself hired as cook at the Commodore, that's how."

"I don't think Sir Nigel would have hired him."

"Not knowingly. Judah knows a thing or two about making himself into someone else. He's been Macbeth, Othello, Caesar, Volpone, Cyrano, and those are the roles that come to mind immediately. You could meet him on the street and think you were making the acquaintance of a stranger."

"Does he need the walking stick or not?"

"I suppose that depends on whether he's in a mood to beat something."

Cole gave her a stern look. "You know what I mean."

"You're asking if he needs it to get around." She shrugged. "Sometimes, yes. Changes in the weather bother him the way they do Sid

Walker. Leastways, that's how it seems."

"Where did he get the stick? It's an unusual piece. The carvings . . . I've never seen anything like it."

"My mother gave it to him. Those are chess pieces whittled into the wood. Pawn at the bottom, king at the top."

"I noticed."

"My brothers remembered her telling them about it. Judah never said. Is it important?"

"Not the provenance of the stick," he admitted. "I've always been curious about it. What I really wanted to know was whether he required it. Wyatt and Will weren't certain. After my first examination, neither was I. I'm beginning to think he gave a fine performance the second time I saw him. The symptoms he affected . . . it's hard not to suspect now that he was making it all up. Setting the stage, so to speak."

Rhyne's faint smile was wry. "That's Judah."

"He must have reasoned that no one would suspect him of traveling to town in his weakened condition. It seems likely that he asked to see me for the purpose of supporting his situation."

"You realize he's already back at the cabin, don't you? If he worked for Sir Nigel, it was only briefly. Wyatt saw him yesterday." Rhyne screwed her mouth to one side as she considered what Cole had said. "What would make

Judah believe anyone would suspect him in the first place? Doesn't it seem unlikely?"

"I think he's faced suspicion before," said Cole.

"Here? In Reidsville?"

"No. At least not that I've heard. I don't know what Judge Wentworth told you, but he mentioned to me in passing that back in Philadelphia, Judah left his position after some sort of incident. It might have been anything, so perhaps I'm making too much of it, but if Judah's a typhoid carrier — and I think he must be — it would explain a great deal. The judge was fairly certain that Judah tried his hand at cooking several different times as he moved your mother and your brothers west. It's reasonable to assume people got sick along the way."

"But they wouldn't have known about germs."

"That's right. They wouldn't have understood the specific cause. Not that many years ago." He rubbed the underside of his chin with his knuckles. "That doesn't mean the people he cooked for didn't come to some conclusions about the source. You said it yourself, Rhyne. He's like a snake. The poison's inside him. I didn't understand until now how accurate you were.

"People would have looked for an explanation for the fever. Judah cooks. People get sick. More important, he never suffers as they do. It stands to reason that now and again he was accused of doing something to the food." Cole shrugged. "Then again, maybe he moved on because the people around him got sick, and he was trying to protect his family. It might have taken him a long time to understand what part he played."

Cole made a steeple of his fingers and tapped the tips lightly together. "What I think is that your mother figured it out. She couldn't explain it, but she *knew.* I wouldn't be surprised to learn that she was infected with the fever at one time. It's hard to believe she could have escaped it. She would have worried about your brothers as well. I suspect that's how they came to believe that Judah was poison, that what he touched or cooked was also poison. She must have explained it to them in the only way she thought they could understand. Later, they told you."

"They told me," she said, grimacing. "They enjoyed telling me. As early as I can remember, they were scaring me stupid with stories about Judah poisoning his other children."

"His *other* children?"

She nodded. "I was ten or thereabouts before I knew for sure there were only ever the three of us." She saw Cole's mouth twitch. In spite of the gravity of their discovery, she also felt the urge to laugh. "It wasn't easy for them to tell me different, but I was going to set Randy's hair on fire so they had to tell me the truth." She turned up her palms helplessly. "That's the kind of boys we were."

Now Cole did smile. He was certain she hadn't caught what she'd said. "Their stories worked. You believed them."

"About Judah? Always. If he started working in the kitchen, I'd usually pretend I was feeling poorly. But it was rare for him to do much besides put the kettle on the stove. Like I told you, it was Rusty, Randy, and then me that did the cooking chores. That's just the way it was." She pressed one hand to her temple and massaged the dull ache that was forming there. "It's like you said, Judah must have known something about the part he had in the sickness. It would have followed him everywhere he went."

"Everywhere," Cole repeated softly, trying to take it in. "I wonder when he got the idea about getting hired on at the Commodore." He realized the answer was unknowable. "Getting ahead of myself again. We should confirm first that he *was* hired."

"Is Sir Nigel well enough to answer questions?"

"I intend to find out."

"You're going yourself? Wouldn't it be better to let Wyatt do that?"

"I have half a dozen patients at the hotel now, but I'll ask Wyatt to go with me if you think that will help."

"He knows Judah," she said. "He might

think of things to ask Sir Nigel that you wouldn't."

Cole agreed. "Very well. I'll speak to him in the morning."

"In the morning? Shouldn't you go now?"

"Rhyne, everything's already been set in motion. This is a runaway train. I can't stop it tonight. I can't stop it tomorrow. As long as Judah's at the cabin — and you said Wyatt spoke to him there yesterday — then he's no danger to anyone. Wyatt will want to prepare the case carefully. I admit to no expertise in matters of law, but what we believe Judah's done might not be a crime."

Rhyne blinked at him. "Not a crime? How is that possible? People are sick; some will die."

"Even then." He held up his hands to forestall her argument. "Let's wait to hear what Wyatt has to say. I doubt he'll venture an opinion until he speaks to Sir Nigel. The Commodore is the place to begin."

Whitley slipped into the typhoid stupor the following morning. Rhyne had been warned to expect it, but she hadn't been able to prepare herself to face it. Cole was already gone when Rhyne carried breakfast to his sister and found her unresponsive. As little as an hour earlier, Cole had been gently teasing Whitley about Digger Hammond as he took her temperature and listened to her heart. It didn't seem possible that Whitley's smile could have faded so quickly or so completely since then.

The stupor marked the beginning of the worst stage of the fever. While the victims lay still and largely insensitive to what was happening, the toxins from the *Salmonella typhi* were poisoning the liver, the spleen, the intestines, and the heart. The extent of the damage could not be known or predicted. One could only wait and see. If the bowels ruptured, death was certain. Other organs could be compromised to a state of such weakness they failed to function properly. Dehydration remained a fierce enemy, but getting liquids into a patient was no small undertaking.

"Swallow, dammit." Rhyne made no apology for her harsh whisper. She wanted Whitley to know her desperation. She spooned more tea between Whitley's lips and massaged the young girl's throat. Whitley coughed as some of the tea slipped down the wrong pipe. Tea bubbled up from her mouth, staining her chin and dripping onto the pillow. Rhyne wiped Whitley's face with a damp cloth and began again, this time using a small bit of bread dipped in the tea to feed her fledgling.

It took nearly thirty minutes to empty the cup into her patient. Looking at the stained pillowcase, Rhyne wasn't certain how much of the liquid she'd truly managed to get down Whitley's throat. Even the neckline of her nightgown was spotted with tea.

After cleaning Whitley and making her as comfortable as she thought was possible, Rhyne carried the breakfast tray back to the kitchen and began her daily chores. No matter how hard she applied herself to the tasks of washing, polishing, or kneading, her mind was never eased for long.

What she wanted to do was shoot something.

Her mind wasn't particularly eased by that notion either, especially when she thought that her most satisfying target might not be some*thing.*

The knock at the front door startled her enough that she burned her fingers as she was pulling loaves of bread from the oven. She set the pans down, pushed the oven door closed with her hip, and still blowing on two fingers, she went to see who the visitor was.

Elijah Wentworth stood on the porch, his hands thrust in the pockets of his black wool coat and his shoulders hunched against the cold. He quickly stepped into the entryway when Rhyne invited him inside.

"Hard to believe spring's coming," he said as he removed his snow-dusted hat. He tapped it lightly against his leg before he gave it to Rhyne.

"If you're feeling poorly, you should know

that Cole's not here."

The judge continued to unbutton his coat. "I know. I saw him at the hotel. I'm here to speak to you. I hope that's all right. Your husband indicated that it was."

Rhyne frowned a little but kept her hand extended to accept Wentworth's coat. "Did he?" She thought of all things requiring her attention, Whitley chief among them, and wondered why Cole would encourage the judge's visit. She certainly did not need the company.

"I can see your husband was incorrect," said Wentworth. He held on to his coat. "I'll just —"

Rhyne took the coat from his hand. "No. You're here. I apologize if I seem less than welcoming. Whitley's taken a turn. Cole doesn't know yet. He was gone before it happened."

"I'm sorry," he said.

Rhyne realized that he had assumed Whitley's turn was for the worse. She supposed he'd read that on her face as well. There'd been a time when the only emotion she'd been able to show was anger, and then she'd used her fists. Now when she was made vulnerable by every other emotion, she could only clench her heart.

She acknowledged the judge's regrets as she hung up his coat and hat, and then she showed him to the parlor. "Please, sit. I have to attend to the bread I just pulled from the oven. I'll only be a moment."

"There's no need for you to rush. I'll go with you."

Rhyne regarded him uncertainly.

"I could smell the bread when I was standing on the porch," he said. "I might have forced my way in if you hadn't invited me. Good. You can still smile. Go on. I'll follow."

Rhyne led the way back to the kitchen and offered the judge any chair at the table. He chose the one opposite of where she was standing and made himself comfortable, but not before he lowered his head over the freshly baked bread and inhaled deeply.

"Has there been some news?" she asked as she wrapped a towel around her hand to lift the loaf pan.

"News?"

"You said you would be making inquiries in Philadelphia," she reminded him. "About my mother's family." She tapped the pan to loosen the bread and then eased the loaf out onto a wire rack. She moved it to the side to make room for the second loaf. "I wondered if you'd heard anything."

"No, not yet. I had replies from Pinkerton and a few colleagues that my telegrams were received. I imagine it will be several weeks before there's information that means something."

Rhyne had to use a knife to release the

other loaf from the pan. She slid it along the edges of the crust, gave the pan a thump, and the bread fell easily into her palm. She laid it on the rack beside the other loaf and covered them with the towel that had been wrapped around her hand.

"You burned yourself," the judge said, pointing to her fingers.

"It's nothing."

"Shouldn't you put butter on it?"

"Cole says butter's for bread." She pumped water into the sink and let it flow over her fingertips. "This is what I'm supposed to do. I can tell you, sometimes it's hard living with a man who knows everything."

He smiled faintly. "I thought you'd be familiar with that."

"Why? Oh, you mean because of Judah." She shrugged. "Judah knows a lot, but he thinks he knows even more. I reckon Coleridge really does." Rhyne removed her hand from under the water and gingerly dried it off with one corner of her apron. "I don't suppose you liked my father much."

"Didn't know him." He paused, sighed. "But you're right. That never stopped me from disliking him."

"It made it easier for you to love my mother." Rhyne saw her frankness made him blink. "I must have misplaced that leash I try to keep on my tongue. That happens from time to time. I'll find it directly."

"And promptly lose it again," he said dryly.

"That's what Cole says." Rhyne filled the kettle halfway with fresh water and put it on the stove. "I hope tea's all right. We're out of coffee. I stretched what we had as much as I could. I heard Morrison's sold the last tin a couple of days ago. Seems people are probably hoarding, worried about when the trains will run again."

"Tea's fine, but truly, I don't want you to go to any —" He stopped because the look she was giving him was the equivalent of a warning shot. It made him chuckle. He sat back in his chair while she leaned a hip against the sink. "I'm recalling a story I heard about you running the doctor off the first time he tried to pay you a visit. Makes me grateful you didn't greet me at the door with your Winchester aimed at my head."

"Runt Abbot might have done it." She'd found the leash so she didn't tell him that Rhyne Monroe had certainly been tempted. Instead, she heard herself come to Cole's defense. "That story about Cole's been exaggerated some, mostly because he never says a word to the contrary. What I did was scare his ornery horse. He had to go after it."

"But you meant to run him off."

"I meant to run him off permanent. He came back, though, with that no-account Beatty boy riding shotgun. Wyatt kind of insisted on an escort. No one knew then that

Cole could hold his own with a rifle."

"And everyone knew Runt Abbot might make the next shot count."

"Could be that's true." She cocked her head to the side as a sound from upstairs caught her attention. "I should check on Whitley. I won't be long." She was in the hallway when she called back. "Mind the kettle."

Rhyne raised her skirts and took the stairs two at time. She hit her shoulder against the doorjamb as she turned too sharply into Whitley's room. The pain made no impact. It was seeing Whitley lying on the floor that jarred her.

Rhyne knelt beside Whitley and felt for her pulse just as Cole had taught her. When she found it, steadier and stronger than she could have hoped for, she finally released the breath she'd been holding. She moved around to Whitley's head and raised it enough to cradle it in her lap. Leaning back against the bedside stand, Rhyne took stock of her situation. She didn't see how she could get Whitley back into bed without help. She regretted telling the judge to mind the kettle.

Rhyne opened her mouth to call for him and closed it abruptly when he appeared in the doorway. He took stock of the situation at once and hurried to join her at Whitley's side.

"Slide your arms under her shoulders," he

said. "I'll lift her legs."

The awkwardness of her position caused Rhyne to struggle more than the judge, but they got Whitley into bed without mishap, and Rhyne rearranged the quilts so Whitley was covered again. She stepped away, putting her hands to the small of her back to lightly massage the area.

"Did you hurt yourself?" the judge asked.

"It's nothing. A spasm." She thanked him for his help. "I should look after Whitley now. I need to get her to take some drink. It's not . . . pleasant. She wouldn't want you to see her."

"I understand."

Rhyne waited until Wentworth was gone, then she bathed Whitley's face and brushed and braided her limp hair. Promising that she'd be right back, she went downstairs to make tea and slice the heel from one of the fresh loaves of bread. It took her just above thirty minutes to empty the cup of tea into Whitley this time, but she thought she'd spilled less than at breakfast. What she needed, she decided, was something like a narrow funnel that would fit deep in Whitley's throat and safely bypass her windpipe. She wondered if such a contraption existed, and if it did, did Cole have one?

Curious, she set Whitley's empty tray on the kitchen table and ignored the rumblings of her own stomach in favor of looking around the surgery. She stopped just inside the door, startled by Elijah Wentworth sitting on the stool behind Cole's microscope.

"What are you doing here?" She wasn't certain that she masked her irritation very well. It wasn't only that she wasn't entirely comfortable in his presence, but that she had no time for entertaining him. "I thought you'd left."

"No," he said. "I left you alone."

Rhyne reckoned that was a lawyerly kind of distinction, and she didn't appreciate it. "I see." She approached the table. "That doesn't explain what you're doing in here."

"I wanted to see them for myself. I heard Cole talking about them to Wyatt." He pointed to the slide. "Is that them?"

"I don't know," she said. "I'd have to look."

He pushed away from the table and turned over his hand, gesturing to the microscope. "Please. I'd be grateful."

Rhyne went around the table and bent her head. She adjusted the focus for her eye and stared at the slide. The rods simply lay there harmlessly, fixed to the slide by heat and stained pink by Cole's application of chemicals. Rhyne straightened and stepped away. She offered him another glimpse. *Salmonella typhi,*" she said.

"Wyatt called them little bastards."

Rhyne nodded. "They are that."

The judge regarded them again. "Fascinating."

Rhyne removed the slide from the clips that held it in place and returned it to the wooden case where Cole kept it and others like it. She put the case back on the shelf.

"Do you really believe Judah caused the outbreak?"

Rhyne turned slowly back to him. "Did you hear that?" she asked. "Or *over*hear it?"

The judge raised an eyebrow, but his admonishing look was softened by his faint smile. "A little of both, I'm afraid. I was intrigued enough by what I overheard to invite myself into your husband's conversation with the sheriff."

"Then you know what I know."

"No. I know what the doctor knows. I asked you what you believe."

Rhyne shrugged as if she had no opinion.

"I believe he caused it," Elijah Wentworth said, watching Rhyne closely. "I believe he did it with malice aforethought."

"Should you be saying that?"

"Why not? What I think has no bearing on anything. There's no statute to account for it. What Judah did won't come before me as a matter of law. Wyatt knows that. Now, so does Cole."

Rhyne felt her stomach churn and turn over. Her eyes darted toward the sink and paced off the distance in her mind. If she was going to be sick, she thought she could make it that far. Her hands curled at her side. She felt the dampness of her palms as her nails scored sharp crescents into her flesh.

"It's because of me," she said, her voice hardly more than a whisper. "If it's true that he did it, it's because of me. I shouldn't have left him."

The judge shook his head. His eyes, so similarly colored to Rhyne's that they might have been a reflection of hers, regarded her with a mixture of solemnity and sadness. "No, Rhyne. You're wrong. Whatever Judah's done — *all* that he's done — it's because of me."

A small vertical crease appeared between her eyebrows as she studied him. He faced her directly, his eyes never wavering from hers. The triangular shape of his face, the narrow chin made broader by his beard, the dark hair distinguished by its threads of silver, she had the odd thought that she was staring at Runt Abbot in thirty years. It should have been a passing fancy only, but it circled her mind like an orbiting moon and struck her dumb when she faced it full on.

He spoke because she could not. "I don't know if I *am* your father," he said. "Delia never told me that I was."

"But you could be." It left her lips as an accusation.

"Yes. I could be. Judah certainly thinks I am."

Rhyne's chin came up. "How do you know what Judah thinks?"

Elijah Wentworth reached in his vest pocket and withdrew a folded piece of paper. He held it between his index and middle fingers. "I found this under my door at the Commodore weeks before the outbreak began." He extended his hand to Rhyne and indicated she should take it.

Rhyne wasn't sure that she wanted it. She reached for it reluctantly and unfolded it even more so. She'd seen few things written in Judah's hand, but the spidery scrawl was immediately recognizable to her. The skin at the back of her neck prickled. She read: *I forgive her sin but not the sin she spawned, the one made in her likeness and yours.*

"You knew he wrote this?"

"I couldn't imagine it was anyone else. Is it his writing?"

Rhyne nodded. "Had you already been given it when you introduced yourself to Cole?"

"Yes."

"So the reports that Judah was seen around town were true."

"It seems so."

"Did you show this to the sheriff? To Cole?"

"No. To neither. Perhaps that was a mistake. I don't know. I wasn't certain I would ever show it to you. Today . . ." He shrugged. "What I heard today changed my mind. I thought I needed to let you know what it's cost you to be my daughter. Judah's hatred was always for me."

Rhyne's brief smile held only the darkest of humor. "Strange, isn't it, that I was the one that took all the beatings."

He blanched but didn't turn away. "I didn't know," he said.

"You knew I was beat regular. Everyone did. You just didn't know I was your child. I reckon that's what's making a difference."

"I still don't *know*," he said.

Rhyne's eyes narrowed. "I doubt there was ever a barber with a razor so sharp that he could split hairs like a lawyer." Her lip curled. "Well, I don't *know* either, and after all this time, I don't think it's all that important."

"He raised you for a boy so he could punish me every time he looked at you."

"He raised me for a boy so I wouldn't become a whore like my mother."

The judge was on his feet and closing the gap between them so swiftly that Rhyne didn't have time to flinch. She stared up at him, her eyes defiant, unafraid of the hand that he was drawing back, yet terrified of the deeply felt regret she saw in his face.

His hand came down, not suddenly, but slowly, deliberately, and then he was cupping her cheek, his touch infinitely tender. "She was no whore. She loved him for a time, and then she loved me. I had her once, but she stayed with him." His fingers erased a tear that spilled over the rim of her lashes. "She was no whore."

Rhyne closed her eyes, shuddered. Although she was certain he would have welcomed her, she resisted the urge to step forward into his embrace. Neither did she sidestep his hand. She waited for him to let it fall away. When it did, she opened her eyes and found he was still watching her.

"She would have loved you," he said. "She would have loved everything about you, but she would have especially admired your spirit. I think she must have had one such as yours. There were glimpses of it when she performed, but away from the stage . . ." He shook his head. "I never knew the breadth of it. That flame was barely a flicker when we met. I can't even say with certainty that Judah quashed it. Look at you. He never was able to take it away from you."

The judge pressed a knuckle against his lips, stilling the quiver that appeared without warning. "She must have surrendered it," he said when he could speak. "She must have given it up."

Rhyne had no idea what to say. The judge was talking about someone she didn't know. "Cole believes she understood that something was wrong with Judah. He thinks she said things to my brothers about it, told them stories to frighten and protect them. She made certain that they did the same for me. That doesn't sound like a woman who lost her courage."

"I would have taken your brothers with me."

"You see her responsibility too narrowly, Judge. She had her neighbors and friends to protect, not only her family. I think you are selfish. She was not."

Rhyne's softly spoken words had the power to knock Wentworth off center. He rocked back on his heels. "I wanted to be everything to her," he said when he recovered. "As she was to me."

Rhyne merely nodded. She did not try to stop the judge as he stepped away and returned to the stool. He had the look of a man who needed to sit. "Would you like a drink? There's whiskey."

He thanked her but shook his head.

"Then perhaps you'd join me for lunch. I was going to heat soup from last night's supper. There's the fresh bread to go with it."

His smile appeared briefly. "Yes, I'd like that."

"Well, come with me then. We don't stand on ceremony here. We'll eat in the kitchen."

Wentworth returned to the chair he'd occupied earlier and contributed very little to the conversation as Rhyne prepared the meal.

She told him how she and Cole came to believe that Judah was the source of the fever outbreak. He'd come too late to Cole's exchange with Wyatt to know the particulars. He listened, intrigued by Rhyne's description of events as a mystery that required attention to detail, specific knowledge, and sudden leaps of intuition.

"Pinkerton detectives," he said when she finished her story. "You and Cole are medical Pinkertons."

Rhyne set a bowl of vegetable soup and a thick slice of bread in front him. "That's a compliment, isn't it?"

"I meant it as one."

"Then you're kind to say so." She sat and picked up her spoon. "I hope you will tell Cole. I believe he would like to hear it from you. He deserves some recognition for his work these last weeks." Her eyes lifted briefly as she thought about Whitley lying abed upstairs. "The circumstances . . . well, you know they have been difficult."

"For you also."

She acknowledged the truth of it with an almost imperceptible nod. "I suppose it is God's small grace that no one has died. I want to believe that Cole's mistaken about the inevitability of it. I reckon that's poor judgment on my part, since he hasn't been wrong yet about the typhoid."

Rhyne saw the judge's hand hitch when the

spoon was halfway to his mouth. Dread filled her empty stomach. "What is it?" she asked. "What's happened?"

Wentworth carefully set his spoon back in the bowl. "Jack Beatty. He moved in with his mother after Sarah Ann and the baby died. She found him this morning. Says his heart just gave out." He pressed his lips together for a moment. "Probably true more ways than one."

All color vanished from Rhyne's complexion. She stared across the table at the judge without really seeing him. She thought she meant to nod, but when she lowered her head, it seemed too heavy to lift again. "So Cole was right."

"Yes. I think he'd prefer it was otherwise."

Rhyne knew that was true. Thinking aloud, she said quietly, "Jack didn't show signs of the fever as early as Whitley."

"I know. I heard Cole tell Wyatt that some people would tolerate it better than others."

"He told me that as well." She glanced up. "Eat," she said. "Your soup will get cold."

He looked pointedly at her untouched bowl but refrained from saying the same to her. He dipped his spoon into the soup and took his first taste. Finding the broth was richly seasoned and dense with carrots, onions, beans, and corn, he quickly took another.

Rhyne fiddled with her spoon, turning it over and over beside her bowl. "Do you know if Cole went to see Evelyn Beatty?"

"Wyatt was the one that told him about Jack. I don't know if Cole intended to visit Evelyn."

"He usually comes home for lunch. Even if he has to go out again, he likes to drop in for a time."

The judge smiled and tore off a chunk of warm bread. "I can think of several reasons why he'd do that, and your good cooking isn't first among them."

The compliment barely registered in Rhyne's mind. "It's already late for him." She frowned a little. "I know there's nothing he can do for Whitley that I haven't, but I wish he knew that she —" Her hand slid from the spoon to the butter knife. She picked it up and pointed it at the judge. "Did Cole send you here this morning?"

Wentworth avoided looking directly at the knife. She wasn't holding it like a weapon but rather as an extension of her accusing finger. "Why do you ask?"

"Whitley would tell you immediately that you haven't answered my question. It seems like something a judge should know."

The judge did. He was hoping not to get snared so easily. "Apparently Whitley has some influence with you."

"She does, yes." Rhyne raised an eyebrow, waiting.

Sighing, Wentworth sopped his bread with

broth. He put it in his mouth, swallowed, and then wiped his lips with the napkin. "It's easier to be on the bench," he said. "There, at least, I'm not distracted by an excellent meal."

Rhyne's eyebrow didn't falter a fraction.

"I offered to come and sit with you," he said.

"Why?"

"You know why. We've discussed the reasons."

"No, that's not what I mean. We discussed them because you're here, but they're not the *reason* you came. Not today. If you hadn't made the offer, who would have shown up?"

He was a long time in answering. "Very well," he said when the knife didn't waver. "Rachel was the likely choice."

Rhyne nodded, expecting to hear just that. What she still didn't understand was why. "Where is my husband?" she asked. She observed the direct question caused the judge some discomfort. He lifted the spoon to his mouth more slowly, and while he continued to eat her soup, she doubted that he was still enjoying it. "I have a right to know."

"He's with Wyatt."

"Of course he is." She realized she had only wanted confirmation of her suspicions. It made her wonder how long she had hidden the knowledge from herself. Had she known something at the moment of the judge's arrival, or had the first hint come later when he didn't leave? "They went to see Judah, didn't they?"

Wentworth nodded. "That's right."

"I reckon they both had some notion that I'd try to interfere if I knew."

"Apparently there is precedent."

She scowled at him. "I don't suppose they mentioned that I might well have saved their necks that time."

"That didn't come up."

"I just bet it didn't. Cole doesn't even own a gun."

"I believe Wyatt intended to give him one. You said yourself that Cole could hold his own with a rifle."

"I don't know about one he's never fired before."

"He seems like a careful man. If I had to guess, I'd say he'd take in some practice before he and Wyatt got as far as Judah's."

That didn't settle Rhyne's jangling nerves. Realizing she was still pointing her butter knife at the judge, she set it back on the table and folded her hands in her lap so they would be out of sight. "How long ago did they leave?"

"I couldn't say. We parted ways at the sheriff's office. Wyatt was going to deputize your husband."

Rhyne's eyebrow had just fallen in place.

Now both of them shot up. "Deputize him? Why?"

"Cole insisted. He wouldn't take a gun otherwise."

"No, he wouldn't," she said softly. "The Lord has a deep well of humor to make a man so smart and not give him a lick of common sense. He knows Judah has no respect for the law." She gave him another pointed look but didn't underscore it with further blame. "I hope Joe Redmond gave him a decent horse this time."

"I'm sure Wyatt would see to that."

"Well," Rhyne said with an air of finality. "There's nothing to be done, is there?" She stood and took up her plate, bowl, and silverware. "Nothing except the chores I still have to do." Standing at the sink, she glanced over her shoulder at the judge. "It'd be a help to me if you'd read to Whitley for a spell. I do that every afternoon, but I'm already late starting the ironing. I do miss taking the linens and Cole's shirts to Maggie Porter."

"It'd be a pleasure to read to her."

"You know not to expect her to respond."

"I understand." He pushed his dishes and cutlery across the table where Rhyne could reach them easily. Wiping his mouth and beard a final time, he stood. "Is there a book in her room?"

"*The Three Musketeers.* I marked it where I stopped reading."

"Dumas is a favorite of mine," he said. He dropped the napkin on the table. "I'll enjoy it. Thank you for asking."

Rhyne saw that he meant it. He wanted to help. There were all sorts of ways a person could assuage guilt, she reflected. She hoped this one gave him some relief. Setting the flatiron on the stove to heat, Rhyne thanked him in turn and waved him off.

Elijah Wentworth read for upward of an hour at Whitley's bedside before his parched throat made him close the book. He smiled at Whitley, begged her pardon for the interruption, and excused himself to seek libation. He recalled that Rhyne had offered him a whiskey earlier. It sounded good to him now. He decided he'd bring it back to Whitley's room and read some more. The girl never stirred once during his rousing recitation, but he liked to think she heard his voice and kept one foot on this side of heaven's door because of it.

Heading downstairs, he ran his hand along the polished banister and let it rest on the newel post while he glanced down the hallway to the kitchen. His angle allowed him to see a small stack of folded linens on the table and a sheet draped over the end of the ironing board. Choosing not to disturb Rhyne, he went straight to the parlor in search of the drinks cabinet.

He poured two fingers of whiskey, held his

glass up to the light, and then poured a bit more. He sipped, letting the whiskey slide smoothly over his tongue and down the back of his throat. It was immediately soothing.

He closed the decanter, put it away, and then stepped back into the hall. His view of the kitchen was better, and he stood where he was for a time to see if Rhyne would notice him. He could admit that he wanted to be noticed. He liked her, liked her fine, and he hoped someday she could say the same of him.

They'd made a good beginning, he thought. The mistakes were all his, and she'd been right to hold his feet to the fire, but he believed she had her mother's forgiving heart, not Judah's bitter one.

He wasn't certain how long he stood there, long enough, though, to recognize that something was wrong. The sheet on the ironing board didn't move. Nothing was added to the stack of linens. He never glimpsed her hand pushing the flatiron to the end of the board. Cocking his head to the side, he held his breath and listened. From the kitchen, there was only silence.

Certain now of what he would find, Elijah Wentworth walked the hallway with as much enthusiasm as a man headed for the hangman's noose. He balked when it came to crossing the threshold. He could see everything at a glance from the doorway.

The folded sheets had never been pressed. The flatiron was as cold as a stone. Its only use had been to keep the draped sheet centered on the board. The laundry basket on the table was more than half full. There was a note pinned to the sleeve hanging over the side of the basket. He could read the bold scrawl from where he stood: *Please mind Whitley.*

Raising his glass, he saluted Rhyne in absentia. *"Fortes fortuna juvat."* Behind his beard, his smile was faintly wistful. "Fortune favors the brave, my dear. It always has."

CHAPTER 16

Rhyne tethered Twist out of sight of the cabin and made her way slowly along the ridge, staying low and using the cover of scrub, pine, and rock to make sure she wasn't spotted. It was the same approach she used the last time she visited Judah, and as on that occasion, she had the advantage that no one was expecting her.

There was a large expanse of open ground to cover before reaching the cabin and she paused, dropping down on her haunches to survey the route she wanted to take. The Winchester lay across her knees.

Irregular patches of snow dotted the valley like spots on a cow. The cycle of melting and freezing had created a glaze of ice on each one of them, and as Rhyne turned her head she had to squint against the sparkle of sunshine glancing off the thin crust.

Sheep and their new lambs grazed on the far side of the stream. There the steep angle of the hillside in relation to the sun meant the quilted landscape was temporarily more green than white. The animals kept their heads down, chewing their cud, intent on filling all four of their bellies. Rhyne suspected they wouldn't notice her when she left the ridge, or if they did, they'd make less noise than if they were penned.

Chickens scratched the ground near the coop, but they hadn't moved close to the cabin. She imagined that meant Judah hadn't taken eggs for his breakfast because he only ever fed the hens at the coop when he was stealing from them. If he could be bothered to do the chore at all, it was his usual practice to throw feed from the porch and watch the furious rush that followed. If he had a hankerin' for chicken that night, the winner was dinner.

Rhyne moved again so she had a wider view of the corral. She'd been bothered from the first that there was no sign of the horses that Wyatt and Cole rode. She'd expected to see them tethered at the front porch. Now that she could see the entire corral, she knew they weren't there either. She scanned the ridge and the hillside, looking for evidence that they were taking as cautious an approach as she was.

Riding out, Rhyne chose the wagon road. She'd reasoned that the men would have taken that route because they'd used it before and it didn't present the same hazards as Colley's trail. She hadn't gone far before she realized she was mistaken. The faint hope that she could catch up with them vanished. It seemed that in spite of Cole insisting that Judah was no longer a danger, he and Wyatt had been in a hurry to reach the cabin. Judge Wentworth had arrived on her doorstep with no purpose but to keep her occupied. She was certain she wasn't meant to discover that Cole and Wyatt had ridden out of town, but once she knew, the judge really had no chance of detaining her.

She couldn't muster any guilt for leaving him. He'd do right by Whitley and as for Whitley, Rhyne had no doubt that she was doing right by her.

Rhyne swiveled around as something glinted in her peripheral vision. She was getting edgy, she reckoned, because it was only sunlight winking at her from another patch of snow. Shaking her head, she went back to studying the cabin, looking for signs of movement, of life.

Smoke curled from the stone chimney, but no one stepped out to get a log from the stack beside the front door. Perhaps it was just a matter of time before Judah appeared. It seemed unlikely that he would have carried in more than a few logs. It was her experience that he minded the trips less than he minded the burden.

At Rhyne's current distance from the cabin,

the windows offered no glimpse to the interior. As she'd done before, she would have to get close enough to press her nose against the glass to see inside. She wondered about the wisdom of going so far if she didn't know with certainty that Cole and Wyatt were already there.

But if they weren't inside, where were they?

Had something delayed them? That was the best possible explanation. The worst was that they were in the cabin, helpless, and Judah had already done something with their horses. It begged the question why he'd bother. Was he so sure that she'd come looking for Cole and Wyatt that he was drawing her like a spider to his web? Of course he was.

"Reckon I'm predictable that way," she said under her breath. Hadn't she once said as much to that no-account Beatty boy? Constant as the northern star. Judah knew her nature well enough to depend on that. "But I know you, too." Right now that gave her narrowest of advantages.

Rhyne rose from her crouch a second time and dropped over the ridge away from the cabin. She took her time making a search of the area, looking for anything that would indicate Cole and Wyatt had crossed her path. On foot, she walked to where Colley's trail met the ridge and looked down the mountainside. As far as she could see, there was no sign of a mishap or any evidence they had come this way.

She wondered if the judge had mistaken their intent, but how could he have when he'd parted ways with them at the sheriff's office? It would have been difficult to misconstrue their plans when Cole was about to be made a deputy.

Rhyne considered the other routes the sheriff could have taken. There was probably no one as familiar with the passes and mountain trails as Wyatt Cooper. She had never explored so far or wide. Hadn't he and Will Beatty been able to track a couple of miscreants all the way to their final resting place?

Beneath her lamb's wool jacket, Rhyne shivered. It caught her unaware. Memory rode on the back of the prickly cold, sneaking up her spine and slipping as stealthily as a shadow into her mind. She turned up her coat collar so that it brushed her ears, although she knew it offered no protection against this sudden chill. When the ice was in her marrow, even a roaring fire was inadequate.

She'd never returned to the site of the attack, wouldn't have known the bodies had been found if Wyatt and Will hadn't reported their discovery. The baby had already been growing inside her, but she hadn't known it then. She thought killing them had been enough for what they'd done to her. It was when she realized she was going to have a child that she was seized by the urge to kill them all over again.

The terrible truth, the one that made her drop to her knees now, was that the killing urge wasn't on account of the child; it was on account of Judah. He knew, *knew* about the baby before she did, and the change in him was as immediate as it was final. What he'd given her, what he'd only ever been able to give her, was tolerance, and then even that became too much for him. Their tenuous bond, as fragile as a gossamer thread, was severed, and Runt was dead to him. He had no use for Rhyne, his whore daughter.

And when he told her that he'd beat the baby out of her, she hadn't fought back.

Rhyne stared at her hands. She clutched the rifle against her thighs. Her knuckles were white from the pressure of her fingers on the stock and barrel.

Judah wouldn't hear her out. She came close to humiliating herself by pleading with him. More than once, he walked away; there was no explanation that could satisfy. In contrast, Cole waited patiently for her to tell him what happened. Rhyne knew a profound sorrow that she never found the words.

Breathing deeply, if not quite evenly, she wondered at her real purpose in setting out this afternoon. She suspected her motives had less to do with looking out for Cole and Wyatt than they did with squaring up with Judah.

She eased her grip on the Winchester and rocked back on her heels. She slowly straightened.

Rhyne walked back to where she'd left Twist and replaced her rifle in the scabbard. She stroked the gelding's nose, whispered a few words, and then set off in the direction of the cabin through the open field, unarmed and no longer afraid.

Cole entered the house by the side door, saw there were no patients, and called for Rhyne. He didn't think too much of it when Elijah Wentworth called back, but he was surprised when he got to the hallway and realized the judge's response came from upstairs.

Cole put his hat on the newel post, leaned the Remington rifle Wyatt had issued him against the wall, and unbuttoned his coat as he climbed the steps. He was shrugging out of it by the time he reached Whitley's room. He stopped just inside the door when he saw Wentworth was alone at his sister's bedside. The judge had his finger marking his place in *The Three Musketeers.*

Trying to suppress his misgivings, Cole regarded the older man expectantly. "Rhyne?"

"You didn't see her?"

Cole shook his head, tossed his coat over the back of a chair, and approached Whitley. He immediately pressed the back of his hand against her brow. She didn't try to avoid his touch. "She's been like this since you've been here?"

"Yes. Mostly. She moved enough at one point to fall out of bed. Rhyne and I put her back. She seemed to be unhurt."

Cole pushed back the covers enough to find Whitley's hand. He put his hand inside hers and squeezed gently. There was no response. He released her, rubbed his brow. It was the judge who put aside the book, stood, and leaned across the bed to replace the blankets.

"I was able to get her to drink some tea not long ago. Rhyne did the same earlier, at least twice. Broth, I think."

Cole nodded. "Good." He glanced at the judge. "Do you mind sitting with her a little longer? I'd like to speak to my wife."

Wentworth frowned. "She's back?"

"Back? You mean she stepped out?"

"I mean she followed you and Wyatt to Judah's."

Swearing softly, Cole immediately crossed the room to retrieve his coat. "Wyatt and I never made it out. There was a small landslide on Colley's trail. We started to go around, but it was too steep. Wyatt's horse lost his footing and almost put them both over the side. We decided to clear the slide instead." One of his gloves fell out of a pocket as he jerked on the coat. He stooped to pick it up. "More rocks came down. I was able to get out of the way in time."

The judge raised an eyebrow. "Wyatt?"

"Smashed his foot. He needed help getting back on his horse. I just left him with Rachel."

Wentworth grimaced, and then allowed, "His foot will probably heal faster than his pride."

Cole had nothing to say to that, although it was undoubtedly true. He slapped his glove against his thigh. It was impossible for him to keep the accusation out of his tone when he spoke. "You told me you could keep her here. It was all you had to do."

"She tricked me."

If the situation were anything but what it was, Cole knew he'd have been amused. That was no part of what he felt right now. "How long ago did she leave?"

The judge fumbled for his pocket watch and darted a look at the time. "It's been a little better than an hour since I realized she was gone. She probably left thirty or so minutes before that."

"Make it two hours then."

Elijah Wentworth nodded.

Allowing for the time it would have taken for her to change into riding clothes, sneak back into her old room for the gun she still kept under that bed, and finally visit Joe Redmond to get her horse, Cole considered that he might not be so far behind her after all.

He stuffed the glove into his pocket. "I have to go."

"I understand." He glanced at Whitley. "I'll be here. I know what to do."

Cole looked from the judge to his sister and then to Wentworth again. His expression gave no quarter. "I have to trust that's the case."

"Rhyne did," Wentworth said gravely. But Cole was already gone; he'd spoken the words to an empty room.

For the first time in her life, Rhyne announced herself at the cabin door by knocking. Common sense made her quickly step aside in the event Judah greeted her with the blunt end of his walking stick, or worse, the old Henry rifle he kept mounted by the bookcase.

"Been expecting you," Judah called from inside the house. "Ever since Wyatt told me you were still alive, I've been expecting you."

It was hardly an invitation, but he'd spoken two sentences without introducing the epithet *whore*. Rhyne opened the door.

"Bring some wood with you," Judah told her. "I had it in my mind to get a few logs, but seems like the Lord always provides."

"Seems like," she said. Rhyne saw at a glance that he had no weapon. The Henry rifle was still mounted; the stick was leaning against the table a good foot out of his reach. She carried in a small stack of wood and set it down beside the stove. She tossed one in. "You cut this yourself?"

"Some. The Beaufort boy takes good money for doing what I can't."

Or won't, she thought. In the interest of sustaining the peace, Rhyne didn't comment. She held her ground while Judah looked her over. There'd been little time for that when he'd seen her before. His attention had been for her Winchester, not her face. She didn't turn away, but neither did she defiantly stare him down. She simply let him take his fill. If there was pain in his wintry glance, he hid it well. Rhyne knew the full range of emotion he was capable of expressing on stage, but none of that was evident now. She wouldn't have trusted it anyway. His indifference calmed her.

"The judge showed me the note you left in his hotel room," she said.

"Sit. You're giving me a crick in my neck." He pointed to the table. "Take a chair over there. Hand me my stick."

Rhyne didn't move. She went on as if he hadn't spoken. "He says I look like Delia. I reckon you always thought so, too."

Judah shrugged. He winced, rubbed his shoulder.

Rhyne didn't allow herself to be distracted. "Did she tell you I was his child?"

"What are you up to?"

Rhyne persisted. "Did she tell you I was

the judge's child?"

"All right," Judah said, appeasement in his tone. "The answer is: she didn't have to."

"Did you ever ask her?"

"I sure as hell wish you'd sit. I don't much like looking up at you."

"You could stand," she said. "I know you can. Your stick wouldn't be so far away if you needed it today." But rather than make him prove it, Rhyne went to the table and hitched her hip against the top. She ignored the chair except to use one of the rails as a support for the toe of her boot. She moved the walking stick behind her, putting it well outside of any grab he might attempt. "Did you ever ask her?" she repeated.

"I didn't have to."

"You didn't?"

"I knew."

"The same as you knew about me?"

His eyes narrowed. "The same as."

Rhyne nodded slowly. "Did you see me coming down from the ridge?"

"I did."

"Thought you might. Thought you might take the Henry down from the wall."

"I saw you weren't armed."

"Could be I got a Colt under my coat."

"Do you?"

"No."

"What do you want, Runt? I thought I knew, but maybe I don't."

"Rhyne," she said. "I'm Rhyne."

He shrugged. This time he didn't wince, and he didn't lift a hand to his shoulder. "Rhyne."

She took off her hat and set it beside her. Her dark hair fell forward, framing her heart-shaped face. She ran a hand through it once, pushing it back from her brow. "Why do you think I'm here?"

"I figured you meant to kill me."

"I figured I might. After what you did to the folks in town . . . well, you deserve it. I haven't changed my mind about that. I doubt I ever will, but it seems I've had time to think that maybe I shouldn't be the one to do it, leastways not before I understand the why of it better." She watched him stroke his beard, his features set thoughtfully. "It seems some of the venom's gone," she said.

He smiled faintly. "Forgot my manners. I should have offered you something to eat."

Rhyne fought down the bile that rose in her throat. Her hands tightened on the edge of the table. It was necessary to keep from reaching for the walking stick and striking him with it. "I was talking about the poison that's inside me," she said. "It never crossed my mind that you'd be any different."

"A man can change."

"Not you."

He began stroking his beard again. "No, not I. *'But I am constant as the northern star,*

574

of whose true-fix'd and resting quality there is no fellow in the firmament.' Do you remember that?"

"I do. I was thinking of it earlier. And what about this? *'I am sorry for thee: thou art come to answer a stony adversary, an inhuman wretch uncapable of pity, void and empty from any dram of mercy'.*"

"Ah, yes. From *The Merchant of Venice.* The Duke speaking to Antonio of Shylock. Am I your stony adversary, Rhyne? Who is sorry for you that you've come to face me? Your husband?"

Rhyne said nothing.

"Where is Coleridge Braxton Monroe? He's not with you."

She didn't answer him, but she also didn't look away.

"You should have never left the stage," Judah said into the yawning silence. "You had such presence there. Like your mother. She could hold any audience rapt, not only these simple miners and shopkeepers. I wanted to take her back east, find work in real theaters. Did you know that?"

Rhyne shook her head. He did have the capacity to surprise.

"She wouldn't hear of it. It was understandable, I suppose, that she wanted no part of the New York stage, but she could have had roles in playhouses in Chicago or St. Louis."

"Not Philadelphia?"

575

Judah smiled thinly. "There, too, but she'd made her escape once. She wouldn't have gone back."

"Escape? You mean because of what you did."

He didn't answer right away, his eyes reflective. "Yes, I suppose I did mean that."

"The judge told me you worked cooking for a family in Philadelphia."

"Did he? I suppose your mother told him that. What else did he say?"

"Very little. He didn't know why you left, for instance." She paused, giving him time to offer an explanation. When he didn't, she went on. "How many people got sick?"

"Five."

Rhyne's eyebrows lifted. She was as taken aback by the number as by the fact that Judah had offered it.

"Three of the family," he said. "Two of the help."

"Did you know you were responsible?"

"No. I still don't."

"You tried your hand at cooking again."

"I had to have money, didn't I?"

"More people got sick."

He shrugged. "Outbreaks like that happen all the time."

"They happened a lot around you."

"Maybe. I don't know. We were moving west. It seemed like the typhoid was everywhere. St. Louis was the worst of it. Delia took sick there and almost died. The babies did."

Rhyne stared at him. "There were babies?"

"Stillborn twins."

So there was some truth in the tale her brothers told her. She should have suspected they hadn't spun it from nothing. They'd have been very young at the time Delia sickened with the fever and probably over-heard more than they witnessed, but they still managed to get the gist of it right: Judah had killed his other children.

Now Rhyne wondered if Judah had also killed his wife. "How did my mother die?"

"You know that. You killed her."

Although it was what she'd expected to hear, what she had always heard, Judah's bald delivery still could make her flinch. She observed the curl of Judah's lip, the pause he took in stroking his iron gray beard, and knew he'd enjoyed getting that small rise from her.

"She didn't die giving birth to me," said Rhyne. "She lingered some."

"I suppose your brothers told you that."

"They did."

"Well, the end was the same, wasn't it? Lingering only meant she suffered for her sin."

"Me, you mean," said Rhyne. "I was her sin."

"That's right. You brought on the puerperal fever."

Rhyne wondered what her father knew about childbed fever. "Did Doc Diggins tell you that?"

Judah shook his head. "Not then, but later. I told him what happened, and he figured it was the fever that took her."

"Then he never suspected it was typhoid."

"No reason that he should. Puerperal fever is what he said."

"I reckon he did, not knowing any better." She watched Judah set his jaw. His hands were now resting on the arms of the rocker, but his white fingertips gave Rhyne the impression that he was holding himself back. "I don't think you meant to kill her." She took no satisfaction from watching him flinch. "I think you meant to kill me. The first time Delia sickened with the fever and lost your twins, that was all nature's doing, but my mind's circling the idea that maybe you had something to do with the second time she took ill. Nature figured in it, sure, but mostly it was *your* nature. You'd seen enough typhoid by then to suspect you had some part in the outbreaks. I bet Delia thought so."

Judah said nothing. His grip on the rocker relaxed. He stopped clenching his teeth.

"You couldn't have been certain that she would get sick again, and you must have realized there was no controlling the consequences if she did, but you risked it because you wanted the child gone. You wanted her free of her sin."

"You don't know anything about it."

Rhyne was aware that what Judah offered wasn't precisely a denial. "Do you want to set me straight?"

He merely stared at her.

"I guess not," she said. "The way I see it, she did die free of her sin. She delivered it to you. What I can't figure is why you didn't kill me right off. You could have told her I was stillborn, and she'd have probably believed you." Rhyne smiled faintly. "Maybe I was noisy from the first."

"Screamed like a banshee."

Rhyne nodded. "And later? After Delia was gone? Why did you decide I could live? You had to find a wet nurse, someone who wouldn't talk later about the daughter you had it in your head to raise as a son. That seems like a powerful lot of trouble for you." Rhyne thought she saw Judah's nostrils flare but couldn't be sure. She reminded herself that he hadn't admitted to anything and that perhaps he never would. She had no evidence to force his hand. Supposition was what she had, most of it coming to her a mere moment before she spoke it aloud.

"The judge thinks you raised me like a boy so you could punish him," she said. "I don't reckon you know if that's true or not. It seems the sort of thing that's easy to keep from yourself." She didn't expect an answer, so she wasn't disappointed when Judah remained quiet. "I told him he was wrong. I thought I had a right to say it since I was the one gettin' cuffed."

"You always did try my patience."

"That's a fact." She was doing it now. "I told him the real reason you raised me Runt instead of Rhyne."

"Oh? I'd like to hear that."

"I figured you didn't want me growin' up to be a whore like my mother." Rhyne remembered how the judge had jumped to his feet when she'd said that. It was telling that Judah remained seated. Elijah Wentworth had risen from his chair to defend Delia. Either Judah wasn't bothered by what she said, or he couldn't be bothered.

"You might be right," he said. "Didn't work, though, did it? Some things are bred in the bone."

Rhyne recalled Whitley saying much the same thing to her, but Whitley had been talking about decency, not adultery.

Judah warmed to the subject. "You took up with the first stranger to see what was under your trousers."

"Strangers," she said. Her stomach curled in on itself, but she pressed on. "There were two."

"Well, then you are the very equal of your mother, aren't you? She had two."

It was difficult to hear him make a comparison of equality. "She was married and took a lover," she said steadily. "I was raped."

"So you said."

"It's true."

"So you said."

Rhyne was reminded that Judah didn't need his stick to jab at her. She felt as if he'd driven his fist hard into her belly. It was difficult to breathe. "I went looking for one of the lambs. Do you remember? A timber wolf scattered the sheep. We thought maybe it took Isolde's lamb."

"I remember. I told you to let it be."

"You did." She'd gone out anyway, needing to know the lamb's fate as much as she needed to track the wolf. "I went upstream, way beyond Robert's Ridge. Took the trail to where I thought there might be a den. I suppose being intent on one thing made it easy to miss the other. I was jumped just a ways off from where I was headed. They thought I was lookin' for them."

"Could be you were just looking for trouble."

Rhyne had already decided he could say whatever he liked. She remained determined to go on. "They got my rifle away from me right off. That'd never happened before. I was purely pissed, Judah. You know I was. I threw myself at the one holding it over his head." She averted her eyes for a moment, the memory of her impulsive act shaming her as much as the consequences had. "There was a struggle. The other fellow grabbed me from behind, and then I was wrestling him to the ground. I don't know exactly what gave me away, probably something he touched that wasn't right. I generally don't go for close-in fighting. Rusty taught me better than that."

"Your temper failed you."

Rhyne knew that it had. "I took a fist," she said, absently touching the bony arch of her cheek. "When I woke, they'd already moved me. It wasn't so much a cave as a deep hole in the face of the rock. I reckon miners blasted it out once upon a time." Her eyes dropped to where Judah's fingers had begun to drum against the arm of his chair. It was the only sign she had that he was becoming impatient, perhaps uncomfortable.

"One of them was grunting over me," she said. "Pounding me against the rock."

Judah made a hissing sound as he sucked in a breath. "Have you no shame?"

There was a time that Rhyne's face would have gone hot. That didn't happen now. Her cheek still felt cool against her fingertips. She let her hand fall back to the table and didn't look anywhere but at him. "I did, but I reckon that was mostly because you thought I should. Not everyone thinks like you do."

"That doesn't make everyone else right."

Rhyne sidestepped that argument. Instead, she said, "The men . . . they took turns."

"You mean you enjoyed the first so much, you invited the second."

"Yes," said Rhyne. "That must be what I mean." She saw that he didn't know what to make of her concession. There'd been no sarcasm in her tone because it was no longer important to her to convince him that she was the one who'd been wronged.

"They had names," said Judah. "You never say their names."

Rhyne wondered if he needed to think of it as personal. It was, but not in the way he wanted to imagine. "Hank and Carl Hardin."

"Brothers?"

"Cousins, I think." Hank had called the other one 'Cuz'. *You got her, Cuz. You got her good. Show her what a man's got 'tween his legs that she don't. Then I'm gonna show her how a boy's gotta take it.* She let the echo of his voice fade away. His rasping, ribald laughter remained with her a bit longer.

"Your bastard would have been a Hardin," said Judah. "Kin to both of them, I suppose."

Rhyne didn't disagree. She couldn't explain why only Carl Hardin could have fathered her child. She needed to concentrate to hear what Judah was saying to her.

"Are they the pair that Wyatt and Will found murdered a ways from here?"

"The same." She nodded slowly. "But I think you knew that."

"If I did," he said, owning nothing, "I also

kept quiet."

"I know."

"You might have been hanged for it."

"Maybe. They were wanted, so it's hard to say. The bounty hadn't been posted yet."

"Dead or alive?"

"Alive, but you heard the sheriff talking about it the same as I did. He didn't seem all that concerned that he'd found them dead. Mostly it was the mystery of it that bothered him."

"Are you thinking about solving it for him?"

"I might. Not today. Maybe not even soon. But someday. Cole thinks he already knows. Will Beatty, too. It could be I'd just be setting their minds at rest."

Judah's chin jutted forward. "Why are you talking about it now?"

"You never let me have my say before, and I needed to tell someone. I was sitting up there on the ridge, trying to decide what to do, when I realized that the person I needed to tell was you."

"Is that right?"

Rhyne reached behind her and drew Judah's walking stick across her lap. She had had his full attention before, but now he was wary. "I know what you did with this," she said. Her hand ran along the carvings in the ebony. Except the tip, the wood was solid and smooth. She didn't have to look at it to make out the shapes of the rook, knight, bishop, and pawn. "After you beat me unconscious, I know what you did with it next."

"You didn't want the bastard."

She couldn't deny that she'd said it, but what she told him now was also the truth. "I think you'd really forgotten I was your daughter, not your son. The baby proved different. I didn't know what I wanted. Except for the once I stood up to you about not parading myself on stage, I guess I hardly knew my own mind. You about beat me senseless then, so I knew what I could expect when you told me you'd get rid of my baby."

Rhyne's hands tightened over the queen and the knight. Ebony was a hard wood, not easy to break over her knee, but the thought ran through her mind. "Leastways, I thought I knew. Cole told me what you did. He found the ropes that you used to tie me down. You must have been worried that I'd come to. It didn't happen, though, and I can't figure if that's a blessing or not. Sometimes I think I remember it, but maybe it's just that I can *imagine* it."

She lifted her left hand and uncovered the knight. She angled the stick so he could see the tip of it but was careful to keep it away from his grasp. "That last pawn," she said. "You see how the ebony's worn there? The wood's brittle from you striking it against things to get attention. I reckon no amount of oil can heal the scarring of a dead piece of wood, even one as fine as this." She retracted the stick, used a fingernail to pick at a hairline crack, and then held up her hand to show him the splinter. "See that? He found some of those inside me."

Rhyne waited, but Judah only returned her stare, his lined expression infinitely harder than hers. "I can't bring myself to believe that you might have done the same to my mother. You loved her once. I have to hope that was enough to make a difference."

Judah struck as quickly as a snake, heaving himself out of the chair and leaping at Rhyne. She was ready for him, had been since the moment she confronted him, and she flung herself sideways so that he grabbed air and not the sleeve of her coat. Never turning her back on him, she retreated until she could put his rocker between them. She held the walking stick in both hands at chest height and kept it parallel to the floor, prepared to swing it in either direction.

"Jack Beatty died this morning," she said. "That's your doing. It was typhoid."

"I don't know how that makes it my doing."

"It's probably better if Coleridge explains." Standing where she was, she could no longer see her husband at the back door, but when her eyes darted in the direction of the kitchen, so did Judah's. He couldn't mask his surprise. He'd been unaware that some time ago his audience had doubled. "Cole?" she called.

He came around the corner so she could see him again. He cradled the Remington in his arms.

"Where's Wyatt?" she asked. She'd been wondering about the sheriff since Cole first began inching his way into the house.

"Around," he said. "He'll be along directly."

She nodded. "I'm going to go around the table and take the Henry down." She gave Judah the widest circle she could. To his credit, he was properly cautious about the rifle in Cole's arms and didn't make a move one way or the other. Rhyne set the walking stick against the wall and removed the Henry rifle. "You keep it clean, Judah?" she asked, looking it over. "You know how dust and dirt can gum it up." She ran her hand along the brass finish and then checked its load. The weapon was properly called a Henry Lever-Action Cartridge Magazine Rifle, and there were folks that swore you could load it on Sunday and fire it all week. They weren't far wrong since it held fifteen cartridges.

"Seems like you might have been expecting trouble," she said. "I don't know that I've ever seen this better cared for except when I was doing it." Rhyne glanced at Cole. "Judah can't shoot worth a lick, but when you can empty this in about half a minute, something usually gets hit." She looked over at his weapon. "Is that a Remington?"

"It is."

"Henry went into business with Remington, you know."

"As a matter of fact, I did."

Smiling, she raised the rifle while Cole continued to cradle his. Her stance didn't waver. Judah's eyes did. "It'd be better if he heard it from you," she said to Cole. "I don't think he has a notion about germs. Probably doesn't know he's got rods in his guts."

Cole nodded when Judah's head swiveled sharply in his direction. "She's right. I might have said it differently, but I couldn't have said it better. You're a typhoid carrier, Judah. Everything we know points to it."

Judah jerked his chin at Cole, unimpressed. "What is it that you think you know?"

"You've been making people sick for a long time. You have a bacterium . . . a germ . . . inside you. It lives in your bowels."

"That so? Well, I've never been sick, so I guess you don't know what you're talking about."

Cole nodded. "It makes what I'm going to tell more difficult to comprehend, but it doesn't make it untrue." In terms so clear and concise that they could not be misunderstood, Cole described the infection, how it was spread, and why Judah presented a danger when he prepared food for others.

"As you discovered," he concluded, "it's an imperfect weapon when you want to use it against an individual. You can't control the timing or the course of the illness. You can't be certain the target of your enmity will sicken or die." He tilted his head in Rhyne's direction and watched Judah's pale blue eyes follow. "If you wanted her dead, Judah, there were surer ways to do it than by poisoning the town. If you only meant for her to suffer, then I'd have to say you chose your weapon well."

Judah's gaze slid back to Cole. "What makes you and her so sure I'm the one that started the fever? What did you say I was? A carrier?" When Cole nodded, Judah went on. "Well, if that's true — and I sure would be interested in how you prove a thing like that — then it could be I'm not the only one. Besides that, I haven't been to town all winter." He rubbed his hip. "And you know I still got the weakness in me from the stroke."

Rhyne snorted. "Too late for that, Judah. Cole might not have seen you jump out of your chair like you had springs in your backside, but I know he caught sight of the end of your leap. Let's not have any more talk about weakness unless it's in reference to your mind."

The corners of Cole's mouth twitched. "There you have it."

"I reckon you think so," said Judah. "But I told you, I haven't been in town all winter. I sent Danny Beaufort in a couple of times.

Now, if you think someone's a carrier, maybe you should talk to him."

Cole shook his head. "We know you've been around. That was clear to Wyatt and me the last time we came out together."

"How's that?"

"The splinter in your hand, Judah. The one that you got from blowing up a stump using a defective fuse from the mine. That cord was what took Ezra Reilly's hand and almost took his life. You were fortunate that all you got was a splinter."

Judah looked down at the appendage as if it offended him. "Hurt like hell, though."

"I'm sure it did," Cole said neutrally. "Wyatt figured you stole the cord from the mine."

"He didn't arrest me, did he? So he must not have been too sure of himself."

"It was more like he thought you got what you deserved."

Judah shrugged. "Being at the mine doesn't put me in town."

Before Cole could respond, Rhyne spoke up. "You left that note I told you about with the judge."

"I *wrote* the note," he said. "You have me there. But that doesn't mean I gave it to him. Ask Danny Beaufort how it ended up under Elijah Wentworth's door." Judah leaned his hip against the table and folded his arms across his chest. He ignored Rhyne in favor of leveling his gaze on Cole. "You look confused, Doctor. You don't know what she's talking about, do you? Rhyne's got her secrets, don't ever think she doesn't."

"He thinks I'm the judge's spawn and Delia's sin," Rhyne said bluntly. "And I'm not inclined to disagree with him. It improves my pedigree."

Unlike Judah, Cole appreciated her dark, wry humor. He didn't attempt to hide his amusement from the older man. "Whether you delivered the note yourself, or had Danny do it for you, hardly matters now. Sir Nigel has sworn to the fact that he employed you at his hotel. There are other employees that will swear to the same."

Rhyne exhaled softly. While not unexpected, Cole's confirmation still had the power to squeeze her chest. "Sir Nigel knew?"

Cole shook his head; his eyes never left Judah's. "No. He didn't see through Judah's disguise. Neither did anyone else. There's a good chance we'll find the clothes and wig he used in the trunks in the root cellar." His expression turned thoughtful as he regarded Judah's stony features. "I expected to find you clean shaven, but I suppose you must have seen Rhyne coming and prepared for her, or perhaps it's only that you missed your beard. You have a habit of stroking it, I've noticed."

Cole's gaze dropped to Judah's wiry beard.

"Do you want to take it off yourself?"

Judah didn't miss the threat implicit in Cole's question. He unfolded his arms, raised his hands, and slowly and gingerly began removing the beard. The glue made the piece difficult to lift away from his face. His skin was stretched and distorted as he tugged.

Rhyne's fingers itched to rip it off his face, but the revulsion she felt at touching him kept her away. She tried not to show her disgust when he smiled at her.

"You didn't realize, did you?" he said, tossing the beard aside.

Rhyne watched it skitter across the table. It looked like a varmint. She swiveled the Henry and fired once. The unnatural creature jumped off the table and fell to the floor where it lay without moving. The bullet splintered wood on the opposite wall.

She kicked aside the ejected cartridge and leveled the rifle at Judah again. Rhyne thought it was probably equal parts fear and astonishment that had made him jump back from the table. Cole, she noticed, held his ground, although his expression had darkened considerably.

"I had an itch," she told him.

"So it seems." He returned his attention to Judah. "Perhaps the next time you're feeling smug, you'll keep it to yourself." He inclined his head toward Rhyne. "She has an itch."

Judah used the back of one of the chairs at

the table to steady himself. He scowled at Rhyne, but he didn't speak to her. In the end, he was the one that looked away. He picked at the remnants of glue on his face, flicked them away, and then rubbed the gray stubble on his jaw with his knuckles.

Cole looked him over. "Rhyne warned me that you could make yourself unrecognizable. I thought of what you'd put on for a role, not what you'd take off. Looking at your face now, I don't think I'd have known you on the street. It was clever of you to shave."

"If you say so." It was an indifferent reply. Even a modest smile would have got him shot.

"It might have worked," said Cole. "In fact, it actually did, since Sir Nigel never once suspected he'd hired Judah Abbot." He paused, giving Judah the opportunity to ask what had given him away, but the man had a better rein on his curiosity and pride than Cole had credited.

Rhyne couldn't help herself as the truth came to her. She chuckled softly, drawing Judah's attention. She used her chin to direct his gaze to his own hand, the right one, where his index finger was cleaved off at the first joint.

"I reckon that what you're missing there is something folks'd take notice of, especially when you're hiring on as a cook." She shook her head. "That's not the sort of thing you can hide. All the chopping and dicing and dressing. They were bound to see it."

Cole thought it was a good thing Judah had no weapon. He looked like a man with an itch. "It didn't cause you to be recognized while you were employed at the Commodore, but afterward, when the sheriff made his inquiries, it was what identified you."

Judah folded the offending hand into a tight fist. "It doesn't mean I did what you said. A man needs to have money in his pocket now and again. There's always something needing fixed. There's feed and seed to buy. I can't always make a trade for supplies. I took work I knew."

"You know mining and acting and building," said Cole. "I understand you tried your hand at a lot of trades, but you took up work that experience had shown would cause harm to others."

"How do you know what experience showed me?"

"You're right. I don't know what lessons you learned."

"Then I guess you don't have anything else to say to me. It's an interesting story, the one about those creatures living inside me, but that's all it is."

"No, I'm afraid not. *That* I can prove."

"Prove? How?"

"Samples. That's why I'm here." Cole's regard was frank. "I need to collect some of your urine, your feces, and your saliva."

Judah didn't blink. "Just show me where you want me to piss, shit, and spit, and as long as you're pointing to your boots or hers, I'm happy to oblige."

"You can make this difficult, Judah, but it won't change anything. I'm not leaving without the samples."

"Where's Wyatt?" asked Judah, his eyes darting toward the windows. "Doctoring doesn't give you authority. Where's the sheriff?"

"He's on the ridge waiting to pick you off if you step outside without me." Cole spoke the lie without a flicker of remorse. He lifted up the collar of his coat to reveal the tin badge beneath it. "I'm standing in for that no-account Beatty boy." He let the collar fall back. "I have a warrant. Wyatt thought that'd be best." Cradling the Remington in one arm, he reached inside his jacket and withdrew a piece of paper folded into quarters. He tossed it on the table for Judah.

Judah stared at it for a long moment before he picked it up. He began to read as he unfolded it, and when he came to the signature at the end, the irony was not lost on him.

Judge Elijah Wentworth had penned his name with a bold flourish and a steady hand.

EPILOGUE

Mrs. Theodore Easter
Above Easter's Bakery on Euclid
Reidsville, Colorado

Coleridge Monroe, M.D.
3 Newton
Reidsville, Colorado

22 July 1885

Dear Dr. Monroe,

After careful examination of the particulars of your position and performance as Town Doctor these ten months past, the Reidsville Physician Search Committee is prepared to retain your services. It is the hope of the Committee that you are desirous of remaining in Reidsville and serving the good folk in this capacity.

The Committee compels me to mention that your extraordinary dedication has not gone unnoticed, especially as it was so evident during the Hard Times of the Fever Outbreak. Further, I must

inform you that fifty-six unsolicited testimonials in favor of engaging you as Town
Doctor were reviewed by the Committee
and provided further evidence of your
excellent character and considerable skill
(and also the good judgment of this Committee in making you the initial offer).

We eagerly await the favor of your reply
and remain hopeful that your interest has
not changed.

Yours truly,
Ann Marie Easter
President, Reidsville Physician Search
Committee

Cole angled the letter on the desktop so
that Rhyne could read it over his shoulder.
He merely smiled when he heard Whitley's
small sound of distress. Impatient for news,
she was leaning forward from the other side
of the desk and trying to read the letter while
it was still upside down.

Rhyne gave Cole's shoulder a light squeeze
to indicate she'd finished reading. "Fifty-six
testimonials, all of them unsolicited," she
said. "That's quite something."

"Yes," he said. "It is."

Whitley craned her neck to get a better view
of the letter. "Where does it say that? I didn't
see that."

Cole and Rhyne exchanged glances as Whitley's avid interest in the letter kept her from

meeting their eyes. Before his sister turned herself inside out, Cole rotated Mrs. Easter's letter so she could read it.

Whitley pointed to the first paragraph. "You might have mentioned that they're asking you to stay — and just ten months in. That's the most important part." She finally glanced up. "You are staying, aren't you? I mean, that's what you want." When Cole raised a single eyebrow at her, she faltered. "Isn't it?"

"You might have considered asking me that before you began your campaign. Fifty-six testimonials, Whitley. That was a lot of work."

She frowned deeply. "I don't know what you mean. Mrs. Easter makes specific mention of them being unsolicited."

"She means they were unsolicited by the committee," said Rhyne.

Cole nodded. "You can appreciate that it's not unreasonable for me to believe you had your fine hand in this."

"Well, I *do* think it's unreasonable," Whitley said. "And I *don't* appreciate it. Further, the judge told me if any suspicion was leveled at my head I should say I'm pleading the fifth. That's the fifth amendment, the one that gives me the right to —"

"The judge?" asked Rhyne. "He encouraged you?"

Cole looked up at Rhyne, shaking his head. "She doesn't need encouragement. She requires legal counsel."

598

Whitley smiled widely. "That's exactly what he said."

Rhyne's own smile was wry. "Of course he did."

Chuckling, Cole found Rhyne's hand on his shoulder and patted it gently. "Now that she has the judge, the Physician Search Committee, and fifty-six testimonials on her side, we're plainly outnumbered. I suppose we'll have to stay."

Rhyne couldn't think of a single reason to be unhappy about it, but on principle her surrender was reluctant. She sighed. "I reckon we will."

"Don't you think it was a little cruel to tease her?" asked Rhyne. She chose from among the small jars of ointments and lotions on her vanity and began massaging the backs of her hands with aloe. When Cole failed to answer her, she looked past her reflection to where he was sitting on the bed composing a letter on a lap tray. He hadn't begun to undress. She tapped the jar against the top of the vanity to get his attention. When he looked up, it was to give her an absentminded smile. He made a sound at the back of his throat that she supposed was a question.

"What are you doing?" she asked, her gaze directed at the lap tray. "And, yes, I can see that you're writing, so you should provide more explanation than that."

"It's my reply to the committee," he said. His tone communicated that it should have been plainly evident.

"Naturally," she said dryly. "You realize the time, don't you?" She saw him frown and consult his pocket watch. His genuine surprise made her smile.

They'd had an enjoyable evening entertaining the Coopers, Will and Rose, and Elijah Wentworth, but the time had gotten away from all of them. It was Rachel, so close to birthing her child that she made Wyatt squirm when she laughed too hard or too long, who finally admitted that she was tiring. Will and Rose left with them, but the judge lingered for a bit after that, spending his time exclusively with Whitley while Cole and Rhyne made short work of removing the last of the dishes and replenishing the drinks cabinet.

Whitley had only a vague memory of the judge reading to her during the darkest days of her illness, but the judge's recollection of those hours spent in her company was clear, and the strength of what one felt and the other knew was enough to forge a lasting bond.

It was Elijah Wentworth that had been sitting at Whitley's bedside and heard the first words she spoke in upward of a week. He would have given her anything she asked for, but all she wanted was water. Unashamed of his tears, he brought her the entire pitcher and called for Rhyne.

In the months that followed, Whitley made sure the judge had a place at their table when he was in town. She also wrote to him when he was away. Their easy friendship and mutual regard confounded Rhyne, and while she sometimes found herself envying them, she remained wary of giving the judge full access to her heart.

It would happen or it wouldn't, Cole told her, and she'd been relieved to realize that accepting Elijah Wentworth as her father was an expectation no one shared, not even Elijah Wentworth. It gave her reason to hope she could be easy around him, that some day she would come to know that he would never betray her trust.

Cole put aside the tray. He leaned against the headboard and cradled the back of his head in his hands. "Where did you go?" he asked.

Rhyne blinked. "What?"

Now it was his turn to smile. "You were reminding me that it was late and then you disappeared."

"I know. I'm sorry. I was thinking about Judah."

"You were? Usually I can tell."

He meant that she wasn't scowling, she supposed. "Well, he came to my mind just as you spoke. That probably accounts for it."

"Do you want to tell me?"

Rhyne hesitated. Talking about Judah reminded her of the limits of her ability to forgive. He'd sickened eighty-seven people, nine of whom died, and the law offered no means to charge him with a crime. The fever had taken Adele Brownlee and one of her whores, the midwife Mrs. Best, Will Beatty's mother, the middle child of Douglas and Margaret Porter, Jack Beatty, Mrs. Wickham of Wickham's Leather Goods, the schoolteacher Thomas Cassidy, and Sid Walker.

Although Cole was able to prove beyond any doubt that Judah was a typhoid carrier, the law lagged behind the science, and there was little that could be done except banish Judah from town for the rest of his unnatural life. He was cautioned against leaving his homestead as well. There was no one in favor of him visiting the horrors of what he'd done in Reidsville on some equally unsuspecting town.

Rhyne didn't know what Judah thought of his punishment. She hadn't accompanied Wyatt and Cole when they'd ridden out to tell Judah what had been decided. He should have thanked them for not telling the town how the fever had come about, but perhaps he knew that they'd kept silent for her sake, not his. The simplest way to be rid of Judah as a problem would have been to inform just one person outside their small circle of what he'd done and watch the wildfire that was gossip take over the town. Wyatt understood his limits as sheriff. Containing a mob of vigilantes was outside of them.

"I could never trust Judah," she said at last. "Or rather I *did* trust him, but only to do things that would hurt me. When I see the judge with Whitley, it reminds me that it should have been different. That it *could* be different."

"So you were really thinking of Elijah," Cole said. "Not Judah."

She nodded. "And you," she said. "I was thinking about you and what you said."

"What I said?"

"That it would happen or not."

Cautious, he said, "Well, I'm certain I meant well."

Rhyne laughed. "You have no idea what I'm talking about."

"I don't, but dare I point out that it's late?"

"If you must." She pushed the jar of aloe back into place and picked up her hairbrush. "You never answered my question."

"I didn't?"

Still watching him in the mirror, Rhyne applied the brush to her hair. "I asked you if you thought it was a little cruel to tease Whitley this afternoon."

"Cruel? Not in the least."

"You've known for months that the committee was going to ask you to stay. They were so eager, they couldn't wait until the end of your first year to make the offer."

His expression was wry. "I imagine the testimonials had something to do with that."

"Could be you're right. Still, if you'd told her the committee's intentions, Whitley wouldn't have gone to the trouble of collecting them."

"I know," he said.

His unrepentant expression made her laugh again. "You're cleverer than my brothers."

Cole climbed out of bed and began to remove his jacket. "How many do you think she wrote herself?"

Rhyne pretended to think about it. "You're very well liked, so I would say not more than fifty or fifty-one."

He was certain he deserved that. "I hope her hand cramped."

Smiling, Rhyne turned away from her reflection in the mirror. She continued to brush her hair as she watched Cole prepare for bed. She thought he was oblivious to her observation until his hands went to the button on his trousers and he glanced sideways at her and grinned. Rhyne had it in her mind to pitch her brush at him, but the urge faded as he correctly gauged her intent and advanced.

The brush fell from Rhyne's suddenly nerveless fingers. Abandoning even the pretense of never surrendering, she gave him her hand without reservation and let him pull her to her feet. She stepped closer, not quite touching him, but feeling the inexorable pull of his body across the small space that separated them. She held his gaze, knew that what she saw in his darkening eyes was a mirror of her own desire.

Rhyne closed the distance. Putting her hands on his shoulders, she steadied herself as she rose on the balls of her feet and kissed him. Cole's arms slipped around her waist; his hands clasped together at the small of her back. His mouth parted. The tip of her tongue teased his upper lip. She pressed a bit harder, touching the ridge of his teeth. He sucked her tongue into his mouth, engaged her body by pulling her hard against him. Spinning them both in a wide arc, he guided her backward toward the bed. She never hesitated once, each of her steps perfectly matching his.

The dance didn't end when they reached the bed, nor was it complete at climax. It wasn't finished even when they lay still and silent and their heartbeats slowed. Every breath was a measure; every touch struck a chord.

Rhyne moved so that she could put her head on his shoulder. She found his hand and laced her fingers in his. "I'm glad I didn't shoot you when I had the chance."

Cole pressed his lips against her hair.

"That's very pretty talk. Are you just coming around to that way of thinking?"

"No, it's been a while."

He smiled. "That's good to know."

"You shouldn't get too full of yourself, though. That'd make you a bigger target."

"Also good to know."

Rhyne moved her head a fraction so she could see him better. He was still smiling. "Is this the dance, Cole?"

And because his own thoughts had drifted in that direction, his arm tightened around her. "Yes, Rhyne, it's the dance. Exactly as I'd imagined."

Nodding, pleased, Rhyne whispered against his ear, "You're very kind to say so."

It was the middle of the night when the No. 473 engine reached the station at Reidsville. John Clay's train made good time from Denver, the fastest ever on the Calico Spur, but then he and the railroad had been paid handsomely to make it happen. For this run his engine only pulled one car, a private one, and the lightness of the load allowed No. 473 to make the climb into the mountains at her top speed.

John Clay had warned his passenger that the whole damn town would be sleeping when he arrived, but Mr. Franklin Benjamin Rhyne of Philadelphia was eager to reach Reidsville, and it seemed he had about as much money to burn as No. 473 had wood in her tender.

The engineer had his own thoughts about what was bringing Mr. Rhyne to Reidsville, but he kept them to himself. It wasn't all that hard to figure out, so he reckoned folks would come to it soon enough. Some people would swear there was better than a passing resemblance to Delia Abbot, though John Clay didn't see it after all these years later, but it was hard to ignore that fine ebony walking stick that Mr. Rhyne used when he stepped onto the platform. If there was another like it in all the world, and John Clay knew there was, then they'd been a matched pair once upon a time.

Elijah Wentworth stepped out of the dark alcove of the station front. "I've been expecting Mr. Rhyne," he told the engineer. "I got his telegram before he left Denver. I know where he wants to go."

John Clay lifted his cap, scratched the back of his neck, and nodded once. "I guess you're goin' to surprise her good, Judge. This time of night, have a care she doesn't shoot first. Evenin', gentlemen."

Franklin Rhyne watched the engineer amble back to his train. Slightly bewildered, he turned to the judge. "Why would she shoot?"

"Why wouldn't she?" the judge said, smiling faintly. He started to explain, then stopped and shook his head. His eyes fell to the walking stick. "I'd leave that behind, though."

Mr. Rhyne's hand closed over the knob, covering the king's crown. "It's a family heirloom."

"I thought it might be." The Pinkerton detectives had finally confirmed what Elijah Wentworth had long suspected. Delia Rhyne had never been anyone's servant. Until she eloped with Judah Abbot *she'd* been the young lady of the house. "I'll help you." He extended his elbow. "Trust me," he said confidentially, taking Mr. Rhyne's arm. "All of us will be better served if your first meeting isn't with Runt Abbot."

The employees of Thorndike Press hope you have enjoyed this Large Print book. All our Thorndike, Wheeler, and Kennebec Large Print titles are designed for easy reading, and all our books are made to last. Other Thorndike Press Large Print books are available at your library, through selected bookstores, or directly from us.

For information about titles, please call:

(800) 223-1244

or visit our Web site at:

http://gale.cengage.com/thorndike

To share your comments, please write:

Publisher
Thorndike Press
295 Kennedy Memorial Drive
Waterville, ME 04901